By AR Bryant

CRAFT BLESSED
A Broken Spirit
A Broken Promise

Published by Dreamspinner Press
www.dreamspinnerpress.com

A.R. BRYANT

A BROKEN PROMISE

Published by
DREAMSPINNER PRESS

8219 Woodville Hwy #1245
Woodville, FL 32362 USA
www.dreamspinnerpress.com

Trade Paperback ISBN: 9781641088459
Digital ISBN: 9781641088442
Trade Paperback published August 2025
v. 1.0

Content/Trigger Warnings

Explicit;

Pregnancy | *Prologue, Epilogue*
Alcohol/Inebriation | *Chapters 1, 21, and 25*
Firearms | *Chapter 2*
Violence | *Chapters 2, 17, and 22*
Death/Murder | *Chapters 2 and 25*
Torture | *Chapter 2*
Severe Injuries | *Chapters 2, 26, and 27*
Imprisonment | *Chapters 4 and 5*
Mild Cheating | *Chapter 6*
PTSD/Panic Attack | *Chapters 10, 13, and 22*
Explicit M/M Relations | *Chapters 10, 16, 19, and 21*
Poison Use | *Chapters 17, 25, 26*
Planned Torture | *Chapter 18*
Planned Genocide/Oppression | *Chapter 18*
Severe Burns | *Chapter 22*

Dishonorable Mentions;

Miscarriage | *Chapters 1, 17, and 27*
Autopsy | *Chapter 4*
Severe Injuries | *Chapter 4*
Serious Illness | *Chapter 4*
Death/Murder | *Chapters 4, 5, 6, and 27*
Child Abuse/Endangerment/Neglect | *Chapters 5, 8, 10, 13, 23, and 27*
Arranged Marriage | *Chapter 5*
Wasting Disease | *Chapter 5 and 7*
Sexual Slavery | *Chapter 6*
Pregnancy | *Chapters 16 and 27*
Death via Childbirth | *Chapters 16 and 24*
Genocide | *Chapter 19*
Animals used for learning | *Chapter 25*
Parental Death | *Chapter 27*
Drug Use | *Chapter 27*

PROLOGUE

"WHERE ARE we going?" Kajaan asked plaintively.

His best friend, Yolotzin, the Prince of Averia, was currently dragging him between the tables and revelers attending the wedding reception. His shaggy red hair kept falling in front of his eyes, and Kajaan impatiently pushed the coarse locks from his face. He felt woefully underdressed in the presence of so much royalty and gentry, his cheeks burning with the knowledge he was wearing a sweat-stained tunic over ratty breeches. He'd been helping the cook in the kitchen, washing dishes and hauling whatever she needed from the larder for the feast.

He didn't belong in this world. The world of gold, jewels, and glamor. Some Illusionist had altered the ceiling for it to appear as if they were outside with the addition of the shimmering green streak of northern lights that were mostly seen in Valvinte. Ignians and Gales had worked together to create floating paper lanterns for light as the evening grew later and darker.

All around them, sharply dressed waiters navigated through the colorful frocks and fine suits with ease. A few hissed at their young prince as Yolotzin pulled Kajaan behind him without a care in the world. Kajaan reached out, desperately trying to undo his best friend's fingers so he could run and hide. Preferably deep in the dungeons after he'd been dragged in front of so many people.

Maybe it wouldn't have been so bad if it was just Averians in attendance. That wouldn't do for King Tonalli's eldest child, though. Princess Saian getting married was apparently a huge deal, and dignitaries from all over the continent had come to celebrate her union to her Fated.

Kajaan could pick out the furs and leathers of those from Pemalia, and the slightly thicker furs and wool from Valvinte. The silks and lightweight cotton from Zothua and Bhyvine. The carefully muted and reserved linens of Nabene.

Kajaan's eyes flitted to the Zothuan prince. He was tall, even at fifteen, dressed in beautiful gold silks that complimented both his blue eyes and brown hair. The teenager caught his eye and impossibly, the man smiled at the sight of a servant's child being pulled around by a child prince. Kajaan stumbled over his feet, and Yolotzin quickly caught him, hauled him back up, and grinned at him.

"C'mon," the prince laughed. "The gardens should be empty."

But why would they go to the gardens?

"I have to work," Kajaan protested, even as Yolotzin dragged him toward the doors. "Tzinny, please, the cook—"

"Won't notice you gone!" Yolotzin interrupted with a giggle. "This is important!"

"What's important?" Kajaan protested. "The wedding already happened!"

Kajaan crashed into Yolotzin's back when the other boy stopped dead in his tracks. He peered up past Yolotzin's shoulder, considering his best friend was already several inches taller than himself, and blanched. King Tonalli stood with his arms crossed over his chest, a severe look on his face. Behind him, as always, stood Kajaan's father. The king's personal guard frowned down at his son, his cheeks slowly pinking, probably from embarrassment. Kajaan immediately dropped his gaze.

"Where are you two going?" King Tonalli asked.

"Outside!" Yolotzin proclaimed with a grin.

"Your friend is not dressed for polite company," the king admonished gently.

"That's not his fault," Yolotzin said, huffing as if it was obvious. "Besides, there's no polite company outside."

"It's too cold to stay outside," Kajaan's father said in a gruff voice.

"It'll be fine for a little bit," Yolotzin argued, stamping one foot. "It's important!"

His voice had risen enough that a few curious lords and ladies were starting to look over. One of them was Duke Ruvyn, and standing beside him was Lord Kende. The lordling regarded them carefully. He was only a couple years older than Kajaan, but he was a smart kid. Kajaan flushed, feeling his ears grow hot. He shook his arm a little, trying to get Yolotzin to release him.

If Yolotzin would let go, he could slip through the crowds and run back to the servants' quarters. His best friend didn't know all of Kajaan's bolt holes and would be unable to follow him if he managed to get out of Yolotzin's sight. Besides, as the crown prince, Yolotzin needed to be seen at the wedding and reception. The moment Kajaan made his escape, his best friend wouldn't be allowed to follow.

"Oh, let them go," the queen's voice came.

She sounded amused as she walked up to her Fated and placed an ever-so-gentle kiss on King Tonalli's cheek. The man melted slightly, slipping one arm around her waist and holding her as close as her poofy skirts would allow.

"Your boy is keeping unfit company again," King Tonalli observed.

"Perhaps if you'd allowed Jeryit time off to get his son fitted with the proper attire, the two would have been able to openly play together," Queen Brekka scolded him gently. "But now you must lie in the bed you made."

King Tonalli just sighed and rested his forehead against her temple. His other hand dropped to her rounding stomach that was just barely concealed by her dress. Kajaan hoped that Yolotzin would be getting a baby brother or sister soon. He knew that his best friend had been praying for it almost every night before bed.

"Yolotzin was very good during the ceremony," Queen Brekka cooed with a smile. "He played his part perfectly. Let him go be a kid."

The king gave a put-upon sigh, then grinned. He nodded to the two boys standing awkwardly in front of him, a glint of amusement sparkling in his eye.

"Off you run," he said. "Don't destroy your suit, young man."

"My liege," Kajaan's father protested weakly.

"Your boy deserves to have fun too. I'm sure he worked hard," King Tonalli said, glancing over his shoulder. "Let's go talk with the Greatblazes. We haven't seen them since young Cadeyrn's Awakening two years ago. I'm told the Senis brought their toddler with them as well…."

The couple walked by, and Yolotzin didn't hesitate. He broke into a run, pulling Kajaan along without listening to his protests that he really should return to the kitchens and help the cook. Instead, Kajaan found himself in the spring twilight. The garden's perfumed air was almost sickly sweet compared to the ballroom's musky odor of far too many people dancing.

Once they were outside the ballroom's bright light, the two slowed to let their eyes adjust to the soft lanterns of the garden. Yolotzin led Kajaan past row upon row of roses and rhododendrons.

Past the perfumed lewisias and lilies. They went deep into the gardens that Queen Brekka loved so much, almost to the pavilion in the center.

Finally, Yolotzin released Kajaan's wrist, and Kajaan pulled it back to his chest, rubbing the slightly bruised skin with a frown.

"What's this all about? It's too dark out here to play," Kajaan protested.

"You're such a fuddy-duddy," Yolotzin huffed, digging his hand into his pocket, sticking his tongue out between his teeth in concentration.

"No I'm not!" Kajaan protested.

He crossed his arms over his chest, scowling at his best friend, well aware that yes, he was being a bit too prim and proper. Kajaan watched as Yolotzin apparently found what he was looking for. The boy produced a pair of large napkin rings along with a wide grin. Kajaan blinked once at his friend and tilted his head.

"Why did you steal those?" Kajaan asked, blinking a few times.

Yolotzin shuffled closer and smiled happily, grabbed Kajaan's wrist again and held it gently in his hand.

"We'll always be together, right?" Yolotzin asked, a sudden vulnerability in his eyes.

"Well yeah," Kajaan said and shrugged. "You're my best friend."

"Good!" Yolotzin proclaimed. He gathered himself to his full height of four feet and shot Kajaan a charming smile. "Marry me. We'll have to make it proper when we get older, but we can make our promises now."

Kajaan flushed, his ears burning as he scuffed his worn boots against the dusty stone beneath his feet. He bit his lower lip and looked shyly up at the prince. They'd been together for their whole lives. One of Kajaan's earliest memories was being held in the queen's arms with her singing down at him while Yolotzin was rocked to sleep in a cradle next to her. He'd never deserved her care and love, only being a servant's son, but Queen Brekka hadn't ever treated him differently.

Instead, she'd encouraged the relationship between the two boys. Kajaan had to wonder if she'd approve of this as well. He stared at his best friend for a long moment while his heart fluttered in his chest. Forever. What if he did something that made Yolotzin hate him? Would their fathers even allow them to make good on that promise?

"Tzin," Kajaan cooed gently.

He was blinded by the brilliant smile Yolotzin gave him. The boy swung their arms slightly and stepped in a bit closer. Their foreheads pressed together, and for a long minute, they just stood together, sharing their breath. He could have this for the rest of his life. Revel in the open love that Yolotzin offered him.

Finally, Kajaan bit his lip and nodded. "Okay," he whispered.

Yolotzin pulled back and bounced on the balls of his feet, grinning madly. He held up one of the napkin rings and started to slide it over Kajaan's hand. It was a bit of a tight fit, and they had to wiggle it quite a lot before it popped over his thumb and hung from his wrist. Then they repeated the process for Yolotzin's matching ring. Kajaan couldn't help but giggle. They did have rings. They just weren't traditional ones.

He still felt a bit shy when he tilted his head up to look his best friend in the eye.

"We're doing this a little backward," Yolotzin finally admitted, admiring their matching rings resting on their left wrists. "But that's okay. It's not the real ceremony we'll have when we're older."

"You mean it?" Kajaan whispered.

"Yeah, Kajie. I mean it," Yolotzin replied just as softly. "You and me forever."

With that, Yolotzin held his hands tight and leaned in to press their lips together. Kajaan couldn't help his squeak, nor could he help immediately melting into his best friend. He wasn't quite sure what was happening, but Yolotzin's lips were so soft and warm. His body tingled and he flushed, staring up at the prince when he retreated ever so slightly.

"I, Prince Yolotzin Navarre-Hamonn, take thee, Kajaan Pernoac, to have and to hold for the entirety of my natural life. In sickness and in health. For richer or poorer. For better or worse. Till death do us part," Yolotzin said quietly, happiness shining clearly in his eyes and in his smile.

"For better or for worse," Kajaan repeated quietly. "Till death do us part."

CHAPTER 1

KAJAAN WAS losing his best friend.

Maybe losing wasn't exactly the right word, but Kajaan was being pushed aside all the same. Prince Yolotzin Navarre-Hamonn had found his Fated in the form of Lady Naias Elrel, and they were currently preparing for their wedding. Five moonturns had passed since they'd met, and neither of them could be happier. Lord Kende had already thrown her Introduction Gala and their Engagement Party. In another handful of moonturns, the wedding would be held, and Kajaan would be serving Lady Naias alongside Yolotzin.

He really shouldn't be as bitter as he was. He should be thrilled for his best friend finding his Fated and completing one of his life's goals. Except all Kajaan felt was crushing disappointment and fear of being left behind. Which was silly, he knew that. He was Yolotzin's secretary, his best friend and frequent lover. There was no real way for him to truly be left behind or forgotten. He'd serve Yolotzin and Lady Naias for the rest of his life, but their relationship was forever changed.

That was how he found himself adrift at the wedding for the youngest son of Duke Ruvyn. Yolotzin had wanted to come, especially after he learned that Lady Naias would be standing for Asyl during the ceremony. She wasn't going to abandon her best friend on his happiest day just to be with her Fated, and Yolotzin wanted to be by her side every second of every day. Supporting Lord Kende was just a pleasant happenstance.

Kajaan could barely recognize his boyhood best friend. Maybe once Lady Naias was able to officially move in with him, he would calm down. Kajaan couldn't understand the near single-minded obsession. He hadn't found his own Fated, and quite honestly, he wasn't sure he was interested. Hadn't been, at least. Not while he'd had Yolotzin with him. They'd slept together countless times over the years, both knowing it was temporary yet both deluding each other it wasn't. Sooner or later, Yolotzin would find his Fated or be matched up with a bride.

Kajaan had still hoped he'd be in the picture once that happened.

Now he knew he wasn't going to be.

The realization hurt. The pain reached deep into his soul and twisted any joy he could muster for his oldest friend. He barely remembered to clap when Lord Kende and Asyl leaned in and exchanged a chaste kiss, sealing their wedding vows.

For better or for worse.

Forever.

Kajaan glanced at his best friend. They'd exchanged similar words to each other once, when they were boys. Maybe he shouldn't have believed their faux vows so much, but the way Yolotzin had repeated them to him as they played husband and husband had delighted Kajaan to no end. The reverence in his voice, the soft look in his eyes… the gentle smile gracing his lips. Kajaan would never have those turned toward him again.

Maybe one day he'd find his own Fated… if he cared to look. Lord Kende just found his own heart's twin only half a year ago, and he was older than him. Not by much, but he was. If Kajaan could believe that he'd be so lucky to find the perfect man that the goddess had made for him, he wouldn't be so bitter. Except that he and Yolotzin had traveled across the continent so many times, and he'd never once felt that tug.

With a sinking heart, Kajaan watched as Lord Kende tucked Asyl's hand into his elbow and escorted him off the dais and away from the priest. Gone was the scared and abused street urchin Kajaan had saved so many years ago. If anyone deserved a happy ending, it was Asyl. The thought didn't help Kajaan's growing loneliness.

With the ceremony completed, the assembled revelers stood and followed the newlyweds out to the reception hall. Asyl disappeared for a few minutes with Lady Naias, likely to decompress from the pressure of being around so many people. He was still incredibly nervous around gentry and royalty. Kajaan couldn't blame him. Not after the treatment he'd received from them for being a Void. Asyl had finally warmed up to him about a moonturn ago, though that was more due to the fact that Kajaan visited Enchanted Waters quite often.

Kajaan carried around a flute of champagne, always watching Yolotzin and the crowd. Sure, he was just a secretary, but he took his prince's safety very seriously. After the attack at Asyl's Introduction Gala that had very nearly killed Lord Kende and permanently injured

Asyl, the man had tightened his security tenfold. The only good that came out of the night was the understanding of how Voids could absorb Craft and redirect that energy however they wanted.

Asyl finally returned to the reception, wearing a blue silk blouse and tight black slacks. He'd put his knee brace on as well, and there was some tightness to his jaw. Lady Naias ambushed him and linked their arms together, marching him over to his new husband, almost completely disguising Asyl's limp. Yolotzin was standing next to Lord Kende, and his face lit up when he saw Lady Naias heading toward him.

Another ache clenched Kajaan's stomach, and he sipped his champagne, turning away from the two couples. He caught sight of Siora canvasing the perimeter of the room, looking grim. Kajaan caught up with the Seer. She flashed him a brief smile before returning her attention to her duties. Kajaan walked quietly next to her for a while, sipping the champagne and glancing over at Yolotzin from time to time.

The prince danced with Lady Naias quite a lot, and when he wasn't, he was doting on her for whatever she needed. Kajaan was usually the one to fetch Yolotzin his drinks, often before his lover knew he needed them. Seeing the pure devotion on Yolotzin's face whenever he looked at Naias hurt. It hadn't been that long ago when Yolotzin had looked at him like that.

"All right?" Siora asked softly.

"Nothing will be the same," Kajaan said quietly.

"No," she replied, "it won't. But you'll survive. Lady Naias is wonderful. You'll love her."

Kajaan wasn't sure about that. Maybe one day he wouldn't begrudge her for being Yolotzin's Fated, but right now he knew he was jealous. Jealous that she got to be with him. That she was chosen by the goddess as Yolotzin's perfect match.

For better or for worse.

Kajaan nibbled on the provided finger foods that he wouldn't remember and didn't pay much attention to anything outside of his duties to his prince. If Yolotzin started looking around for him, he went to his side immediately. It was nearly midnight when Lord Kende thanked everyone for their attendance and announced he and his husband were retiring for the night. Lady Naias was going to be staying with them, so she said farewell to Yolotzin. It fell to Kajaan to get his best friend home safely.

At some point Yolotzin must have consumed a fair amount of alcohol. He wasn't sloppy drunk but had definitely hit the maudlin and unbalanced phase. Kajaan ignored all of his sad comments about missing Naias already and the expectations that had been placed on him since birth. The knowledge that he'd be taking over the kingdom ever since he'd been able to understand what that meant, and that he'd have to have heirs. That the moment he married he could no longer indulge his wanderlust. He'd be stuck in the castle, with the exception to royal events he'd attend, dealing with politics day in and day out.

At least Kajaan had been able to change his occupation. He wasn't a guard like his father, despite his best efforts at forcing him to wield a sword. Though he owed that bit of fortune to his morose best friend arguing for him when it would have been easier to ignore Kajaan's distress.

Kajaan got Yolotzin securely inside the Craft carriage and wrapped his hands around the steering wheel. He focused on his Craft, locating the shallow energy inside him, and tapped it. His fingers tingled as his meager power leapt to his command, filling the Craft carriage's engine.

It rumbled to life, and Kajaan steered it toward Alenzon Castle, leaving Ruvyn manor and Lady Naias behind. The rocking of the carriage must have lulled Yolotzin to sleep, as he heard his friend's slight snores behind him. The silence of the carriage didn't improve Kajaan's mood. It just helped him dwell on his future position within the castle.

The trip back to the castle took a good half hour, and Kajaan was starting to fade by the time the carriage trundled up the driveway. Powering a Craft vehicle not once but twice for an extended period of time was a massive drain. He would be sleeping really well tonight. Kajaan drove the vehicle around back, where the other carriages were stored near the stables. He removed his grip with a heavy sigh and stretched his arms above his head, arching his back, groaning when he felt the popping resonate from his spine.

"Wake up, Tzinny. You gotta sleep in your own bed," Kajaan said.

He turned and shook Yolotzin's shoulder. His friend groaned and his eyes opened, unfocused and blinking blearily up at him. Kajaan made a mental note to get Yolotzin to drink some water before he truly succumbed to sleep.

"Sleep with me tonight," Yolotzin said, yawning.

"You're engaged. I'm not sharing your bed," Kajaan scolded him.

"Nah, just sleep," Yolotzin said. "Please, Kaj?"

"Walk to your bedroom under your own power and I'll consider it," Kajaan said.

Yolotzin nodded and smiled. He playfully bumped into Kajaan as they walked into the castle and made their way through the corridors to the royal wing. There they climbed the stairs to the third level, where the royal family's bedchambers were located. Luckily, Yolotzin had one of the first rooms, with his sisters across the hall from him in their suites with their families.

Queen Brekka hadn't produced another son, and after several failed pregnancies, she and the king had stopped trying. In the end, it resulted in the queen absolutely doting on her youngest child and only son. The prince's bedchambers were decked out in lavish silks and the furniture hewn from beautiful purple heartwood. The chaise lounge and armchairs in his parlor and study were upholstered with a delicate-looking velvet, though it was a bit sturdier than it appeared.

Then, of course, there were the prince's books. He had turned into a bibliophile like his mother, and he'd spent many an evening curled up on his lounger with a book cracked open across his knees. Kajaan always joined him when he could, enjoying the quiet hours slipping by with the crackling fire to keep them company. There was no fire burning in the parlor tonight.

Kajaan pulled down the blankets, grateful it was getting warmer. They were entering spring, and she was coming with a vengeance. No more heavy comforters or bed warmers to have to worry about removing. At least the Ignian inventors were working on something they called central heating. They promised some sort of contraption that could be turned on to emit hot air. It didn't make any sense to Kajaan, but he'd be glad to use it all the same.

Kajaan fetched a glass of water while Yolotzin undressed, albeit a little unsteadily. He stared at his best friend until the entire glass was drained. After taking the glass back, Kajaan retreated to the en-suite bathroom to refill it from the waiting ewer and set it on the nightstand.

As soon as Yolotzin got into his bed, his eyes drifted closed and he burrowed into the covers. Smiling fondly at his best friend, Kajaan tucked him in and, even though he shouldn't, he pressed a kiss to his temple. He knew he was making his separation harder on himself, but Kajaan couldn't seem to help himself.

"Love you," he whispered as he stood.

The only response he got was a small snuffle, and Kajaan figured he was all right with that. He turned and left the prince's room for the last time. Even though he and Yolotzin had grown up together and were unofficial lovers, Kajaan was still expected to sleep in the servant's quarters, which were located on the first floor in the opposite wing to the royal family's.

Granted, his room was nicer than almost all the others and private, unlike the maids, cooks, and general groundskeepers' were. That was most definitely a perk that Kajaan did his best to not grumble about despite the distance from his lover. Even when he had to trudge to his own rooms in the middle of winter, shivering and hating that one of his responsibilities was to make sure that Yolotzin got safely to bed.

What he hadn't expected this late was to see three people heading toward the main hall of the castle from the direction of his room. Kajaan paused, blinked once. Blinked again. Then he bowed properly, showing deference to the three men. King Tonalli stood before him, austere and slightly detached as always. He shared Yolotzin's brown hair but had blue eyes instead. Ignians always made Kajaan slightly nervous, and the king always seemed taller than his already imposing six foot five.

In short, the king scared him.

To the king's right was his secretary, Yannat. He was just as haughty as the king, though at one point he hadn't been quite so stuck-up. The man was a full foot shorter than Kajaan with intense green eyes that didn't miss much of anything. It looked like he needed to shave his head soon. The usual shining dome was starting to look scruffy.

Then to the king's left was the Captain of the Guard. Also known as Kajaan's father. If King Tonalli was imposing, he had nothing on Captain Jeryit. Built like a mountain, Kajaan's father stood at six foot eight, more muscle than sense, cropped brown hair, and piercing brown eyes. Much to his father's disappointment, Kajaan looked nothing like him. Weedy, ginger, pale green eyes, and a half foot shorter. His mother had passed them on to him, from what he'd heard from the maids and Queen Brekka while he grew up.

Kajaan never had the pleasure of knowing his mother. She'd died bringing him into the world, bleeding out while his father desperately got them to a Healer. It was probably why his father hated him so much. Always pushing him to do better, even when Kajaan's tutors had nothing but praise for him. Pushing him to hone his Craft and learn how to fight with a sword, even though Kajaan was much more comfortable with a quill.

Instead, Kajaan pulled further and further away from his father's cold indifference as he grew older. Running around with Yolotzin and keeping him out of trouble had developed slimmer muscles, needing to be agile rather than rely on brute strength like his father had wanted. Spending more time with Yolotzin's tutors, learning anything and everything he could about being the best secretary that he could be.

Yolotzin had treated him with love and kindness despite everyone telling the young prince to stay away from Kajaan, insisting that the little ginger boy would be a bad influence on their prince. Yolotzin ignored them all, offering Kajaan his friendship instead of disgust. Kajaan refused to be anything less than perfect for his prince.

"Kajaan," the king said tartly, "I was wondering if you were coming home at all tonight."

"I had to see Prince Yolotzin safely abed before I retired, Your Majesty," Kajaan said, not daring to rise from his bow. "He didn't want to leave the wedding until Lady Naias was ready to depart."

King Tonalli snorted derisively. "That marriage is cursed. To a Void. Why my idiot brother hasn't disowned him or disposed of the Void, I don't know. At least the Healer's the youngest and most useless out of that brood."

"Asyl is quite the skilled alchemist," Kajaan said, stung by the harsh words and a little alarmed at King Tonalli mentioning disposing of someone. "He's a good man who's already suffered so much and deserves to be happy."

Behind the king, his father cleared his throat and shook his head. Kajaan glanced at him and scowled before schooling his features and returning his gaze to the floor. Right. Don't contradict the king, even though it was his nephew he was talking about. Even though Duke Ruvyn had clearly blessed Lord Kende and Asyl's union. He'd even proudly attended the ceremony tonight with his wife and the rest of his children.

There was a moment of tense silence while King Tonalli eyed him up and down before sneering at him. The air around them warmed, and Kajaan's heart did its best to break out of his chest. Nervous sweat prickled along his forehead, and Kajaan closed his eyes, trying to not tremble too openly.

"I have a task for you," King Tonalli said.

The king was giving him a task? Kajaan folded his hands together on the small of his back as he straightened, trying to look interested instead of panicked. The last time the king had asked him to do something, he'd been away from the castle for a moonturn. Yolotzin had nearly been a basket case by the time he'd returned, and it had taken Kajaan several hours to reassure his best friend that he was all right.

"Whatever Your Majesty needs," Kajaan said.

"You will take this missive to King Cadeyrn Greatblaze," King Tonalli said, handing Kajaan a thick scroll that Yannat passed to him. The king's seal in red wax glittered up at him in the low candlelight.

"May I ask why this can't be sent via a messenger?" Kajaan asked carefully.

"You are the messenger," Yannat said, snorting as if Kajaan had said something amusing. "Prince Yolotzin is occupied with his Fated and their upcoming wedding, and Lord Kende is helping him arrange it. Currently, you're not needed. When you get back, your duties will have changed to something befitting your station."

A cold shudder ran down Kajaan's spine. He didn't like the sound of that. What would his duties be changed to? Obviously he'd expected he'd be taking care of Lady Naias as well as Yolotzin, but Yannat was making it sound as if that wasn't the case. He flicked his gaze over to his towering father, who just stared at him with an unreadable expression. Somewhere in the back of his mind, Kajaan realized with horror that his hands were visibly shaking.

Would they really separate him and Yolotzin?

"You will be leaving immediately," the king said.

That snapped him back to attention immediately.

"Sorry?" Kajaan asked, blinking a few times.

"You will be leaving now," Yannat repeated, this time definitely sneering at him. "Your clothing has already been packed and the carriage loaded. You'll be taken towards Zothua and Paelfjord Castle as soon as the door closes behind you."

"But," Kajaan tried protesting, "it's been an incredibly long day. Surely a good night's sleep would be preferable before I see King Cadeyrn."

"The trip is a week long," Jeryit rumbled. "How you sleep tonight doesn't affect you one way or the other. You're to stop in Sestella the night before you have your audience, where you can refresh yourself."

"What about Tzinny?" Kajaan asked.

That had been the wrong thing to say. Both the king and his father got dark looks on their faces while Yannat just smiled gleefully. Kajaan tried to not shrink back, shivering at how the two overwhelming men were glowering at him.

"I'll handle him," King Tonalli said. "You need to leave now."

Kajaan opened his mouth to protest before he thought better. He snapped his jaw shut and bowed to him. Muttering the usual platitudes and farewells to the king, Kajaan spun on his heel and all but stomped down the hallway toward the stables again. How dare they! He debated running up to wake Yolotzin and let him know he was going to be gone for a while, but the footsteps behind him told Kajaan that he was being followed.

Probably so he couldn't do exactly what he wanted to do. Why were they separating him and Yolotzin? Had he somehow just been a sort of temporary companion that had been endured until Yolotzin found his Fated? Had that been the king's plan all along? Let the prince have his playmate until it was time to grow up and start producing offspring? Kajaan's heart ached. There wasn't even a way to send Yolotzin a message. All his correspondence was read before it was released to him.

Screening Yolotzin's mail had been one of Kajaan's duties. Was Yannat going to take over? The thought made Kajaan feel slightly sick, knowing that his life was going to be irrevocably changed in a fortnight. Goddess, he hoped it was just taking on more responsibility with his prince and his fiancée and he wasn't being tossed away. Maybe he could send a message to Lord Kende asking him if he knew. Or at least have him tell Yolotzin what happened.

Tell him that Kajaan hadn't just abandoned him.

He should have never left Yolotzin's room. He should have just steeled his heart and crawled into bed with him one last time. Maybe then he would have been able to properly say goodbye in the morning before he was sent out on this task.

Heart beating in his throat, Kajaan stopped beside the traditional carriage that had been hooked up to two beautiful horses. On the back were a couple of his steamer trunks, lashed down tight. At least they and the coach looked suitably worn, so hopefully they wouldn't attract too much attention. The coachman looked bored and cold if how tightly he'd bundled himself was any indication. Kajaan turned to see his father towering over him.

"Am I at liberty to know what the missive is about at least, since I'm being thrown out so hastily?" Kajaan asked, unable to keep the snark out of his tone.

His father growled low in his throat. "No." The man glanced up at the coachman before Jeryit's tone dropped, and his face seemed to soften. "Be careful. Highwaymen have been aggressive lately. Use your Craft to protect yourself if you need to. If it comes down to it, unhitch one of the horses and flee. Your missive is the biggest priority. Don't be a hero."

Kajaan couldn't keep his surprise off his face. That sounded like legitimate concern for him from his father. He blinked a few times at the man before giving him a jerky nod. Before he could say or do anything that spoiled the moment, Kajaan spun and climbed into the carriage. The moment the door shut, Jeryit smacked his hand against the carriage twice, and the driver snapped the reins.

He was on his way to Zothua.

For better or for worse.

CHAPTER 2

FOUR DAYS into the ride and Kajaan couldn't remember the last time he'd been so bored. He'd briefly opened the trunks the first day when they'd stopped for dinner. A cursory look had revealed no reading material had been packed for him. That had confused him. He'd been sure his father was involved in the packing. It was hard to miss the fact that Kajaan liked reading. Hell, there were always a couple of books sitting on his nightstand.

The second day he'd gone through the trunks a little more critically, and away from the watchful eye of the coachman. The man was always watching him closely, as if he'd take off running with the missive and any gold he could get his hands on in the middle of the night. It was odd that he didn't know the driver who'd been assigned to him, and the man refused to converse with him at any length.

Kajaan knew pretty much everyone in the castle, he liked knowing who was around his prince, and yet this man was unknown to him. It put him on edge, and the driver shut down all his attempts at conversations during the quiet moments. So Kajaan rifled through the trunks when he was able to get a moment away from the man.

His snooping hadn't eased his mind.

The top layer contained his jackets and slacks, folded neatly to prevent too much wrinkling. Most of them were his rattier ones, the ones he wore when he was going to the less suitable areas of Alenzon. He'd spied the outfit he wore to Tillet's all those years ago when he'd freed Asyl. Kajaan hadn't worn it since. If it hadn't been his favorite at the time, he would have burned the damn jacket. But underneath a few changes of clothes, what he saw puzzled him.

Sheets. The rest of the trunk was packed full of plain white sheets. Kajaan had repacked the first trunk quickly, trying to make it appear as if he hadn't noticed. The second trunk was more of the same. Clothes that were nicer, more formal, and much more conducive to meeting the neighboring king hadn't been packed for him. Why pack so little of his clothes and include so many sheets that were completely useless to him? It didn't make sense.

The pouch of coins that was usually included on his trips was also missing. Sure, he wasn't truly anyone important, but why hadn't he been given something? Did the coachman have the funds necessary for their stay at the inn once they reached Sestella? Somehow, Kajaan doubted it. He hadn't brought his own coin purse with him when he attended Lord Kende and Asyl's wedding. It wouldn't have been needed at all, considering he was driving and was at a friend's home.

He didn't have a copper to his name. The realization washed over him, as if he'd gotten ice cold water dumped over his head. No money, no good clothing that could prove that he had money, a suspicious driver…. Something inside him screamed that he was in danger, and he was inclined to believe it.

Anxiety had put him on edge for several hours, though it seemed stupid once he thought about his situation a bit more. They were on a well-traveled road, and he could see other people at almost all times. Nothing could happen to him without someone noticing. Still, he figured he shouldn't totally disregard the feeling in his gut.

When the driver stopped briefly in a bordering town on the third day, Kajaan slipped out of the carriage. He found the post office and cringed inwardly when he asked if he could send a letter collect. But who to send it to? He couldn't send it to Yolotzin. Any incoming mail would be intercepted and read, and Kajaan would be left adrift. The only other people he knew he could trust were also part of the castle. It didn't matter who he sent the letter to in Avitou. His name would surely have been flagged by now and any correspondence he mailed read. A sense of abandonment and helplessness coursed through him.

Was this how Asyl felt when he woke up chained to a bed? Alone for far too long, rejected by his parents for being born a Void, and no one around to watch his back. Knowing that no one was likely looking for him, no one to miss him when he didn't come home at night. No one to care when he was…. Kajaan's mind shied away from the violence that had been afflicted upon the lordling's person.

He could write to Asyl, Kajaan realized with a jolt. Their relationship was better than it had been a few moonturns ago, as in, they actually had one. Kajaan purchased the paper, ink, and wax seal that would be collected at the time of delivery. He scribbled a quick message, trying to be as concise about what had happened as he could. Hopefully Asyl would understand and forgive him when the messenger arrived and demanded however much it was going to be to accept the letter. He knew that Asyl could pay for it. Enchanted Waters was doing well, and he had a lord as a husband and a duke for a father-in-law.

Kajaan instructed that if the letter couldn't be hand delivered to Asyl at Enchanted Waters, then they needed to take it to Lord Kende Ruvyn. As an afterthought, he gave them Lady Naias Elrel's name. If the first two weren't able or willing to take it, maybe she would hear his name and realize something was amiss. Especially since he was sure Yolotzin was upset about his disappearance. The two of them had rarely been apart, and now that separation could quickly become permanent. Kajaan really wanted to be wrong.

The messenger tucked the letter, his lifeline, into his vest and turned toward the attached stables. It was all Kajaan could do to not beg the men to let him come along instead of sending the letter. But the missive King Tonalli had given him weighed heavily in the carrying case belted to his waist. There was nothing else he could do. Help would arrive… or it wouldn't. It might not matter in the end, and he had to accept that possibility.

By the time Kajaan snuck back into the carriage, he spotted the messenger trotting out of the city, already on his way. Kajaan wished him good speed and that his horse wouldn't lame. The coachman arrived as the messenger faded into the distance, and hopped on, smelling heavily of alcohol. Kajaan winced but said nothing, curling up in the carriage and staring out the windows. It was all he could do as he stared at the mind-numbing scenery of rolling hills, fields of wheat, corn, or cows.

He wanted to be home.

Kajaan blinked when the coachman swerved off of the well-beaten and heavily used road onto a lesser-known trail the following day. He pulled his thoughts away from the letter he'd penned to Asyl yesterday and forced himself to pay attention. There should be no reason they'd be on this road. They still had three days of traveling to get to the royal city of Sestella. Why was he deviating from the route? There was no way this was a shortcut. The driver was Averian; he wouldn't know the rural pathways that cut through the rolling hills of Zothua.

The carriage rocked violently when its wheel hit a rock, throwing him around like a rag doll, and he flung out his arms to try and catch himself. What the fuck? The horses were galloping now instead of the leisurely canter that they'd been at for the last four days. The shabby carriage rattled around him, threatening to fall apart on the next jolt. Kajaan opened the window to the driver, quickly taking in the absence of any sort of civilization around them.

"What's going on?" Kajaan asked.

"Nothing to worry about," the coachman said. "Shortcut."

"Shortcut my ass. Turn around and follow the main thoroughfare. We should be following the direct orders from our king, not off gallivanting as if we were minor lordlings," Kajaan scolded him, frustration taking over the fear roiling in his gut.

"I can't do that," the man replied.

"Like hell you can't!" Kajaan snapped. "Turn around right—"

His words died in his throat as the coachman turned and pointed something at him. For a second, Kajaan didn't quite recognize the weapon. It had a hollow barrel attached to a polished wooden grip and a trigger. The weapon had a faint acrid smell to it. As soon as he realized what it was, Kajaan scooted to the back of the carriage, not exactly proud of himself for how badly his hands were shaking.

An Ignis flintlock. Like many other Craft-operated tools, this one didn't require the user to be an Ignian to be used, as it held its own charge. Pulling on that trigger would ignite the explosive black powder inside and launch a small metal ball that was packed into said powder.

Apparently the Ignis inventors had gotten the idea when a granary exploded. Something to do with surfaces and small particles and how they reacted quickly to fire. Why they had made such a deadly weapon was beyond Kajaan. Most elemental Craft Blessed were more than dangerous enough with their abilities.

Such abilities had passed over Kajaan, leaving him essentially helpless in situations like these. He wouldn't be able to reach out and flood the barrel to render the powder useless or swirl the dirt path ahead of them to mud to force the driver to focus on the horses in order to keep them safe.

"Sorry," the coachman said. "You're a really nice kid, always talking to me as if we were equals, making sure I ate and didn't push the animals too much. But I've got a job to do, and it includes you being quiet."

Kajaan nodded a few times earnestly. He could be quiet. The coachman grunted his assent and shut the partition. As soon as he was cut off from the outside, Kajaan felt panic overtaking him, his heart thundering in his ears. It seemed his worst fears really were coming to fruition. He really wasn't going to the castle; it had all been a ruse to get him isolated and away from Yolotzin. But why? What would his death even serve? He wasn't anyone of any note. Was it really just personal?

"Use your Craft to protect yourself if you need to. If it comes down to it, unhitch one of the horses and flee."

But I don't have a strong Craft!

The thought hit Kajaan hard. He could change the composition of a limited amount of liquids from time to time, sure. That's how he'd gotten Asyl free. He could drive Yolotzin all around their home city of Alenzon in a Craft-powered vehicle and not run out of energy. But he wasn't a fighter. He could passably wield a sword thanks to his early training, but Kajaan much preferred to wait and talk his way out of situations. Talking his way out of this would be impossible. The desperation in the driver's voice and his wild eyes indicated a man who was teetering on the edge.

Kajaan closed his eyes as the ride got bumpier until he was certain they weren't even on any sort of known path. He might not be able to fight or use his Craft, but he knew patience. Once he got the opportunity to try and flee or appeal to the man's better senses, he would do everything he could to defuse the situation. Kajaan struggled to keep his breathing even. His life was forfeit if he passed out like a damsel in the queen's romance books.

The carriage began to slow. Kajaan slid to the door and put his hand on it, keeping a careful eye on the closed partition. He hadn't thought about throwing himself out of the vehicle while the horses had been galloping, but now that they weren't going at a breakneck pace, maybe he could jump.

And go where?

He was dead twice over. Even if he was able to run, the coachman could run him down with the horses or shoot him from a distance. His Craft was useless, so he couldn't rely on that whatsoever to help protect him. The coachman must have felt or heard Kajaan unlatching the door. The partition banged open, and the flintlock was pointed at him again.

"Don't," the man warned.

"I'm dead either way," Kajaan said, an odd sense of calm settling over him.

Pain seared through him as he flung his body weight into the door. The crack from the flintlock echoed over the hills, and Kajaan's ears started ringing. He tumbled out of the carriage and rolled a few feet away from the startled horses. Luckily, the coachman had to settle the horses before he had the chance to load the weapon again.

That left Kajaan with a few seconds to think of what to do. His upper arm burned as he pushed himself to his feet, his vision going black around the edges, his body protesting with each movement. He must have taken longer to recover from his fall and the injury than he thought as he looked toward the prancing horses.

The flintlock was pointed at him for a third time. Kajaan didn't think, he just reacted. He flung out his uninjured hand toward the man, freezing him in place. The body was 70 percent water. All the water in his muscles, blood, fat…. Kajaan tapped into that and held the man still. Exhaustion was quickly tugging at his limbs, making his knees weak. Kajaan had never really been able to get proper rest and recover his energy when he attempted to sleep in the rocking carriage. But he had to try.

Thinking about what he wanted the water to do, Kajaan winced as the man began to scream. His body bent at awkward angles, joints popping free and bones fracturing, trying to obey what was demanded of them. The driver's hand flopped over to unhitch the horses from the carriage. That gave Kajaan his means of escape. The next was to unarm the driver. His wails and sobs were nearly unbearable, but it would be over soon.

As soon as the flintlock went sailing off to the side, Kajaan released the man, gasping. The black spots in his vision receded ever so slightly as he stumbled a few steps toward the front of the carriage. He had to leave. Now. Kajaan had no idea where he was going to go, but he couldn't stay here.

Trying to ignore the driver's wretched weeping, Kajaan rushed forward and soothed the horses as much as he could. The scent of his blood, the driver's screams, and the unfamiliar report of the flintlock had driven them near to panic. He grabbed their lead, pulling the duo away from the carriage. There was nothing here that he needed to bring with him past the potentially fake missive.

If there was anyone at all nearby, they would have been alerted by the man's screams, if not the fired shot. He had to get out of here before anyone came by. There was no way in hell that they'd listen to him before rendering judgment and either arresting or killing him. Kajaan wasn't even entirely sure he was legally in Zcthua anymore. Focus. His head felt light. Between the use of his Craft and the blood loss, it was a miracle he was still standing.

Just as Kajaan got the remaining harness off the horses, he heard shouting. His heart plummeted, and Kajaan spun to see who was nearby. There were six men rapidly approaching on their own mounts, in livery that Kajaan recognized. His naive heart leapt upon seeing them before his suspicion kicked in. Why were members of King Tonalli's guard here?

He got his answer when four of them pulled out their own flintlocks and aimed them at him. Tears sprang to Kajaan's eyes. Why had they slated for him to die? Was he a scapegoat for some other plan, or was he just a pest to be eradicated?

He didn't even know if Yolotzin would ever know what happened to him.

If Yolotzin knew how much Kajaan loved him.

For better or for worse.

Please, goddess, Kajaan prayed for the first time since he was a child. *Please, Lady Ilyphari, I won't stand in the way of your will. As much as I wish it had been me Yolotzin was Fated for, I won't interfere. Just let me survive this so I can love and support him as his confidant.*

As the seconds passed and the men steadied their aim, the weariness that had seeped into Kajaan's muscles eased. His fingers tingled with power, and he felt a warmth expand in his chest. Instinctively, he knew that he didn't have access to this wellspring of power for very long. Kajaan flung out his hand and stunned the six men and their horses, freezing them in place.

Just as he did, he finally realized what he'd done, not only to these six men, but to the driver as well. There was an incredible amount of rules on how to not use an elemental Craft that was taught the day after their Awakening.

Ignians weren't allowed to tamper with anyone's body temperature, Gales couldn't take someone's breath from their lungs, Gaians weren't allowed to manipulate the minute amount of metals in a human body.… And Aquans were forbidden to manipulate the water inside a body.

Even if he survived this, his life was forfeit. Even if he got back home, got back to Yolotzin and tried to seek asylum with the church, he would be hanged. Maybe he could make his case of self-defense against the coachman, but he truthfully didn't know if the six men were here to kill or protect him. If there was any chance he got home and to a trial, he could plead his case and explain how terrified he'd been and was running on instinct.

Yolotzin would understand. He'd be able to feel Kajaan's emotions and know he wasn't lying and had truly panicked. But he wasn't ever going to see Yolotzin again, was he? Tears fell from his eyes even as he held the twelve bodies in thrall. He had to do something. He couldn't just hold them forever, and even if he tried holding them until he got out of his sphere of influence, they could easily catch up to get into range and shoot him. But he refused to kill them.

Swallowing hard, Kajaan slowed the blood flowing through the men, trying hard to not feel too guilty at their frantically rolling eyes and startled looks. Rendering them unconscious without killing them was going to be a small window, but he had already likely killed the coachman who'd finally stopped sobbing. He wasn't going to add to his body count. When the guard's eyes began to flutter closed, Kajaan would release the man and his mount. The horses' reactions ranged from stamping to screaming, and two of them bolted, throwing their riders to the ground.

Finally, the last guard's eyes glazed over. Kajaan released them, the power at his fingertips vanishing between one heartbeat and the next. Bone-deep exhaustion washed over him, and the world spun as Kajaan crumpled. He wasn't unconscious, but he needed a minute or two to breathe and get his bearings once more. The two horses he was stealing were prancing in place, the earlier soothing forgotten.

Breathing was hard. His chest ached as Kajaan forced himself to his feet, and his vision grayed out on him. Blood soaked his sleeve, and Kajaan tried to ignore the throbbing around the wound. He didn't want to look at it. Somehow, he managed to mount one of the horses, riding bare and sliding on her sweat-slicked hair until he got his seat. His arm ached, and Kajaan looked over at the crumpled guards.

A few of them were already stirring.

Kajaan kicked the horse he was on into a trot, weaving the fingers of his good hand into the mane. He hadn't ridden bareback before, but at least he was a skilled rider and had an excellent seat. It didn't take him too long to figure out how to balance himself and sit properly. There was shouting. Angry shouting, if Kajaan could determine it over the wind and thundering hooves.

Something tugged him to head north by northeast. Kajaan didn't know what, but he wasn't going to question whatever instinct was telling him to ride in that direction. All he knew was that Sestella and Paelfjord Castle was east of Averia, and that was the direction the coach had been heading for the last few days. He kicked the mare into a gallop, heart pounding as hard as the hooves on the earth below.

It was almost loud enough to cover the other horse's approaching gallop.

Kajaan glanced over his shoulder and immediately regretted that he did. Two of the guards had recovered enough to pursue him, weapons at the ready. One of the raised flintlocks cracked and missed. Kajaan crouched low to the horse and urged the mare on. The earlier run had already tired the creature, and tapping into the beast's body, he could tell there wasn't much left in her. He had to pull back else he ran the risk of the mare's heart bursting.

As much as Kajaan wished he valued his life over a beast of burden, he couldn't do that to this magnificent, innocent creature. Just as he started to pull back, to urge the horse into a trot or a canter, he heard another crack and felt something hit the area between his shoulder blade and neck. There wasn't any pain, almost as if he'd been pegged by a rock.

The force of the blow unbalanced him, and already weakened, Kajaan pitched forward. He tumbled off the mare and hit the ground, much like one of Reina's rag dolls. Kajaan couldn't draw in a full breath, wincing from the tightness in his chest. It would have been kinder if he'd struck his head on a rock and immediately died from the fall.

At least he was lying on his back. Now the pain settled in; a deep, harsh biting pain in his shoulder that set not only the entire area on fire, but up his neck and along his jaw too. Somewhere in the back of his mind, he registered the feeling of his clothes getting damp. He could hear the horse he'd been riding stamping and braying. Shouting. Angry, incredibly angry shouting. Kajaan had never heard anyone so enraged before. He knew it was likely directed at him. Well, he'd put up a good fight, he supposed.

His vision swam, and Kajaan knew in his last few moments, he was fine shedding a few tears. He'd never truly told Yolotzin how much he loved him. He'd never get to say goodbye. A velvety nose snuffed near his face, and he felt the warmth of the creature's breath ruffle his hair. At least he was going to die under the open, cloudless sky.

And what a beautiful day it was.

Dimly, Kajaan heard more voices add to the shouts. Screams of pain, indignant curses. As his vision began to fade, Kajaan ignored whatever was happening with the two guards nearby. He wanted to go out thinking of his first and oldest love. Someone jostled his injured arm, shooting searing pain through his body. Kajaan didn't even have the energy to cry out as his vision went black.

Chapter 3

"Hey, Asyl. There's a courier here for you," Prenta said cautiously from the workroom door.

Asyl looked up from his potion and nodded. She flashed him a hesitant smile and retreated quickly. He had to force himself to not roll his eyes. Another Aquan who was terrified to touch his cauldrons. Asyl hadn't understood it with Naias, and he most certainly didn't understand it with Prenta or Binty. Olire offered him a small smile, knowing full well the front store ladies thought it was best to leave the brewing to the Voids.

Ruffling the teenager's red curls, Asyl untied the apron he now donned while brewing. He draped it over his workbench, dropping off his Ignis gloves at the same time. There. Mostly presentable, though definitely sweaty, Asyl entered the front of the store where he indeed saw a courier hovering awkwardly at the end of the counter. He approached the man, seeing he was a fellow Void, and smiled faintly at him. Thankfully it seemed like he had steady work and wasn't a complete pariah where he lived.

If the man's surprise was anything to go by, the courier hadn't expected a Void to be his contact.

"Lord Asyl Ruvyn?" the courier asked.

A small thrill ran through Asyl, and his smile grew. He didn't care about the title, but taking Kende's last name had been heady. Hell, Asyl had bounced around their bedchambers when Kende handed him the official paperwork confirming that his name had been changed. It had taken his lover several hours—and orgasms—later to wear him out enough that Asyl could sleep for the night.

"That's me. How can I help?" Asyl asked politely.

"I have a collect letter for you," the courier said, glancing over at Prenta as she rang up another customer. "It's three gold."

Asyl wanted to blanch at the amount. He managed a small cough instead. "Excuse me?"

"I'm from Kierton," the courier said. "It's a three-day ride. One gold a day, and it was sent collect."

"From who?" Asyl demanded, folding his arms.

He wasn't going to look at or touch the letter at all until he knew. If he even so much as expressed interest in the letter, then he could be liable for the price anyways.

"Kajaan Pernoac," the man said. "He instructed that if I was unable to deliver to you, then to go to Lord Kende Ruvyn, and then Lady Naias Elrel. He was insistent that one of you three needed to read his letter."

Kajaan? The thought that the man was contacting him of all people threw Asyl for a loop. He had no idea why the prince's secretary was writing to him when he could have Prince Yolotzin relay any messages. Asyl stared at him for a minute before he nodded. Something was going on, and if Kajaan couldn't speak freely with the prince, then maybe Asyl was his next best bet.

The one good thing over the last year was that he no longer truly needed to worry about money. Enchanted Waters was doing better every moonturn between private orders and the storefront. Having a lord for a husband certainly helped as well, but Asyl didn't like depending on him for everything. He snagged the requested three gold from the cash box and avoided Prenta's questioning gaze. Asyl handed the courier the money and received a thin letter.

As soon as Asyl had the letter in his hands, the courier saluted him and all but fled the store. Asyl inspected the letter and shrugged before finally breaking the seal. He skimmed over the letter and stopped halfway through. As he reread it, this time intently, Asyl's heart pounded in his chest and worry started to bloom in the back of his mind. He had to get home and show the letter to his husband.

Asyl darted into the workroom and grabbed Olire's shoulder.

"Turn off the burners. I don't want you unattended in here with the Plates," Asyl said. "Then either help Prenta or go home."

"But the potions will spoil!" Olire protested, obviously not understanding.

"That's fine," Asyl replied, shaking his head. "It's fine. I need to leave, and I won't have you hurt."

"Tsela will be here soon!" Olire complained.

"Two hours isn't soon," Asyl chided. "Please do as I say."

The boy pouted at him but nodded. Asyl kissed his forehead, grabbed his messenger bag containing his research, and ran out the back door. Trying to flag down a carriage or wait for Toemi would take too long, and he wasn't that far from home. Asyl ran through the barely warm spring evening, realizing he'd left his light cloak behind. At least he was wearing his brace, keeping his knee stable during his run.

Asyl darted up the stairs to the manor and pushed his way through the heavy doors, aware that he probably looked like a panicked, sweaty mess. Nothing like how a proper lord should look or act. Birgir, as always, sneered at him as he approached, his mouth set in a hard line.

"Kende," Asyl said, too overwhelmed to consult his bond.

"Now, young man—" Birgir began to scold him.

"Where's my husband?" Asyl snapped.

"Upstarts—"

"Asyl," Kende said from the door of his study.

Turning away from the rude steward, Asyl rushed over to his husband and held out the letter.

"How quickly can you get Prince Yolotzin here?" Asyl asked.

Kende frowned and took the letter from Asyl. His husband wrapped an arm around his shoulders, pulling him close to his body. Asyl automatically nestled into Kende's chest, shifting his weight to take pressure off his injured knee. Even as his love's warmth spread through him, banishing the fear that had gripped him during his run, it also meant that Asyl could feel Kende's reaction. His husband went very still, and he cursed under his breath.

"Siora," the man called. "I need Tzin here immediately. Tell him anything to get him here, but within the hour."

"Yes, sir," Siora said from behind Kende.

She and Linel had been working with Kende for Naias and Prince Yolotzin's wedding. Sending out RSVPs, making sure the florist, bakery, catering, venue, and everyone else who was involved had everything they needed. It was a much bigger affair than his own wedding, considering the crown prince was involved, and the two women and Kende were being run off their feet trying to keep everything on track and dealing with issues quickly.

Asyl couldn't say he was too upset that Linel wasn't always following him around anymore, but he did miss her company from time to time. Linel actually talked to him and would bounce ideas for his shop back to him when he was in a planning mood. At least he didn't have to deal with a perpetual bodyguard anymore.

Not since his mother had been arrested.

His father had visited her in prison until she gave birth to his infant sister. The baby was handed over to Lord Lairne without any question, though apparently Ilfa had screeched at him for how he was abandoning her. Lairne's divorce from her became final a week later. The last Asyl had heard about her, she'd fallen into a deep depression, though she held firm to her beliefs that Voids should be rounded up and incarcerated.

Asyl got to babysit his newest sister, along with his other young siblings, quite often, much to Kende's delight. Being a minimum of thirteen years older than his siblings was hard at times, but he was making an effort to be involved with his estranged family. Even if he did struggle to relate to his giggling and girl-obsessed ten-year-old sister.

At least his father genuinely seemed like he wanted Asyl in his life again, actively inviting him to family dinners and parties. Unlike his mother, who'd tried to kill him. Sure, she'd had some ulterior motives, but at least she faced him herself instead of getting someone else to do her dirty work for her.

Asyl didn't realize he was trembling until he felt Kende's lips in his hair, his lover gently whispering nonsense, trying to calm him.

"What'll happen if… if…." Asyl trailed off, unable to voice his concern.

Kende gently shushed him and led him into the study, where Linel was working on the design of the wedding program and food cards. She smiled sweetly at him, though she likely knew full well that Asyl was distraught. He didn't even really know why.

Sure, he and Kajaan had a tentative friendship, and the man had proved himself by rescuing him over four years ago. But why the thought of him in danger had upset him so much, Asyl couldn't quite figure out.

Kende sat on the couch and pulled Asyl sideways into his lap. He tucked him close to his chest, humming and kissing his head. Sometimes he dipped down and kissed his face or lips. It wasn't meant to be sexual, nor did Asyl take it that way. Just knowing Kende was here for him, comforting him, was enough to calm Asyl's anxieties.

Siora arrived with the prince close to an hour later. The man looked a bit harried and more than worried. In fact, he seemed rumpled, and not quite as put together as he normally was. There was a faint darkness around his eyes and a shadow along his jaw.

"Cousin," Prince Yolotzin said.

"Hey, Tzin," Kende said. "We got a letter from Kajaan."

"Kajaan?" Prince Yolotzin asked, looking frustrated. "Why would he mail you? The bastard disappeared a week ago—"

"Read it," Kende interrupted gently, handing him the letter.

Frowning, Prince Yolotzin took the letter from his cousin and took a deep breath before opening it. His face grew darker the more he read, and Asyl could only imagine what his reaction was going to be.

My Dear Lord Asyl Ruvyn,

I hope this letter reaches you well. I apologize in advance for having to send it collect, but I'm currently in a bit of a bind. The King, his advisor, and my father ambushed me after we left your wedding and decided I needed to call upon King Cadeyrn Greatblaze of Zothua to deliver a missive with contents that I have no knowledge of. I currently have no identification or funds, and when I inspected what had been packed for me, no proper clothes or anything personal. The coachman isn't someone I know, and the carriage itself is shabby and unmarked.

Maybe I'm worried about nothing, but I can't help but feel like something's wrong. I snuck away from the carriage to send this to you, and I don't have much time. Please make sure this letter, or at least the contents, get to Tzin. Make sure he knows I didn't intend on leaving without saying farewell. I couldn't. My father followed me to the carriage to make sure I couldn't. I didn't even get to my room, so I couldn't leave a note anywhere there either.

I was assured I was only going to be gone for two to three weeks. If I don't come back... well. You know.

I wish you and Lord Kende nothing but the best. Give Tzin all my love and well wishes for his marriage to Lady Naias.

Thank you.

"What the fuck," was Prince Yolotzin's reply.

"It is incredibly concerning," Kende said.

"Only three people knew where he went," Asyl said. "If something happened to him…."

"No. Nothing's happening to him," Prince Yolotzin spat. "I'm demanding the truth from my father. He's been dodging me ever since I started asking around to figure out where Kajaan went. Maybe I'll ambush Captain Jeryit. He and Kajaan haven't had the best relationship, but if Kajaan's in danger…."

"Unless he was part of the planning," Asyl whispered.

The look he got from the prince made him cringe and duck his head. Kende cleared his throat, drawing Prince Yolotzin's glare.

"You have to be aware that it's a possibility, cousin," Kende said. "Leave the letter here. We'll keep it safe."

"But...," Prince Yolotzin faltered.

He looked down at the crumpled letter in his hands and gently smoothed it out. His eyes got a little shiny, and Prince Yolotzin sniffed, staring at the potential last words of his best friend and lover. Asyl felt his heart break for the man. To have someone so close be ripped away without being able to say goodbye.... Asyl had almost been in the same position during his Introduction Gala when Kende had been stabbed with Void blood and nearly died as the poison ate away at him.

"We'll keep it safe," Kende repeated gently. "I promise you. If he doesn't come home, I won't contest you for ownership."

This time, a few tears dropped from the prince's eyes. He let out a choked noise and nodded, thrusting the letter at Kende. Asyl quietly took it from him, standing. He wrapped his arms around Prince Yolotzin's waist and hugged him. The prince was a couple inches taller than his husband, and their bodies fit all wrong, but with the hug he got back, Asyl knew his action had been the right one.

"Oh Goddess, what if he's gone? What'll I do?" Prince Yolotzin said.

"Pick up the pieces of your heart and move on," Kende replied. "Lady Naias will understand if you need to delay the wedding to mourn your best friend."

"I truly thought he and I would be Fated," Prince Yolotzin whispered. "We've been together for so long. I just thought it would snap into place once Father relinquished the kingdom to me."

"Maybe you weren't for reasons that'll become clear in the next few years," Kende offered. "Who knows why the goddess forges the bonds that she does, but they always seem to make sense in the end."

"Like Lady Ilfa and Lord Lairne?" the prince said caustically.

Asyl stiffened and took a few steps away. "They did love each other before my Awakening failed. Only after that did she seem to become twisted."

Prince Yolotzin sighed, seeming a little chastised and said, "Sorry. That wasn't exactly fair."

"No, it wasn't," Kende said. "You know as well as I do that Fated relationships very rarely fail, and usually it's due to outside influence. Such as what happened with Ilfa. Hell, it's more common for a marriage to fall apart when one of them finds their Fated."

"Do you think he's not my Fated because this was going to happen?" Prince Yolotzin asked.

"I don't know," Kende replied. "This may have happened even if he was. You know your father hasn't exactly enjoyed the fact that the two of you were practically inseparable as children and haven't grown much further apart as adults."

Prince Yolotzin chewed on his lower lip and nodded. He turned toward the door and took a deep, shaking breath before nodding again. With that, he stood up straight, squaring his shoulders, and left the room. Asyl knew damn well the man was going to go on a tear to find out what happened to his best friend. Looking up at his husband, Asyl winced slightly seeing the blatant worry on his face.

"Will he be all right?" Asyl asked.

"Goddess, I hope so. He's the only heir, so I doubt King Tonalli will do anything to him," Kende said and grimaced. "Just as long as he hasn't lost his mind."

CHAPTER 4

KING CADEYRN Greatblaze of Zothua stared at the letters on his desk, pushing his glasses up the bridge of his nose. The damn things slid far too much, making reading a massive pain. Behind him, he could hear the scratching of a pen and knew his secretary, Quillin, was hard at work drafting a preliminary terse letter to the nearby kingdom of Averia. He was pretty sure that's who the young man in the dungeon belonged to, though he didn't know anyone in the castle with bright red hair.

That meant the man was either an imposter or some sort of bandit. He glanced at the scroll that the redhead had been carrying and scowled at the broken seal. What in the hell had possessed him to ride out a few days ago in the small hours of the morning, going farther and harder than he usually did? He'd nearly left his retinue in the dust, pushing his mount as hard as he could.

At least his gexena, Maeeri, had enjoyed the run and hadn't been bothered with the extra weight of carrying a second passenger. Not once had Cadeyrn thought his mount couldn't handle the added burden. Maeeri stood at a full twenty-two hands and had the insane muscle definition to go with it. She would be a formidable dam once he started breeding her.

The thought kept circling in his head. But why. Why? It made no damn sense to him. Eventually Cadeyrn growled and removed his glasses so he could press the palm of his hands to his eyes, hating the headache he felt starting to bloom between his brows. The scratching behind him tapered off, and he heard Quillin move slightly.

"Anything I can help with?" he asked in his perpetual soft voice.

"No," Cadeyrn snapped. Silence reigned in the small room for a few minutes before the king snarled at himself. "Yes. I can't find the reason for why I did what I did."

"What you did. You mean saving the kid downstairs?" Quillin asked.

"Yes," Cadeyrn said simply.

"I can try to help there," his advisor's teasing voice said.

Cadeyrn lowered his hands to stare balefully at Ameyalli as they entered his study. His advisor was a delightful person who always challenged his decisions and truly made him think about his choices if they didn't believe he was thinking clearly. Right now their influence wasn't entirely wanted. Especially with that teasing smile playing on their lips.

"Please, do tell," Quillin said, a lilt of happiness in his words.

Trying to not roll his eyes at the Fated couple, Cadeyrn fought his smile. Truthfully, he enjoyed both his advisor and secretary and had thrown them a huge wedding once they'd announced they were Fated for each other. Quillin got to his feet and gently kissed Ameyalli's cheek, causing them to blush lightly. The couple before Caderyn was almost half his age, and Ameyalli wasn't used to public affection. Or any sort of affection that didn't happen in complete privacy.

"All right, then," Cadeyrn said, leveling a look at the Seer. "Tell me why I did what I did."

Ameyalli's face broke out into a smile, and they simply said, "He's your Fated."

Thank the goddess Cadeyrn didn't have anything in his hand, else it would have shattered on the ground. He stared at the Seer and their Fated in numb shock for a minute before he snorted and shook his head. His heart pounded at the words, and Cadeyrn resolutely tried ignoring it. The moment they'd uttered the words, everything seemed to slot perfectly in place.

Fifteen years ago, he would have loved to hear those words, would have loved to believe that the goddess hadn't forgotten him. But he wasn't a newly crowned monarch anymore, aching for someone to love and hold during those first stressful years.

"That's not possible," Cadeyrn said flatly.

"Menea wasn't your Fated," Ameyalli said. "It was an arranged marriage, and you two fell in love after a couple of years. It's not the same."

"I'm not attracted to a *boy*," Cadeyrn snapped.

He quickly got to his feet, making his chair screech backward and nearly tip over. Neither of the two in front of him so much as winced, more than used to his blustering. Because in the end, it really was just frustration leaking through. He'd never be able to live with himself if he hurt Quillin or Ameyalli, even accidentally.

"He's not a boy, he's a man," Ameyalli replied as calmly as ever. "Why did you ride out on Maeeri with a retinue and Healer prior to dawn?"

Cadeyrn glowered at them, trying to intimidate them into dropping the subject. It was practically impossible, but he had to try. Ameyalli was one hell of a force of nature. One that Cadeyrn usually respected. Right now, he didn't want to hear it.

"Why did you ride as if the very devil was on your tail?" Ameyalli pressed.

"Because I felt like I needed to," Cadeyrn snarled at them. "There's no reason to it. I just did. I felt like I needed to ride, and I kept people with me just in case something happened."

"And something did. Out of all the acres, leagues, miles, whatever you want to use to measure the distance, finding the man and saving him should have been damn near impossible. Did you notice that his horses were pointed in the castle's direction? He was riding to you as you were to him," Ameyalli said, their voice still maddingly calm.

Cadeyrn clenched his hands into fists as his heart beat harder in confirmation of their words. He focused inward to try and breathe in deep to calm it, hating that the room seemed to grow warmer. His control over his Craft hadn't been tested for at least a decade. And now hearing three simple words had thrown his discipline out the window.

There was no way the man several floors down was his Fated. It wasn't possible. The goddess wouldn't grant him a second love. Not after he'd failed to keep his wife safe.

"You charged Tonalli's guards without even giving them time to explain," Ameyalli continued. "But then you saw the man. You got off Maeeri and immediately went to his side and called for the Healer. I saw how you cradled him. How panicked you looked when he didn't respond to your touch."

A cold feeling settled in the base of his spine at the remembered horror. Seeing the redhead covered in blood, his face pale and lips blue, had nearly sent Cadeyrn into a rage. Only feeling the slow yet steady heartbeat under his hand had kept him grounded.

His Healer, Tamya, had gotten the wounds to stop bleeding and stabilized the young man, but that hadn't completely eased Cadeyrn's racing pulse. The man's blood had coated his hands, arms, and chest by the time they had returned to Paelfjord and Cadeyrn finally relinquished him to his Healer.

Then he'd interrogated the guards who had been about to kill the redhead. They'd claimed he was a criminal that escaped custody. When Cadeyrn had pressed on why corporal punishment and running him down in a foreign country was his sentence, the men had balked. Until one of them had told Cadeyrn that the redhead had used his Craft to manipulate others' bodies. That was a universal crime, agreed on by every kingdom, but something about how they said it made Cadeyrn doubtful.

Desperate men made desperate decisions that might not always be morally correct. Cadeyrn had claimed jurisdiction since they were on his land, and he sent the guards packing, having some of his own escort them back to the border. He'd instructed them to sweep the area to look for anything suspicious. They found the coach and the ruined corpse that was sluggishly dripping blood from the driver's seat onto the dirt below.

According to his Healer pathologist, the man's cells had burst, and the bones in his arms were broken at weird angles. She'd been confused at the autopsy until Cadeyrn asked if an Aquan manipulating a body would result in the damage. That had silenced the entire morgue, and his pathologist stared at him with wide, terrified eyes. No one wanted to run experiments, even on animals, to try and figure out, and she refused to give him a definitive answer to his question.

"If he truly is a criminal, then there's nothing between us anyways," Cadeyrn said flatly, feeling the anger leak from him. "I have to think of the kids first. Would they even be ready to understand that I have a man as my Fated?"

"Plenty of people are bisexual or pansexual," Quillin said with a shrug. "Why would it be such a big deal if our king was too?"

It wasn't an issue for him. Cadeyrn had been interested in the exercising guardsmen as much as he was watching the ladies giggle during soirees. He'd wanted to wait for his Fated, but his aging father wanted to make sure the line of succession was secure. Cadeyrn hadn't protested too loudly. His wife had been beyond gorgeous with a wicked sense of humor.

Then she'd given him four wonderful children and was gone well before her time.

"Fayette and Rodolfo are *six*," Cadeyrn said. "How can they understand?"

"They'd understand their daddy was falling in love and happy again," Ameyalli whispered.

"I won't disgrace Menea's memory," Cadeyrn snapped.

"It's been four years," Quillin said, "and I know for a fact she'd want you to pursue this. She said so herself when she realized she'd lose the fight. Don't deny it. I was in the room with you."

Cadeyrn closed his eyes and hung his head, letting all his breath out and collapsing back into his chair. All the anger and frustration that had risen in him flowed away. He remembered the moment as if it was yesterday. Holding Menea's skeletal hand, withered from the ravages of her unending fever. Her eyes bright and voice steady, even as her body slowly wasted away in the warm autumn evening.

Promise me you'll love again.

He did. He loved their children without any hesitation. He loved his advisor and secretary, even though they were currently annoying him. His Healer, his staff, Maeeri. They all held pieces of his heart and affection, and he gave it freely. Cadeyrn was content to live the rest of his life sleeping alone in his bed. It wasn't as if his body had stirred for anyone.

Until he'd panicked seeing the crumpled man with red hair and pale skin littered with freckles, a stark difference from anyone living in Zothua. Touching him had roused a soul-deep urge to protect another who wasn't his child. Even now he knew the man was below and could pinpoint exactly where he was in the castle. It was distracting to say the least.

But he'd already failed the goddess once. He hadn't been able to properly take care of Menea, and she'd died because of it. All the money and Healers in the world hadn't been able to break her wasting fever. He hadn't been able to help. What kind of husband failed the mother of his children, let alone someone who could be his Fated?

"The goddess gives us our Fated for a reason," Ameyalli said. "Maybe he's meant to heal your heart and give you strength until the end."

"Then he's got one hell of a burden," Cadeyrn said.

"You're a good man, Cadeyrn. These last four and a half years have been awful for everyone. The kids included," Quillin said.

Cadeyrn winced. Thaddaeus was old enough to remember his mother and her passing, though he was just now grasping the permanence of death. In the beginning, he had asked for her during dinner or when Cadeyrn was trying to teach him something new. Every time he asked, especially now when Thaddaeus was slowly understanding he'd never see his mother again, it tore at his heart. Burying his wife had been a special kind of torture.

She'd just turned thirty when the fever grasped her. Thank the goddess for his nannies. He wouldn't have been able to deal with four kids all under the age of ten and care for his ailing wife at the same time. Even now he could still see her fever-glazed eyes as she looked up at him, her hair plastered to her skull with sweat. How thin and wasted her body had become after fighting the fever for weeks. It was possible she might not have ever fully recovered, even if she'd beaten the fever.

Being bound to her bed would have killed her just as readily as the fever did.

Small, hurried footsteps echoed through the open door that led to the hallway. Cadeyrn quickly wiped his cheeks to get rid of the few tears that had escaped and composed himself. He knew that gait, and he stood, quickly rounding his desk. Quillin and Ameyalli both retreated to the window of his office as Fayette burst into the room.

Her large smile lit up her green eyes that resembled her mother so much. It made Cadeyrn's heart ache, seeing a bit of his wife in his child. The nanny had put her silk-soft hair up in two cute little buns, and sometime during the day, she'd lost her shoes. Or more likely kicked them off in the gardens, if the mud on the hem of her kaftan was any indication.

"Papa!" she squealed, running over and launching her tiny body at him.

Cadeyrn caught her underneath her arms and swung her up in front of his face. He planted his lips on her stomach and blew a raspberry. She squealed, laughing and squirming in his arms. There was no force on this earth that would cause him to drop her now. Tucking his precious, giggling cargo on his hip, Cadeyrn kissed the top of her head.

"What is it, darling?" he asked.

"The man's awake!" Fayette squealed. "He talks funny."

Looking up at his secretary with a frown, Cadeyrn asked, "How and why were you down there?"

"Ro and I snuck in! We wanted to see him and his red hair!" Fayette giggled, oblivious to Cadeyrn's frustration. "It's so bright, Papa! Like your fire!"

"Oh, is it?" Cadeyrn said, attacking her sides with crooked fingers. His tickles caused another round of high-pitched squealing laughter from his daughter. "Well, then. I suppose I should go talk to him."

"I wanna come!" Fayette proclaimed, latching on to his shirt with her small fists.

Her face was set in what Cadeyrn assumed was an imitation of his glower. It was absolutely hilarious on a six-year-old girl. Cadeyrn couldn't help his snort of laughter, and he kissed her forehead.

"You really do?" he asked.

"Yeah! He's really pretty, Papa." Fayette giggled.

A small blush rose on her cheeks, and Cadeyrn suppressed a sigh. She was only six, so he knew that she was only finding how he looked pleasant and there wasn't any true attraction. Still, he understood the lure of a first crush. Cadeyrn looked at his secretary and advisor. They were watching him with amused smiles on their faces, and Quillin had a hopeful air to him as he gazed at his Fated. The two were trying to have a child of their own, but Ameyalli was having a hard time conceiving.

Cadeyrn bounced his daughter on his hip gently as he grabbed the opened missive they'd retrieved from the redhead. After a moment's thought, he tucked it into his belt. Just in case he needed his other hand free if Fayette got too squirmy.

"Well then, sweetheart. Shall we go see him?" Cadeyrn asked.

His daughter nodded eagerly, grinning at him, showing off a gap in her mouth. She was growing up so fast, already losing her milk teeth. Thaddaeus was her age when Menea died, and she'd happily held her son's tooth in a skeletal hand. She barely got to experience the joy of him becoming smarter and showing hints of the man he'd someday become. She'd never see any of her babies to adulthood.

The thought sobered him, and Cadeyrn planted another hard kiss on Fayette's forehead as he left his office, his secretary and advisor trailing after him. She clung to his white button-down shirt, babbling away about one thing or another. He listened with one ear, not hearing anything that he really needed to pay attention to. She mostly was going on about the bugs she and Rodolfo had found that morning after breakfast. Their nanny had probably been beside herself once she realized the two troublemakers were tromping around outside.

None of the other castle staff approached him as he descended the spiral stairs leading to the second floor. Unlike most castles, this was where the bedchambers were. His was the farthest back, with his valet's room attached. Speaking of the man, Inti was hovering near the grand staircase that led down to the entrance hall. He didn't say anything but instead smiled faintly when Cadeyrn passed by him.

The whole castle likely knew that their prisoner was awake. Gossip spread through the serving staff like wildfire, and Inti often made sure he brought the most reputable news to Cadeyrn at the end of the day. Immediately if it was an emergency, but otherwise his valet saved it for when he was helping Cadeyrn get ready for bed. Cadeyrn turned and walked down a small passageway that was mostly hidden from view, tucked underneath the staircase.

Visitors, dignitaries, and messengers rarely saw the door, let alone the hallway behind it. This led to the dungeons, and it didn't surprise Cadeyrn that his kids knew about it, though it made him wary. His father had probably felt the same way when Cadeyrn had discovered the hidden door in his youth. Granted, his father was a little more predisposed to apoplexy than he was. The spiral staircase to the dungeons was long, and the air chilled the farther they went.

Fayette shivered in his arms, and Cadeyrn barely had to think about invoking his Craft to project an aura of warmth. His daughter snuggled into his side, humming happily and whispering how much she loved him. If only he didn't feel like such a failure. At least this he could do with barely a thought or drain to his reservoir.

The dungeons had their own living space that the staircase spilled out into. He had permanent guards stationed down here, with rotating breaks for them to be able to leave. Otherwise the men stayed underground. They wore Ignian-enhanced armor that kept them warm and their suits dry. Currently, the stove was burning brightly, and one of the guards was cooking something to share with the rest of the crew.

Cadeyrn ignored them as he walked past them, through the hallway that branched off into an expansive sleeping quarter, and finally through the jailer's office. There was another door in here that led up to a hallway that most prisoners were walked through. That way they wouldn't know that their jailers had plenty of comforts down here. Or that there was a pathway right into the heart of Paelfjord Castle.

He nodded to the jail master and slipped into the wide, arched hallway that had been carved through sandstone. Jail cells lined the walls as he walked down the length, ignoring the moans and pleas to be set free. Why was Fayette wandering around down here alone? He knew that theoretically she would be safe, since all prisoners were restrained properly, but it only took one mishap for everything to go wrong.

Trotting down to the second level, where the more dangerous offenders were placed, they were met with silence. That was better. Cadeyrn headed for the last cell on the right, where the man they'd rescued was placed. One of his guards stood near his cell, pike in hand. Cadeyrn gave a curt nod to dismiss him, and the guard retreated halfway down the walkway, close enough if he was needed, but far enough for some privacy.

Cadeyrn stood in front of the bars and looked down at the gangly ginger in front of him. He was weedy, and his skin had seemingly paled even further in the few days he'd been unconscious. There was a spattering of freckles that Cadeyrn wanted to caress. His eyes were wide, slightly downturned, and the color of fresh spring grass. The vibrant red hair that Fayette adored was styled in an undercut with a bit extra on top.

His high cheekbones and straight nose were nice, as was his strong jaw. Not to mention his sweet full lips. Cadeyrn wanted to figure out what it felt like pressing their mouths together. To kiss him, finding out what he tasted like. What he sounded like when he moaned or sighed. Desire coursed through him, startling Cadeyrn. He hadn't had such thoughts since his wife started to take ill five years ago.

So why was his gut clenching and his cock stirring? He knew the answer to that question, even as he didn't want to believe it or listen to himself. Ameyalli was right. This was his Fated, and if he wasn't careful, if the bond perceived anything in their conversation as a rejection, they'd both be in for a world of hurt. Cadeyrn wasn't sure he was remotely ready to open his heart once more, let alone deal with the issue of figuring out who this unknown man was.

Cadeyrn shifted Fayette to his other hip, trying to hide a small readjustment to stay comfortable. His prisoner was curled up into a ball, though he'd looked up at their approach. His hands were bound together in shackles that covered his entire forearms, holding them together with a small one-inch-thick chain. He'd been dressed in a simple white tunic, sleeping pants, and thin-soled slippers. The clothes he'd arrived in were good for nothing but stoking the cook's fires.

The man was watching him in return, almost warily. He had to tilt his head back to look him in the eye from his position on the ground. For a second, the redhead's eyes snapped to Cadeyrn's Ignis Craft mark and something that looked like fear coursed behind his eyes as his body went rigid. Cadeyrn fought a frown. Why would he be scared of his mark? The man before him was an Aquan, and surely he'd been around other Ignians.

Out of the two of them, the stranger clearly had the advantage if they came to blows. Not that he could defend himself with the restraints that had been bespelled by Healers to sever the Craft Blessed from their reservoir and well. It was a bit curious that the man seemed to fear Ignians, but that was a conversation for a later time. Right now, Cadeyrn watched quietly as the redhead managed to roll up into a sitting position.

"Do you speak Averian?" the redhead rasped.

The man licked his lips and swallowed hard, probably trying to bring moisture to his throat. All it did was make Cadeyrn slightly more uncomfortable, seeing the quick flash of his pink tongue. Though, at the man's words, Cadeyrn rolled his eyes. Typical of an Averian, coming to a country that he likely didn't speak the language of. Nor well versed with the current monarch.

"Of course I speak Averian," Cadeyrn said, switching his dialect. Ameyalli and Quillin would be able to understand, but his daughter and the guard likely wouldn't. "Your kingdom isn't *that* far away."

"I wasn't sure. The little one...." He trailed off, looking at the child and smiling gently at her.

It was a fond and sweet smile. Something that a father would give his child or an uncle to his niblings. Clearly the redhead adored children with how his whole face softened when he regarded the little girl. Fayette giggled and buried her face into Cadeyrn's shoulder. He suppressed the urge to roll his eyes again. Out of all the children, Fayette would be the easiest to win over, and the stranger had apparently already accomplished that with one charming smile.

"She's at the beginning of her teachings. Now, who are you?" Cadeyrn demanded.

His question seemed to strike something in the redhead. He sat up straight, rolling his shoulders down and back as well as he could with the restraints on. Looking past the sweat-stained clothes and slightly haggard appearance, Cadeyrn could see the man as being someone of importance. Maybe some sort of nobleman, even. He had the posture down right.

"My name is Kajaan Pernoac. Secretary to Prince Yolotzin of Averia. I was sent here by King Tonalli to deliver a missive—" The man's face drained of the rest of its color, making the spatter of freckles across his nose and forehead stick out. "—Oh Goddess, the missive. Please tell me that it was still on me."

Cadeyrn grabbed the missive from his belt where he'd tucked it and showed it to the man. Kajaan sighed audibly and slumped back against the wall.

"Does Prince Yolotzin have his secretary often dressed as a pauper?" Cadeyrn asked acerbically.

Kajaan's face flushed red now. Interesting how quickly his skin colored, making him easier to read. Cadeyrn's traitorous thoughts wondered if he flushed down his neck to his chest when he was aroused. He cut off his thoughts before he became more indecent than he was now. For the goddess's sake, he had his daughter with him!

"No, sir. See, I was sent here by the king, but he had someone else pack my belongings. We were on our fourth day of travel, so I was simply wearing travel clothes," Kajaan said, biting his lower lip. "I had outfits appropriate for meeting King Cadeyrn Greatblaze upon arrival."

Fayette looked between Kajaan and him, likely having picked up only the names, though she wouldn't quite know who was who except for her father. She stuck her thumb in her mouth, clearly sensing something wasn't quite right and trying to quell her anxiety. Cadeyrn gently pulled her hand from her mouth and reached over to Ameyalli. They placed a small sweet in his palm, and he handed it to his daughter. It was designed to be chewed on for a while, replacing the need for a pacifier or thumb sucking.

Maybe he indulged his daughter a little too much, but already she was breaking her habit. Instead of sucking her thumb every week like she was at the beginning of winter, she was closer to once every three weeks. She was relying less and less on infantile comforts and learning how to process her emotions in a healthier manner. Soon the habit would be broken completely, and Cadeyrn wouldn't have to worry about her teeth growing in wrong.

"Tell me what happened," Cadeyrn said. "Why were you being chased?"

"I don't know!" Kajaan replied, obviously distressed. "All I know is that it was the afternoon when the carriage driver decided to go off the main road and speed along some pathway. When I tried talking to him, he pointed a flintlock at me." Terror flitted over his face, and Kajaan's eyes got a bit shiny. He started breathing heavier and shook his head to try and continue. "Once the horses slowed to a reasonable pace, I tried to jump out, but he shot me."

"Your arm," Cadeyrn said simply.

Kajaan nodded, glancing down at where he'd been shot. There was a small scar there shining a soft pink against his white skin. Tamya had struggled to get Kajaan's body to heal at first. As much as Cadeyrn was loath to admit it, Kajaan had nearly died several times.

"Luckily I was able to incapacitate him, and when I was getting the horses unhitched, others came after me. I truly don't know why they wanted to kill me. I don't even know what the missive said, so if they'd taken it, the message would have been lost," Kajaan said.

"The guards said you used your Craft to hold them," Cadeyrn said.

The redhead inhaled sharply, his eyes widening. He sat back slightly, and once again Cadeyrn could see distress forming on his face. His body began to tremble, and Kajaan hung his head. It took a minute for the man to compose himself to speak once more, though his hands were still visibly shaking.

"I did," he admitted quietly.

Behind him, Quillin hissed out a long breath. Admission to anyone about an elemental Craft Blessed controlling another's body was a death sentence. Confessing to a king, queen, or council member was subject to immediate termination. Instead of ordering the man's death, as he would have been well within his right to do so, Cadeyrn simply watched Kajaan shake, obviously distressed about what he'd done.

"Why?" Cadeyrn asked. "Revenge for being shot? He made you angry and you lashed out?"

"No!" Kajaan shouted. "He'd already loaded another round and was going to shoot me again. I… I didn't see any other way out. I really didn't want to hurt him, so I had him unhitch the horses from the carriage and then throw away the flintlock."

That would explain his injuries. Kajaan was likely not trained on anatomy as much as Healers were, so he probably hadn't had the knowledge to manipulate the man's body in a more natural manner.

The redhead licked his lips nervously, his eyes shiny with unshed tears and face stained with the ones that had already escaped.

"Is… is he okay?" Kajaan asked. "He was screaming…. I was hoping he'd passed out."

"He's dead," Cadeyrn said bluntly.

That got Kajaan to crumple as if someone had cut his strings. He curled into a tight ball, covering his face with his hands. It looked a bit awkward with the restraints, but Cadeyrn could appreciate the redhead not wanting to openly cry in front of strangers. The man's shoulders shook as he sniffled, trying to regain his composure.

Cadeyrn waited quietly until the trembling man stilled. Fayette stared up at him with her large eyes, the hard candy clacking against her remaining milk teeth. After a few more minutes, Kajaan took a deep breath and sat back, his hands falling limp into his lap. His eyes were red and puffy, his nose had run, and the manacles had tear tracks on them.

If their conversation could wait, then Cadeyrn would have walked away to give the man his privacy to collect himself in peace. The fact that Kajaan was upset about taking a life despite having lashed out in self-defense spoke volumes about his character. He was proud that his Fated was someone who didn't take another's life easily. Cadeyrn pushed that thought to the back of his mind. He couldn't afford to think of the redhead in such a manner until he truly knew who he was.

Which meant more questions.

"The other guards?" Cadeyrn asked.

"I held them too," Kajaan said, "and their horses. I didn't want to strand them completely or drop them when I let go. I cut off circulation to their brains for just a few seconds. Only until they passed out, then I let them go. I got on the horse, and I took off. But obviously they recovered quick enough to catch up and I got shot again."

Cadeyrn stared at the smaller man in front of him with something that felt like respect. He'd not only controlled one man, but held six more and their horses for long enough to incapacitate them? On top of that, he'd blocked blood flow for a limited time, trying to reduce the amount of damage to them. Sensing blood flow in each individual could be hard for a trained Healer who was touching their patient as organs took priority. For an Aquan to do such careful work while holding twelve beings at once and for varying lengths of time?

Behind him, he could hear Quillin mutter an oath under his breath. Beside him, Ameyalli just hummed happily, as if they weren't bothered at all by what Kajaan just told them. A small shiver ran down Cadeyrn's spine as he thought about the scope of the man's abilities. What he could be capable of if he didn't have those manacles on.

"You must have a very powerful Craft," Cadeyrn said.

Kajaan snorted. "I'm one step above a Void. Sure, I have a Craft, but it's weak."

"What you just described to me is not something someone with a weak Craft could do," Cadeyrn said. "Besides, you owe your life to a Void."

Something akin to amusement twisted Kajaan's features for a second before he looked up at him. "What do you mean?"

"You'd drained your Craft so thoroughly, your soul was dying. So one of our Voids took the energy from another Aquan and poured it into you," Cadeyrn explained.

Kajaan's eyes lit up, and he smiled faintly. "I've seen that before."

Cadeyrn tilted his head. As far as he knew, Averia treated their Voids as if they were scum. It had been the same here before Cadeyrn took over from his father. After a long twenty-year campaign, the Voids in Zothua were nearly revered and always sought out by Healers. They could be crucial to the healing of a patient and were quite handy when a Craft Blessed lashed out with their Craft while out of their mind with pain, grief, or illness.

Surely he would have known of a Void getting any sort of recognition. If this Kajaan was to be believed and he really was Prince Yolotzin's secretary, then the Void was somehow attending court—which was highly unlikely if not impossible. Or had it been some lucky Void who'd been in the right place at the right time?

"When?" Cadeyrn asked, finding himself truly interested.

"I attended an Introduction Gala for Lord Kende Ruvyn's Fated. He was attacked and poisoned with Void blood. But his Fated is a Void himself, and he'd also been attacked by a Harvester and Ignian. He was able to put that energy and what others offered to him into removing the poison and refilling Lord Kende's reservoir and well," Kajaan said with a smile. "It was oddly beautiful."

Interesting. He had no idea the duke's son had found a Void as a Fated. He had no idea that Voids were even blessed with a Fated. It seemed that even after twenty years, he still had quite a bit more to learn about their non-Craft cousins. Cadeyrn made a mental note to talk with Ameyalli about it later. See if any Fated couples here involved Voids.

Cadeyrn studied the man for a minute and sighed, shifting Fayette slightly on his hip. She was still fixated on her candy, though her wide green eyes kept switching between Cadeyrn and Kajaan. For the few blessed minutes they'd been down here, she'd remained still. With any luck she wouldn't be getting bored any time soon.

"How do you propose I verify who you are?" Cadeyrn asked.

Kajaan blinked and nodded toward the missive. "That, I hope, should at least have some proof."

"You said you didn't know the contents, though, correct?" Cadeyrn asked.

Kajaan nodded. Well, this was going to be interesting. Cadeyrn tossed the missive through the bars, letting the scroll land with a clatter at Kajaan's feet. He didn't need to wait long for the man's reaction. Kajaan rolled to his knees and shuffled forward, positioning the scroll on the ground and unfurling it. He frowned and pushed the scroll away, revealing the whole letter.

That had no writing on it whatsoever.

"I don't understand," Kajaan said. "Why's it blank? I never let it out of my sight! The coachman wouldn't have been able to swap it out. I would have heard him stop the carriage or come in and woken if I was asleep. The one time I was in a town, I had it on my hip to make sure it wasn't altered or stolen. But…. But why's it *blank*?"

Kajaan scrabbled at the edge of the scroll, picking up the paper and inspecting the wax carefully, tilting it slightly a few times. That was something Cadeyrn hadn't expected him to do. Each king's wax seal had a specific color to it when it hit the light just right. It helped protect against forgeries. This one shined gold against the red wax. As soon as it flashed, Kajaan inspected the stamp, then the underside of the wax where Cadeyrn had peeled it away from the rest of the scroll.

"It's authentic," Kajaan murmured. "I don't…. What's going on?"

"That's what I'd like to know," Cadeyrn replied tersely. "Why would your king send you on a sudden trip with a blank missive, where his real intent was seemingly to kill you? Or were the guards we talked to correct in saying you're a criminal who was trying to escape his death sentence?"

The man's head snapped up, his eyes wide as his jaw went slack.

"You can't believe that!" he protested.

"I don't know what to believe," Cadeyrn said, making his voice grow cold and harsh. "All I know is that there's a man who claims to be Prince Yolotzin's secretary, though he was dressed in clothes befitting a lower middle-class man. He was being pursued by six men and had just killed the coachman who was driving a pretty dilapidated coach. He's got a blank scroll that somehow seems to be legitimate, and he continues to claim ignorance to whatever message King Tonalli wanted to send."

"*Please*," Kajaan begged, "please send for Tzin. He'll clear up the issue surrounding my identity. I can't claim what King Tonalli was doing, but Tzin will vouch for me. We grew up together. I've always taken care of him, and we've hardly been separated. I—"

Kajaan twitched when Cadeyrn held up a hand, stopping the panicked tirade. Cadeyrn didn't really know Prince Yolotzin, so anything Kajaan would try to say to prove his identity was worthless. He also really didn't want to give Tonalli any excuse whatsoever to come into the castle. Taking an information inquiry and twisting it to visit was the man's specialty, though the old man rarely left Avitou anymore.

"I've never seen you when I've visited King Tonalli, so I can't trust your word, since I've always seen Prince Yolotzin without you at his side," Cadeyrn said. "All I know is that a suspicious man was caught in my country. One who admits to using his Craft in forbidden measures yet claims that he's innocent. You will stay here until I get word back from King Tonalli."

Recognition dawned on Kajaan's face as he stared up at him. True, Cadeyrn wasn't wearing his regalia—much preferring simple light-colored silk slacks and lightweight button-down shirt when not holding court—so someone unfamiliar with him would likely have thought he was part of the staff. Kajaan blinked rapidly a few times before shuffling and bowing as best as he could on his knees.

"King Cadeyrn," he gasped out, "please show mercy. I mean you no harm."

"We'll see," Cadeyrn said.

With that, he turned and walked away. His heart ached with every step that separated him from his Fated. Kajaan needed comfort and reassurance that he would be all right, but Cadeyrn wasn't going to provide that. Not until he knew for sure exactly who Kajaan was. He had to protect his children. Criminals lied all the time to get out of punishment.

Except that he didn't need Quillin to tell him that Kajaan hadn't lied once.

CHAPTER 5

AT LEAST he was fed during his captivity. Trying to eat with the restraints on was awkward, but he managed. The meals he got three times a day consisted of a small loaf of coarse bread, a slice of meat that changed with every meal, and a piece of fruit. Water he got whenever he needed, which was nice. As soon as the jug was empty, the guard would tap out a pattern with his pike, and another would come by to swap out jugs.

Of course, his perpetual guard would come into his cell with the second, his pike trained over Kajaan's heart in a pretty obvious message. If he moved in any manner the guards didn't like, he'd be impaled. It had gotten a little fraught the one time Kajaan had sneezed when the straw kicked up dust. Luckily he only sported a small rip in his shirt rather than a blade through his ribs. After that, the guards were careful to not disturb the straw.

Since there was nothing else to do, Kajaan ran through his conversation with King Cadeyrn constantly. He shouldn't have told him he'd used his Craft on the men despite his gut telling him he'd be safe around the tall Ignian. That made his life forfeit no matter what. Even if Yolotzin came here and managed to convince the king who he was, he'd still violated the cardinal rules.

Knowing the coachman was dead caused pain to lance through his heart every time he thought about it. How could he have done that? Killed someone. Sure, it was probably a mercy after the first manipulation, but that hadn't been Kajaan's intent! He'd just wanted to get away. Get somewhere safe.

He was a murderer. That wasn't up for debate. He could claim self-defense and try to plead his case, but it wasn't a good one. It was his word against a dead man and six guards he'd essentially tortured. No, he'd been dead the moment King Tonalli had cornered him in the hallway to his room. Anger burned in his gut at the thought.

How could his king do this to him? To his son! And not just King Tonalli, but how could his own father be okay with this? They didn't have a great relationship, but Kajaan was the only thing Jeryit had left of his mother. Had his father loved her so little that he was fine with Kajaan's death? Or was it because she was dead that his father simply didn't care for him and was glad to be rid of him?

A range of emotions swirled around him. Going from being angry, frustrated, to devastated and upset was exhausting. Kajaan found himself sleeping a lot. Not like there really was much else to do. None of the guards that came near him to deliver food or water, nor the ones posted by his cell spoke Averian.... Or at least feigned ignorance when he asked.

Goddess, had he really asked the fucking *king* of all people if he spoke Averian? He truly hadn't meant to insult the man, but even though he carried himself with grace and power, he'd been dressed simply. Almost as if he'd been a clerk or another staff member. But no, turns out the damn king dressed in the plainest clothes available during his down time.

The plainest clothes, but the most gorgeous face. Much to Kajaan's frustration, the man's face swam into his vision almost as constantly as Kajaan relived their conversation. He'd been near speechless upon seeing him, his strong patrician features and beautiful sparkling blue eyes. Years ago, he and Yolotzin had gone south to the Duparthon Sea, and the shallow waters looked the exact same as King Cadeyrn's eyes. His chin-length brown hair looked silky with how it had shone in the light.

What he could see from the body hidden from him, Kajaan figured King Cadeyrn kept in good shape. Very good shape. If he had more privacy, Kajaan might even be tempted to take himself in hand at the memory of the king. The moment their eyes had met, he'd felt something stir in his soul. Something that told him that King Cadeyrn would protect him.

But that was ridiculous!

Wasn't it?

Why would the king protect him? He wasn't even a citizen of this kingdom. He was a damn criminal, for goddess's sake. His execution was all but guaranteed. Kajaan wasn't even sure why he was still alive. He'd admitted to the fucking king of all people what he'd done to his attackers, and yet he still drew breath. Maybe King Cadeyrn wanted to take his time with Kajaan's execution.

The thought made him shudder as memories he tried to suppress floated to the front of his mind.

"Goddess, you're such a baby! Stop sniveling and get back here and face me like a man!" Torbid snapped at him.

He'd tried to get away, but the old man grabbed his arm, his palm searingly hot to the touch. Kajaan couldn't help but scream as his flesh sizzled and burned.

"For fucks sake, use your Craft to protect your skin! You should be able to counteract the heat and no longer be at risk for any burns," his tutor sneered.

The older man kept grabbing at his arms, his shoulders, even his face once, demanding that Kajaan call his Craft quickly. He refused to listen to Kajaan when he said he couldn't. That it took a while for him to draw from his core. Torbid had simply called him lazy, stupid, common. That he wasn't fit to be a drudge, let alone the prince's secretary.

Torbid refused to let a Healer examine Kajaan's wounds and try to treat them. Refused to give him salves to help with the burns or the agony that accompanied them. Only until Kajaan could protect himself and truly let himself submit to his training would he be granted access to a Healer or medicine. There were many nights where Kajaan curled up on his bed and sobbed from the pain.

That was when Yolotzin would come into his room and soothe him. He'd bring burn salves he stole from the infirmary to coat the angry red and weeping sores, and a pain reliever to help him sleep. Once he was medicated, Kajaan always expected his best friend to leave him, but Yolotzin would refuse. He'd lie down behind Kajaan and just hold him, trying to stifle his own tears. As a Sympathetic, he'd been able to feel Kajaan's agony as if it was his own.

Was it any surprise that they'd been each other's firsts for a lot of things? First kiss, first time undressing in front of a lover, exploring each other, making love. But they were never meant to be Fated. Never truly meant to be together, no matter how much the two had deluded themselves. Always thinking that maybe they just needed more time before the goddess blessed them.

It was one of the main reasons they traveled, after all. To gain experience, knowledge, and just try to understand the world better, all the while trying to improve his international relations with the other kingdoms. Hoping that maybe after visiting this dignitary or that duke that something would click. Or learning a new language. A new culture. Trying out new foods, dances, ceremonies, or celebrations. And yet nothing had triggered an activation for their bond. They just apparently weren't meant to be.

The image of King Cadeyrn holding his daughter on his hip with obvious love and affection in his gaze pushed those thoughts aside. Why did the king have to be an Ignis? Just being around him made Kajaan nervous, and he was glad the man hadn't visited since. Much like how being around King Tonalli unnerved him. He couldn't stop remembering how easily it was for his tutor to burn him, demanding he protect himself.

Just the thought of touching an Ignis made him break out into a sweat and feel like he wanted to vomit. So why in the hell did he want to submit and lie underneath those broad shoulders with just the memory of King Cadeyrn? The man was nearly a half foot taller than him and could most definitely throw him around easily with those thick arms of his. He should have been completely imposing and terrifying. Instead, Kajaan found him attractive.

Kajaan scrubbed at his face and sighed, sitting up on the loose straw mattress. He stared glumly down at the new tray of food that had been brought while he'd been tossing and turning. Running his hands through the patchy scruff that was growing on his chin, Kajaan winced. He hated his inconsistent facial hair, but he knew damn well the guards wouldn't give him a blade to shave.

Instead, he pulled the false missive close and ripped another tear into it. Eleven notches. Eleven meals. He'd been down here for almost four days now. No more royal visits—not even from the little girl and boy who had been oohing and aahing over him before he woke. Once the little girl returned with King Cadeyrn, Kajaan figured the boy was probably her brother. The Sympathetic and Seer that had been with the king never came back either.

Kajaan picked at the food he'd been given after using some clean water to rinse off his hands, sighing listlessly. At least the meat appeared to be some ham, which was nice. It tasted much better than the turkey and didn't dry out his mouth. He ignored the footsteps approaching his cell, keeping his eyes and head down. Likely another rotation of the guard that stood outside his cell.

What was even the point? He was in a cell, his arms bound together with barely any movement possible. It wasn't like he was able to get free without taking his arms off at the elbow. The metal was some sort of specialized compound, and Kajaan couldn't feel his Craft at all. No matter how deep he reached, he couldn't invoke it. These had to be dampeners, though he'd only ever heard about them and had never encountered such an item before. That was fine by him. He didn't want to kill anyone else.

"The king requests your presence," a soft voice came through the bars.

Kajaan looked up to see the slightly pudgy man he'd seen next to King Cadeyrn. He was fairly homely looking, round in all the nicest places, with soft-looking brown hair and eyes. In his hands were fresh clothes and what looked like a bar of soap. Kajaan sat up, blinking a few times. He hadn't thought the two with the king had been able to speak Averian.

"All right," Kajaan said.

He stood with some difficulty as the man unlocked his cell. The brunet walked over, looking around with open curiosity on his face. He didn't comment, however, and stood about a foot away from Kajaan. It wasn't like he'd been able to decorate his cell, Kajaan thought uncharitably. He'd done his best to keep everything neat and as clean as possible.

"You will not use your Craft for any reason. If I feel you reaching for it, you will be incapacitated," the man said, his soft voice giving his words an extra layer of danger.

Kajaan simply nodded his agreement. After a moment, the man nodded in return and stepped forward, placing the bundle on the straw mattress. He produced a key from somewhere and unlocked the restraints around Kajaan's arms. Kajaan breathed a sigh of relief, suddenly feeling whole again. He knew his Craft was there, he could feel it, but as he promised, he didn't reach for it.

There was another awareness he felt too. Upward and toward the right, gently teasing the edge of his curiosity. It made him want to go investigate. Curious. Kajaan had never felt any sort of pull like that before. Maybe it was the same kind of intuition that had him riding north however many days ago he'd been shot.

The brunet handed Kajaan a rough washcloth and bar of soap. He eagerly took the items, grabbed the nearly full pitcher of water, and retreated to the corner where the chamber pot sat. Kajaan wet the cloth, using as little water as possible, over the refuse pot and scrubbed the soap against the cloth. He scoured his skin, rinsing the towel as needed when it got to be a bit too grimy.

Not once did he think about the man who was still in his cell as Kajaan pulled off his shirt and then pants. He couldn't bother himself to care about being nude in front of him or the guards outside his cell. All he cared about was that he was clean. He rinsed out the cloth completely and wicked away the remaining soap, feeling ages better than he had that morning. Kajaan used his hands to wash his face and simply wet his hair, not bothering to actually wash it. That would take more water than he had left.

Dripping wet, Kajaan turned to face the brunet. The man was smiling gently and held out a large, fluffy-looking towel. He seemed completely nonplussed and at ease around another naked man. After taking the terrycloth with a small thanks, Kajaan dried himself off, beginning to shiver in the gloom of the dungeon. He was given a pair of close-fitting breeches and a simple green tunic. Kajaan slipped his feet back into the soft-soled white shoes he'd been wearing since he woke.

"Hands behind your back, stacked on top of each other," the brunet instructed.

Kajaan sighed and turned away, doing as he asked. He was able to keep his shoulders in a neutral position this way, and he looked like he'd just folded his arms behind him. From the front, at least. Kajaan felt a pang of loss when the restraints were fitted back on. His Craft slipped out of reach completely again. Not that it really had much of a presence in the first place.

The brunet held his bicep and led him through the cell doors. Kajaan walked quietly next to him, hating that his first few steps were a bit unbalanced. He had tried to pace the cell as much as he could, but that didn't make up for the amount of exercise his body was used to, and his muscles had atrophied slightly. They ascended a set of stairs and passed more cells.

Once they were in the jailer's office, he was turned and led up a steep, narrow staircase. This led to a small landing with a guard posted. The guard opened a door upon seeing the two of them, and Kajaan stepped out onto a gravel pathway, trying to stealthily steady his breathing. The sun was shining, and Kajaan immediately raised his face to it, closing his eyes as the heat of the day thawed him out. His companion gave him a minute to soak in the warmth before firmly tugging on his arm to get him walking again.

They were to the side of Paelfjord Castle, Kajaan finally realized as they walked through a beautiful rose garden on a multicolored gravel pathway. The castle itself was made of smoothed sandstone, decorated with small arched windows that held panes of stained glass in a multitude of colors. There were several curious holes in the castle walls that Kajaan couldn't quite figure out what their purpose was.

The holes were much too small and ineffective for them to be arrow slits or tar chutes. The answer came in the form of a small brown bird. It flitted up to the hole, seemed to hover in front of it, then burrowed inside. The realization startled Kajaan. They were birdhouses. In the castle walls itself? He supposed since the castle wasn't made of wood, they'd be able to confine the creatures easier. Still, knowing that animals were seemingly encouraged to call Paelfjord home was surprising.

He was led around to a side door that opened into a massive kitchen. A multitude of workers were bustling around, preparing one dish or another. The floor beneath him was a sort of fieldstone, he thought. A nice, soft gray to counteract the polished yellowish beige sandstone. Their kitchen table and counters were made from a beautiful white wood, and a large oven pushed out plenty of heat, making him break into a sweat.

Kajaan's stomach rumbled at the smell of the pastries, meats, and spices in the air. He firmly tried to ignore it, as the brunet didn't give him a chance to stop and inhale. Once out of the kitchen, Kajaan was led through a series of white wood doors, until finally he found himself in the throne room. They were approaching the throne from the side, and Kajaan perked up, tuning in to the conversation when he heard a familiar voice.

"—concerning letter that was mailed to one of our nobility," Yolotzin was saying. "I was hoping that perhaps he's arrived, and if so, I could speak to him if he's still here."

The two of them walked into the room just enough that he could see his best friend in some of his finest clothes standing a few paces ahead of Lady Naias, and Lords Asyl and Kende. Sitting on the throne in his near full regalia was King Cadeyrn. He wore a flowing black silk thawb and leather boots. His orange Bisht had shimmering threads stitched into it in some overarching pattern, making it appear as if it was on fire when he moved, and his crown was studded with a multitude of gemstones that gave it the same effect. Kajaan couldn't help his shudder at seeing it, remembering how Torbid's palm got the same look right before grabbing him.

Sitting on what was normally the queen's throne was a young boy dressed in a saffron chiton with jeweled sandals and armlets. He was older than the two kids that had run away when he woke days ago, but he had the same eyes as the king. They sparkled with a keen intellect, and Kajaan knew that the kid would be a nightmare once he started getting older. The boy was probably the prince, learning how to oversee visiting dignitaries.

King Cadeyrn's eyes flickered past Yolotzin toward Kajaan and the man who'd fetched him. He gave a small nod and the man holding him let go. Was he…. Kajaan gave the soft-spoken man a bewildered, hesitant look. His heart lifted when the Sympathetic gave him a small smile and Kajaan realized he was being given the reunion he sorely needed.

"Tzin!" Kajaan called out.

Yolotzin spun and upon seeing him inhaled sharply. Heedless of his arms tied behind him, Kajaan rushed toward him. The prince met him halfway, his strong arms wrapping around Kajaan and holding him tight. Kajaan pressed his face into Yolotzin's neck, breathing in deep. As always, his best friend smelled like lemon and strawberries, calming and comforting him. If he whimpered and silently cried a little, Yolotzin didn't comment.

"Oh, Kajaan. I was so scared," Yolotzin whispered in his ear.

He began to rub his hands up and down Kajaan's back, slightly too roughly for it to be comforting. Kajaan only nodded, unable to stop the tremors that racked his body. He'd been terrified as well, but he didn't quite trust himself to speak at the moment. Just trying to not audibly begin crying was taking all his strength. He wanted to hold Yolotzin tight, bury his face in the man's chest, and not come up for weeks.

"So this *is* your secretary, then," King Cadeyrn said blandly.

"Yes," Yolotzin said, his voice stronger after he cleared his throat. "I feared for his safety, though I don't know why my father would risk Kajaan's life."

"I have an idea about that," King Cadeyrn said, leaning forward and putting his elbows on his knees.

"Majesty," the woman at his side interjected softly, touching his shoulder with two fingers.

He turned toward her, leaning back, and they swapped back to Zothuan for a whispered conversation. Kajaan pulled away from Yolotzin just enough to look up at him. The prince wasn't looking at the king and his council. All of his focus was on him. Yolotzin's hands came up, cupping his cheeks. He gently wiped away Kajaan's tears with his thumbs, his gaze soft and full of affection.

Yolotzin tilted Kajaan's head up and bent down to place a soft kiss on his forehead. Kajaan sighed ever so softly, melting into his best friend's affection. He opened his eyes to look up at him, wishing they had the privacy to share a more intimate kiss. Guilt tore through Kajaan, remembering that Lady Naias was here and that their fun was over permanently. She was his Fated, yet Yolotzin held him in his arms instead.

"Very well," King Cadeyrn said and sighed, turning back to the group. "Prince Yolotzin, how much do you know about your father's plans for my kingdom?"

Yolotzin shuffled to the side so he could face the king while still holding Kajaan. The thought made him smile faintly, though it also put him in the perfect position to see Lady Naias. She just watched them with a small smile on her lips, her eyes shiny. Once she noticed Kajaan was looking at her, she caught his eye and her smile warmed and became friendlier.

Did she really not mind how close they were? Was she not threatened by his proximity to her Fated? Or was it more of a matter of trust? Kajaan had resolved to not do anything that would jeopardize Yolotzin's relationship with her, considering that his best friend had been looking for his Fated ever since he learned about the concept. The fact that he ended up with someone who would understand the depth of their friendship shouldn't have surprised Kajaan. Yet he still assumed the worst.

"Not much, regrettably. My father has been having me take over more duties to run the kingdom and has put me in charge of reaching out to most of the other kingdoms to keep our relations well, but he's never talked to me about Zothua," Yolotzin said.

"And his attitude toward us?" King Cadeyrn asked.

"Neutral, I believe," Yolotzin said, sounding confused.

Lady Naias made a small noise, and Yolotzin turned to look at her. She gave her Fated a curious look and took a small step forward, curtsying politely toward the king in a silent request to speak. The king inclined his head toward her, his face impassive.

"If I remember correctly, there were some issues around ten years ago," Lady Naias said.

King Cadeyrn nodded and glanced over at the boy beside him. The child blinked and turned to his father, tilting his head slightly. Did he understand what they were saying? A kid with an ear for language could most definitely be bilingual at his age. Kajaan had already picked up a rudimentary amount of Valvintian and Bhyvineese before he was in his teens.

"King Tonalli has constantly pushed the borders of our kingdoms. He wants more, though I'm not entirely sure why, since the lands nearest to the border are mountainous and unusable scrub land. Perhaps there are metals or gemstones in the mountains, or maybe he has plans to utilize the scrub land, but since he refuses to share his plans, I've rebuffed him every time. Ten years ago, my son Thaddaeus was born," King Cadeyrn said. At that, the boy on the other throne gave a shy smile and a small wave, straightening as much as he could. "King Tonalli came to me a week afterward with another request. This time, he wanted to enter my son and his daughter, Princess Reina, into an arranged marriage."

Both Yolotzin and Kajaan stared at King Cadeyrn for a minute before Kajaan made a small noise of disbelief at the back of his throat. Kajaan most certainly didn't remember that proposal being talked about through the halls. Almost everything the king did was subjected to gossip, but not this venture. A marriage proposal would have been talked to death by everyone, even as unlikely of a pairing as these two would have been.

It wasn't often that a marriage proposal was requested while a child was still in their cradle, but it did happen. Such proposals were rare and mostly restricted to the more reserved monarchs, albeit with children that were usually much closer in age. Nabene was the one most likely to enter in such contracts, with Pemalia close behind. Though that was more of a frantic bid to keep supplies importing into their barren country. Nabene was just backward.

"But I'm the youngest," Yolotzin said slowly. "Both of my sisters are older than I."

"Yes. So tell me why I should have approved a marriage between my son and a woman thirty years his senior?" King Cadeyrn said.

Yolotzin shook his head, frowning. "That makes no sense. Even if the marriage happened right when your son turned eighteen, my sister would have been nearly fifty."

Besides, hadn't Princess Reina found her Fated twelve years ago? She wouldn't have been available for a marriage to the prince. Fated pairings negated any arranged marriages unless both parties agreed to walk away. King Tonalli must have planned on King Cadeyrn's rejection and used it as an excuse to act like a child.

King Cadeyrn nodded. "And that is why I rejected the proposal without even considering it. No offense to your sister, but I would not saddle my child with a woman who would be past her prime, be unable to bear him children, and quite likely leave him with many lonely years." When Yolotzin nodded his understanding, King Cadeyrn continued. "King Tonalli wasn't happy in the least. He raged about how I was being discourteous, and I, of course, made the mistake of calling him out on it. He's been oddly quiet the last ten years, but now...."

"He sent Kajaan to... what? Make you suspicious?" Yolotzin asked, sounding incredulous. "To be a spy without even knowing what he was looking for?"

"To kill me on Zothuan soil," Kajaan said, fresh fear gripping the base of his spine.

"What?" Yolotzin yelped, looking down at him. "Why would Father do that?"

"Because he's your childhood friend," King Cadeyrn said simply. "Upon learning your friend was killed in a foreign land under suspicious circumstances, you may have been spurred to enact revenge on the perceived offending party or kick up trouble by demanding restitution."

"But that doesn't make sense," Yolotzin protested. "He was with and pursued by Averian guards. Why would I have gone after Zothua if Kajaan had been killed by our own men?"

"It wouldn't take much to alter the facts, I'm sure," Lord Kende said from behind them. "Especially if King Tonalli has spies in the area. Or if Kajaan was never recovered, he could make the reports say whatever he wanted. Who would have known better if there were no witnesses? Would you have ever doubted your own father? Or would you have taken his word at face value?"

"But I wouldn't urge my father to wage war on a neighboring country just because Kajaan went missing," Yolotzin protested hotly.

Even as he spoke, Yolotzin's arms tightened around Kajaan as if he couldn't bear the thought. Kajaan grunted and squirmed slightly, pushing back and making Yolotzin release him, though he didn't go anywhere but a step away. It was just far enough to be able to look him in the eyes easier.

"You would, though," Kajaan told him quietly.

"He's right. The only reason you don't think that now is because he's alive and safe next to you," King Cadeyrn said simply.

"Father is already unhappy that I left to come here," Yolotzin said. "We'll return, and you can remind him that he was the one who sent you, and it was his men that attacked you. We'll get this all cleared up, and I can reinstate you as my secretary, no matter how much Father wants to push his lackey into that role."

Someone behind them snorted, and Kajaan thought it was most likely to be Lord Asyl. Kajaan appreciated the man's obvious distrust of anyone in authority except for Lord Kende and potentially Yolotzin. He heard a sharp hissing noise, and a quick glance over Yolotzin's shoulders revealed Lord Kende scowling at his husband, who was in the middle of an eye roll. King Cadeyrn sighed heavily.

"And what would stop him from having Kajaan detained or killed some other way after you return? Why do you think he waited ten years to try and assassinate Kajaan?" Cadeyrn asked. "Do you really think he'd just let it lie? With you knowing that his plot failed?"

There was silence in the room for quite a while. Yolotzin just looked puzzled, his hands absently resting on Kajaan's arms, rubbing his thumbs in small circles. Finally it was Lady Naias who cleared her throat and lifted her chin. She seemed slightly perturbed about what was being implied, if not outrightly said.

"It's because of me, isn't it?" she asked softly, a small quaver in her voice. "Because Yolotzin found his Fated."

"Quite probably," King Cadeyrn said. "I think, in his own twisted way, King Tonalli knew how much this would hurt you, Prince Yolotzin, so he waited until you found your Fated. That way she could comfort you and help you through the grieving process of losing your best friend. Maybe it would have dampened the need for revenge, or maybe he was counting on her to encourage justice. We'll never know, and frankly, I'm glad for it."

Yolotzin's hands drifted to Kajaan's shoulders, gently squeezing them as he looked down at him. Kajaan watched his friend, seeing the despair and hurt in his eyes. He knew that the prince had always done his best to respect his father, taking what he said at face value and believing him to be a decent person. Hearing all of this was challenging his entire perception of who his father was.

It couldn't be easy, trying to come to terms with a father who had plotted to kill his best friend solely to start a war with one of Averia's neighboring kingdoms. Maybe some of his off-colored comments and actions would be viewed in a whole new light. Yolotzin had a lot of soul-searching to do, and if Kajaan evaluated the other three Averians in the room correctly, his prince wouldn't be floundering alone. Lord Asyl would be happy to pop the bubble of parental adoration and trust.

"Either way, it doesn't matter. Kajaan can't return to Averia, much less Alenzon," King Cadeyrn said. Yolotzin looked at him, bewildered. The king tilted his head to address Kajaan. "It might hurt less to hear it from you than from me."

Of course the king would tell Yolotzin if Kajaan refused, he knew. The fact that King Cadeyrn was even giving Kajaan the courtesy of telling his best friend what he'd done was incredibly kind. Kajaan didn't know very many Ignians outside of the castle, but his relationship with Jaclyn, Torbid, and King Tonalli had made him believe they were quick to anger and would use secrets to their advantage—often as cruelly as possible. King Cadeyrn seemed to be an exception.

"Kaj?" Yolotzin asked quietly.

Taking a deep, fortifying breath, Kajaan drew himself up straight and looked his best friend in the eye. Apparently Yolotzin knew this was something bad, if how tightly he was gripping Kajaan's shoulders was any indication. The smallest of frowns tugged his lips down, and Kajaan hated seeing the look of pure worry on his face when Yolotzin was usually such a carefree soul.

"The carriage driver shot me while I was trying to get away. I only just barely escaped the six guards with my life before King Cadeyrn's people found and rescued me," Kajaan said, trembling with the knowledge of what he had to say next. Tears pricked at his eyes, and Kajaan struggled to breathe as he tried to drag in enough air to finish his explanation. Luckily, the king and his friend waited patiently, letting him build up his confidence. Finally he managed to say in a fragmented voice, "But to do so… I used my Craft on them."

Lady Naias gasped, and her hands flew to cover her mouth, her eyes going wide and immediately filling with tears. Yolotzin's face fell, and he looked crushed, his fingers digging into Kajaan's skin. Behind him, Lord Kende muttered an oath and dropped his head, one hand coming up to cover his eyes. Only Lord Asyl looked puzzled, trying to search the others for any hints as to the significance of his words.

"You didn't," Yolotzin said in an anguished voice. "Goddess, Kajaan, please tell me you *didn't*!"

Kajaan's vision swam as his tears began to fall unchecked, and he slowly bowed his head, unable to stop his lower lip from trembling. He couldn't look at Yolotzin, couldn't see the anguish and horror on his face. His best friend's grip had tightened to the point of pain, his knuckles going white. There would be ten oval bruises waiting for him in a half circle that night.

"What does that mean?" Lord Asyl asked in a low voice.

"It means he used Craft illegally to manipulate someone's body," Lord Kende said just as softly.

"That's stupid!" Lord Asyl snapped immediately, loud enough to bounce around the throne room. The man's vehemence brought a small, unsteady smile to Kajaan's face. Even though Lord Asyl had been raised as his father's noble heir until his Awakening failed at thirteen, it seemed his court manners had been forgotten in his anger. "His life was in danger! Why shouldn't he be allowed to protect himself! There should be exceptions to the rule for such events!"

"Asyl, it's forbidden for *anyone*, especially for elemental Craft Blessed, to mess with someone else's body," Lord Kende said, obviously trying to placate his husband. "It's an automatic sentencing."

"So, what, Kajaan should have let himself get shot again? Or killed? What else could he have done? He did what he needed to do in order to survive," Lord Asyl said, his frustration making him grow louder.

"I killed one of them," Kajaan said hoarsely. "What now?"

"Self-defense," Lord Asyl replied as sharply as his sneer. "Do you know how many times I nearly killed a man in a fight to protect myself when a john thought I was worth less than the shit on his shoe?" Lord Kende made a strangled noise, and when Kajaan looked over, Lord Asyl had his arms folded tight across his chest, his face a mask of pure rage directed at his husband. "Besides, how many times do you or Gojko alter people's bodies on a daily basis to heal them? I do alterations with my own potions, so why aren't Healers rounded up, jailed, and executed for their so-called crimes? Why hasn't Enchanted Waters been raided? They know it's run by a Void!"

"Healers are exempt so long as they're helping," Lord Kende said.

"That still leaves me and any other non-Healer alchemist in a sticky spot, even though we're helping too," Asyl snarled. "Besides, what if someone *wanted* to commit suicide and was healed physically, but in the end it causes more harm than good because their head's not right? That's not exactly helping if the person wanted to die!"

Lord Kende paled visibly, and he gripped Lord Asyl's upper arms. He was almost frantic in his motions as he gently shook his husband. Even Lady Naias looked stricken, trying to wipe away the tears streaming down her cheeks.

"Sweetheart, please," Lord Kende said urgently, almost begging, "don't say things like that."

"Your Void is correct," King Cadeyrn said, breaking into Lord Asyl's frustrated growl. "It doesn't make a lot of sense, does it. Desperate men make desperate decisions that might not always be morally correct."

"What are you saying?" Yolotzin asked, looking at the king.

He sounded seconds from crying. Oh, his sweet, gentle-hearted prince. Kajaan had wished so many times that he could have redone that day he'd nearly been assassinated. That he could have had the courage to face down his death. That he hadn't used his Craft to manipulate the driver and kill him. Hearing him now, Kajaan wished he'd slept in Yolotzin's bed and avoided King Tonalli completely. If he had, maybe he'd still be in Avitou Castle, sighing over Yolotzin's relationship with Lady Naias.

"I'm saying that instead of an immediate death sentence, the situation should be examined first. For instance—"

"Majesty!" the woman next to the king interjected frantically, her eyes wide.

King Cadeyrn waved away whatever concern his advisor was going to say. "They need to understand, Ameyalli. Do you know how my wife died?"

"Fever," Yolotzin choked out.

The man nodded. "I am an Ignis, as you can see. In her final days, I used my Craft to try and lower her body temperature to break her fever and spare her organs from failing when the Healers were unable to help her. Should I die for my actions in trying to save the one I loved? The law says I should, since I'm not a Healer, even though I was trying to do something to help her."

"Why are you telling us this?" Lady Naias asked warily.

"Because I don't believe Kajaan should die," King Cadeyrn said with a shrug as if it was that simple. "But if he returns to Averia, he will. Either for some hairbrained reason King Tonalli will come up with, or because he used his Craft to save his life. Kajaan isn't one for keeping such a secret when confronted about what happened."

"Even though he killed someone?" Yolotzin asked.

"Even though he killed someone," King Cadeyrn confirmed and nodded toward Lord Asyl. "Your Void friend understands."

Lord Asyl nodded, the anger seemingly gone from him. His husband still held him tight, running one hand through his Fated's long, silky black hair. Kajaan knew that their relationship had been touch and go a few times due to what Lord Asyl had suffered through during his time on the streets. His angered words had likely hit Lord Kende a little too hard, and he needed reassurance from his husband.

"Does that mean… can these shackles be removed, then?" Yolotzin asked.

King Cadeyrn nodded and gestured to someone behind the Averians. The brunet who'd escorted Kajaan up moved forward, and he felt the click reverberate up his arms. As soon as he felt the restraints leave, Kajaan flung his arms around Yolotzin's chest, clutching at his back. He needed to try and comfort his best friend as much as he could in the little time they had left together.

Except, now that he could feel his Craft seep back into him, Kajaan felt that pull again. Something told him he should go to the throne and acknowledge his Fated. No, that was ridiculous. He and Yolotzin had been to Paelfjord Castle many times, even if Kajaan kept to the servant areas rather than accompany Yolotzin in his audience with the king—and queen when she had been alive. Surely he would have known if he was Fated to someone here.

Kajaan ignored the tug, reveling in the feel of having Yolotzin in his arms again.

"What's next?" Yolotzin asked. "If he can't come home…."

"Kajaan will stay here," King Cadeyrn said. "We're not so far away that you can't come to visit him once every few moonturns. I won't deny you your relationship with him."

"Thank you," Yolotzin said, squeezing Kajaan tight for a second.

"He was your secretary, correct? Thaddaeus could use one here soon. His tutors are trying to schedule his lessons at the same time, and Quillin is, unfortunately, too busy with me that he cannot give Thaddaeus the consideration he deserves. It's caused quite the mess," King Cadeyrn said and sighed heavily. "While they all know Averian, Kajaan will be expected to learn Zothuan if he stays."

If he stayed. It wasn't like there was anywhere else Kajaan could go. Sure, he could try to find his mother's family up in Valvinte, but that could be a wild goose chase for all he knew. Pemalia was just depressing and a harsh place to live, and Nabene would be hostile toward him once he revealed he preferred the company of men. Bhyvine and Zothua really were his only choices, and Bhyvine cuisine really wasn't a favorite of his. Too spicy.

Besides, if the king was making good on his promise and he could become the young prince's secretary, then he'd have the perfect excuse to stay. He'd be somewhat close to Yolotzin, and with any luck, they'd be able to see each other frequently enough. Then once King Tonalli passed on and Yolotzin took over, he'd be able to return home! He could endure a few years here in the meantime.

It really wouldn't be *that* long of a stay.

"I can do that," Kajaan said softly.

"He's an excellent secretary," Yolotzin said proudly.

"I agree," Lady Naias said with a smile. "He's great if something comes up too. He never panicked whenever I saw him work and someone decided to try and throw a wrench in his plans."

Her praise flustered Kajaan, and he ducked his head to hide his blush. He'd never expected her to pay any sort of attention to him, even though he'd been working on taking over her schedule as well the closer they got to the wedding. It had just been something he'd done, as it would be expected of him once they were married. Kajaan had never once thought she'd noticed.

Their wedding!

Kajaan gasped and pulled away, looking up at a startled Yolotzin.

"Will I be able to attend your wedding?" he said urgently.

"I don't know," Yolotzin whispered, grimacing.

"Maybe. If we try to get diplomatic immunity and a special pass for you," King Cadeyrn said kindly. "Are other kingdoms supposed to be in attendance?"

"Yes," Lord Kende said. "We haven't quite finished with the invitations yet, so they haven't gone out. Right now, the plan is for the wedding to be held roughly mid to late summer."

"Plenty of time to work it out," King Cadeyrn said, nodding.

Yolotzin cupped the back of Kajaan's head, very gently scratching the base of his skull. Kajaan's eyes drifted closed, and a full-body shiver ran through him. He was unable to stop the longing sigh that escaped his lips. It was a hot spot that Yolotzin had found by accident years and years ago. Kajaan slumped bonelessly into Yolotzin, who rumbled with laughter, continuing to scratch at his scalp. At this point, Kajaan didn't even care if Lady Naias was jealous at the obviously intimate familiarity and touch.

"We'll see each other again," Kajaan finally mumbled sometime later.

The buzz of voices around them fell into silence. There'd been some sort of conversation that he'd completely missed. Hell, Kajaan wasn't sure he was interrupting anyone at the moment. All he could concentrate on were those wicked fingers rubbing and scratching at his scalp and the base of his skull. Kajaan could truly die happily in his best friend's arms, so long as he continued his teasing assault.

"I don't know how many times I'd be able to take two and a half weeks off," Yolotzin said sadly. "The castles are a week apart."

"For a horse," King Cadeyrn interrupted.

There was something off about his voice that Kajaan wasn't able to discern. He opened his eyes and looked over at the king. The man was watching the two of them with heat evident in his gaze, though his lips were pulled back into a slight grimace. It made Kajaan nervous, able to feel his raw jealousy. But jealousy over what? Or was that anger over their very obvious close relationship? Kajaan knew same-sex couples were equal in Zothua, so he didn't think it was disgust.

"Come. Let me give you a gift. Just don't let your father get his hands on it," King Cadeyrn said.

The man rolled seamlessly to his feet, his Bisht billowing around him. The material shimmered, consuming his body in flames. Kajaan winced at the imagery, and Yolotzin squeezed him gently before letting go, his fingers slipping from Kajaan's hair. He took his hand and followed the king as he gestured for them. Lady Naias came up on his other side and smiled, grasping his other hand.

Her acceptance made Kajaan's head spin. Surely she had an idea of how Kajaan felt toward Yolotzin? Did she truly not care? Or was she kind about it because he was being removed from the picture altogether? He knew Lady Naias only marginally, generally staying away from her when she was with Yolotzin. He knew he'd be beyond jealous about their relationship, so he'd just avoided the situation. Now he wished he'd spent more time with the two of them.

Considering he'd rarely ever see them again. If he'd known that he would be losing his best friend in a more permanent sense, he would have treasured every minute they'd still had together. Instead, he'd just assumed incorrectly that they'd be together forever. Now he'd miss out on so much. Maybe their wedding. Definitely their first kid.

Pain flashed through his gut. He shouldn't have isolated himself. Shouldn't have pulled away from Lady Naias. He should have treasured every moment he could have had with his best friend and his Fated. Kajaan squeezed their hands tight and swallowed hard, blinking rapidly. Lady Naias's other hand grasped his forearm, ever so gently returning his distressed squeeze.

The king led them through the back gardens, wordlessly showing off the vibrant and foreign plants that were native to the area. A few were similar to the plants growing in Alenzon, but not many. Avitou Castle had a similar garden, with plenty of trees and gazebos to hide in if it started raining. Out here, where the Laiyi Desert stretched out for miles, there wasn't much need for such permanent or heavy coverings. Instead of gazebos, there were small areas that held benches shaded by trees or a silk-covered pergola with gorgeously carved deep purple wood supports.

Kajaan inspected the carefully cultivated plant beds as they walked, surprised to see plenty of plants that weren't in bloom mixed in with those that were. He identified a few that he knew were late-summer bloomers and even a few that flowered in winter. Kajaan had to give the master gardener props for making sure the beds were constantly in bloom without looking too crowded.

The fragrance was sweet and spicy, much like the roasts that the chef had been working on when Kajaan had been escorted to the throne room. All it did was remind Kajaan that he hadn't eaten much before he was brought up, and he didn't know how long ago his last meal had been. As if on cue, his stomach growled at him, twisting uncomfortably. The scent made him slightly nauseous, as if that would make him more inclined to eat something.

The gravel pathway they took eventually led them from the gardens to the stables. From there, Prince Thaddaeus broke away and ran deep into the stalls, calling out a name. King Cadeyrn smiled at the boy's excitement, not bothering to scold or call him back. Clearly, the prince had a beloved creature or stable hand in here. Outside of the Averians, nothing here would hurt Prince Thaddaeus—and none of Yolotzin's party would lift a hand to the child.

Kajaan wasn't sure why he was surprised upon seeing that the creatures kept here weren't horses. Instead, he was faced with fanged muzzles. Their pelts looked like someone had bred an Averian horse with the zebras that roam Pemalia—dark stripes cutting through black, brown, or gold hair. The creatures easily stood up toward twenty hands, with their antlers giving them even more height.

Neither the height nor the sharp, protruding eyeteeth bothered Kajaan the most. He really wasn't sure if his apprehension came from their six legs or the uncanny intelligence that lurked behind their eyes. He distantly wondered if the rumors of gexenas bonding deeply with one rider, almost like a Fated bond, was true. They certainly seemed aware enough.

Gexenas were the pride and joy of the Zothua kingdom. They'd been carefully bred over generations to become the perfect mount. Apparently the third set of legs had been a freak mutation, and when that gexena had performed much better than her siblings, she was deemed the founding dam of the breed. Since then, the breed only improved through careful breeding. Their excess bulk, extra set of legs, and height allowed them to easily outrun an Averian racehorse.

Zothua never sold or traded an intact gexena to another kingdom, even though they were completely incompatible with horses, despite their similarities. They guarded their creatures with a rabid obsession, and Kajaan could understand why. Gexenas were scarily fast mounts, and their sharp, extra-long eyeteeth and dangerous antlers helped them rip into their opponents.

Kajaan had heard plenty of tales where a gexena killed just as many foes as her Zothuan rider in a skirmish. He hadn't believed it before. Now he could. The visiting Averians were watched carefully with each stall they passed, a couple of the terrifying things kicking the walls of their stalls with cloven hooves.

King Cadeyrn led them through the large stable, passing several gexenas without so much as blinking an eye. Behind him, Kajaan could hear Lord Asyl exclaim in wonder at the six-legged beasts. Of course he'd find the beasts exciting, and the man immediately started asking Lord Kende question after question. Apparently he'd never seen one before and wanted to know *everything*.

The king seemed completely at ease around the gexenas, unafraid of one lunging over its stall door and tearing out his throat. After all, who knew what whims or harebrained ideas these creatures experienced. Kajaan had been on the biting end of an ornery horse enough times to keep a healthy distance from the damn things. Sure, he rode with Yolotzin plenty of times, and he was an excellent rider, but then he usually only had to stay mounted on the horse, not worry about gathering and walking it through the stable.

They were led to a stall near the back with a gexena currently lying down, apparently dozing. King Cadeyrn whistled softly, and the gexena's oval horse-like ear flicked. It raised its head to see who was calling it before rolling onto its belly and then standing. This gexena was very much a male, Kajaan noted as the creature shook hay from its shaggy hide and antlers before it tromped over to the door. The gexena snorted, his head bobbing once or twice.

"This is Hariam," King Cadeyrn said in introduction. The gexena extended his head over the stall door, nosing at the king. He didn't hesitate before putting his hand on the beast's nose, rubbing between his nostrils. "He has the same dam as my Maeeri, though I had to geld him when he was young and couldn't control his temperament."

"He's gorgeous," Yolotzin said softly.

King Cadeyrn leaned in toward the stall and patted the gexena's long neck and beckoned for Yolotzin to come forward.

"Let him smell you. They're omnivores, but don't give them table scraps. Raw meat, produce, and hay is best for them. Hariam will easily travel about two hundred miles a day. Probably about one-fifty if he's carrying two or luggage," King Cadeyrn said.

Despite Kajaan holding on to Yolotzin's hand tightly, the prince slipped away and stepped up to the hell spawn. He held out his hand, palm flat to the creature's large nose as if he was offering a carrot to a horse. Hariam leaned in, taking several long whiffs before swinging his head up and down a few times. Apparently the creature approved of the man. Yolotzin simply smiled and patted the soft nose, taking another step closer to the gexena. He made a small noise low in his throat.

"He's quite calm, isn't he?" Yolotzin asked, a slightly dreamy quality to his voice.

His remark made King Cadeyrn look at him a little oddly before he smiled. "Yes. After we gelded Hariam, he's become quite docile and friendly."

"You poor thing, you were upset because your rider died. That's why you were acting out," Yolotzin murmured, reaching out and stroking the gexena's neck.

King Cadeyrn turned toward him, his head tilting to one side. He stared at the prince for a long minute before saying slowly, "They hadn't been together long, though he reacted to her the best. They'd been making good progress, but then she was bucked off by another gexena she was trying to train. The fall killed her instantly, so she didn't suffer."

"So you gelded Hariam because he wasn't compatible with another rider?" Lady Naias asked.

"We did try, my lady. I sent the call out to any eligible rider who wasn't paired with a gexena. I can't remember the actual number of people who tried to bond with Hariam, but it was definitely in the hundreds," King Cadeyrn said with a heavy sigh. "It wasn't an easy decision. He'd hurt a few of the unbonded riders, and gelding had to be considered. Hariam hasn't chosen another rider to bond with, but he'll still be an excellent mount. There just won't be that deeper connection."

"You might want to rethink that," Kajaan said with a soft smile, recognizing the look on his best friend's face.

Being a Sympathetic, Yolotzin could easily read into the emotions of others and instinctively know when he was being lied to. On rare occasions, a Sympathetic was able to communicate mentally if they had skin contact and a strong connection with their target. Since Yolotzin had managed to forge a deep bond with Kajaan, they'd been able to share memories with each other a few times, but it was incredibly taxing on the prince. They'd really only opened that bond when one of them was trying to make a point the other was having a hard time understanding.

Right now, Yolotzin had the same serene expression as he petted Hariam's neck. Almost as if the beast understood him, Hariam lowered his head and dropped it onto Yolotzin's shoulder, huffing out and relaxing. Yolotzin didn't even seem to notice, his other hand coming up and gently scratching behind Hariam's ears. They were in their own little world together, completely oblivious to anything else around them.

"Goddess," King Cadeyrn whispered.

"Is that bad?" Naias asked nervously—likely from how close those tusks were to Yolotzin's unprotected back. Kajaan wasn't a fan of Yolotzin's vulnerability either. "Is he safe?"

"Completely. Hariam is open to accepting a pairing with Prince Yolotzin. I've never seen a gexena pair up with a rider before taking a few laps around the ring," King Cadeyrn said with a small upward twitch to his lips. "Your Fated is completely safe, my lady. If Prince Yolotzin is in danger anywhere near Hariam, he'll do anything he can to protect him. Nobody but the prince will be able to ride him. Perhaps eventually, Hariam will accept you as a solo rider, though you'll have to have many rides with the prince before he'll allow it."

A delighted smile broke out on Lady Naias's face, and she nodded to him. Kajaan turned when he heard movement behind him and saw Lords Asyl and Kende approach. Lord Asyl's eyes were slightly red, and Kajaan wondered what had happened between them. Last he'd been paying attention to the couple, Lord Asyl had been completely smitten with the gexenas.

"Yolotzin, we have room in our stable for your gexena. We were talking to one of the stable hands and learning what we'd need to do to modify the last stall to make him comfortable. That way your father won't have easy access to him and can't bar you from him," Lord Kende offered.

Finally, Yolotzin moved away from Hariam to look at them. The creature lifted his head at the same time, seemingly understanding that his rider's attention was needed elsewhere. His large nostrils flared, taking in the scent of the two that just came up to their small party. Hariam regarded the humans calmly, a small flick of his ear being the only thing distinguishing him from a statue.

"That would be best," Yolotzin said, blinking several times.

Trying to come out of the bond he'd been forging with Hariam was bound to take him a while. Kajaan gently nudged Lady Naias toward her Fated, and she walked to his side and took his arm in hers. He smiled almost drunkenly at her, a naked fondness on his face that made Kajaan's stomach twist. The feeling of being replaced was nearly overwhelming, and Kajaan tried desperately to push it away. He could admit to himself that he was jealous, even if it was grudgingly.

If only because Yolotzin would never look at him like that again.

Kajaan swallowed hard and looked away. Movement caught his eye, and he noticed that King Cadeyrn was watching him. Something flared in his gut, spreading warmth down his arms and legs. The king's expression was gentle, thoughtful. There was no pity in his gaze, for which Kajaan was grateful. He didn't need the man's compassion for his longest relationship ending in a giant ball of fire.

"Stay for the night," the king said kindly to the visiting Averians. "It's too late in the day to get back to the next city, and it'll give my tack master time to change Hariam's barding to Averian colors. Horse tack won't work on a gexena, so we'll give you what's already been made for Hariam."

"Thank you. Between Hariam and keeping Kajaan safe, I'll always be in your debt," Yolotzin said, sounding more like himself.

King Cadeyrn gave him a slightly predatory grin. "Don't think I'm being completely selfless. You *are* the heir of Averia, after all."

With that, he swept out a side door, where Ameyalli and Quillin were waiting for him.

Chapter 6

Dinner had been delicious. Yolotzin refused to be separated from Kajaan for longer than the time it took for him to use the bathroom, always holding on to his hand or arm. He insisted on sticking around and keeping Kajaan company when he took a longer, much more thorough bath, even if he didn't join Kajaan in the hot water. The prince even insisted he should be the one to wash Kajaan's hair, fussing about how long it was getting and how much his pathetic scruff had grown in these last few days.

Roughly a week's worth of patchy stubble wasn't a beard, but it felt so much nicer when Yolotzin so very gently shaved him. Kajaan had long given up on protesting that he could tend to himself, letting his best friend fuss and pamper him. This would be the last time they'd have such intimate contact. The realization that he wasn't going to see Yolotzin every day kept coming back into his mind with a stab to the heart. Tears welled in his eyes each time, yet he refused to openly cry.

It was hard enough shoving his emotions aside to keep a passive face. Trying to hide them from a Sympathetic was damn near impossible. If the guilty and tortured glances Yolotzin gave him from time to time were any indication, Kajaan knew he'd failed. If he gave in to his despair and hurt, it would likely set off Yolotzin, and he'd do his damndest to try and figure out a way for them to live together again no matter what either king said. As much as Kajaan wanted that, it wouldn't be fair to Lady Naias.

Besides, the longer he didn't have those awful Craft-suppressing restraints on, the stronger the tug got. It was getting harder to ignore and harder not to just give in and follow where the tug was leading him. Kajaan had a sinking feeling he knew damn well who the goddess had chosen for him, and he truly didn't want to acknowledge it. Still, he couldn't help but keep glancing in King Cadeyrn's direction during dinner, hoping his furtive looks weren't noticed.

They'd been served classic Zothuan dishes, with the staff explaining what was in them as they were being set on the table. Likely to avoid any allergies or dietary issues. The contents of one dish had made Kajaan a little nervous to try, which included the liver of an exotic blue bird called a han-han. He had stared at the weirdly colored dish, but the kids ate it without any sort of protest, and Kajaan found the organ meat tender and quite flavorful.

After nearly a week in the dungeon, Kajaan hadn't been able to eat much. After the first plate had been placed in front of him, he'd asked how many courses there were, and to be served a minimal amount of each. That way he could try everything and not be overly stuffed or sick, but also reduce the amount of waste. King Cadeyrn had seemingly been pleased with his thoughtfulness and honesty, and Kajaan's plate had been adjusted. Yolotzin had been upset to learn how little Kajaan could eat, but he didn't say anything, regarding him with a pained expression.

At least the children had brought a certain amount of levity to the meal. The twins spoke rapidly in Zothuan, the little girl unable to sit still, constantly shifting from sitting properly to rolling onto her knees, to flopping back onto her butt. Eventually she wiggled her way onto her father's lap, who just smiled indulgently at her and kissed the top of her head. He didn't seem to mind that she was making it harder for him to enjoy his meal.

Lady Naias had a gleam in her eye watching the twins, the incredibly shy Princess Marika, and the polite Prince Thaddaeus. The boy was doing his best, in halting Averian, to try and talk to Lord Asyl, who sat across from him. Lord Asyl had unending patience talking with the boy, all gentle smiles and careful listening. He didn't quite have the parental yearning that his best friend had in spades, but he was sweet enough to the young prince.

Princess Fayette dropped off right before the dessert course, which consisted of a sweet flaky pastry with a nut mixture smeared between a few layers. It was stickier than all hell too, and Kajaan hadn't remembered the last time he'd been grateful to get such a small portion. The youngest boy, Prince Rodolfo, snatched up his twin's piece and subsequently ran from the room, gooey fingered and his cheeks bulging like a chipmunk's.

It felt good to laugh.

Now Kajaan stood listlessly in the bedchamber he was given. Quillin, the man who'd fetched him from the dungeon, had told him that this would be his room for the time he was at the castle. In other words, his new sanctuary. It didn't feel like his. He felt like an intruder, looking at the green stained-glass window and at the little balls of light that hovered on the ceiling. Those were quite fascinating, and Kajaan wasn't quite sure how to use them. Quillin hadn't bothered giving him an explanation.

At least his room had a nice view of the gardens, even through a heavy green tint. The bathroom itself was spectacular, and instead of the flagstone flooring that was almost everywhere, his quarters were made with black marble streaked with gold. The wood was different too. No longer was the furniture made out of some white wood, but rather a deep brown. His sheets were the same color as the smoothed sandstone walls.

The bathroom had a large enough tub to comfortably fit two and had runes etched along the bottom. Yolotzin had figured out earlier that they were triggers to heat a covered portion of the tub's curved bottom to warm the water. There was also a covered toilet that sluiced itself with a quick pull on a lever to wash away the waste. Above the tub and the sink was a small dial that spouted out water, usually lukewarm from the sun's heat.

Kajaan had never seen such casual luxury. Avitou was still relying on chamber pots and maids hauling up bucket after bucket of water to heat over the fire. This castle, which was likely older than Averia's, had modern fixtures and plumbing that Kajaan found himself impressed by. He wasn't quite jealous, considering he was the one to be staying here, but he was definitely awed.

In all his and Yolotzin's travels, he'd thought Averia was the farthest ahead technologically. He hadn't been privy to the other castle amenities, always staying with whichever duke they were visiting. Their methods had always been similar to Avitou's. Now he really wasn't sure. Perhaps he'd done himself a disservice by always insisting on staying behind while Yolotzin was busy schmoozing with the kings and queens.

Kajaan was staring at himself in the mirror of his en-suite bathroom when he heard the knock on the front door. He'd been given a pair of loose, flowing sleep pants to wear, and Kajaan didn't think about not having a shirt on when he opened the door. King Cadeyrn was on the other side, and he seemed startled at seeing Kajaan's bare chest, jerking back slightly. The pull that he'd been experiencing all evening came back with a vengeance, nearly making Kajaan stumble. Instead, he swayed slightly and inhaled sharply, shaking his head.

"May I help you, Your Grace?" Kajaan asked with a proper bow.

"Follow me," King Cadeyrn said.

He turned and strolled down the hallway without looking to see if Kajaan would obey. Kajaan hesitated and stumbled after him, unable to take his eyes away from the man's broad shoulders. Kajaan's fingers twitched, and he fought the impulse to reach out and trace the shapes on his back just to see how defined he was. The man must do something to keep himself in shape. Or perhaps he carried his kids a lot, if the ease of how King Cadeyrn held his daughter was anything to go by.

King Cadeyrn suddenly stopped in front of another door, and Kajaan snapped out of his daze. What in the hell was wrong with him? The last thing he needed to do was come on to King Cadeyrn and be thrown back into the dungeons for his impertinence. Not once had the king made any sort of indication he'd welcome such an advance.

Oblivious to his distress and not so much as even glancing back at him, King Cadeyrn rapped on the door. The same three quick knocks that had summoned Kajaan from his inspection of the bags under his eyes. It took a minute for the occupant to open the door, though Kajaan was blocked by the king from seeing who'd been assigned to sleep inside.

"Majesty," Yolotzin's voice came. "How may I help you?"

"I apologize," King Cadeyrn said simply. "Your rooms were mixed up. Someone else will be sleeping here tonight."

Kajaan stared up at the back of the king's head in confusion. There had been absolutely no such miscommunication. He knew that from how Quillin had shown him around his quarters, telling him that new clothes and toiletries for him would be delivered to him within a week. Lessons to learn Zothuan would start in two days, giving Kajaan a day of rest. The secretary was quite thorough and had been quite transparent about what to expect.

"Okay?" Yolotzin said slowly, clearly seeing through King Cadeyrn's lie. "Give me a moment."

"No need," King Cadeyrn said. He stepped to the side, and the two friends were able to see each other again. A small, almost sad smile formed on the king's face. "Good night."

With that, he turned and strode away, not waiting for any sort of response. Kajaan watched him leave, thinking how good he looked in the simple buttoned shirt and slacks he'd changed into for dinner before Kajaan turned his attention back to his best friend. Yolotzin had been watching him, and a slow smile spread across his face. He was dressed in a similar pair of sleeping pants, his chest also in view and an absolute delight to see.

"Come in," Yolotzin said, standing back.

Feeling almost like he was being set up, Kajaan entered Yolotzin's room. As soon as the door clicked shut, Kajaan found himself in Yolotzin's arms.

"Finally," the man breathed.

With that, Yolotzin dipped his head down and kissed him. Kajaan moaned and returned the gentle, seeking kiss, pressing in close. He wrapped his arms around his best friend's neck, holding him tight. Yolotzin tilted his head, pushing harder against him, his tongue seeking entry, licking along Kajaan's lips. Kajaan parted his lips, easily submitting to the prince without a second thought. For his lover of sixteen years, it was easy. Especially when he felt Yolotzin's hand sink into his hair and hold him firm.

Yolotzin tugged his head back, and Kajaan couldn't stop the whimper escaping him from the sharp points of pain, baring his neck to his love. He had always liked a bit of rough in bed, something that Yolotzin had quickly learned and was quite happy to oblige. Kajaan's heart raced, his body warming to Yolotzin's affections. He wiggled his hips against his lover's, delighted to feel an answering hardness.

"Nothing visible," Kajaan said, panting.

The prince snorted. "Haven't left anything visible yet."

Kajaan smiled and grunted when he felt a few sharp yet gentle nips on the side of his neck, hot air puffing against the sensitized skin. The hand in his hair kept him from moving too far away, and Kajaan couldn't help gasping and writhing against Yolotzin. Each gentle tug sent painful pleasure shooting down his spine, straight to his cock. He was so hard he ached, and there was nothing more he wanted to do than lie back on the bed and spread his legs.

But he couldn't. He couldn't give in to his temptations. Couldn't give in to what his body and soul craved. Yolotzin wasn't his anymore. Hadn't been his for moonturns, and if Kajaan bent over now, he knew he'd always wait for the next time his best friend visited and he could get Yolotzin alone. It wouldn't be fair to him. Wouldn't be fair to Yolotzin. And most importantly, it wouldn't be fair to Lady Naias.

Tears pricked at the edges of Kajaan's eyes as he reached up and put his hands on Yolotzin's chest, ever so gently pushing against him. They had to stop.

"Tzinny," Kajaan breathed, "if you don't stop, I fear you'll regret what we'll do."

His best friend groaned, and his hands relaxed. He shifted and rested his forehead on Kajaan's shoulder, sliding his hands down to rest on Kajaan's near nonexistent hips. The prince's body relaxed into his, and Yolotzin gently kissed Kajaan's neck over the bite marks. They panted together until their hearts stopped racing and rational thought came much easier.

"I probably would," Yolotzin said. "With as much as I adore Naias, you're right. Though she does know what you mean to me."

"She does?" Kajaan repeated, startled.

Since Yolotzin didn't seem inclined to move, Kajaan slowly ran his fingers through the man's soft hair. He'd always been envious of the prince's brown hair and how silky it was. Kajaan's own locks were coarse and not exactly pleasant to play with. Nowhere near as desirable as Yolotzin's hair was. He was envious that Lady Naias got to touch him freely for the rest of their lives. If this was to be their last night, Kajaan would touch almost every inch of his beloved prince.

"I told her on the way here. She said she deserved to know why I was so upset that my secretary was gone, and I agreed. So I told her, and since Kende and Asyl were in the carriage as well, they also know," Yolotzin said, leaning into Kajaan's touch. Kajaan didn't bother telling his best friend that he figured Lord Kende knew full well what their relationship was like—and that if he knew, then Lord Asyl surely did as well. "I told her how close we've always been and how we experimented with each other, before eventually becoming lovers."

"It's not like we were exclusive, though," Kajaan teased him.

Except, he had been. Even though it had killed him time and time again to watch Yolotzin charm his way into another man's pants or a lady's skirts, Kajaan had never taken another to his bed. His heart had only ever belonged to Yolotzin.

For better or for worse.

It was definitely worse now. Kajaan had to remind himself they'd been six when they recited the marriage vows to each other, and that had been boyhood folly. Even then, Kajaan had known that there wouldn't be anyone else for him but Yolotzin. Always being tugged along by the prince. Staring after him with wonder in his eyes and a fantasy in his heart. Wanting to be together forever and eagerly repeating the words Yolotzin had heard earlier in the day.

Tears surged to the surface, and this time they wouldn't be denied. Yolotzin was touching his bare skin, so there was no point in hiding them or his heartbreak. As intimately connected as they were, the man would pick up on his distress no matter how hard Kajaan tried suppressing it. He shook as Yolotzin straightened and gently pulled him close, holding him as if he were something precious.

"No," Yolotzin said gently, "but I do love you. I'll always love you."

"I love you so much," Kajaan whispered.

Did Yolotzin even remember their nighttime little faux wedding when they were boys? Probably not. It had been so insignificant in the grand scheme of things. Yolotzin had much more important things to remember now. Most notably, his Fated. He'd been so busy once he had his Awakening, though he'd somehow still carved out a small amount of time for Kajaan.

"Naias did say, though, that if I were to ever be unfaithful to her, she'd rather it be you than someone only interested in bedding a prince," Yolotzin said with a small laugh.

Kajaan couldn't help it. He gave a bitter, hiccupping laugh as the tears came freely. He buried his face in Yolotzin's chest, trembling in his arms. It was time. Time to officially break away and go their separate ways. To patch over the cracks in his broken heart and face the reality that Kajaan had been stubbornly avoiding.

He would never call Avitou home again.

"We were supposed to be forever," Kajaan managed to choke out.

"I wish we could have been," Yolotzin whispered, kissing the top of his head. "Maybe once I'm crowned in a few years, I'll be able to pardon you and bring you home."

"And watch you be madly in love with Lady Naias? You'll probably even have kids by then," Kajaan said, trying to not be bitter about it. "I don't know if my heart could take that."

His words were met with silence for a long time. Kajaan hadn't quite meant to verbalize what he'd been feeling for the last few moonturns since Yolotzin had found Lady Naias. He'd always kept his thoughts to himself, even when Yolotzin had touched him and asked him what was wrong. His best friend had always taken the "I'm fine" lie, knowing damn well Kajaan wasn't being truthful. Perhaps since he'd been such a tempest of emotions, Yolotzin hadn't been sure what was going on.

"Then maybe some distance will be best for both of us," Yolotzin finally said. Kajaan winced. He sniffed and looked up at his best friend. The prince smiled sadly at him and cupped his face. "Who knows. Maybe you'll find your Fated here, and you'll love them as intensely as you once did me."

"Don't say that, as if my love for you would be so easily forgotten," Kajaan chided him.

"I know it won't. After all, I can recognize that I still love you deeply, despite my growing relationship with Naias," Yolotzin said.

He leaned down, and they exchanged a gentle, languid kiss. It wasn't any deeper than parted lips seeking each other, but it ripped Kajaan's fragile heart apart all the same. After a long time, Yolotzin broke away and took Kajaan's hand in his. He led him to the bed and crawled on, tugging on Kajaan's arm. Kajaan was reluctant to follow, chewing on his lower lip.

"I don't think I'm up to having sex tonight," Kajaan managed to say.

"Just let me hold you," Yolotzin said.

Hold him one last time. Even when his best friend came to visit, they'd likely never get this chance again. Yolotzin might not be able to visit before his wedding, and afterward, he'd share his bed with Lady Naias. One last night. One last kiss. One last embrace. One last chance to form bittersweet memories that Kajaan could try and clutch to when he spent the rest of his nights alone.

Sure, he hadn't slept with Yolotzin every night, but a good majority of them he had. Especially when they were on the road. Kajaan nodded jerkily and crawled after his best friend onto the soft mattress. Yolotzin pulled the covers over them, and Kajaan was surprised to realize that it had been growing darker in the room. Indeed, the balls of light floating at the ceiling were dimming.

"Those are fascinating," Yolotzin murmured, echoing Kajaan's thoughts. "Maybe you could see if King Cadeyrn would be willing to export them."

"I'll ask when I know him better," Kajaan replied.

He curled up on his side, facing Yolotzin. It was natural to fit their bodies together, twining their limbs and snuggling up close. Yolotzin had one of his legs between Kajaan's, and Kajaan draped his leg over his best friend's hip, slotting them perfectly. Once again, Yolotzin's hand was in his hair, tangling his fingers in his coarse locks, the other hand resting on Kajaan's ass almost possessively. In return, Kajaan was cupping Yolotzin's face with one hand, his other arm draped over the brunet's waist. It was warm, comfortable, and incredibly soothing.

"You didn't tell King Cadeyrn that you already know a bit of Zothuan," Yolotzin teased him.

"You didn't either," Kajaan remarked, smiling. "But it's only written words. I'm not great at speaking or listening to it."

"Still. You'll be able to *impress* him," Yolotzin said.

"Why are you saying it like that?" Kajaan asked, frowning at him.

Yolotzin chuffed, giving him a peck on the lips.

"Because you've been watching him," Yolotzin said. "He's intriguing to you."

"He's an Ignian. Of course I'm watching him. I still have scars from Torbid's training," Kajaan replied flatly.

"It's not the same. You're not regarding him in fear. You were checking him out when he was walking away." Yolotzin chuckled.

Kajaan blushed and glanced away, biting his lower lip. His best friend snorted and laughed harder, scratching Kajaan's scalp and pulling him in close for another soft kiss.

"I'm not going to jeopardize my position here by hitting on the completely straight king," Kajaan said and sighed. "No matter how handsome he is."

Yolotzin cocked an eyebrow and laughed quietly. "Handsome, huh? Don't bank on the straight thing, though. He watched you as much as you've watched him all day."

"What do you mean?" Kajaan asked.

"He kept glancing at you. While we were in the throne room, in the stable, at dinner…." Yolotzin trailed off, smiling.

"You're seeing things. You don't want me to be alone now that you've found your Fated, so you're projecting," Kajaan protested.

"I wasn't the only one who saw it," Yolotzin teased. "Kende commented on it too."

There wasn't much Kajaan could protest about that. He cleared his throat and ducked his head, burrowing into his best friend's throat. Since he hadn't been privy to that conversation, he couldn't deny what had been said. If Lord Kende had seen it too, then it was probably true and not just Yolotzin's wishful thinking.

"I'm surprised Lords Kende and Asyl came," Kajaan said, trying to divert the subject.

"Of course they did," Yolotzin replied, sounding surprised. "Asyl looks up to you, you know. After he got over his initial distrust of you, I think he formed a bit of hero worship."

"I'm hardly a hero," Kajaan argued.

"You are to him, and that's all that matters. You saved him from spending the rest of his life as a sex slave, which might have ended with his murder," Yolotzin said gently. "Tillet has been interviewed extensively by Macik. I'm pretty sure he manipulated Tillet to confess more by reading his moods and calling him out on his lies."

"What did he find out?" Kajaan asked, not sure if he wanted to hear the answer.

Truthfully, he hadn't really thought much about Tillet and Lady Ilfa for moonturns. Ever since their arrests and Yolotzin's betrothal, Kajaan hadn't really had the energy to keep up with the two criminals. He'd briefly noted the birth of the youngest Seni child, but he'd had plenty of other things on his mind. Namely, Yolotzin leaving him.

"Asyl wasn't his first. Just his longest captive. Apparently he'd sell his pets, as he calls them, once they started getting a little too old. He and his Fated just liked how Asyl looked, so they kept him longer. Tillet didn't know what happened to the other boys he sold, but he at least gave Macik names to follow up on," Yolotzin said.

"Fucking disgusting bastard," Kajaan growled. "Please tell me he didn't hurt anyone after Asyl."

Yolotzin drew in a deep breath and sighed heavily. Just like that, Kajaan knew the answer. As much as he didn't want to hear it, the victims deserved to have their stories told. His stomach clenched in anticipation.

"He did. Two other Voids," Yolotzin said, his voice barely above a whisper. "Tillet killed one himself. The other he sold."

"Goddess," Kajaan whispered, nestling in deeper. He began shivering, needing his best friend's warmth and comfort. The doubts hit him a second later. "I should have said something. Talked to Macik or done *something*. I might have been able to save them."

"Don't think like that," Yolotzin chastised him. "Macik might not have believed you, you know that. He's open-minded, but he still needs his lieutenant's permission for an investigation like that regarding gentry. Besides, Voids are only just now gaining recognition, and solely because of Asyl saving Kende's life from a Craft Blessed."

"I'd been ignoring his invitations for a couple years before I went," Kajaan admitted.

"You couldn't have known," Yolotzin said, kissing the top of his head and scratching his scalp. "It's easy to think about the past and beat yourself up about it. Asyl has never blamed you for taking so long to find him, you know that."

"I suppose," Kajaan muttered, sighing. "It just sucks knowing."

"Think about it this way. If you had found Asyl sooner, Tillet might have taken more victims, and Asyl might not have run into Naias when running from you. If that didn't happen, then he might not have ever been found by Kende, and their relationship would have never flourished, Tillet and Ilfa wouldn't have been stopped, and it would be possible it would take even longer for me to have found my Fated," Yolotzin said.

"So you're saying that if I wanted you longer, I should have gone to one of Tillet's parties sooner?" Kajaan teased weakly.

That earned him a sharp slap to his ass, and Kajaan yelped, jumping.

"Maybe." Yolotzin snickered. "But that would also mean that Asyl wouldn't have nearly torn Birgir a new asshole."

Kajaan leaned back to look at his love, smiling at the glint in his eye.

"Oh, do tell. I don't understand why Lord Kende keeps him around," Kajaan said, wanting the details.

"Sympathy, maybe? The old man is close to retirement and wouldn't be able to get employment elsewhere. Asyl got your letter and apparently worked himself up into a state. From what Olire says, Asyl just ran back to the manor, not bothering to call for Toemi or wave down a hired carriage," Yolotzin began.

"I doubt a hired carriage will stop for a Void, even if it's for Lord Asyl," Kajaan broke in. "His knee, though…."

Yolotzin winced in sympathy and nodded. Lord Asyl had been walking all right today, so any damage done that night had probably healed. Nothing would have stopped Lord Kende from taking excellent care of his beloved husband.

"True," Yolotzin relented, shrugging. "Birgir was apparently affronted when Asyl didn't let the footman open the door and didn't quite look the part of a lord's husband and tried scolding him. Asyl wasn't having it, and that's when he gave Kende your letter and got me involved. He was the one who planned the whole trip in less than a day after Father blew me off. When Birgir tried stopping him and demanding he let those below his station handle the day-to-day necessities and that he needed to be proper, Asyl ripped into him to the point where Kende had to intervene and nearly sedate him."

Kajaan blinked several times, staring at Yolotzin. He'd seen the underlying anger Lord Asyl possessed while he'd been defending Kajaan for using his Craft. Still, it was so outside of how he usually perceived the alchemist that it was bizarre. The Lord Asyl Kajaan knew was even-tempered and sweet, but maybe he'd only talked to Lord Asyl on his good days. He'd seen a glimpse of Lord Asyl's dedication when his husband's life was on the line, though Kajaan would never have thought that fervor would be directed toward him.

"Lord Asyl handled all the preparations?" Kajaan asked.

Yolotzin smiled and nodded. "Yeah. He had me go get Naias and run a couple errands for him, not caring whatsoever that I'm the crown prince. Hell, he even glared at Kende when he tried to protest and have Siora handle the preparations instead."

Kajaan laughed softly. "Lord Asyl certainly doesn't behave like he's a noble, does he? Rank doesn't seem to matter to him."

"It's refreshing, honestly. He knows I'm his prince, but Asyl treats me the same as everyone else. I think he's the best husband for Kende. Kende always cared a bit too much what others thought of him," Yolotzin said. He blinked and tilted his head slightly, kissing Kajaan's temple. "Speaking of him, would you let Kende take a look at you in the morning? I'm sure King Cadeyrn's Healers are just fine, but I'd feel better having my cousin's opinion."

"Whatever makes you feel better for leaving me here," Kajaan said softly. "But you know King Cadeyrn won't hurt or upset me. It'd be stupid for him to."

Yolotzin stared at him for a moment before he hummed. "Why do you think that?"

Kajaan rolled his eyes. "You're smarter than that. Just think about it."

"I'm tired," Yolotzin complained pitifully with a small smile. "Or maybe I just want to hear you talk about your theories about why you're safe."

"What did King Cadeyrn do to try and save his wife?" Kajaan countered, raising an eyebrow.

"Used his Craft," Yolotzin said and made a noise low in his throat before sighing, closing his eyes. "If you tell me he's mistreating you, then I can use that against him."

"One letter to the world council and he'd be dethroned and executed. They wouldn't care to investigate or talk to him as to why he did what he did. They'd just make an example out of him, telling the whole world that kings aren't exempt from the rules. Then they'd either crown Prince Thaddaeus or install an advisor until he becomes of age. Whichever they do, there'd be unrest, and your father would have the perfect opportunity to try and take over," Kajaan finished.

Yolotzin sighed heavily and nuzzled their foreheads together, kissing the tip of Kajaan's nose.

"I'm going to miss you at my side," Yolotzin said. "I'd gladly have you as my advisor rather than my secretary."

Kajaan smiled faintly. "I'd rather just be your secretary. But I won't be your side piece."

Yolotzin smiled, almost sadly. The orbs had gone completely dark now, and Kajaan's night vision had taken over. It was plenty dark in the room, but he was just able to make out the features on his best friend's face from their proximity.

"That's probably for the best," Yolotzin admitted in a whisper. "But I'm still going to demand hugs and cuddles when I'm able to."

As if to illustrate his point, Yolotzin squeezed Kajaan's ass and pulled him tight to him. Kajaan snickered into his chest, breathing in his love's lemon-and-strawberry scent as he finally allowed himself to drift off to sleep.

CHAPTER 7

"YOU'RE SULKING," Ameyalli said quietly as they entered Cadeyrn's study.

Cadeyrn sighed, keeping his focus on the letter that had come in that morning with Neerian's pathetic tithe. The man was short by quite a significant amount, and as such had sent along a letter explaining why. According to him, the new safety standards that Cadeyrn was implementing for granaries and factories had taken out a hefty chunk of his reserves, not to mention from what he'd brought in that quarter. Cadeyrn wasn't sure how much of that he believed.

What he did believe was that Neerian thought he'd be able to get away with not properly paying his tithe and trying to wiggle out of his responsibilities. Cadeyrn had already started drafting a letter to his auditor to send out an agent and poke around. The safety standards shouldn't take that much gold or time to implement, so labor loss would have been minimal. Hell, maybe a couple platinum total for all of Neerian's buildings. He knew the old lord was stingy, but not like this.

"I'm working," Cadeyrn said with a huff. "Today got derailed and I haven't had time to go through everything."

They both looked over when the study door opened again. Instead of Quillin, who Cadeyrn had fully expected, he was pleasantly surprised to see his eldest son. The boy shut the door firmly and quickly scurried over, hopped into Cadeyrn's lap, and leaned against him. Cadeyrn wrapped one arm around his son's waist, marveling at how big Thaddaeus was getting. He wasn't showing any signs of slowing down either. It made Cadeyrn wonder how tall his son would end up once he was done with his last growth spurt.

"Hey, kiddo," Cadeyrn said warmly.

"Hey, Papa," Thaddaeus replied, sighing softly.

"What's on your mind?" Cadeyrn asked, grateful for his son's interruption.

Thaddaeus just shrugged and looked up at Ameyalli. Maybe Cadeyrn was a bit too hasty to feel relief at seeing his son slip into his study.

"Just felt like I should be here," Thaddaeus said, sounding a little puzzled.

Cadeyrn frowned but shrugged and hugged his son tight for a moment, returning his focus to the papers on his desk. For a long few minutes, no one spoke while he scratched out a few more lines with his quill.

"He'll be faithful," Ameyalli finally said into the silence.

There was something odd in their voice that made Cadeyrn look up. They didn't have that faraway tone that denoted Ameyalli was currently embroiled in a Vision. No, they were just watching Cadeyrn with a shrewd look in their eye and a small smile curving their lips.

"You need a relationship to be faithful," Cadeyrn said flatly.

"Who?" Thaddaeus asked, looking up at him.

Cadeyrn was about to tell his son to not mind when Ameyalli answered for him. "Kajaan. He may love the prince, but that will pale in comparison to the love he'll have for you."

"He doesn't even want to acknowledge the bond," Cadeyrn protested.

"And because he didn't approach you, you organized for him to spend the night with his former lover," Ameyalli said and sighed. "You do understand he's vulnerable in his position right now. He's not going to make the first move. It'll be on you to activate the bond and begin to court him."

"I don't understand," Thaddaeus said quietly. "What bond?"

"Kajaan is your papa's Fated," Ameyalli replied.

Hearing it again made Cadeyrn's chest ache. He wasn't wanted by his Fated, he knew that. Kajaan loved Prince Yolotzin with all his heart. There was no room in there for him. Besides, it was for the best. He'd seen the hope on Kajaan's face whenever he looked up at his prince. The moment he was no longer Prince Yolotzin and became King Yolotzin, Kajaan would leave Paelfjord far behind and never look back.

"If it was safe to send him home, I would," Cadeyrn said flatly.

"I thought Mom was your Fated," Thaddaeus whispered. The boy wrenched himself from Cadeyrn's grasp and spun, his face flushed with the frustration Cadeyrn could easily see. "How can you push your Fated away? Everyone always talks about how wonderful it is!"

"Yes, my liege, why are you pushing your Fated away?" Ameyalli asked in their infuriatingly soft voice.

"I won't kill another lover," Cadeyrn snapped. He flung his quill onto the half-written letter, not caring about the splashes of ink that marred the words. "I already killed Menea. I don't see why the goddess would grace me with a Fated."

Thaddaeus just stared at him, his eyes wide, tears pooling along the bottom lid. Ameyalli gently put a hand on the prince's shoulder. They weren't that much taller than Thaddaeus anymore. Only about a half foot. Sooner rather than later, the prince would tower over his advisor, all gangly and awkward until he grew into his adult bulk.

"You didn't kill Menea," Ameyalli said firmly. "That was the fever, and you know it."

"I didn't try hard enough," Cadeyrn protested. "I should have reached out to—"

"To who?" Ameyalli interrupted, sounding angry now. "You wrote to Healer after Healer and even brought some over from Averia and Bhyvine to try and treat Menea. They all told you the same thing. They couldn't heal her. They couldn't get her fever to break. Sometimes bad things happen."

"If I could have broken the fever," Cadeyrn said weakly, scrubbing his face and burning eyes, "maybe they would have been successful."

"You did all you could," Ameyalli said, their voice gentling once more. "With all your resources, all your power, and all your love, you did all you could."

They gently pushed at Thaddaeus's shoulder. The boy didn't hesitate, running back to his father. Cadeyrn found his lap full of his son again, though this time Thaddaeus was straddling him, hugging him around the neck and holding him tight. As if he'd fall apart if Thaddaeus didn't halfway strangle him.

"Ames," Cadeyrn said quietly, "I don't deserve this."

"Everyone deserves a chance to be happy," Ameyalli replied quietly.

The three stayed still for a full minute before Thaddaeus sniffled and Cadeyrn realized that his son was likely struggling with the conversation. From briefly thinking that his father had purposely killed his mother, rather than her wasting away. He wrapped his arms around the boy and held him close, reveling in the knowledge that for now, Thaddaeus needed him for comfort. These moments were numbered, Cadeyrn knew.

Soon Thaddaeus would slip off his lap and out of his arms for the last time, and he wouldn't even know.

And it would probably be sooner than Cadeyrn would be ready for.

"What do you think, Thad?" Cadeyrn finally asked.

His son sat back, wiping the tears from his cheeks before he pouted up at him.

"I miss Mom," he stated and let out a shaky laugh. "But the babies deserve to have happy parents. And you're not as happy as you were with Mom."

Cadeyrn's heart ached. He didn't realize Thaddaeus had a lot of memories of Menea before she fell ill. He hoped that Thaddaeus wouldn't lose them, no matter how old he got. Cadeyrn chewed on the inside of his cheek for a moment, regarding his son carefully. There was no resentment in the boy's countenance.

"You're all right with it?" Cadeyrn asked.

Thaddaeus just nodded. "He's your Fated. Why wouldn't I be?"

"They're not a complete guarantee. We can walk away if we both agree that it would be better," Cadeyrn argued gently.

"It wouldn't be. You'd still be lonely," Thaddaeus said and shrugged. "Besides, I think he needs it too. He seems sad a lot of the time."

Yes. Kajaan was sad every time his prince's attention wandered from him. Cadeyrn had caught that as well. The agony of losing his most loved person, even if it wasn't as truly permanent as death, though this seemed crueler. Kajaan wilted minutely every time Prince Yolotzin wasn't focusing on him. Lady Naias had seen it, acknowledged by the pain in her eyes as she watched them.

Cadeyrn wondered if she felt guilty that she was Prince Yolotzin's Fated. Not that there was much to do about it. The prince was absolutely smitten with her if the look on his face after bonding with Hariam was anything to go by. But at the same time, he'd seen Kajaan's devastation. The pure heartbreak and desolation on his face had been the only thing stopping Cadeyrn from laughing at Lord Asyl's sneezing fit right before the two had joined the rest of the group.

But it had also been the driving factor for him to invite them to stay the night. Courtship regulations from Averia required the prince and his Fated to sleep apart until their wedding night, so Cadeyrn intervened. He could give Kajaan one last night with his lover before he was left behind.

"It's time, Cade," Ameyalli said quietly. "The future is uncertain. Something big is coming, and it concerns both you and your guests."

"How will it turn out?" Thaddaeus asked, shifting in Cadeyrn's lap to look at the Seer. "Everything will be okay, right?"

Ameyalli smiled faintly. "It doesn't work like that, sweet. There are so many possibilities of what the future can bring based on the choices we make today. Though there are a few impressions that are constant."

"Do we need to be careful?" Cadeyrn asked warily.

Seers were quite possibly the most enigmatic of all the Craft Blessed. Their Visions were tricky to interpret, even for one as competent as Ameyalli. Nothing was ever set in stone, though Ameyalli insisted that specific events were always to happen, no matter how hard the Seer might try to prevent it. It was just the minor details that changed. Perhaps such an event was in their future.

"Not exactly," Ameyalli said, their voice gaining a dreamy quality, "but Kajaan will be very important. He needs to master his Craft before his return to Averia. Many lives will depend on it."

Cadeyrn couldn't help it. He hugged Thaddaeus tight for the amount of time it took for the boy to wheeze out his protest. Trying to woo Kajaan, help him with his Craft, and juggle going to Averia along with his children to attend a wedding wasn't going to be an easy task. Oh yeah, then there was the minor issue of continuing to keep an eye on his kingdom.

Coming out of this upcoming dire event alive was going to take a minor miracle.

CHAPTER 8

"KENDE, LOVE, are there any bans on Zothuan medical books?" Lord Asyl asked as he entered the room.

Kajaan was sitting nude on the vanity stool, a towel between his bare ass and the fabric. He'd followed Lord Kende to his room right after breakfast for a complete physical examination, while Lord Asyl had vanished with one of the footmen. Now he knew what the young man had been up to. A large tome was split open in one hand, his other blindly shutting the door, almost all his focus dedicated to the words on the page.

Lord Kende didn't respond to his husband, his eyes closed as he used his Craft to check Kajaan over thoroughly. It was weird, Kajaan had decided about an hour ago. He could feel the man's touch like a warm caress along each one of his organs and muscles. He felt almost feverish and would have been worried if Lord Kende wasn't currently cupping his face with his eyes closed, concentrating. He'd never experienced such warmth in previous healings and had to wonder if Lord Kende was just an exceptionally strong Healer.

At the silence, Lord Asyl looked up and froze before he blinked once, taking in the scene. No anger passed through his expression at seeing a naked man with his husband. Instead, he quietly shut the large book and set it on the vanity before walking over and perching on a small settee. Apparently used to what was happening, Lord Asyl didn't bother talking again. Instead, he smiled faintly at Kajaan, who returned the gesture. Even if Lord Kende couldn't hear them, silence made it easier for a Healer to work.

A small twitch of Lord Kende's brow was the only tell that he was pulling away from Kajaan's body and back into himself. The man's green eyes opened, and he frowned down at him as the internal warmth died down to a normal level.

"That's curious," Lord Kende muttered. "Give me a moment to breathe, but there's something I want to check before I call it good."

"Let me get dressed while you do that. I'm not going to give Lord Asyl a show," Kajaan teased them.

Lord Kende startled and turned to see his husband, who snickered, wiggling his fingers in hello. The smile that softened his lips made Kajaan's chest ache with a deep longing. He quickly turned away and tugged on the clothes he'd been given. They were made of the same breathable material his sleep pants were, though Kajaan wasn't too surprised.

Even in early spring, he could tell the air was warmer here. He and Yolotzin had never traveled through Zothua during the summer since the heat was rumored to be nearly unbearable for the more mild citizens of Averia. Bhyvine was even worse. Instead, they'd traveled either north to Valvinte or stayed in Averia during the warmer seasons.

"You don't need to call me Lord, you know," Lord Asyl said with a smile. "Goddess knows I don't act like one pretty much ever."

"You were born one, and married into the title," Kajaan said simply. "You are a lord twice over despite your protests. Especially since Lord Seni has revoked your disownment."

Lord Asyl groaned and shot his Fated a pathetic look with a pout. "Make him stop."

Lord Kende snorted. "I've been trying to get him to drop my honorifics for nearly thirty years. I wish you luck, love. Was your search in the library fruitful?"

Almost as if that was a trigger, Lord Asyl popped off the settee, gathered the tome, and handed it to his husband. Once Lord Kende started rifling through the pages, Lord Asyl went off on a huge tangent about how Zothuans used different herbs to concoct the same potions he brewed at home, how some were more effective than others, and how he wanted to experiment with his mixtures. It seemed as if he was going to go on for hours, but Kajaan knew they didn't have that long.

Lord Kende swooped down and lightly kissed his husband's lips. Lord Asyl fell quiet with a gentle moan, arching up toward his Fated, chasing his affection even when Lord Kende took a step back.

"Why don't we ask Quillin about any bans on their medical books and herbs that they use? I'm all for you experimenting and using your ingredients in the most effective manner you can, but let's get that information first before you set your heart on something you can't do," Lord Kende said gently.

"Okay," Lord Asyl said, nodding. He took the book back from his husband and looked at Kajaan, who'd been watching them with a faraway smile. "What did you want to recheck?"

"Kajaan's Craft," Lord Kende said.

Kajaan regarded him curiously. "What's wrong with it?"

"I'm not sure. It seemed dim," Lord Kende replied, shrugging.

The Healer cupped his face again, though this time he kept his eyes open, their eyes locking. Kajaan could feel the man's warm touch slip deep into his chest, oozing almost as if it was honey on a cold day. It wasn't invasive, but it wasn't comforting like it had been before either.

Something in him wanted to shove Lord Kende away and run. He'd never had a problem with how Healers felt before and clearly hadn't objected to the probe earlier. So why now? Kajaan felt his heart lurch, and he gripped the edges of his seat tight, forcing himself to stay still.

"What do you mean by dim?" Lord Asyl prompted.

"I mean there's something not quite right," Lord Kende said.

"According to King Cadeyrn, I drained myself past my reserves. They had to have a Void come and transfer energy from another Aquan into me," Kajaan offered.

"That's not the problem," Lord Kende said, his brows furrowing. His eyes grew distant, not really seeing anything anymore. "The transfer was a success, though I'd suggest slowly draining that foreign power so your body can regenerate your native energy."

"There's a difference?" Kajaan asked, surprised, "I thought it was all the same."

"Each Craft is unique to each person. Almost like a fingerprint," Lord Asyl explained. "Underneath that is an essence that's universal, but it can take some time to strip the unique parts away. Either form can be transferred over, though I only used the white essence to help heal Kende."

Lord Kende shrugged. "There's a lot about this kind of energy transfer that's not researched at all in Averia. The Healers here may have more complete information since they haven't been persecuting their Voids for decades. Asyl's been talking with Duke Vitalis as well to gain his insight, but it's been slow."

"So I should use my Craft a little each day?" Kajaan asked.

"Yes," Lord Kende confirmed and tilted his head before he continued in a low voice. "But… wait. Why is your reservoir so small?"

"I'm really only one step up from being a Void," Kajaan said bitterly. "My Craft has been incredibly weak ever since my Awakening. I honestly don't know how my Awakening didn't fail."

"No," Lord Kende murmured, scowling briefly. "That's not it. There's a massive well here that's untapped. You should have leagues more power than you do. Your reservoir is tiny, but there's plenty of space. It's almost as if it's been stunted."

"How would that have happened?" Lord Asyl asked. "Isn't it just something that's blessed on Awakening?"

"Not exactly. There's a certain amount immediately available, sure, but it wouldn't be wise to give a teenager free rein over an elemental Craft. Proper training and usage strengthens the bond between a human and their Craft, stretching out their reservoir to what it's supposed to be. Basically, what's going on is because of this block, Kajaan can't store the power his body is capable of generating, so most of it goes to waste or just doesn't generate. Your Craft is stagnant," Lord Kende said, finally releasing Kajaan's face.

Finally feeling like he could breathe, Kajaan took several gulps of air, eyeing the Healer warily. He slowly edged away from Yolotzin's cousin, trying to fight back the panic rising in his throat. Lord Asyl noticed and tilted his head, pouting slightly.

"Everything okay, Kajaan?" Lord Asyl asked.

"Just trying to tamp down my fight-or-flight reflex," Kajaan admitted with a weak smile. "For whatever reason, Lord Kende focusing solely on my Craft made me panic."

"Odd," Lord Kende murmured. "It shouldn't. Checking your reservoir and well is the same as any other bodily check. Is there something that happened after your Awakening that could have made you fearful of your own Craft?"

"Idiot child! If you can't invoke your Craft almost instantly, how will you be any use to the prince?"

"Goddess, why did my wife have to die and leave me with a nearly useless son?"

"You'll never be worth anything if you can't control yourself! Your burns are your own damn fault. Stop crying, you little matricidal brat."

Kajaan pushed the echoing sneers to the back of his mind and shrugged.

"Maybe. My trainer gave up on me pretty quickly," Kajaan said, trying for some levity. "Said I was useless and there was no point to train me after a few moonturns."

He did his best to not fidget and rub the barely visible burn scars along his arms. At least his face had healed without marring, so he wasn't too disfigured. Yolotzin had never judged him for the odd patches along his body. It made undressing with him for the first time easy.

"That's ridiculous," Lord Kende snarled. "Everyone has a specific link to their Craft, and your trainer should have worked with you to find it, rather than expect you to pick up his methods immediately. A good trainer would have never abandoned you."

"Never said he was good," Kajaan pointed out.

A timid knock echoed through the room, and a footman poked her head in.

"Excuse me, masters. It's time," she said gently.

Those last two words couldn't hurt any more. Kajaan waited for the Fated couple to leave the room first before he took a deep breath and followed the footman to the great hall and main doors. Out front, Hariam stood next to the carriage, nearly dwarfing the vehicle. The horses seemed a bit shy around the gexena, but they didn't try to bolt, barely prancing where they stood.

Kajaan was startled to realize he recognized the driver. Toemi had come with them. He supposed it made sense, thinking about it. If Lord Asyl had been the one to put everything together, then he'd absolutely use his husband's resources rather than the castle's or hiring a driver. Less interference from King Tonalli that way.

Kajaan stood on the wide, generous porch that led to two curving staircases, hugging a beautiful fountain of the goddess Ilyphari that was currently spouting water into the air from her forehead where a Craft Mark would be. King Cadeyrn was already there with his advisor and secretary, and Kajaan found himself pausing next to the man. Not close enough to touch, but he didn't walk farther than where the king was standing.

This was it.

Kajaan's heart clenched, and a lump formed in his throat. He was having a hard time catching his breath, and if the glances he kept getting from King Cadeyrn said anything, he wasn't hiding his distress very well. Lord Asyl tapped Quillin on the shoulder and handed the medical tome back to him, asking about bans on books and plants. That drew King Cadeyrn's attention, and Lord Asyl told them about his profession as an alchemist and his shop, Enchanted Waters.

As a final gift, King Cadeyrn gifted Lord Asyl the medical tome, and Quillin politely said that no bans against medical books or herbs were in effect. He pulled out a small notepad from his breast pocket and wrote down some contact information. Apparently a couple were Harvesters, one a Healer, and another a Sympathetic for Lord Asyl to reach out to about his curiosity. The Void was nearly bouncing after he said his proper thanks, bowed, and pelted down the stairs to catch up to his husband, who laughed upon seeing the pure delight on Lord Asyl's face.

Lady Naias was standing next to a Zothuan guard, dressed in breeches to ride instead of her usual skirts. She'd always been a fairly practical lady, and Kajaan wished he could hate her for it. Clearly Yolotzin was taking what the king said to heart and trying to expose Hariam to his Fated quickly. Speaking of, where was he?

"King Cadeyrn," Yolotzin said from behind them. He circled the small party and bowed properly. "Thank you so much for your hospitality and gifts. I will cherish Hariam as much as I hope you cherish Kajaan."

"Thanks for putting me in the same category as a mount," Kajaan said dryly.

"As if you're not hoping to get mounted," Yolotzin shot back.

Kajaan coughed, his cheeks and ears flaming. He wished he wasn't quite so close to being a prisoner, else he'd retreat somewhere and pretend Yolotzin hadn't just said that in front of the *king*, of all people. To his horror, King Cadeyrn began laughing. It was hearty and joyous and wonderful to listen to. Kajaan immediately found himself addicted, and his face warmed with something other than his mortification.

"You are always welcome here," King Cadeyrn said kindly. "Don't worry about Kajaan. We'll take good care of him."

Mollified, Yolotzin came to stand in front of Kajaan. He cupped his face, tilting it up to him just like what Lord Kende had done not too long ago. The prince stood there for a few heartbeats, quietly regarding him, before dipping down and pressing a kiss to his lips.

"Farewell for now," Yolotzin whispered, their lips brushing together as he spoke. "For better or for worse, Kajie."

Kajaan had never really thought a breaking heart was physical. He knew, as his barely held-together heart tore into tiny pieces, that he'd been wrong. Pain lanced through his chest, numbing his extremities, and the lump in his throat grew, making it even harder to breathe. With a great effort, he managed to hold back the agony that coursed through him.

This hadn't been how he wanted to learn that Yolotzin remembered their boyhood vows.

With another quick peck, Yolotzin released him and trotted down the stairs. Kajaan managed to hold it together as Yolotzin beamed at Lady Naias and mounted Hariam. He didn't break apart as Yolotzin and the guard helped Lady Naias mount behind him and cuddle up to him, her arms wrapping around his waist, a gleeful look on her face. His control began to waver once Toemi cracked the reins and the group began to depart. Leaving him behind forever.

Yolotzin didn't look back.

Despite knowing how incredibly rude he was being, Kajaan turned and bolted without a word. How he made it back to the rooms he'd been assigned without being able to see anything, he had no idea. He collapsed onto the bed and wept, a gaping hole in his chest where his fragile heart lay shattered.

CHAPTER 9

KAJAAN WAS an incredibly smart man. That was the conclusion King Cadeyrn came to after watching the man almost to the point of obsession. He'd been amused to learn that Kajaan had some rudimentary knowledge of Zothuan so long as it was written down. Though why neither he nor the prince had said so was a curious thing, it really didn't matter in the end. Kajaan took to his language, culture, and legal lessons like a duck to water.

It made King Cadeyrn want to see about getting other language experts in here to see how many Kajaan could pick up, and how quickly. In a single moonturn, he'd gone from talking Zothuan slowly and struggling with the pronunciation of most words to speaking as well as Thaddaeus did.

And the change Kajaan had made in his son!

No longer was Thaddaeus the quiet, almost surly boy he'd become in the last couple of years. Kajaan had got all of Thaddaeus's tutors together, sat them down, and handed them each a new schedule for the prince before the first week was out. He'd altered the schedule heavily, changing almost everything that they'd been doing. According to the translator who'd been attending, there was quite the explosion, and a few of the instructors had shouted at Kajaan.

He'd just let them rage themselves into exhaustion before explaining his motives. That Thaddaeus deserved to still be a child, and children should be allowed to have fun. Even if they were the heir to a kingdom. Kajaan claimed it would help his attention span and would likely motivate the boy to study better and be able to retain information easier. He also speculated it would help with Thaddaeus's blatant rejection of trying to learn the more intricate laws.

After all, Kajaan had stressed, Thaddaeus was only ten. He hadn't even gone through his Awakening yet, so his status as crown prince wasn't assured. It had taken him less than a half hour to convince the tutors to try Kajaan's method for two weeks after their posturing. Perhaps some of that was the tutors hoping the schedule would fall apart so they could take over again. They had underestimated Kajaan.

Instead of seeing each tutor once a week for an all-day learning session, Kajaan had split the prince's time into two-hour chunks across the week. Now Thaddaeus would see two different tutors each day between breakfast and lunch for their allotted time. He'd see each of his tutors three times a week, giving him more time to learn and absorb what he was being taught rather than trying to cram it in his head.

The boy's afternoons were dedicated to physical well-being. Riding, swordplay, endurance training, and even meditation. With these activities, Kajaan insisted on involving all of Cadeyrn's kids. Fayette and Rodolfo had been overjoyed to be able to spend more time with their elder brother, but then again, the twins always wanted to do anything that allowed them to run nearly unchecked outside.

His eldest girl, Marika, was a different story. She'd always been quiet, even as a toddler, and Marika preferred to spend her time in the library, reading anything she could get her hands on. If Kajaan could bring her out of her shell, Cadeyrn would be grateful. He'd been trying for the last four years to get Marika to confide in him, but it hadn't worked yet.

Even though Quillin had fully expected Kajaan's plan to fail, Thaddaeus surprised them all by absolutely loving his new schedule. His demeanor changed almost immediately, and he started gaining more energy and began to talk more during meals. Cadeyrn couldn't have been happier, seeing the joy back in his son's eyes. His tutors had been stunned but ultimately receptive of the changes and were much more willing to listen to Kajaan after another week.

Cadeyrn found himself worrying about Kajaan quite often. As much as Ameyalli insisted that Kajaan was his Fated and that their love would be vast, he really wasn't sure how to approach the man. While he most definitely felt a tug toward him and craved his approval, it seemed like Kajaan wasn't returning his interest. He'd understood how much Prince Yolotzin and Kajaan meant to each other the moment they'd had their reunion in the throne room.

But his farewell.

Prince Yolotzin had likely meant to not be overheard, but Cadeyrn had caught his words anyways. Had the two been planning on marrying before Lady Naias came into the picture? If so, it wasn't really surprising that Kajaan had fled and holed up in his room for the rest of the day. Cadeyrn had hovered outside the door a few times when the agony he felt through their tenuous bond became unbearable, listening to Kajaan's muffled crying, poised to knock. Every time something held him back, telling him that the comfort he wanted to give wouldn't be welcomed.

To him, Kajaan was clearly the one more distraught by their parting, having to pull away from the prince he loved so deeply without another bond to sustain him. Anger had burned in Cadeyrn at Prince Yolotzin's casual dismissal of his lover, but Ameyalli had soothed him. Prince Yolotzin had his Fated. He was moving on, not because he didn't love Kajaan as much as Kajaan loved him, but rather because of the bond Ilyphari had formed the moment the prince took his first breath in this world.

Even still, Cadeyrn wasn't sure if the grief of losing his lover, because it was a harsh loss, was reducing Kajaan's awareness of his own potential bond. Cadeyrn wanted to hold Kajaan in his arms and make him confront the tug between them, but again, he knew that right now Kajaan was in a delicate place. He'd basically just been exiled from everything he'd known and was thrown into a foreign country with no friends or old comforts.

That didn't stop his children from trying to get Kajaan to play with them. Except for Marika. But she'd gladly read with him if he made an effort to sit next to her with a book. When Kajaan was with the children, his joy came back, and he'd begin laughing and get involved with their shenanigans. Something told Cadeyrn that Kajaan hadn't had much of a childhood. With how tightly he'd tied himself to Prince Yolotzin and how easily he played with the kids….

Cadeyrn didn't want to think about what might have happened in Kajaan's childhood to rob him of his youth. Speculation would only hurt their bond in the end. His spies hadn't really dug up much about Kajaan when he asked them to look into him. Just that his father, Jeryit Pernoac, was the captain of the guard, his mother died during birth, and Kajaan was raised alongside Prince Yolotzin once the prince was born a few moonturns later.

The sparse knowledge available made Cadeyrn even more curious about Kajaan's past. Plenty of things must have happened that had either been forgotten or never remarked upon that made Kajaan the man he was today. No one lived in a castle with royalty without gossip about them. Especially someone like Kajaan, a man who'd loved one so far above his station so deeply that he often retreated into himself when he wasn't occupied.

A COURIER WAGON arrived early in the morning one moonturn after the Averian delegation left Paelfjord Castle. Wayra, the captain of the castle's guard, fetched Cadeyrn from his study. A letter accompanied the shipment addressed to him. It was a simple note from Prince Yolotzin letting him know that he'd personally packed a good portion of Kajaan's rooms, leaving the furniture and bedding behind. He acknowledged that a lot of the clothes likely wouldn't be appropriate anymore but wanted to give Kajaan the decision to do what he wanted with them.

Well, at least he was thoughtful about Kajaan's things. Hopefully the shipment would help brighten his mood for even a little bit. Or help him assuage his grief and settle in more firmly here. Cadeyrn consulted their bond and followed it to the library while the couriers carried the trunks up to Kajaan's room assisted by Wayra's men. There were five of them in total, and they looked to be in much better condition than the ones they'd found at the dilapidated carriage where they'd first encountered Kajaan.

Curled up on a couch near Marika, Kajaan had a book in his lap, though he seemed to be dozing rather than reading. Poor guy was probably not sleeping very well still. Not that Cadeyrn really blamed him. He didn't sleep great while traveling either, and he at least had his family or staff with him. He'd hoped Kajaan would have calmed by now, but the redhead still seemed to be on edge. Having trouble sleeping. Barely eating….

Cadeyrn worried he'd made the wrong choice. He no longer wanted to walk away from his Fated, even if Kajaan still didn't acknowledge their bond. But seeing him in such obvious distress day in and day out bothered him. Clearing his throat, Cadeyrn approached the two of them, smiling when Kajaan's head popped up. He was grateful that Marika gave Kajaan the peace he needed to relax and fall asleep near her.

"A shipment arrived for you today," Cadeyrn said softly. "Prince Yolotzin packed a good amount of your stuff. I had them delivered to your room."

Kajaan blinked sleepily at him a few times before his eyes lit up and he nodded. He got to his feet and gently tugged on Marika's braid as he placed his book on the end table. No one would bother it until Kajaan placed it on the return rack. He watched as his Fated left the room, his shoulders slumped as if the weight of the world was pressing down on him even as he held his head high.

"Hey, Papa," Marika said quietly.

"Hey, sweetling," Cadeyrn replied, plopping onto the couch next to his daughter. He grabbed the book Kajaan had fallen asleep reading and smiled at the title. It was a geographical breakdown of the kingdom, including imports, exports, and a whole host of information about the gexenas. It seemed his Fated took learning about Zothua very seriously. "How're you doing this morning?"

"A bit sleepy," Marika said and shrugged. "Kajie had us running all over the gardens yesterday."

He'd heard. Cadeyrn grinned at the memory of hearing his littles screaming and hollering as they ran down the aisles of plants. For a while, he'd even stood on his balcony and watched the five careening around the gardens without a care in the world. It had been a fantastic and well-needed break.

"The terrible two were quite filthy when they came in," Cadeyrn said with a chuckle.

Miski had been beside herself, seeing the twins covered in dirt. She'd managed to wrestle them into the bath after threatening the two with no dessert for a week if they didn't cooperate. The woman was ferocious when it came to taking care of her charges and trying to keep them presentable. Not that Cadeyrn really minded all that much. They were kids. He didn't care if they were grubby and ran amok for a few more years.

Though perhaps he shouldn't be quite so apathetic about Rodolfo and Fayette running around in the nude now that they were six.

His daughter giggled and smiled at him, swinging her legs as she flopped back against the couch. It was good seeing her smile again. He should have found someone to help him with his kids sooner. Though maybe it was specifically Kajaan's influence that was helping his kids. The man belonged here, no matter how much Cadeyrn felt guilty about having to keep him in Zothua. He had no doubt in his mind that Tonalli would try to kill Kajaan again if he set foot anywhere near Averia.

He scooted close to Marika and pestered his little girl for long enough that she huffed and started reading her book out loud. She was getting to be a proficient reader, and the story she was engrossed in was some wondertale about a knight protecting her princess from goblins. It was pretty cute, Cadeyrn had to admit.

After a few hours passed, he finally admitted to himself that he was restless. He wanted to check in on Kajaan and see how he was doing in his unpacking. Cadeyrn kissed Marika's cheek and tried to casually walk toward Kajaan's suite. Maybe he wasn't totally successful if a quick grin shot his way by Simthe was any indication. He debated on if he really wanted to interrupt his Fated as he climbed the stairs toward his rooms.

His choice was easy to make once he arrived. The door was already ajar, and Kajaan sat in the middle of his reception room, surrounded by open trunks, holding a book loosely in his lap. It was a well-loved book from the state of the spine, and Cadeyrn was unable to stop himself from entering the room.

"Everything all right?" he asked softly.

He hadn't wanted to startle Kajaan since he looked pretty lost in thought. It didn't work. Kajaan jumped, his head snapping up, and Cadeyrn felt a pang of guilt for not coming by sooner. Kajaan's eyes were red and his cheeks streaked by tears. He quickly wiped his face dry and looked back down at the book in his hands.

"Just hurts more than I thought it would, Your Majesty," Kajaan said.

"It's a huge and incredibly sudden change," Cadeyrn soothed him, crouching down next to Kajaan. "And it was fairly violent too. I'd be more worried if you were completely unaffected by all of this."

He reached out and lightly touched the scar on Kajaan's arm that was left behind by the ball projectile. At his touch, Kajaan jerked away, nearly falling over. Maybe he'd just been startled, but the implied rejection stung and the bond radiated pain, constricting his gut. Instead Cadeyrn just smiled gently at him.

"Give yourself time. If you want, Quillin or Ameyalli can help you go through your clothes to see what would be appropriate attire here. Your winter clothes will be practically useless. It never gets that cold," Cadeyrn offered, "unless we travel north, of course. But even then, you might have new outfits."

He wanted so badly to commission his tailor to create a whole new wardrobe for Kajaan. Even the heavy cotton and wool for their winter seasons that would halfway be a waste if Kajaan kept his old clothes. They weren't of Zothuan design, so Cadeyrn wanted them gone, but it wasn't his choice. He wouldn't, couldn't, take his Fated's agency away from him.

"Prince Thaddaeus has already come by and offered to help. He wants to teach me some more Zothuan at the same time while I teach him Averian. It'll just be for articles of clothing, but it'll be good practice," Kajaan said.

Cadeyrn's smile widened. "That's a great exercise."

Kajaan shrugged. "It helps making games out of learning. His tutors have picked up on my methods too."

"Have you been a secretary to other kids or helped plan their lessons?" Cadeyrn asked.

He settled himself on the floor next to his Fated, trying to appear smaller. There were occasions where Kajaan still regarded him with a fearful gaze, and it hurt every time. The redhead snorted and shook his head, his eyes sparkling with amusement.

"Tzin is the youngest in his family. His cousin, Lord Kende, is also the youngest, and Duke Ruvyn never looked at me twice if he could help it. I've only had one position in the castle, and that was as Tzin's secretary," Kajaan explained.

"Yet you're great with kids," Cadeyrn pointed out.

"I love kids," Kajaan said simply. "I just paid attention to Tzin's nieces and nephews and what I enjoyed as a kid myself. There's a lot of books on child development that I read too."

"You're very scholarly," Cadeyrn remarked.

"Gotta be," Kajaan replied, tilting his head as he studied Cadeyrn. "Had to do something when Tzin was busy attending socials where I wasn't wanted. Staying behind, sitting in the carriage and reading, or stationed with the other carriage drivers in an isolated room was quite common for me. Otherwise I likely would have gone crazy."

"Can't have that," Cadeyrn said with a soft smile.

"Some of the drivers picked up needlework or knitting," Kajaan said absently, slowly falling into one memory or another.

Cadeyrn felt his heart thud oddly, and his breath hitched as he watched Kajaan. The tug intensified, urging him to lean forward and stake his claim on Kajaan. To kiss those lush lips that had fascinated him ever since he first saw him. He was curious to know what it was like to kiss someone with stubble. Would he like it? He hoped so, considering Kajaan was his Fated and he'd always been the amorous sort.

Kajaan's face flushed as their eyes met, and the redhead's expression cleared as he returned to the present. The man was leaning toward him, almost as if the tug was physically pulling him, urging him closer. His pupils dilated just a fraction, and Cadeyrn found himself moving closer. Kajaan's eyes flickered up toward the Ignis mark on his forehead and he pulled away, his face paling slightly.

His Fated cleared his throat and very deliberately set the book aside with exaggerated care. He rolled to his knees and pawed through the nearest trunk. Several more books joined the one already on the floor, and a few different piles started to form. Cadeyrn wanted to ask after their order, but the view of Kajaan's back was pretty nice too. He was slim, though a bit underfed, as Kajaan was still having a hard time eating. Cadeyrn really needed to get a few pounds on him.

For a long time, they sat in silence while Kajaan worked. Every once in a while, Kajaan would get to his feet and place whatever he was holding somewhere around the room or disappear into the bedroom briefly. The piles of books slowly migrated to the shelves along the wall, in an order that only Kajaan understood. Cadeyrn got to his feet and wandered over, tilting his head to look at the titles.

They were romance novels. Lots of them. Sure, there were a few textbooks and science journals on the bottom shelf, but a vast majority of them were romance. He refused to comment, not wanting to make Kajaan feel judged or insecure on his preferences.

"What's your favorite?" Cadeyrn asked instead.

Kajaan wandered over with another armload of books. He glanced at Cadeyrn and slowly added what he had to the shelf. For a minute he was quiet, and Cadeyrn didn't press, figuring his question would go unanswered. Once his arms were free, Kajaan reached out and touched one novel that had an impressively faded spine.

"This one. I know it's silly, but I really like reading stories that are happy at the end," Kajaan said sheepishly.

"Nothing wrong with that," Cadeyrn told him. "I can understand the compulsion of feeling good at the end of a story or series."

"What do you like to read?" Kajaan asked, almost shyly.

"Wondertales," Cadeyrn said without hesitation. Kajaan had opened up just slightly toward him, so he would return the favor. "Fantastic creatures, faraway places. Whole worlds that the author just… dreamed up. It's fascinating how their minds work."

Kajaan nodded. "I can see that. Queen Brekka had a lot of romance novels in her rooms. So when I spent time with her, I ended up reading them."

"Can't those novels be pretty… explicit?" Cadeyrn asked.

"She has a separate shelf for those," Kajaan replied, laughing. "One she kept me away from until I was of age."

"Sensible yet fair," Cadeyrn judged with a smile.

A crack about the queen needing romance novels to supplement her relationship with Tonalli stuck in his throat. He didn't know if Kajaan would be insulted by it, or if he would leap to her, or worse, Tonalli's defense. Cadeyrn wondered how long his Fated would be loyal to the man who forced him into exile. If he was loyal now.

Kajaan glanced at him and turned back to the trunks. He closed and latched two of them, then scooted them toward the wall. The room had filled up with small trinkets within the last few hours. Cat statues of varying materials, small animals carved out of gemstones, beautifully cut stones resting in bowls, hand-sized canvases expertly painted in an abstract style, small plants that Cadeyrn wasn't quite sure had been packed into the trunks or had just been sent with them. It made the suite feel warmer and intimate. More lived in.

While he didn't entirely think of Kajaan when he looked at everything, he suddenly understood that Yolotzin had loved his secretary very much even if he hadn't outwardly expressed it during his visit. On his own, Kajaan would have never been able to afford all these beautifully made tchotchkes. He must have received a good amount of them as a gift from his lover. As cruel as Yolotzin's departure had been, he now wondered if the prince had partially done it to protect himself.

Cadeyrn was about to comment on how nicely Kajaan was putting the place together when he heard the man make a distressed noise low in his throat. He turned to his Fated and quickly trotted over to his side, resisting the urge to sweep him into his arms. Kajaan was kneeling in front of one of the trunks, cradling a small tarnished and deformed band in his hands. There was a fairly large jagged cut, and the ring had been pulled apart, almost as if it had been stuck on something.

"What is that?" Cadeyrn asked softly, kneeling down next to Kajaan.

His Fated's eyes were shiny as he stared down at the ring in his hand. It was too large for it to be a traditional ring, but too small for a bracelet. Kajaan licked his lips, his whole body trembling slightly. Without thinking, Cadeyrn reached out and rested his hand on his Fated's back, ever so gently rubbing up and down his spine. He probably couldn't offer much comfort, but he could at least make sure Kajaan knew he was there.

If he could take some of his pain away, Cadeyrn would count himself content. Kajaan sucked in a shaky breath and curled his fingers around the ring.

"At Princess Saian's wedding, Yolotzin stole a pair of napkin rings," Kajaan whispered. "He dragged me outside during the reception and proposed to me. It was… silly. Childish. But we exchanged vows to each other from what Yolotzin had heard that day."

Fuck. No wonder Kajaan was so devastated. From what he'd overheard a moonturn ago, he had a feeling that Yolotzin remembered that night too. Cadeyrn frowned, a memory tugging at the edges of his mind. He'd attended Princess Saian's wedding. He remembered arguing that he shouldn't have to attend. Sure, he was Zothua's crown prince, but he wasn't *important.* His father had played along that Cadeyrn was given permission to stay home. Then the morning of his departure, he was ambushed and pulled from his bed by Wayra's father and literally tossed into the carriage.

He'd sulked for a good chunk of the voyage, and he'd resolutely ignored a lot of what had happened around him. Sure, his father had been able to make him attend, but he couldn't force Cadeyrn to pay attention or be mentally present for everything. It was all he could do at the time as a frustrated teenager who had to keep appearances. Kajaan was nearly ten years his junior by his informant's report. That would have made his Fated quite young indeed.

The memory came back to him in a rush. Watching a child Prince Yolotzin run through the ballroom, carelessly hauling a young redhead in stained work clothes behind him. The boy had looked at him, his eyes wide, face pale, and obviously terrified. At the time, he hadn't known if it was because he wasn't supposed to be there and was going to get into trouble, or if he'd been mortified from being around so much gentry.

"I remember that night," Cadeyrn said with a smile. "I saw you with the prince. You were a really cute kid."

Kajaan's face went red, his ears and neck pinking. He darted a glance up at Cadeyrn, biting at his lower lip. Cadeyrn's heart skipped a beat, fighting back another surge of want.

"What kid isn't cute?" Kajaan protested weakly.

"Oh, my dear, there are plenty of ugly children out there. They usually turn into striking adults, though," Cadeyrn said.

"And the gorgeous kids grow up ugly?" Kajaan teased.

"That is your opinion, not mine," Cadeyrn said.

The two of them shared a brief chuckle. They slowly fell silent, and Cadeyrn reached out to cup Kajaan's chin. He tilted the man's head up toward him. The bond sang between them, bouncing back and forth, echoing louder, pulling them closer, urging them to start solidifying their bond and recognize what they were to each other. Kajaan slowly wet his lips, his breath coming a little quicker.

Noise erupted in the hallway, and the two of them sprang apart. Kajaan cleared his throat as he shoved the napkin ring into his pocket. Cadeyrn backed off quite a few steps, breathing slowly to calm his racing heart. It was good they were interrupted. He didn't want to take advantage of Kajaan's distress to further their bond. Besides, they really should talk about it first.

Thaddaeus came running into the room, flushed, but excited to help Kajaan with his Zothuan. Fayette and Rodolfo were right on his heels, thankfully dressed and hollering their excitement. Cadeyrn retreated toward the door, not wanting to try and figure his way through this budding relationship in front of the kids. It was awkward enough between the two of them that adding his children would make it nearly unbearable. Thaddaeus already knew that Kajaan was his Fated, and he might be a little aggressive in trying to do some matchmaking.

The redhead seemed startled with the children's exuberant shouts and energy, shooting Cadeyrn a panicked look. Laughing, Cadeyrn walked out of the room, abandoning him to his fate. The noise from the chaos followed him out to the hallway and down the hall to his own rooms. Cadeyrn left his door open, grabbed a book, and curled up on the settee in his reception room. He didn't read exactly, just sat there and listened to the shouts of delight and laughter drifting from Kajaan's suite.

Kajaan's laugh was lovely to listen to. Light and melodious. Movement caught his eye, and he looked up to see Marika hovering in his doorway. She was clutching a book to her chest, regarding her father shyly. Cadeyrn smiled and patted the cushion beside him. Within seconds, she was clambering up to sit next to him, and nestled into his side before she cracked open her book again.

Warmth settled in Cadeyrn's chest, delighted that his daughter came to him for the first time in quite a while. He draped an arm over Marika's shoulders, being careful to not pull any of her beautiful brown hair, and held her close. They settled in together, the other three children running down the hallway between his room and Kajaan's to show their father the "exotic" clothing they adored. Cadeyrn opened his book on his knee, a feeling of contentment growing in his chest.

Kajaan was exactly what he and his kids needed.

Chapter 10

Spending time with the kids was incredibly soothing, though it was stressful and loud at the same time. Kajaan felt himself relaxing the more he spent time with Prince Thaddaeus, Princess Marika, and the twins. Princess Fayette proudly declared that Kajaan was to be her secretary as well… as soon as she needed one. Right now the young girl sent her nurse into a tailspin when she snuck out of the castle with her brother to play in the expansive gardens.

At least Kajaan didn't have to personally worry about cleaning or mending their clothes. Though the kids seemed to understand that if they were going to play anywhere near any of the thornier plants, they would be at risk of getting scratched. So, instead of needing to call a Healer and a seamstress, they just needed a Healer. Kajaan hadn't expected to see the six-year-old twins sprinting around the rose gardens completely nude, cackling like the devils they were as they avoided Miski and several palace guards.

Kajaan had tried to not laugh and failed miserably.

That didn't exactly endear him to the twins' nurse, who looked like she sucked on lemons hourly. He found that he really didn't care, so long as the kids were happy. Though he most definitely got an amused yet slightly disapproving look from King Cadeyrn at his snickering when the two told their father about it at dinner that night.

Eating meals with the king and his kids was another thing Kajaan had to get used to. Quillin and Ameyalli sat with them as well, along with some of their staff. That included the head Healer, Tamya, who tended to the children when they got scratched up; King Cadeyrn's valet, Inti; and the captain of the guard, Wayra.

King Tonalli would have never hosted such meals. If there weren't any dignitaries visiting, he'd take his meal in his study or parlor. Queen Brekka took her meals in her room when she did decide to eat. Both Princess Saian and Reina ate with their families in their respective suites, never bothering to invite their siblings or parents to join them. There were no family dinners anymore. The Navarre-Hamonn family had fractured years ago.

Funny how Kajaan hadn't really acknowledged it until now.

So, even though he was sitting at the long table that most assuredly could seat several dozen, it was surprisingly fun. Kajaan carved out small bites of his peach and whipped cream dessert, trying to prolong mealtime. Princess Fayette ran out of steam, so Prince Thaddaeus picked up the chatter, eagerly talking about his history lessons that he'd started taking an interest in now that he wasn't listening to an eight-hour lesson.

Princess Marika seemed all right to just hold up whatever book she'd read that day when it was her turn to share, though she was forbidden to read at the dinner table. Prince Rodolfo was a quiet child as well when he wasn't pelting around the castle and being a general pest. Or maybe it was due to him practically falling asleep at the table, his forehead planting in a smear of cream.

The wet *plop* signaled the end of dinner. Miski somehow knew that one of her charges had crashed and bustled in, gathering a drowsy Prince Rodolfo in her arms and using him to get Princess Fayette to follow her. Princess Marika slid off her chair and hugged the book to her chest, trotting off to either the library or her room. One by one, the others departed for their nightly routines. Soon, it was only King Cadeyrn and Kajaan left at the expansive table.

"Are you settling in a bit better?" King Cadeyrn asked.

"Yes, Your Majesty. Thank you," Kajaan replied politely.

King Cadeyrn simply sighed at him and shook his head. "You can just call me Cadeyrn or Cade. We don't need to be formal to each other. Not when…."

Not when we're Fated. Kajaan flexed his jaw slightly, looking down at the polished surface. He clenched his hands into fists as he fought with that nugget of information. For the last moonturn, he'd struggled with the knowledge that he and King Cadeyrn would be the perfect couple. Kajaan forced his hands open and rubbed the half-moon circles in the palm of his hand with his thumb.

A week had passed since his belongings had arrived from Avitou. He'd felt immensely more settled once he had his trinkets and gifts decorating the room around him. Not that it was a substitute for Yolotzin's presence, but the familiarity definitely helped ease his homesickness. Especially when he could read his inappropriate books late at night after the children had gone to bed.

Now he just needed to find an escort that would take him to Sestella to browse for any new novels. Perhaps Zothua had books that were never imported into Averia. That idea had excited Kajaan. He didn't even have to worry about funds. Yolotzin had sent along a nice, hefty purse with his belongings, and King Cadeyrn paid him a generous wage for his secretarial work. Kajaan assumed at some point he'd be moved over to the servants' quarters, but Quillin never said a word. It was odd, being so close to the royal family. It was nothing like Avitou.

Thinking about Yolotzin and what used to be his home didn't hurt nearly as much as it used to. Being assimilated into the Greatblaze family, because that's exactly what was happening, was helping soothe that ache even more than his belongings Yolotzin sent. It helped fulfill something he hadn't quite realized he needed. He adored the children. Ameyalli and their dry humor was so refreshing compared to Yannat and his snide remarks. Even Quillin and Wayra were kind to him, and not in the "I have to because my king told me to" way.

He'd been here for five weeks. They were well into spring now, and the temperature was starting to climb during the middle of the day, lingering in the afternoons and evenings. Already it was quite a bit warmer than it would be in Alenzon. Hell, sometimes the city still received snow for another moonturn. What a difference a mountain range and a week's travel made in terms of weather. Kajaan was already phasing out his old clothing from home.

No. Not home. Averia. Averian clothing was too warm, even the lightweight summer cloths. Silk was much kinder and more breathable, and the Zothuan cotton was a looser weave. A few outfits had just shown up, carefully folded, on his bed about a fortnight past. Kajaan had put them away, not really thinking about it, trying to cling to his proper Averian attire.

Until the latest heatwave that had just broken today. Kajaan had excused himself in the middle of a meeting with Thaddaeus's math tutor, so sweat-drenched and uncomfortable he could barely breathe. One of the guards had suggested he wear the Zothuan clothes that King Cadeyrn had commissioned for him while handing him a large mug of water.

Both the guard and tutor had looked pretty smug when Kajaan returned in the light silks. While he was given short or sleeveless tops and loose pants, many of the natives were wearing warmer clothes. Still, they were kind enough about him adjusting to the heat. It didn't help that

Kajaan adored how the clothing felt against his skin. Even the cotton was disgustingly soft. How would he ever be able to wear Averian clothing again without it feeling like it was chafing?

"Kajaan?" King Cadeyrn's voice was gentle.

Blinking out of his thoughts, Kajaan looked up at the man. He hadn't moved, watching him curiously. Goddess, but he was a handsome man. His eyes flickered up to the encircled candle flame Mark on his forehead, and the familiar clench of horror gripped his stomach. By the time he was able to return his gaze to King Cadeyrn's, the man was frowning slightly.

"Does my status bother you?" King Cadeyrn asked.

"What status?" Kajaan rasped, licking his lips.

His heart was beating out a steady tattoo, betraying his panic as surely as his heavier breathing. King Cadeyrn simply frowned and sat back in his chair, folding his arms across his chest.

"The fact that I'm an Ignis," he said bluntly. Kajaan couldn't help his flinch, and he looked away, curling in on himself. After a minute of awkward silence, the man continued, "Is it because Tonalli is one too?"

"Not just," Kajaan said, looking everywhere but at King Cadeyrn. "It's… I'll get over it."

"I hope so," King Cadeyrn replied.

His voice was gentle without any hint of reproof in it. He sounded genuinely concerned about Kajaan's distress. There was no way he could tell this man what had been done to him. He should be over it by now anyway. Eighteen years was a long time ago. Kajaan was barely aware he was rubbing the scarring on his arms. Right now they weren't easily visible against his pale skin, but that wouldn't be the case in a couple more moonturns once his skin darkened.

There was a reason he'd always worn long-sleeved shirts in Averia, even in the height of summer. Yolotzin had never complained that Kajaan scheduled for them to go north during the warm seasons and south during the cold. Kajaan was never comfortable showing off his arms, and his best friend understood why without needing to be told. Until now. When he knew that he'd gain more attention if he stubbornly continued to wear sleeves.

Once the rest of his arms tanned during high summer, then his scarring would become startlingly visible. He'd be about as striped as a gexena. Maybe King Cadeyrn would have gotten the truth out of him by then. If not, Kajaan knew he'd be interrogated about his scarring. Probably. Most likely. King Cadeyrn didn't seem like the kind of man to not know everything about his Fated. If anything, Princess Fayette would be curious enough to ask, and not understand that it was rude in the way only children were.

Kajaan got to his feet, knocking his chair back with a screech. He winced from the loud noise, and he sketched a quick bow to the king before turning and trying to not run out of the dining hall. His hands shook as he tucked them into his pant pockets, his breath wildly uneven. He couldn't do this. Whatever Ilyphari was thinking, pairing the two of them together, she certainly didn't factor Torbid into the mix. King Cadeyrn didn't deserve to have a Fated who was scared of him. Of something about him that he couldn't control or change.

Just as Kajaan couldn't control or change how useless he was as an Aquan, no matter how much Kende believed that he'd been stunted.

He made it to the main hall before he heard footsteps behind him, rapidly approaching. Kajaan turned slightly to see King Cadeyrn trotting after him. For a second fear spiked through him, white-hot, and his mind flashed panic, his scars throbbing in remembered agony. The only thing that kept him from fleeing was the look on the king's face. Pure concern and an openness that King Tonalli would have never shown.

Once the man caught up to him, he didn't manhandle Kajaan. Didn't touch him or shout at him, demanding answers. Instead, he ever so gently herded Kajaan up against the wall. King Cadeyrn didn't fully block him in, but he stood only inches from him. The man's breath washed over his face, and Kajaan did his best to not shudder and suppress the thoughts that eagerly sprang to mind with the king's proximity.

The one incredibly annoying thing about having a Fated was how the body automatically reacted. His cock was already leaping to attention, the traitorous thing. He felt a sense of rightness slowly override the fear as they silently shared the same air, the bond pulling him toward King Cadeyrn, urging him into the brunet's arms. He was so warm. Comforting. Like a fire in a hearth rather than a rampaging wildfire. Kajaan resisted only barely.

"Yes, Majesty?" Kajaan asked quietly.

"You don't need to call me that," King Cadeyrn gently chastised him.

Kajaan smiled weakly and shook his head. "I'll keep the honorifics. Did you need something?"

It kept a degree of separation between them. With the slight look of despair on King Cadeyrn's face, the man knew it too. King Cadeyrn would tire of chasing him soon and finally give up. Then they could sit down and talk about breaking the Fated bond between them and live out separate lives within the castle. Kajaan would move to the servants' quarters. The king would be able to take a new lover. One that would love the kids as if they were their own.

Kajaan was just the help. He was just their secretary and would remain so until it was safe to return to Avitou. Or maybe he wouldn't. People went missing over the mountains all the time. He wouldn't have to face the pain of watching Yolotzin with Lady Naias. Something must have betrayed his thoughts as King Cadeyrn gently touched his arm. Kajaan twitched but didn't pull away, keeping his features placid. If his breathing got a bit harder from the contact, he could blame it on the Fated pull rather than the fear that curled in his stomach.

"Is what I am that bad?" King Cadeyrn asked.

"You're a king," Kajaan said, deliberately misunderstanding. "I'm nothing. It's a bad match."

"We're a match sanctioned by the goddess. It can't be a bad match," King Cadeyrn said firmly.

"I've seen three Fated couples end poorly," Kajaan sniped, scowling at him. "It's not a guarantee, so don't try to placate me with false platitudes."

"How did they end poorly? I'm sure there were extenuating circumstances that led to their breaking," King Cadeyrn replied, not rising to the bait. Even his voice was still even, damn him. "Three matches out of how many in Averia? In Alenzon? You can't judge everyone by a minority. You can't believe that we'll turn out the same way."

"I am below your station!" Kajaan snapped, almost shouting now. "I. Am. *Nothing*! You deserve someone better for your kids!"

"You're the one who's gotten them to smile again!" King Cadeyrn replied, his voice sharp, though he didn't debase himself by falling into a shouting match. "Thad was turning into a problem child, and I had no idea how to help. Marika is talking more. The twins aren't getting into as much senseless trouble or destruction since you've redirected their energy. That's *your* influence. So don't you *dare* say that you're not good for our kids!"

Kajaan's retort caught in his throat as he stared, wide-eyed, up at the king. They were breathing hard, chests heaving and slightly brushing against each other. King Cadeyrn was watching him carefully, as if Kajaan was on the brink of a meltdown. Kajaan wondered if he might be, with how fast his heart and mind were racing and how hot he felt.

"*Our* kids?" Kajaan asked weakly.

"They're yours as much as they're mine," King Cadeyrn replied in a near whisper, forcing Kajaan to calm and listen. "Once we seal the bond, they automatically become yours too, in the eyes of the law."

Something in his chest eased. Kajaan wanted that. He wanted kids so much it hurt sometimes. The joy he took at seeing Princess Marika come out of her shell, or watching the twins run around the gardens in varying states of undress, was something he'd never felt before. He felt so much pride when Prince Thaddaeus came running up to him after a lesson, proudly proclaiming he finally understood something he'd been struggling with. Or when Prince Thaddaeus's tutors came to him to tell him how well the boy was doing with his new schedule.

Kajaan had been researching and planning on finding a surrogate soon. Yolotzin was giving it until his birthday before he gave up the search for his Fated and married Kajaan. They had wanted a ton of children to raise together with minimal help from a nanny. Probably more than they should, simply because Kajaan adored littles so much and Yolotzin wanted him happy. Cuddling an infant, *his* infant, was the second highest thing Kajaan wanted in his life.

So to suddenly be a father of four children, one of which probably still remembered his mother, while wonderful, was terrifying. He'd never measure up to the late Queen Menea. She had been a force of nature, helping King Cadeyrn with the humanization of Voids, making sure they were equal citizens with equal rights, all the while pushing for a larger family. She'd been the king's perfect partner as a Seer, able to help guide king and country better than the previous advisor.

She'd also been from Pemalia, a cherished daughter of one of the chiefs, and was terribly missed. The family had never blamed King Cadeyrn for her death and mourned her loss like the tragedy it was. Kajaan doubted his own father would mourn his death if he even cared to acknowledge him anymore. At least marrying Queen Menea had been advantageous for Zothua. If King Cadeyrn truly wanted him—and Kajaan struggled to see why he would want to—he'd gain nothing.

No alliances. No dowry. No stability or protection. There was no point in acknowledging their bond. Kajaan shook his head.

"We can't," Kajaan protested ever so weakly. "You gain nothing by claiming me."

"I'd get you," King Cadeyrn whispered.

Oh, Goddess help him. Kajaan felt his knees grow weak even as he stared up, stunned, into his Fated's eyes. He realized a second too late that his own were brimming with tears.

"You can't just *say* something like that!" he cried out, hiccupping on his next breath.

Kajaan clapped his hands over his mouth and nose, staring up at the man before him. King Cadeyrn looked conflicted, torn between wanting to comfort him and stepping away. His Fated was revolted by him, Kajaan knew. Of course he would be. He was a king, for the goddess's sake. Showing such raw emotion in public was beyond shameful and unbecoming of royalty. Kajaan ducked his head, his shoulders trembling.

A gentle hand slid into his hair, another curling around his shoulder. He found himself being pulled into a warm chest, and on his next stuttering breath, Kajaan knew that it was his Fated who was holding him. Silently offering him comfort while Kajaan struggled with the idea that if he just said yes, if he simply tilted his head up and sought out the king's lips, he could have this comfort and support forever.

Forever.

You and me forever.

Fresh agony laced through Kajaan's heart. How could he pledge himself to another man when he'd already exchanged vows with his best friend? It didn't matter that they'd only been six. It didn't matter that they had napkin rings instead of real ones. It didn't matter that there hadn't been any witnesses or an officiant present.

Because those vows had never meant anything.

The idea that he could have real vows, real promises with the man currently pulling him in closer caused his mind to snap out of his grief. The man who had shown him nothing but kindness, giving him space when he needed it, and always moving away when Kajaan started to panic, was his. If it was anyone else, Kajaan would worry that he'd just be desperately throwing himself into a new relationship to try and forget the pain of Yolotzin leaving him.

But this was his Fated. They were meant to be together. Everyone in the castle was likely baffled as to why Kajaan hadn't jumped on the chance to be with the king. Who wouldn't? Kajaan… apparently.

"We were going to begin planning our wedding this fall," Kajaan said, his voice muffled by his cupped hands. "We'd had plans on finding surrogates the moment our vows were sealed, since we'd already spent so much time traveling and being together."

"Oh, Kajaan," the king murmured. The man's large hand began carding through his hair, his arm wrapping around his shoulders. Kajaan shivered, and he threw his arms around King Cadeyrn's chest, clutching the back of his shirt. If the man was surprised, he didn't show it. He just held Kajaan tight, enveloping him in a comfortable warmth. "Would Lady Naias have been invited to your wedding?"

"Probably," Kajaan whispered.

The wedding of the crown prince would have been huge, even if both of them really just wanted something small. All the higher born gentry and their age-appropriate children would attend from every corner of Averia. Then, of course, dignitaries from the other countries, except for maybe Nabene since their union would have been between two men. Lord Kende would have attended with Lord Asyl… and Lady Naias would have been invited as a part of the Elrel clan.

"Then isn't it better that their meeting happened now than on your wedding day?" King Cadeyrn asked, not unkindly.

He hadn't even thought of that possibility. He and Yolotzin greeting everyone who attended their wedding as was proper, watching nervously as his brand-new husband fidgeted next to him because he could feel the tug. Seeing him search for someone else when Kajaan would be *right there* would have been painful. Having Lady Naias come up, escorted by her parents or whomever was her companion for the evening. Her and Yolotzin's eyes meeting.

And knowing… knowing that the marriage license would be voided only hours after it was signed. Kajaan pressed harder into the king's chest, trying to erase the memory of something that never happened….

"Oh Goddess," Kajaan gasped.

"Perhaps she moved a little fast, a little recklessly, because she knew that her time was almost up. That to avoid even worse heartbreak, she couldn't be delicate," King Cadeyrn suggested. "Not that there may have been a way to be more delicate than the prince meeting her at a gala."

Kajaan hated how reasonable that sounded. He squeezed his eyes shut and reluctantly nodded. Sniffling, Kajaan started to pull away. For the briefest second, King Cadeyrn resisted but allowed him to retreat. Not looking up at the man, Kajaan wiped his eyes and sniffed a few more times, clearing his throat.

"I'm a mess," he whispered. "I don't know what to do."

"One day at a time. One step. One breath. Count them and keep moving to the next one. It'll still hurt. It'll always hurt. But it won't be so debilitating the longer it's been," the king replied.

Of course he'd know. Kajaan raised his gaze to look the man—his Fated—in the eye. He felt his shoulders relax. Maybe his vows with Yolotzin when they were boys didn't matter at all anymore, but he did have an opportunity here. An opportunity to love four wonderful children and maybe grow to love the man in front of him. King Cadeyrn hadn't seemed bothered by his mini-breakdown, hadn't seemed to care that Kajaan had cried and snotted on him. Even now, he didn't look annoyed or embarrassed, just concerned.

Kajaan licked his lips nervously, and he noticed King Cadeyrn's eyes flick down to catch the movement. The man breathed in slow and deep, shifting slightly, but not to crowd Kajaan or move away. Kajaan dropped his eyes to avoid looking at him, instead fixating on the wet mark staining the silk shirt King Cadeyrn wore.

"Your shirt," Kajaan said weakly.

"It'll be fine after it's washed," King Cadeyrn replied, shrugging. "Don't worry about it. I'm glad yours fits well enough. I had Inti use the sizing you wore down in the prisons as an estimate."

"They're very comfortable," Kajaan said. He was beyond grateful the king was all right with him completely changing the topic. The last thing he wanted right now was to keep talking about Yolotzin. "Much more comfortable than my Averian clothes."

"It's also a wonderful color on you. The blue really brings out your hair," King Cadeyrn said, a gentle smile gracing his lips.

"It matches your eyes," Kajaan said with a quiet laugh.

The king gave a mock gasp, and Kajaan rolled his eyes, smiling a little more at the obvious jest.

"I never noticed," King Cadeyrn proclaimed softly.

Kajaan reached up, and the man went very still. As if he was a rabbit being approached by a predator. Perhaps in a way, he was. Kajaan could hurt him endlessly if he so chose. Not that King Cadeyrn wouldn't retaliate if that happened, but suddenly he understood that his Fated wouldn't strike first. It was in his nature to be gentle. Hadn't that been one of the reasons he'd shared what happened with Queen Menea? Other than to give Yolotzin blackmail.

King Cadeyrn's hair was just as soft as Kajaan had predicted it would be with how it shone in the light. It wasn't oily or greasy. Impossibly, his hair felt like his silk clothing and about as delicate too, slipping through his fingers like fine sand. Kajaan's breath caught, and he looked the man in the eye.

Kajaan would be the first to admit that he was still a hot mess. Still mostly hung up on Yolotzin. Missing Avitou even though there really wasn't much to miss anymore with his lover's attention elsewhere. Trying to come to terms with the fact that he had a *king* for a Fated. And that said king was an Ignian. His hand shook slightly as he realized that he'd have to tell King Cadeyrn about Torbid soon if they were to build on their relationship.

But the warm hand cupping his cheek was nothing like the one time Torbid had grabbed his face with his burning hot hand, leaving him with massive blisters and charred skin. That had been the end of his so-called tutelage with the man. Yolotzin had screamed and screamed about the damage while Kajaan could barely do anything but breathe until Queen Brekka had called for a Healer and viciously fired Torbid behind King Tonalli's back. Luckily, Kajaan hadn't scarred at all—at least physically. He could still smell his burning flesh and feel the blinding pain from time to time.

Kajaan took that one tiny step forward, staring up at the king. The man didn't move, just watched him quietly to see what he'd do. Taking a deep breath, Kajaan lifted on his toes and tilted his head. He delicately pressed their lips together in the most chaste of kisses. He felt a jolt of happiness through their strengthening bond even as Cadeyrn hummed low in his throat. The king held still, though doing so must have been close to torture, allowing Kajaan to explore at his own pace.

Or maybe to not bring Kajaan to his senses. Tightening his grip on King Cadeyrn's hair, Kajaan ran his lips across the brunet's before pressing in for another kiss. This time, the man responded, pushing back gently. They took their time, getting to know the shape of each other's lips and how they best fit together. Kajaan took a step back with Cadeyrn's gentle urging, leaning against the wall. He slid back down to his feet, smiling faintly when his Fated chased after him.

Kajaan was the one who parted his lips first. He expected King Cadeyrn to surge in, eager to taste him, dominate him. Neither happened. The king was apparently loving taking it slow, if the joy radiating through their bond was anything to go by. His face was tilted a bit further up as King Cadeyrn kissed Kajaan's lower lip and then stilled, teasingly worrying the flesh between his teeth. Kajaan couldn't help the snort of laughter that escaped him.

With a smile, Cadeyrn let go and planted one last lingering kiss on his lips. Kajaan closed his eyes, his head spinning from his Fated's affection, as tame as it was. It felt so good, so right, to be in his arms with barely anything separating them. The scent of cinnamon and oak with the slightest hint of ink enveloped him. It was intoxicating in a way that lemon and strawberry had never been. There was no hiding that King Cadeyrn was a man, and one who didn't care to mask his natural scent with perfumes.

It was tempting to try and pull King Cadeyrn even closer and melt into him. To try and incite his Fated into a frenzy as he submitted, body, mind, and soul. Said soul sang at the idea even as King Cadeyrn kissed him once again, echoing the pure unadulterated bliss he felt from his Fated. He wanted to keep the man in his arms happy. To keep or bring back that roguish smile even during a hard day. Making him laugh after a frustrating consult with a petitioner and calming him.

He wanted to make King Cadeyrn his.

If they were alone, Kajaan would have dropped to his knees and sought out Cadeyrn's cock. Taking him to the root and reveling in the heaviness on his tongue and the saltiness of his essence, regardless if it made his jaw ache. He'd deal with a bit of discomfort to have the man in his mouth while being enveloped by his Fated's natural musk.

A small, weak noise escaped him as he dreamed about what his lover would taste like or do, if Kajaan offered his mouth. Maybe he didn't quite care that they were making out in the great hall. Not if he had something better to do with his mouth. King Cadeyrn's bulk could hide a lot of their indecency while Kajaan was pushed against the wall. Besides, what guard would interrupt their king from taking his pleasure with his Fated?

A flash of pain on his lower lip pulled a sharp gasp from Kajaan, and he snapped back to reality. To their gentle, languid open-mouth kissing. Or what had been gentle before the king had bitten him. King Cadeyrn was slowly pulling back, an amused smile on his face. The man's pupils were blown, and there was a flush on his cheeks. While his lips weren't exactly red and swollen from kissing since they'd been gentle, there was definitely an indecent look about him.

"Good night, Kajaan," King Cadeyrn whispered.

With that, the man stepped back, turned, and strode away. Kajaan stood there in shock for a minute before his legs finally gave out. He slid down the wall into a small heap, unable to stop staring ahead of him, his breath coming quickly. What had he almost done while drunk on their bond? Trying, or offering, to blow the king in front of guards, servants, and anyone else who walked by?

The thought of doing such an act made his gut clench as a pulse of arousal coursed through him. Kajaan wasn't sure if that came from him or his Fated, but either way, he was a little startled at his exhibitionist streak. Maybe he could sneak into the man's study and crawl under his desk to part his pants or duck under his thobe to get to his ultimate prize. Wouldn't that be exciting, teasing and edging King Cadeyrn while he was in a meeting?

Kajaan bit his lip, staring down at his hands. What was wrong with him? He was achingly hard just from theorizing about what to do with his Fated. Not memories of what he and Yolotzin had actually done. Those hadn't even crossed his mind once during his musings. No, all he wanted right now was to find King Cadeyrn and say yes. Would the king think he was too desperate if he did that and made him wait to seal the bond? Or would they fall into bed together and end up with Kajaan pinned to the mattress?

That sent another shudder through Kajaan. The stone floor chilling his backside and legs reminded him of where he was, and Kajaan managed to get to his feet. He hunched slightly, as if that would hide his arousal that was completely unrestricted by the thin silk trousers he wore. Kajaan ducked his head, refusing to meet the eye of any of the stationed guards. At least none of them were obviously staring at him or chuckling as he passed them.

Suddenly mortified, Kajaan felt his face heat even as his stomach churned unhappily. He'd been somewhat used to being stared at and having servants and guardsmen whisper about him behind his back before. Being a prince's steady lover over the years brought that kind of frank speculation pretty quickly. Especially since he'd openly been with Yolotzin since their mid-teens. But Yolotzin was still only a prince. Sure, the crown prince, but he wasn't the *king*.

But now, this time, he was an interloper. Even worse, he was a foreigner, exiled from his birthplace solely because of his relationship with the prince. He was a complete unknown to everyone here, and they had no reason to trust him. Had they thought it was hilarious to watch the pathetic charity case melt under the king's attention, or did they think he would be a threat to the crown?

The attraction definitely wasn't one-sided. Not with the soft gaze, flushed skin, and harsh breaths that King Cadeyrn shared with him moments ago. No matter what he thought he saw in the king, no matter if they might truly be Fated, the servants would have their own gossip and opinions. Kajaan was sure that there'd be a hundred different variations of what happened in the hall floating amongst the staff tomorrow.

Kajaan shuddered as he listlessly climbed the stairs toward the royal wing, every part of him drooping. What should he do? Some part of him wanted to desperately believe that yes, Cadeyrn wanted him as his Fated. That they were truly meant to be together, and what he felt through their bond reflected that. But at the same time, he was just the weak excuse of a guard's son. He couldn't even wield a blade effectively.

Another part of him wanted to run. He knew without a doubt that if he told the king that he wanted to move into Sestella and live on his own, he'd be able to. Hell, King Cadeyrn might even arrange for him to have help packing up his belongings and moving. Maybe if he did that, then the man would give up on this "Fated" business, and they could walk away from each other without the agony of an unrequited bond. He doubted it.

But Kajaan didn't want to leave either. He slumped against his suite door, blindly locking it behind him. Thoughts of how King Cadeyrn looked after making out with him drifted back to the forefront of his mind, and he felt an undercurrent of desire course through him. His body thrummed at the memories of his Fated's hands on him, pleasure sparking his blood to rise once again.

Groaning, Kajaan stumbled past the reception area to his bed and flopped down on the horsehair mattress. Just recalling what the man looked like and how gently he'd treated him roused his ardor once more. Now that he was alone, Kajaan wiggled out of his silk trousers and kicked them off, his slippers following in short order.

He rucked his shirt high up on his chest as he plucked at his nipples with one hand, the other roaming over his stomach, just touching for now. A spike of pleasure hit the back of his mind, causing the room to spin around him. Kajaan let out a soft moan, closing his eyes, imagining that he wasn't touching himself. King Cadeyrn was. Those big, strong hands sliding over his stomach, sides, hips, and down his waist. Between his legs to explore his inner thighs.

Forcing his legs apart, King Cadeyrn settled in between them, ignoring Kajaan's weak protests that he wasn't worth it. The man shoved his face into the crease of his hip, breathing his musk in unashamedly as he grasped Kajaan's prick in one of those large, slightly callused hands. Kajaan arched, letting out a breathless cry as the hand on his cock sped up, fisting him furiously. A hot tongue lapped at his balls, tenderly playing with the sac before heading down farther.

Kajaan loved, *loved*, getting rimmed. It wasn't one of Yolotzin's favorite things to do, but maybe King Cadeyrn would like it. That wet heat stroked over his entrance, and Kajaan couldn't stop his choked sob as his orgasm hit him. His cum splashed over his chest and stomach, striping his chest with his release. Panting hard, Kajaan opened his eyes to stare at the beige sandstone ceiling as he shivered from the strength of his orgasm.

He lay there for a few minutes, his body and cum cooling, sweat rolling down his forehead. Pleasure echoed in his mind, washing over him, and Kajaan groaned, almost feeling like he climaxed again as his back arched. Completely drained, Kajaan managed to push himself to his feet after a few minutes and was startled to see the amount of cum that coated his hand and stomach. Well he definitely needed to clean up now.

Kajaan stumbled into the bathroom, his legs feeling as if they were barely going to support him. He washed up, slowly becoming aware of additional contentment and tiredness lingering where the extra jolt of pleasure had come from. Kajaan stared at the basin, gripping the edges of the stone sink, and tried to clear his thoughts. He knew what those extra emotions were, didn't he?

King Cadeyrn was his Fated, and their bond was forming the longer they spent time together. Touching each other so intimately had strengthened it, allowing each a glimpse into their partner's emotions. Whether that would fade over the night or not would be answered in the morning. At least until their next romantic encounter, where their bond would strengthen even further, pushing them to seal their connection.

He was fairly certain that penetrative sex with the king would be a lot of fun. If the man showed even an ounce of patient understanding that he had tonight in the bedroom, he'd be a wonderful bed partner. Even better if Kajaan could convince him that he liked it a bit rough. Just the thought of being impaled on a hot, hard cock after only the bare minimum of preparation—especially after a dry spell—made his spent dick twitch in interest.

Kajaan ran his still damp hands through his short hair, making it spike up at odd angles. He blew out a hard breath, watching his cheeks puff out like a chipmunk stuffing its face full of nuts. Right now, he really didn't have the energy to question what was going on. If they'd continue to acknowledge the bond or if they'd walk away. Kajaan wasn't sure which one he wanted more right now.

Kajaan made it back to the bed and collapsed onto the soft sheets. He burrowed underneath the thin cover, burying his face in a pillow. Spring was so much warmer here, and Kajaan was trying to acclimatize to it. Right now, while the kids still had quilts on their beds on top of any other sheets, Kajaan was kicking his single off as he slept. Which was a shame, really. He truly loved making a nest out of his blankets when he wasn't sharing his bed with another.

Chapter 11

Sleep eluded Kajaan as he tossed and turned, trying to lie still in positions that he knew were comfortable and soothing. None of them turned his brain off as he debated about what to do in the morning. Would he and the king go back to acting like nothing happened? Would the man expect him to walk into his arms the next time they saw each other? He ran himself in circles, plagued by what-ifs, finally dropping off when the sky began to lighten.

Thankfully it was Saturday, which meant that Kajaan didn't have anywhere to be, so his restless and sleepless night wouldn't impact anything vital. He woke up almost more exhausted than he was last night around midmorning, which was unfathomably late for him. Groaning, Kajaan found that once again he'd kicked the sheets off the bed and that he'd rolled to the edge of the mattress.

Despite trying to go to bed at a decent time and completely sober, his head throbbed angrily at him. Kajaan put his head in his hands and pressed his palms against his closed eyes, hoping a bit of pressure would stop the pounding. The sun pouring in through the window certainly wasn't helping one bit.

Kajaan got to his feet and managed to dress despite his lethargy and pounding headache. His mind was quickly crowding with thoughts and his doubts, making it hard to think. He needed to talk to someone who wasn't King Cadeyrn, Kajaan finally decided. But who? There was no way he could talk to Yolotzin. He was too far away. Quillin was always fair, but he rarely left King Cadeyrn's side, and that's exactly who Kajaan wanted to avoid. Ameyalli wasn't always around the king, but they reported only to him just the same. Besides, they were firmly for him and King Cadeyrn relenting to their Fated bond.

Both of them would likely tell King Cadeyrn anything he said to them even if it was in confidence and especially if it was his doubts. The kids most definitely weren't to be trusted, solely because they were children. Kajaan didn't know any child who kept a secret. He and Yolotzin certainly didn't when they were boys. Even if he did consider talking to them, the children wouldn't really understand the turmoil Kajaan was currently facing. They'd just want their papa to be happy.

His head throbbed and Kajaan groaned, rubbing it. First he should visit a Healer. He barely paid attention to what he had put on; he just knew it was lightweight since the air was already warm with the morning sun. It almost felt like he really was hungover, though Kajaan knew for a fact he hadn't touched any alcohol. King Cadeyrn kept his dinners dry for the children's sake.

As Kajaan slid his feet into a pair of plain sandals, he realized that a Healer was exactly what he needed. They were under oath to keep their patient's confidentiality. It didn't matter if King Cadeyrn tried to bully them into telling him what Kajaan said. They had to refuse unless Kajaan okayed it, and King Cadeyrn would know that. The only time that oath was broken was if they feared for the patient's or another person's safety.

Feeling marginally better with his decision, Kajaan slipped from his room and headed down the stairs. Paelfjord Castle had a fairly expansive medical wing. The entire castle staff used the facility, and even citizens of Sestella and the surrounding areas were able to request to be seen. Denials were rare, especially if the person's life was in danger, but minor cases were often given a referral to another nearby clinic.

Avitou would never have such a system. Maybe once Yolotzin took over, but right now, only the royal family could use the castle Healers. The staff had to go out and find an outside Healer, even if they'd been injured on the job and needed medical attention faster than getting into a carriage and heading to a clinic. Kajaan supposed that's what the healing potions his father had purchased were for.

Kajaan found the internal door for the Healers and quietly slipped in. There were a handful of people waiting in the lobby, and Kajaan bypassed them, trying to not stare or seem like he was too nervous. Many of those gathered weren't part of the castle staff, and he got plenty of curious looks. He figured that King Cadeyrn hadn't really told anyone in Sestella that he was here, and his red hair and pale skin definitely stuck out.

"Can I help you?" the Healer behind the reception desk asked kindly.

"Um, yes," Kajaan stammered quietly. "I need to talk to someone… confidentially. I'm… confused, I think is the best word. I don't know how to put it, but my mind is acting off."

The woman's smile slipped from her face, and she regarded him seriously. When she spoke, her tone was kind and soft, but firm enough that Kajaan knew she was already sizing him up if he needed to be restrained. "Are you having violent thoughts?"

"No," Kajaan breathed. "Nothing like that. Everything's just… jumbled. Racing. I can't get it to stop, and I couldn't sleep last night."

She nodded and gestured for him to sit. Since he'd brought Prince Rodolfo in once for an injury, the staff knew who he was. The boy had taken a spill in the gardens and cut the palms of his hands and his knees up pretty good. He'd taken the pain like a champ and barely cried while they waited for Tamya and King Cadeyrn to see the boy. Kajaan had all but fled once the king had shown up.

Kajaan sat for about twenty minutes while those in the lobby were called back and others filed in. It seemed the castle employed a good amount of Healers to make sure no one had to wait for very long. It was nice seeing how much thought King Cadeyrn put into taking care of his citizens. He only wished that King Tonalli would do the same for his.

He rubbed his temples and curled in on himself, trying to get the pain to back off even a little bit. At least he couldn't feel anything foreign in the back of his mind like he had last night. Their bond must have diminished, not yet strong enough to withstand so many hours apart. Someone touched his shoulder, and he jumped, looking up into the face of the royal Healer, Tamya.

"Come on, Kajaan," she said gently, "I was wondering if I'd see you today."

She had been expecting him? Kajaan followed her into a hallway lined with several doors on either side. One was ajar near the back, and Tamya gestured for him to enter and sit. He did so, folding into a simply made wooden chair. The Healer shut the door behind her and sat across from him, crossing her legs at the ankles and regarding him kindly.

"So what's going on, Kajaan?" Tamya asked.

"I have a feeling you might already know. Why did you think I'd come to see you today?" Kajaan asked weakly.

The Healer grinned, and she sat back in her chair, looking completely relaxed. Much like Kajaan, she was dressed in soft silks, though hers were bleached white to denote her Healer profession. It was a tradition that Zothua and Bhyvine had implemented years ago, though it hadn't quite caught on with the rest of the kingdoms. Tamya tilted her head as she regarded him for a long moment.

"Because you and Cade had a very public fight before he kissed you last night, and you looked pretty distraught about it afterwards," Tamya said.

"Distraught might be the best word," Kajaan muttered and groaned, covering his face with his hands as he curled in on himself. "I'm so confused, and I don't know what to do."

"Start with what happened after Cade left you on the floor. Don't think he didn't get a lecture about that from Inti this morning. He should have made sure you were all right," Tamya suggested.

Kajaan snorted and shook his head, dropping his arms to his legs. "He didn't need to. But I don't understand why he's pursuing me instead of just breaking the bond outright. It's not like I'm worth anything and can bring anything to the relationship. I have nothing resembling a dowry."

"Start from what happened after Cade walked away," Tamya repeated.

Knowing she wasn't going to let him gloss over what happened made him blush. He kept his gaze set firmly on the ground as he told her what he'd done after he holed up in his room, his fantasy, and how he'd felt the entire time, including the sudden extra orgasm, and ending with how he'd been unable to sleep.

Tamya listened without any sort of reproach in her expression. Just nodding at certain points, silently encouraging him to continue. Once he was done, the room was silent for a good long while. Kajaan had included his doubts and how he felt like he should just walk away and try to distance himself. Even when he voiced leaving, she didn't scowl at him like she thought he might.

"Where is Cade now?" Tamya asked.

"In the library. Why?" Kajaan replied.

She stared at him as he watched her, confused. Finally it dawned on him. No one had told him where King Cadeyrn was. He leapt to his feet, shaking his head. The bond hadn't faded overnight. If he focused on it, he could feel a gentle current of concern in the back of his mind, overtaking the subtle contentment that he'd been feeling this morning.

"No, no, no! The goddess is wrong. I'm *nothing*. I barely even have a Craft, and I'm from Averia. I'm just projecting because I'm lonely and he's been nothing but kind to me," Kajaan protested.

"Are you?" Tamya asked ruthlessly. "The goddess doesn't make mistakes, Kajaan. You are Cade's Fated, even though you're trying to fight it. Why?"

"Because I'm not good for him," Kajaan nearly shouted. "I can't do it."

"Cade has a lot of love to give. Did you ever see him with his wife?" Tamya stared at him until he shook his head meekly. "Then you don't know how tactile and attentive he is. He's spent the last four years alone, not seeing anyone and living a half life."

"So I'm the backup," Kajaan said bitterly. "He needs another wife, not an ordained whore."

Tamya's eyes flashed angrily, and she snarled at him. "Do you truly think Cade would see you that way? Why do you think you're so unfit for this position? The twins absolutely adore you, Thaddaeus is happier than he's ever been in the last four years, and Cade has smiled more lately. Marika even talked some the other day without prompting! You're bringing life back into this castle and into their lives without even being with Cade, so you're more than a body to take pleasure in. And knowing our king, he's said exactly what I have to you too."

Fully chastised, Kajaan dropped back into the chair and curled up again. He ducked his head so he didn't have to look Tamya in the face. Yes, King Cadeyrn had given him quite the argument last night, and Kajaan had wanted to ignore all of it. Kajaan just wanted his life to go back to what it had been.

"I'm scared," he finally admitted.

"I know," Tamya replied, her voice soft once more. "I know you are, Kajaan. You do have some valid concerns. You're not native, but then again, neither am I. Zothua is a lot gentler than Averia. It doesn't matter that you're not nobility. Even if you two weren't Fated, it wouldn't matter. No one will stand in Cade's way if he wants you."

Sighing, Kajaan rubbed his face with his hands. He was tired. He hated being scared, hated feeling like he constantly needed to run. A gentle outpouring of affection came through their bond, easing his aching head. It felt really nice, though Kajaan still felt a bit wary.

"My head hurts," he finally whispered.

"It's possible the bond is mistaking your turmoil and nerves for a rejection," Tamya suggested. "You know how to fix that."

Either convince King Cadeyrn to break the bond or accept it. Those were his only options unless he wanted to get sicker and sicker. He'd never heard of anyone actually dying from the rejection since it happened so rarely and one of the parties eventually capitulated. Hell, even Lord Asyl submitted to the goddess's will and accepted his bond with Lord Kende. The two had been so happy ever since.

Was it finally time for him to do the same?

Just take the leap. See what happened.

For better or for worse, right?

After a few minutes where neither of them spoke, there was a gentle knock on the door. Tamya called for entry and Ameyalli slipped in. Kajaan barely looked up at them, figuring he already knew why they were here considering he could feel King Cadeyrn's concern. It hadn't gotten any stronger or overbearing, thankfully.

"Cade's worried about you," Ameyalli said firmly, though their voice wasn't unkind. "He sent me to check on you."

"Kajaan is having a few doubts with their bond," Tamya supplied.

Kajaan groaned. This was exactly what he didn't want to have floating around or reported back to the king. So much for confidentiality. Though maybe just coming here had started those rumors. He didn't know. Why couldn't he go back to being invisible like he'd always been? It was so much easier than always being put in the spotlight and having everyone watching and speculating about his movements.

"I see," Ameyalli said and sighed heavily. "I struggled with my own bond." When Kajaan looked up at them, they nodded and smiled. "I did. Why would Quillin want me? My body wasn't formed right, and I have a lot of scars from surgeries from when I was a child. We may never have children of our own, and he wants a whole herd of them while also not wanting to use a surrogate. I believed I was useless to him, and I'd just been promoted to being Cadeyrn's advisor. Fraternizing with the secretary, I thought, was going to be grounds for dismissal.

"But you know what? It all worked out. I'm happy. We're both at peace with what we bring to each other. Sure, we're trying to have kids, but I know he won't ever hold it against me if we never do. Because that's what being Fated means. It's working with each other and leaning on them, knowing they'll be there to catch you."

Tamya seemed delighted at Ameyalli's words, smiling up at the advisor. Kajaan could only shake his head, looking between the two of them.

"You two come from the same rank," Kajaan said slowly. "I was only raised in Avitou castle because my father works there. If he hadn't, we might have been middle class at best. I'm not fit for anyone in nobility, let alone a *king*."

"Did you think that might be what Cade needs, though?" Tamya asked. "He might need an outside perspective, both nationality and class-wise. Someone to remind him there's more to life than what's in his office."

"Maybe," Kajaan finally admitted, ducking his head.

"But you want to try," Tamya said softly.

Kajaan flushed. He flexed his hands a few times into fists before he ever so slowly nodded. He did. All his life, he'd played it safe. Followed Yolotzin around, keeping his bed warm and never even trying to look outside their relationship for another. Always wanting his love and fidelity, always believing that they'd be together, and not entertaining the idea that there'd be a time they'd be apart.

Accepting King Cadeyrn as his Fated and beginning a relationship with him didn't quite feel as much of a betrayal as it used to. Now he almost felt selfish, looking to the man to be his support. Except wasn't that kind of what Tamya and Ameyalli were suggesting? Besides, they both had the entire staff of Paelfjord behind them. And the kids. They wouldn't be alone and could give each other the strength they needed to succeed.

He thought back to his conversation with King Cadeyrn last night. How he believed that Ilyphari had broken Kajaan's heart in a spectacular way in order to save him even more sorrow and pain later on. That the goddess wasn't the best or kindest at guiding her children, sometimes needing to resort to a heavy hand, but she always did it with their future happiness in mind.

I'd get you.

Once, even a few days ago, such words would have terrified him. Now they warmed his chest as he thought back to King Cadeyrn's easy smile and gentle eyes. What would happen if he tried? The worst that could happen would be that he failed and they'd end up awkward around each other, leading to Kajaan moving out and maybe trying again with someone else. The best? Ending up in an open, exclusive, loving relationship that Kajaan had always wanted.

He just had to have faith.

"Come," Ameyalli said, holding out their hand.

Kajaan reached out and took it. They hauled him to his feet and smiled up at him. For all their presence and personality, Ameyalli was fairly short, at roughly five and a half feet. They tugged on his hand, and Kajaan found himself following the Seer out of the Healer wing and toward the library where King Cadeyrn waited. Kajaan barely had time to wave farewell to a smiling Tamya.

No one stopped them as Ameyalli marched Kajaan across the castle to the library. Not even Quillin, who looked amused, tried to stop them. Being around the countless books, breathing in the smell of pressed paper, ink, and leather relaxed him. He knew damn well where Ameyalli was taking him, and that he would have likely been able to find the king on his own without their assistance. Though he might not have had the courage to.

The large Ignis was curled up on a plush-looking couch, a small novel in his hand. It looked like he was reading more for pleasure than work.

"Cade," Ameyalli said.

He looked up and smiled, seeing the two of them.

"There you are," he said warmly.

Kajaan flushed, realizing that smile was mostly for him. He bit his lower lip and stumbled when Ameyalli none too gently shoved him toward the couch. The Seer trotted off a second later, causing King Cadeyrn to snort out a small laugh. Swallowing down his embarrassment from how he'd acted the night previous, Kajaan perched stiffly next to King Cadeyrn on the couch.

Nothing was said, and Kajaan wasn't sure if that made it worse. King Cadeyrn simply returned to his novel, almost dismissively. But he'd wanted him here, right? Slowly, he found the tension leaving his body and he scooted back, getting comfortable. Once again, King Cadeyrn was letting him set the pace. Not watching him to make him nervous. Letting him control how far they went even just to sit and read in the library.

As soon as he fully relaxed, King Cadeyrn slid his hand over and found his. Their fingers twined together, and though Kajaan's heart felt as if it was going to beat out of his chest, a sense of rightness settled over him.

This was where he was meant to be.

Chapter 12

For the next fortnight, King Cadeyrn seemed to make it his mission to get Kajaan to relax more around him. Maybe Ameyalli had said something to him, or maybe he'd truly felt all the panic that Kajaan had gone through and knew he needed to ease into their bond. Kajaan was still baffled that it was even happening, figuring he'd wake up at some point and their developing bond would be gone and it would have all been some sort of cruel joke. Every day that passed, his fears faded a little more.

One afternoon, King Cadeyrn coaxed Kajaan to the back of the castle where the barracks and training grounds for the royal and city guards were built. The newer recruits were beginning to clean up the practice ring, skin shiny with sweat. Kajaan hesitated, staring wide-eyed at all of the shirtless men, nearly falling over his feet when King Cadeyrn tugged him over to the sergeant. A sword was pressed into his hand, and Kajaan realized that the king was intending to use some sort of weapons practice as a bonding exercise.

Kajaan was firm in his refusal, too many bad memories surfacing of facing down older recruits as a child. Some of his anxiety must have either shown on his face or bled through their bond as Cadeyrn's face softened and he smiled at him instead of getting frustrated. Instead of joining his Fated in the ring, Kajaan sat on a nearby bench with Thaddaeus, watching the sergeant put King Cadeyrn through an advanced set. Seeing the power behind his controlled swings was oddly comforting. King Cadeyrn was strong and knew how to handle himself.

Afterward, Kajaan inspected King Cadeyrn's callused palms and rubbed a soothing lotion into the skin. The king was far too experienced to have raw skin or blisters, but it felt nice to take care of his Fated, even if it was fairly useless. Cadeyrn just smiled at him the entire time, his skin still flushed from the exercise. Their moment was interrupted by the twins running over and jumping all over them.

They spent their evenings together, in either one of their rooms or the library. King Cadeyrn was a huge bibliophile and loved to read wondertales, much like Princess Marika did. They both loved stories of going to different planets where the flora and fauna were nothing like they were here. The only difference was that the princess liked her stories to have dragons or unicorns in them, whereas King Cadeyrn was a little less picky about the contents. He didn't seem to care where they were written either, so long as he could read it.

By the end of the second week, Kajaan was curling up into his Fated's side, enjoying his own book with the man's arm around him.

The good-night kisses were his favorite parts, though. They were chaste and quick, and Cadeyrn always wished him pleasant dreams before leaving him at his door. It made Kajaan feel giggly every night, and most nights, he felt that joy rebound back to him. He was becoming sappy, and suddenly Kajaan could understand how Yolotzin's feelings for him vanished so quickly.

Or maybe not exactly vanished, but were overshadowed. That made a bit more sense, considering he knew he still loved his prince—it just wasn't the same anymore. His focus was changing with every smile Cadeyrn directed his way. Every time one of the kids laughed or happily chattered at him for one reason or another. For the first time in a very long time, Kajaan felt settled and at peace.

It really didn't come as a surprise to him when Quillin found him one afternoon and told Kajaan that Cadeyrn was waiting for him upstairs in the study. By this point, their kissing was starting to get a little heavier, with roaming hands finding more delicate areas that shouldn't be fondled around the children. When said children interrupted their more passionate moments, it was hard to pull away.

This time it seemed the man wanted privacy, since Quillin didn't follow Kajaan upstairs to the study. He could only hope that perhaps they'd actually get to some heavy petting and start to learn each other's hot spots and then exploit them. They hadn't quite talked about when they wanted to seal their bond, so perhaps that's what Cadeyrn had planned. Unless someone was screaming bloody murder, Ameyalli or Quillin could handle any requests, and Miski could handle the kids.

When he entered the study and was told to shut the door behind him, Kajaan smiled slowly and locked it. He leaned back, cocking his hips slightly, delighted to see the gleam in Cadeyrn's eye. Kajaan was more than ready to play a little dirty, and it looked like his Fated was more than ready to play the game.

Cadeyrn scooted back in his chair and patted his knee. Oh hell yes. This had always been a kind of fantasy for him, though it was always King Yolotzin who wanted him on his lap. His Fated beckoning him was better. Much better. Kajaan crossed over to him and plopped down, sitting sideways and draping his legs over the armrest. He wrapped his arms around Cadeyrn's neck, his smile turning somewhat shy.

There wasn't anything to worry about as one of the king's beefy arms wound around his chest to hold him close, the other running up and down his side. Kajaan leaned into him, and submitted to the languid kisses that Cadeyrn pressed to his lips. He slowly teased them open, nipping his lower lip and groaning as if this was all he needed.

Without a single doubting thought, Kajaan parted his lips for the king's curious tongue. His exploration was just as slow and thorough as his chaste kisses, taking the time to map out and memorize everything about Kajaan's mouth. All his teeth, and even the slight scarring he had on the inside of his cheek where he'd bit quite a few times growing up to keep quiet, nothing was left out.

His Fated tasted heavenly. They were going slow, learning how each other kissed and liked to be kissed. Since they'd both only ever had one partner prior, it wasn't too hard to find a new rhythm. Kajaan was a little more aggressive than he usually was, trying to provoke Cadeyrn to be a bit rougher with him, and the man easily gave him what he wanted, squeezing him closer.

Kajaan had nearly forgotten the hand on his side until Cadeyrn gently slid it up his sleeveless tunic. A low groan escaped him, and he wiggled a little in his Fated's lap. An answering bulge in the king's pants told him how much he was enjoying this too. The man's hands were callused, a reminder of all the hours he spent in the ring with a sword, and they scraped over Kajaan's soft skin, sending pleasure sparking down his spine.

Holding back a groan, Kajaan briefly disentangled himself from Cadeyrn so he could straddle the king's hips, though he didn't push their bodies flush. Not yet. He could rock slightly against the man's thighs, and Cadeyrn had quite a bit more access to his body this way. Their lips clashed together once again, feverish and eager for more, and Cadeyrn's hands roamed his body once more. Eventually he'd get around to exploring his Fated's chest and abs in return. Once he wasn't so enamored from kissing him….

The king's hand pulled away for just a moment, tenting his tunic and stretching it a bit tighter across his body. Kajaan felt heat radiate over his side, and he shifted slightly on the man's lap, a little too preoccupied with kissing his Fated that two and two weren't adding together. An unnaturally warmed hand touched his chest, and the old warnings he hadn't needed in years began screaming in the back of his mind.

CHAPTER 13

CADEYRN HAD forgotten how nice it was to have a pliant lover in his arms. With their weight on his lap and feeling their warmth seep into him. As an Ignis, he always ran hot, but Kajaan ran cool. He was refreshing to hold in his arms, and all Cadeyrn wanted to do was squeeze Kajaan to him and never let him go.

The more time they spent together, the more Cadeyrn was loath to walk away in the evenings. He probably wouldn't last much longer before he led Kajaan to his suite and into his bed. That would be a fresh new challenge he needed to research first, though. Or perhaps Kajaan would be all right with just sleeping together with sex coming later.

Cadeyrn thought kissing another man would be awkward or off-putting after having only kissed women. That had been one of many reasons he'd cornered Kajaan a fortnight ago and kissed him in the great hall. Turns out, Kajaan shaved consistently and his beard grew in very slowly. His face was almost always smooth, but even the slight rasp of their good-night kisses felt nice.

He just wasn't sure what to do once the clothes started coming off. From his own experience, he knew the theory of how to please Kajaan with his hand, but he had no idea if there was more to it than that. If Kajaan had a pussy, he'd already know what to do and there'd be no hesitance on his side. Taking a partner with the same equipment as him was going to need a bit more research.

Or a very awkward talk.

Ameyalli had given him a romance book from Valvinte weeks ago. For a minute, Cadeyrn had stared at them with an eyebrow raised. They'd leaned in and whispered in his ear that it featured two men and was quite explicit. To help with his research, they'd giggled, hugging a second copy to their chest and trotting off to their quarters. Quillin had laughed himself to tears with his Fated's antics and shamelessly asked him if it was any good the next day.

Cadeyrn hadn't read it yet. It was hidden under his pillow, mocking him every time he went to lie down and sleep for the night. One day he'd read it. It had to be soon, though. The urge to consummate their bond was growing, and Cadeyrn found himself not wanting to wait. Kajaan was the reason he was trying to take it slow. The man was still skittish sometimes, yet he seemed to enjoy Cadeyrn's kisses quite a bit.

Tonight, though, Kajaan had freely come to him while he was in his office with a sweet smile. His eyes had lit up in unabashed excitement when Cadeyrn had patted his leg and had even locked the door. It had occurred to him that maybe Kajaan needed to be touched as much as he did himself. The more tactile he was, the faster Kajaan leaned into him and became more open to receiving his advances.

Now he had his Fated in his lap, his scent enveloping him and clouding his thoughts. Who knew how intoxicating roses smelled? Cadeyrn squeezed Kajaan tight to him as he reveled in how soft his Fated's skin was. It was nothing like he'd imagined all those nights during his boyhood when he peeked at the guardsmen practicing out in the yard. His Fated was damn near hairless and smooth, his body giving slightly under his touch. Kajaan wasn't a musclebound swordsman, and that was just fine to him.

Cadeyrn was glad that Kajaan preferred the more pacifist path. Using his mind and wits to outsmart teachers much older or learned than him, or simply ignoring those who tried to intimidate him. His Fated was so strong, and Cadeyrn couldn't be prouder of having such a man by his side. Especially now that Kajaan was more than willing to have Cadeyrn touch him. His reservations about Cadeyrn being a king and an Ignis seemed to have faded away with the time they spent together.

The last day had been hard on his sweet Fated, though. The twins had run him ragged during their afternoon physical exercise, and even Marika joined in to exasperate him further. As he rubbed Kajaan's side, he could feel the bunched muscles resist his touch. Well, he knew an easy way to help with that. Cadeyrn pulled a hand back, not bothering to break the kiss and tell Kajaan what he was doing.

Menea had liked it when he warmed his palms during a massage to help target those extra sore areas. She'd said it relaxed her muscles and helped the tension of the day melt away, always leaving her sleepy and content. Trying to raise twin toddlers on top of their other two while running all her programs and trying to get pregnant had taken a lot out of her. He'd given her warm massages almost every night. With how stiffly Kajaan was holding himself, Cadeyrn figured he could benefit from this as well.

Everything had been going fine until he put his Craft-heated hand back onto Kajaan's chest, just under his left breast. There was a beat where Kajaan went completely still, the pleasant, warm contentment coming through their bond fracturing into irrational fear. Before Cadeyrn could pull away and ask what was wrong, Kajaan was alternating frantically pushing at him and trying to climb him like a tree to get away. His eyes were wide, wild, and panicked.

Terror radiated from his Fated, and Cadeyrn quickly dropped his Craft, trying to hold on to Kajaan so he didn't fall backward and whack his head against the desk or stone floor as he struggled. He made soothing noises, but none of them seemed to reach his Fated, and being restrained almost seemed to make it worse, with Kajaan making an odd keening sound.

The one thing that could be classified as "bad" about their relationship was their size. They were closer in height than Cadeyrn was with his late wife. Cadeyrn's mistake came in the way of misjudging distances and getting clocked in the face by Kajaan's elbow as he thrashed and pulled to try and get away. He earned a knee to the gut, and Cadeyrn finally let go instead of trying to hold Kajaan against his will.

Kajaan rolled off his lap, hit the ground, and scrambled to his feet. Ignoring the pain in his stomach and whatever was trickling down the side of his face, Cadeyrn shot to his feet. His Fated was already halfway to the door, his mind a churning mess of panic and fear. There was no way in hell he was going to let his Fated out of this room while he was practically blinded in his current state.

There were a lot of stairs, and while the castle was Kajaan's home, he wasn't going to risk his Fated's safety. He could potentially slip or accidentally cause another to fall down the stairs, and there was no guarantee that Kajaan would just retreat to his rooms. What if he managed to get out of Paelfjord, dodge all of Wayra's men, and end up on the streets of Sestella? Cadeyrn would like to think his subjects would regard Kajaan kindly, but he was clearly a foreigner. There weren't any Zothuan-born citizens with the red hair and pale skin that Kajaan had.

The locked door gave him the half second he needed to reach Kajaan.

Grabbing his Fated's arm made him give a strangled shriek, and Kajaan spun, putting all his weight into leaning away and down, frantically scratching at Cadeyrn's hand to try and let him go. Cadeyrn held on a little tighter, not wanting Kajaan to crash to the ground once again.

"I'm not fast with it, please don't burn me!" Kajaan cried out.

"Kajaan, I'm not going to hurt you," Cadeyrn said, his heart clenching painfully.

"Please," Kajaan begged him, panting hard.

He slowly shrank toward the ground, tears filling his unfocused eyes as he stared at where Cadeyrn was holding him. Kajaan's entire body trembled as he struggled to breathe evenly. If he wasn't careful, his Fated was going to pass out. Making gentle noises low in his throat, like he'd done for his children when they were small, Cadeyrn loosened the hold he had on Kajaan, rubbing his thumb along his white skin.

"Kajie. Darling," Cadeyrn murmured, pulling him close.

It took a little doing with his Fated still trying to pull away, but he was able to get Kajaan close enough that he could wrap his arm around the redhead's waist. His breath still came in harsh gasps, even though his eyes seemed to be clearing. They weren't darting around so much, and focusing on Cadeyrn's face rather than his hand. Cadeyrn continued to murmur gentle words, mollified to see Kajaan start to come down from his frenzied state.

The panic in the back of his mind eased, and Cadeyrn squeezed Kajaan tight to him, letting go of the harsh grip he had on his Fated's arm. He winced, seeing faint bruising forming on his pretty pale skin. He'd call for Tamya soon. Kajaan began to relax, his body settling heavily into his arms as his breathing evened out. Cadeyrn knelt, picked him up, and walked back to his chair. This time he had Kajaan sit astride him, and the redhead leaned into his chest, nestling his face into Cadeyrn's neck.

Cadeyrn pressed gentle kisses to the top of his head, marveling at his coarse hair. Averians generally didn't have the hair Kajaan had, instead leaning toward darker colors. The color of his hair made him think of the women from Valvinte. The northern kingdom's people were vibrant and incredibly friendly. It was one of his favorite places to visit, and he often went there during the winters to watch the snow drift lazily from the skies with the kids, even though he was usually freezing.

Kajaan nuzzled into his chest and shuddered one last time, blowing out a harsh breath. He slowly sat up, avoiding looking up at him, biting his lower lip. Cadeyrn didn't dare restrict his movements, not wanting to prompt another panic attack. Kajaan held his body as if it was a massive weight, his shoulders slumped and his head bent forward, his chin tucked up against his chest.

"Sorry," Kajaan whispered.

"What happened?" Cadeyrn asked softly, cupping his cheek and forcing his Fated to look at him. "Who burned you? What did you mean by not being fast with it?" Kajaan winced and looked away, continuously chewing on his lower lip. "Kajaan. I know you insist your Craft is weak, but now you're mentioning that you can't call it quickly. That's another thing entirely. Please, who burned you? Why would they burn you?"

Kajaan shuddered and stared down at their laps, picking at his thumbnail for a long while before finally coming to a conclusion and nodding, drawing in a shaky breath. Cadeyrn could feel his Fated's resolution through their bond, and a spark of pride warmed his chest. He had no qualms that this would be an easy topic, but his Fated was going to be brave enough to talk about it.

"My teacher at Avitou believed in an aggressive training method. He'd make his touch so hot it would burn my skin on contact unless I could invoke my Craft and cool his hand quickly enough before he grabbed me," Kajaan said softly.

Rage flared quickly in his mind, and Cadeyrn had to take a few calming breaths before he went off on a tangent and scared his Fated again. He closed his eyes and pulled Kajaan back into his arms, kissing the top of his head again. Kajaan simply molded to his touch and demands, not protesting or insisting that he didn't need to be coddled. Maybe he knew that Cadeyrn needed his Fated. Or maybe he was just too drained to resist.

"So he would burn you when you failed?" Cadeyrn asked.

"And I always failed," Kajaan murmured. "I couldn't invoke my Craft fast enough, so wherever he touched me, he burned me."

Cadeyrn snarled and tilted Kajaan's head up. He kissed his lips gently, holding him tight, as if he could take his old pains away with enough passion. Cadeyrn took Kajaan's wrist in his hand and extended his arm, inspecting the fair skin there. He'd felt the raised skin during their stolen moments together and assumed the blemishes were from before his Awakening and hadn't said a thing despite his curiosity.

Now that he was looking at them.... Cadeyrn wrapped his fingers around his Fated's arm, and the long-faded scars lined up with his hand.

Poorly, but they were definitely similar enough in shape, and he thought he could identify a palm or two. Cadeyrn had much bigger hands, and he was suddenly glad that his father hadn't thought of the same training method.

"You shouldn't have these," Cadeyrn said finally. "What kind of bastard Healer left you with scarring? There should be no reason you couldn't have been healed completely."

"I wasn't allowed to be attended to by a Healer," Kajaan said.

Breathe. Don't hurt your Fated. Just breathe. In for four. Hold for four. Out for four. Hold.... Nope, he was still seeing red. Kajaan wheezed, and Cadeyrn realized he'd been nearly crushing his Fated to his chest. With an effort, he gentled his grasp, though he demanded a few frantic kisses from Kajaan to reassure himself that his smart redhead was all right. Kajaan didn't seem put off by his needs, and Cadeyrn couldn't detect any added distress through their bond.

"So the bastard burned you, refused you treatment, and left you with physical and mental scars," Cadeyrn snarled, "and a fear of Ignians."

"Pretty much," Kajaan whispered.

"What made him stop?" Cadeyrn asked. "The kind of man who can torture a child wouldn't just stop on his own."

"Tzin," Kajaan replied simply. Cadeyrn felt a rush of gratitude toward the young prince. The man had protected his best friend, even though he'd likely also just turned thirteen. "Torbid grabbed my face once and… the damage was really bad. Like, potentially life-threatening bad. He left me in the courtyard after that session. All I remember is the other servants whispering to each other as I cried, and then Tzin was at my side, screaming at them.

"They were fine ignoring me, but they wouldn't ignore the crown prince. I was already out cold by the time the Healer arrived, but Tzin told me later that his mom had Torbid out on his ear an hour later while I was recovering in her bed."

"Oh, Kaj," Cadeyrn whispered. He could feel the ripples of pain and fear from his Fated as Kajaan recounted the memory. Cadeyrn placed tender kisses on his forehead, eyelids, cheeks, and eventually his lips. Kajaan clutched at his shirt, leaning into the affection, needing it almost desperately. "Is that why you essentially live as a Void?"

Kajaan shrugged and nodded. "I don't really ever invoke my Craft if I can help it. It's embarrassing since it takes so long, and I can't really do anything with it unless it's small stuff."

"I don't believe that for a second," Cadeyrn said. "You held six men and their horses. Not only that, but you were able to work delicately enough to stop each individual's blood flow until they passed out. That's something only an insanely powerful Craft Blessed can manage. Yet you did. You're not weak. When we go to Prince Yolotzin's wedding, I want to meet your old teacher."

"Why?" Kajaan asked warily.

"So he can feel what it's like to be burned, unable to defend himself, and refused any medical help," Cadeyrn replied darkly.

"It's okay," Kajaan tried cajoling him.

"It's not okay! You just had a massive panic attack when I warmed my hand to try and give you a massage. So much so, I'm surprised all the Sympathetics in the castle haven't beaten down the damn door trying to figure out what happened and make sure you're all right," Cadeyrn said, shaking his head. "You were unfairly hurt as a child. No man in their right mind would ever put a child in a position to be hurt so needlessly during training."

"That was his way," Kajaan said, shrugging. "Torbid trains all Aquans the way he did me."

"Does the king know?" Cadeyrn asked.

"Of course he does. He hired him," Kajaan replied.

Cadeyrn closed his eyes and tried counting his breathing again. It was easier to manage the near all-consuming anger this time, and he cupped Kajaan's face. He leaned in and brushed their lips together, needing the intimacy to soothe his temper once more. Kajaan was here, safe, in his arms. His Fated melted into his touch, sighing quietly.

Before he could sink into his Fated's embrace, Ameyalli's mostly forgotten warning surfaced in his mind. Kajaan needed to master his Craft, and soon, for the sake of others' lives. The only major upcoming event Cadeyrn could think of was Prince Yolotzin's wedding. Only a fool would try to start something at a royal wedding, but then again, there were plenty of fools in the world.

Besides, even if Kajaan wasn't destined to help in some way, Cadeyrn thought that mastering his Craft would go a huge way toward building Kajaan's confidence. He shifted his Fated and nuzzled the top of his head, curling Kajaan in close again. His lover laughed gently, more of a huff than anything, but eagerly cuddled against him.

"Would you be willing to work with an Aquan trainer?" Cadeyrn asked softly.

"Why?" Kajaan asked.

"Just to see what they think. I still don't believe your Craft is as weak as you believe it to be," Cadeyrn told him.

"Lord Kende did say something about my reservoir being abnormally small when he did an exam while he was here. He'd focused specifically on my Craft, but I haven't really thought much about it," Kajaan said.

"Let me call up a few trainers to work with you. You can have a session or interview with each one of them and pick who you want to work with. They will be Aquans, not Ignians, and you will never be barred from getting help from our Healers," Cadeyrn said. "Though they should never put you in the position to need one."

"If that's what you think is best," Kajaan murmured. He jolted backward, and Cadeyrn felt a flash of alarm through their bond. "You're bleeding."

"Don't worry about it," Cadeyrn whispered, pulling Kajaan flush to his body.

Kajaan frowned up at him this time, the slightest amount of irritation radiating from him. His lover reached up and tapped around his temple, making him wince. Kajaan's fingertips were dark with his blood. Cadeyrn grabbed a cloth that he used to wipe ink off his hands. Kajaan carefully cleaned the blood from his wound before wiping up what had run down his face. There was a bit of blood spattered on both of their shirts, but there wasn't much he could do about that anymore.

Cadeyrn hummed and lightly kissed his Fated again now that Kajaan was satisfied. He wrapped his arms underneath the man's ass and stood, picking him up once more. Luckily Kajaan didn't seem to mind being manhandled so often, as he didn't protest. Instead, Kajaan wrapped his arms around Cadeyrn's neck, legs around his waist, and rested his head between his own arm and Cadeyrn's neck. Cadeyrn angled himself so he could unlock the door and open it without letting his Fated go.

Quillin was standing alone in the hallway, nervously wringing his hands.

His secretary must have kept everyone else away or from interfering. Cadeyrn managed to give him a small smile, and Quillin simply nodded. They walked undisturbed down to Cadeyrn's quarters, where he gently laid Kajaan onto his bed. Kajaan didn't let him go, and Cadeyrn barely hesitated before he crawled on top of him, rolling onto his side so he could tuck his Fated as close to him as he could.

For the rest of the evening, Cadeyrn quietly relayed his orders to Quillin, who didn't even bat an eye at him. The man sat at the desk in his room and made a list of things to do. It was oddly peaceful, with Kajaan wrapped around him and slipping in and out of sleep. Panic attacks wore even the strongest person out. Cadeyrn didn't bother trying to get up, not wanting to leave his lover alone for even a minute.

A rumor of their high emotions and early respite must have made its way through Paelfjord. Before the hour was up, all four of Cadeyrn's kids had crawled into bed with them. Fayette managed to worm her way in between him and Kajaan, wrapping her tiny arms around the redhead's neck. Marika propped her book up on Cadeyrn's side, reading quietly as Thaddaeus plastered himself to Kajaan's back. Rodolfo decided he wanted to sleep on top of his twin, nestling in close.

Kajaan didn't even stir.

CHAPTER 14

GODDESS, KAJAAN wanted to puke.

It had only been a couple days since he'd told Cadeyrn everything that Torbid had once done to him. The king had surprised him, being incredibly gentle, constantly giving him reaffirmations and affection when he was obviously upset. While he knew that his Fated wasn't a callous man, feeling his anger at how he'd been treated, and then feeling the man's love for him went a long way for Kajaan's trust.

But his care hadn't stopped once they left the study. No, the king had publicly taken care of him, retiring to his room to work instead of sending Kajaan off to recover on his own. Which would have been completely understandable; he had a whole kingdom to manage after all. The rest of the day had passed in relative calm, with the children napping with them, then listening to Marika read one of her wondertales until dinnertime.

Cadeyrn had continued to tend to him afterward, kissing the scarring on his arms that night after the kids had been ushered to their rooms. He'd insisted that Kajaan spend the night with him in his bed. Just to sleep. Though Kajaan wondered if he wouldn't have minded something a little more to take him even further from his memories.

It was to ease his mind, Cadeyrn had said. Kajaan didn't quite believe that was the reason, or at least all of it, but it was nice being held so much again. It wasn't how he and Yolotzin had always cuddled, but having Cadeyrn's arms wrapped around his chest and held tight against his hard body made him feel more secure than he'd ever been before. He'd briefly thought about how traitorous that was, and was about to spiral in the darkness. One sleepy kiss from Cadeyrn on his shoulder stopped him, and he'd settled right down.

He was home.

Kajaan didn't know how Cadeyrn had done it, but yesterday, several Aquan Craft teachers had arrived at Paelfjord for him to meet after lunch. He'd been ushered to one of the larger side rooms with

Quillin to observe, but not participate in, Kajaan choosing his teacher. The king's secretary was there just to make sure nothing escalated and to report back to Cadeyrn of Kajaan's choice.

The men Kajaan shrank away from immediately. While they weren't taller than him, they'd carried around an air of authority that brought back unpleasant memories. He refused to let another man have power over him or hold his future in his hands. Unless it was Cadeyrn, of course. But Cadeyrn never really ignored Kajaan's requests. He was a bit brash and fast acting, yes. But he listened.

Out of the two women, the younger one seemed surprised and a little irritated she was having to teach an adult the basics. She'd started to spit out rude comments about how inept he'd have to be to seek training as an adult until Quillin barked at her to be quiet and to be cognizant that not everyone was fortunate to have a private tutor.

The normally placid and kind Sympathetic losing his temper had been a sight to see as he'd dressed her down and then had her immediately escorted from the castle. Kajaan had a feeling she wouldn't be working as a teacher for a long, long time. Not unless she left Sestella and went to a far-flung city. Even that might not spare her from the rumor mills.

That left the final person and his newest teacher, Rhionne Laltine. She was an older woman, barely five feet, and her gray hair nearly brushed the ground behind her steps. Before she even said anything to Kajaan, who at the time was concerned about having to reject all the teachers before her, she just studied him.

Then she startled him with her words. "This is just as much of a recovery of the heart as it is your Craft."

Without a word or explanation from him, she'd understood exactly what he'd needed. Kajaan simply nodded, and just like that, he had a personal teacher once again. Rhionne tapped her cane against the stone floor, declared she'd be back in the morning, and left the castle faster than Kajaan had expected from the older woman.

Quillin had taken Kajaan up to the king's study after that, declaring that Miski could take care of the children for the rest of the day. Cadeyrn was delighted that one of the teachers had met Kajaan's approval, and Kajaan spent a good rest of the day in the man's lap, tucked against his Fated. Cadeyrn hadn't seemed to mind working around him one bit. He could feel the man's joy and excitement at Kajaan finding someone he could trust.

Trust.

Kajaan had once been worried about Cadeyrn touching him in fear of being burned, but it never truly occurred to him anymore. Not after he accepted that Cadeyrn was his Fated a fortnight ago. Kajaan was safe with him, and Cadeyrn was nothing but patient and kind. Perhaps that should have instilled a sense of confidence in him, but Kajaan still felt unbalanced by everything that had happened in the last few moonturns.

Nothing would erase the fact that he'd killed a man. When he brought that concern up to Cadeyrn last night, his Fated had hugged him tight for a second and then kissed the nape of his neck. He'd seemed to debate about something before finally telling Kajaan about the first time he'd killed someone.

Cadeyrn had been helping defend his carriage from highwaymen during a return trip from another kingdom, with a very pregnant Queen Menea inside. He could have sat back and let the guards handle their assailants, but he'd felt compelled to protect his wife and unborn child. He'd been trained to wield a sword, after all.

Cadeyrn had never regretted what he'd done. The thieves could have run the moment he stepped out with his sword, but they'd persisted in their attack. So they lost their lives for threatening his pregnant wife. It was as simple as that for Cadeyrn.

Knowing that he wasn't judged by what he'd done made the pain a little easier to bear whenever it came back to haunt him. At least it had only been one man, and the other six guards had survived. Well, survived his hands at least. Kajaan wasn't quite sure if the other six had made it back to Averia or if they were being held somewhere or helping fertilize a field.

Today he was ensconced with Rhionne in a small room near the kitchens that had been cleared of almost everything. He sat across from her with a large wide-rimmed bowl full of water resting on the floor between them. They were sitting on thick pillows, designed specifically for Aquan training. The fabric was completely waterproof and would dry quickly, aided by the warm air.

Zothua produced more Aquan Craft Blessed than the rest of the world. Likely because of the environment and the need for water. Though that didn't quite explain Pemalia having an unnatural amount of Ignians, given its harsh environment. Or Valvinte with her excess Harvesters when the land was already lush with vegetation. It would have made a bit more sense for Pemalia to have more Harvesters and Valvinte to have more Gaians.

Kajaan rubbed his sweat-slicked palms on his pants, swallowing hard as he stared down at the bowl of water. Ever since the door had shut, his anxiety had ratcheted up, and no amount of Cadeyrn's gentle reassurances through their bond was helping. Rhionne hadn't said anything for the past five minutes, and the longer she sat and watched him, the more nervous Kajaan got.

"What are you so scared of?" she finally asked.

Even though her tone was gentle, Kajaan still flinched. She didn't raise an eyebrow or scold his baseless reaction. Instead, Rhionne had given him a gentle tilt of her head, reminding him that she expected him to answer her question. Kajaan had to swallow several times to try and rid himself of the lump in his throat so he could speak.

"Failing," Kajaan replied after a long minute, "and punishment when I do."

She clicked her tongue at him and shook her head. "When you expect failure, you will fail. Why are you so scared of failure that it's all you can think of to the point where it's consuming you?"

Kajaan looked at her for a moment, wincing at her gaze. Her expression had hardened, yet her shoulders were relaxed, and her hands sat loosely in her lap. She didn't seem angry. Or at least if she was, it wasn't aimed at him.

"My former trainer was an Ignis," Kajaan said slowly. "He'd punish failure with burns and deny me a Healer."

Rhionne made a noise of disgust, and Kajaan immediately lowered his eyes to stare at the floor. He chewed on his lower lip, wondering if he'd already screwed everything up. If she'd get to her feet after realizing that Kajaan was an unworthy pupil and leave in a huff. He was thirty-one. He should have gotten all the training he needed when he was thirteen.

"No Ignis should teach an Aquan," she finally said. "Only those who share the Craft should teach each other. It seems to me that it was set up this way to ensure your failure and to train you to be scared instead. Tell me, are you scared of all Ignians?"

"Yes," Kajaan whispered. "Except…."

"Except for our king," Rhionne said with a smile. "He's been much happier since you came here."

"Is it that obvious?" Kajaan asked, desperately trying to steer the conversation away from him.

"For those who watch, yes. Tamya is my grandbaby, and she's been keeping a close eye on you two. Now, from what I'm seeing, you were truly trained in three things: to fear Ignians, that failure brings pain, and to be ashamed of your Craft. You purposely weren't taught *how* to invoke your Craft properly, so you struggle to use it, which in turn has left your spirit aching."

"Don't know about that last part," Kajaan murmured.

"Tell me. How strongly do you feel your bond with our king?" Rhionne asked.

Kajaan stared at her a moment, baffled by the non sequitur. He was still struggling a bit with the knowledge that Tamya was her granddaughter and that his early training had a much more sinister purpose to it. He'd been stunted on purpose? Had Jeryit known? Had he been a part of the planning? Kajaan pushed those thoughts away, shaking his head to bring him back to the present. He'd talk to Cadeyrn about those thoughts later.

"It's stronger when he's nearby or if we've interacted recently," Kajaan replied.

"And yet it should be at full strength constantly. Your soul is grabbing on to his Craft, trying to fill what should be yours," Rhionne said.

"How do you know that I'm just not weak? Not everyone can be strong like Cadeyrn," Kajaan said.

The old woman sighed. "Tamya told me how you came to arrive here. She didn't perform the autopsy on the coward who tried shooting you, but she read the report once it became common knowledge in the castle that you're our king's Fated. She also told me how you stopped six men and their horses. That is…."

She trailed off and breathed in deep. There was something akin to reverence in her expression. Kajaan cringed, hating the look. How could she even look at him without reporting him to the council? Maybe she was of the same mind as Cadeyrn was and believed that breaking the strict laws of elemental Craft Blessed should be viewed on a case-by-case basis.

"I prayed to the goddess for help," Kajaan said. "She worked through me so I could protect myself. I still don't know why, other than to probably give Cade time to arrive. I wasn't really aware of what I was doing."

"Perhaps she did. Or perhaps she unlocked your spirit and encouraged your Craft to work at its full potential. You are ruled by fear. Perhaps you weren't aware of it while you were in Avitou, or you just weren't challenged to face it, but you are actively holding yourself back," Rhionne said. "Unfortunately, because of how that Ignian bastard trained you, we have to start at the very beginning. You at least know how to invoke your Craft, so we're not at the freshly Awakened training stage, but damn near close."

"It takes some concentration and time to do so," Kajaan said.

Rhionne nodded. "It does, yes. But what your trainer neglected to tell you, whether on purpose or unintentionally, I don't know which, is that once you know how to invoke your Craft, you don't need to search for it."

Kajaan stared at her for a minute in disbelief. She patiently waited as his brain slowly processed what she said. He'd been stunted on purpose. Lord Kende had been right. Cadeyrn had been right. Kajaan had just never thought about trying to talk to someone with an elemental Craft to learn how they invoked their abilities so quickly. He'd thought it had been him who was lacking and had wanted to hide away out of embarrassment.

"Oh Goddess," Kajaan whispered.

Rhionne nodded. "You see now. Who knows how strong you really are. Though I will say, if the goddess only unshackled you and filled your well and reservoir, you are going to be incredibly strong. Perhaps that's why your teacher or whomever hired him decided to stunt your growth. Perhaps he was scared of your potential. Right now, what I see with you is a boy only a few moonturns from his Awakening. You may quite possibly breeze through everything and find that once we get started, your reservoir will quickly expand.

"But you need to be prepared that we may never be able to see what you were supposed to be. The reservoir stops growing once you leave your teens. It's possible it's too late. It's possible you'll be somewhere in the middle, or that it'll take many years for your reservoir to be at where you should be now. Do you understand me?"

Kajaan did. "There's no guarantee what this will bring."

"Unfortunately, yes," Rhionne said. "I don't want you to be disappointed and think that training a few times with me will unlock the full potential of your Craft. Or get frustrated with yourself for not progressing quickly after a moonturn or two. This will take time, and you must be patient with yourself. Tamya can examine your Craft every week to see if your reservoir is expanding or not to give us an idea of what's happening. We will train every day, and after a moonturn, we will discuss the results with King Cadeyrn and see if we want to keep going."

"Okay. I'm good with that," Kajaan said.

Rhionne finally smiled at him, her eyes sparkling, and he caught a glimpse of what a beauty she'd been in her prime. He could see bits of Tamya in her face, mostly with the dimples and how much her ears lifted when she grinned, making her quite expressive. His teacher nodded and took a deep breath, making sure she was sitting properly.

"Now, how do you feel when you invoke your Craft?" Rhionne asked. "What physical changes occur?"

Physical changes? Kajaan looked at her, confused. Nothing about him changed when he invoked his Craft. He shrugged, feeling useless even after her reassurances. Between them, the water began to ripple and warp before a column stretched up toward the ceiling in a shimmering pillar. When it splashed back down into the bowl, not a drop escaped. Kajaan stared at her in surprise. She hadn't even blinked.

"Invoke your Craft. Move the water around in the bowl," Rhionne instructed.

Kajaan nodded. He closed his eyes briefly and dove deep into himself. He'd expelled the foreign Craft that had filled his well and reservoir in small spurts to help him clean off the foam from when he shaved, but past that, he hadn't really used it. Cadeyrn was right when he said that Kajaan lived as if he was a Void. His Craft had never been strong, so he never saw the point in using it for daily tasks.

It took him a bit longer than usual to remember how to invoke his Craft. He'd been so consumed with the children, he hadn't used it in a moonturn or so. As soon as he tapped into his well, his fingers began to tingle, and Kajaan gestured toward the bowl. It was a miniscule ripple that met his push, but it was there.

A small voice in the back of his mind whispered how pathetic he was. He was over thirty and yet still couldn't do much more than what he'd just done, whereas his teacher had made a column. Instead of offering him a scathing remark, Rhionne nodded as if she was satisfied by what she saw.

"Did anything feel different?" she asked. "Your hands specifically."

"Um. Yeah. My fingers tingle," Kajaan said.

"Good. That's the physical manifestation of your Craft affecting your body," Rhionne said. "I personally feel a bit of pressure between my eyes. It's not pleasant, but it is what it is. Now. Move the water in the bowl again, except don't search for your Craft."

"How?" Kajaan asked, staring at the water.

He pointed at it, but not even a hint of movement met his gesture. Rhionne smiled kindly at him, and Kajaan felt something between his shoulder blades relax. For once during his Craft training, Kajaan didn't feel belittled when he failed. Or that he was in danger of being hurt because he couldn't perform perfectly the first time.

Rhionne was subtly encouraging him to ask questions and to try and learn as much as he could. Giving him a safe place to fail in minor, insignificant ways, after trying to do what she requested. At the same time, she wasn't fully holding his hand, letting him try and figure out how to use his Craft first. Training with her was already worlds away from Torbid telling him to shut up and listen.

"Your fingers tingle. Think about that. Think about the sensation it creates, how your body reacts to the feel of the buzzing," Rhionne instructed.

Kajaan stared at the bowl of water. Instead of diving into himself, he thought about the soft tingling sensation in his hand as if he'd restricted the blood flow for a while. He remembered one summer when he and Yolotzin were still boys playing in the garden and he'd caught a bee in his hand. It had stung his palm, but not before he felt the beating of its wings against his skin….

Yolotzin had laughed at him, as boys do when their friend gets hurt in a non-life-threatening way. A small smile crossed Kajaan's lips at the memory. The sound of clapping startled him, and he jumped. He looked up at Rhionne before realizing that his fingers were actually tingling rather than him trying to think about it.

The water in the bowl had plenty of ripples in it now. He could feel the slow drain on his reservoir as he held his will to disrupt the water. Kajaan let it go, the tingling in his hand fading away, and the bowl stilled once more.

"What did you think about?" Rhionne asked.

Kajaan felt exhausted, looking at her. The light in the small window had dimmed. How long had he been trying to figure out his shortcut? A shortcut he should have been taught over half a lifetime ago. It didn't matter anymore. He could learn.

"Bees," Kajaan said. "Tzin and I caught one once, and it felt similar enough."

"Good," Rhionne praised him. "That association will help. Now, let's take a breather so you can rest and center yourself again."

Kajaan nodded, giving in to his exhaustion. He leaned forward onto his elbows, curling into himself a bit as he hung his head. After a few minutes, he heard his teacher's gentle encouragement to try again. Kajaan sat up straight and rolled his neck and shoulders before starting to concentrate. Someone knocked on the door. Rhionne clicked her tongue in frustration but nodded to Kajaan.

"Yes?" he called.

"Kajie, you've got a letter," Thaddaeus said meekly, poking his head into the small room.

"Can it wait?" Kajaan asked.

"It's from… um. Avi…. Avitou? I think that's how it's pronounced. Papa wants to know what it says," Thaddaeus said.

Rhionne sighed and waved her hand in approval. She got to her feet, heavily relying on her cane to do so. Kajaan quickly jumped to assist her, offering her his hand. She took it, her grip surprisingly strong. As soon as she was steady, the old woman smiled up at him, patting his hands.

"Then we'll pick this back up tomorrow," Rhionne said. "Don't let King Cadeyrn keep you up too late. You need proper rest between your lessons."

Kajaan flushed a deep red and stammered out a promise and his thanks as she left. Beside him, Thaddaeus looked confused, staring after her. He turned his innocent little face up at Kajaan, tilting his head.

"Why would Papa keep you up late? Does he have you working with Quillin on a project?" the boy asked. "Or are the tutors giving you problems again?"

The innocent questions made Kajaan blush harder. He cleared his throat and shook his head, avoiding the boy's gaze.

"Where's your dad?" Kajaan asked.

Thaddaeus smiled up at him and waved for him to follow. The boy took him up several flights of stairs to Cadeyrn's office but hesitated outside the closed door. Kajaan knocked and slipped inside once he got permission to enter.

Cadeyrn sat at his usual desk with his glasses on with Quillin standing behind him, pointing at some letter they were going over. His Fated looked exasperated, and his hair was mussed, as if he'd been repeatedly running his hand through it. Quillin just seemed tired.

"If Lord Neer—"

"If *Lord Neerian* thinks I'm going to help him out of the mess he created with his subjects, he's sorely mistaken," Cadeyrn interrupted. "I'm not going to give him funds that he should have so he can mismanage or hoard once again, and not actually help his people. Send a few blacksmiths, thatchers, and builders to Barian with soldiers to defend them. Maybe hire one of the better trained secretaries who isn't on assignment right now to help coordinate everything. Just because Neerian is an idiot doesn't mean his people have to suffer homelessness after the fires."

"I'll get the letters started," Quillin said. "Do you want to use journeymen or masters? I'm sure we've got plenty of journeymen available, and they could use the experience."

"One master in each field to oversee their work, I think, but I agree on using mostly journeymen. They'll do well with a master to check their work. The college will likely know of a good alumnus for a secretary. That position I want to send someone with good experience and temperament. Make sure you factor in pay for their skill levels as well. They should either be compensated for their time or have their expenses completely paid," Cadeyrn said.

"Or," Quillin said slowly, "Lord Neerian pays for all of their expenses. That way, he's held accountable, at least partially, for his negligence, and it's not all coming out of the royal coffers."

"Oh, I was thinking we could fine him to the moon and back for allowing the fire to even happen," Cadeyrn said in a dangerous growl. "There should have been no reason at all that Ignians and Aquans couldn't have gotten to that first fire in time to put it out before it got too big. He blatantly ignored our safety regulations we sent out earlier this year and almost got people killed. Thank the goddess everyone got out in time, but some memorabilia can't be replaced, and those people are now homeless."

"Make him pay for the rebuilding and compensate those whose homes were lost along with the ones that have to take off of work because of the fires," Kajaan suggested. "They shouldn't have to pay to rebuild their homes because of another's neglect. That way those families aren't at risk of poverty, are able to eat, and hopefully find adequate shelter. If not renting a place, then staying at an inn. Better than being on the streets."

Quillin hummed. "A few businesses were burned down as well. Many of those who were evacuated are out of jobs."

"So he pays their salaries until the businesses are back up and running after incorporating the new safety standards so this doesn't happen again. The victims' jobs should be secured and their wages guaranteed since they weren't the ones responsible for the fire," Kajaan added.

"That is going to be one steep price," Cadeyrn observed.

"Like you said, he was neglectful," Quillin replied, sniffing.

Kajaan had never seen his Fated's secretary ruffled before. Sure, he'd lost his temper with that Aquan teacher, but this was a man on a mission to make someone pay for endangering lives. The stark difference, including Quillin's placid mask, made Kajaan wonder how dangerous an enemy he could be. Maybe Quillin just got really frustrated when something was mismanaged so horribly wrong.

The secretary snatched up the map from Cadeyrn's desk, nearly crumpling it, and a thick stack of blank paper before he huffed and flopped into his chair. He dipped his pen in ink and began writing furiously. Kajaan raised an eyebrow at his Fated, who simply gave him a slight, yet tight, smile.

While Quillin scratched out his first letter, Cadeyrn rang the small bell that was installed in the wall. They waited only a few seconds before a young page came running into the room. He gave the king a proper bow, his eyes flicking over to Kajaan curiously. Kajaan hadn't met many of the younger secretarial staff. Mostly because the boys and girls were always running from one end of the castle to the other before going home after their short shifts.

"Quillin will have some letters for you in a moment. They need to be delivered as fast as you can," Cadeyrn said to the boy. "Then let your supervisor know that you're going to take the rest of the day off. If he has any concerns, he can talk to me."

The boy nodded, and he hovered next to Quillin's desk. He didn't seem anxious, silently standing there with his hands folded behind his back. Only the slight scuffling of one foot betrayed his impatience to complete his task. Cadeyrn sat back in his chair and removed his glasses. He pinched the bridge of his nose for a moment before actually smiling up at Kajaan.

"The two of you together will be frightening," Cadeyrn said.

"Why do you think that?" Kajaan asked.

Cadeyrn simply grinned at him, and Kajaan found himself unable to stop from returning his Fated's smile. The king looked positively gleeful, his eyes sparkling as he regarded him.

"You formed a plan together within minutes on how to settle this issue," Cadeyrn replied. "If Thaddaeus can learn from you, he'll be a formidable king indeed."

"Don't discount yourself, Majesty," Quillin said, handing a sealed letter to the page and waving him off. The study door slammed behind the boy in his exuberance. He sat back and grabbed another letter from a drawer in his desk, then handed that one to Kajaan. "This arrived today with our western merchant caravan."

Kajaan approached and looked down at the letter. It was postmarked as being from Avitou castle, but the handwriting wasn't Yolotzin's. He frowned as he took the letter from Quillin, tilting his head slightly, trying to place the penmanship. Cadeyrn's arm slid around his waist, and Kajaan found himself being pulled onto the man's lap.

The king really was insatiable when it came to physical affection. If he was nearby, Cadeyrn had to be touching him, regardless of who was around them. Kajaan really didn't mind. In fact, he thoroughly enjoyed having his Fated manhandle him. Yolotzin was slightly taller than him, but he had more of a runner's build, whereas Cadeyrn was bulkier, nearly a half foot taller, and had combat training. Moving around a smaller, thinner man was probably child's play for him.

Not that Kajaan really resisted him.

"Lord Kende wrote this," Kajaan said, finally realizing why the handwriting was vaguely familiar. Siora tended to write a lot of his outside correspondence. He had addressed a few personal letters to Yolotzin himself, but anything official went through his secretary. "Tzin might have given him some information he overheard."

"Why isn't it from the prince, then?" Quillin asked.

"So that it wasn't intercepted," Kajaan replied and sighed. "I'm sure King Tonalli is watching Tzin like a hawk and isn't letting him send any letters without them being opened and read first. If he knew Tzin was writing to me, it could put him in danger."

"You think he'd hurt his own son?" Cadeyrn asked, sounding startled. "His heir?"

"I wouldn't put it past him," Kajaan said. "Tzin is mostly blind to the king's darker side. But he could poison Tzin so he was bedbound for a while, effectively stopping him from sending out intelligence. Or have him visit another kingdom for one reason or another."

Cadeyrn nodded and tapped the envelope, clearly getting impatient. Kajaan looked at the seal and got confirmation that the letter had indeed come from Lord Kende's household. The wax was a soft blue and had the Enchanted Waters stamp instead of the Ruvyn crest.

So Lord Asyl had touched this as well. Kajaan frowned, wondering why the note had changed so many hands, risking it getting lost. Perhaps Yolotzin had given his letter to Lord Asyl, and he'd sealed it before handing it off to his husband. Or had he secreted it to Lady Naias, who sealed the letter and handed it to Lord Asyl to give to Lord Kende so he could post it?

Why would Yolotzin go through so much trouble? Why wouldn't he just seal the letter himself and give it to Lord Kende to send off? Was the situation at the castle that dire? Was the prince really that heavily watched right now? The implications worried him a little bit, and Kajaan felt a curl of unease rise inside of him. Cadeyrn hugged him a little tighter, sensing his worry.

Taking in a deep breath, Kajaan broke the seal and pulled out the letter. The page had once been folded over and over again, heavily creasing the edges. Tracing the lines, Kajaan deduced that the letter had once been folded into a small square. It had been subterfuge, then. Carefully hidden from King Tonalli and changing several hands to get out safely.

The letter itself was filled with what appeared to be random clusters of numbers, periods, and hash marks in a varying pattern. The unease multiplied, and Kajaan immediately began chewing on his lower lip. To go through so much perceived trouble to send this to him? Having the envelope passing through so many hands had been a carefully calculated move. Letting Kajaan know who was safe to write to? He didn't know.

Behind him, Cadeyrn grunted and reached for his glasses. He put them on and looked over Kajaan's shoulder again, resting his chin on his Fated's head. Kajaan couldn't stop the small smile, even as he leaned back into the man's warmth despite his growing unease.

"What is this?" he asked.

"A cipher," Kajaan said. "This could be bad."

Kajaan set the paper on Cadeyrn's desk and wiggled off his lap. Before he could run out of the study, the king cleared his throat and Kajaan paused at the threshold.

"If I could, may I borrow your promise ring as well? I promise I'll return it," Cadeyrn said.

Confused, Kajaan stared at him for a long moment. Quillin looked between them, frowning slightly. What was he talking about? He didn't have a promise ring. The only ring he'd ever been given was.... Kajaan bristled slightly. Cadeyrn wanted him to hand over Yolotzin's faux wedding ring? But. It really was worthless. Not just in value, but in what it represented as well.

Kajaan slowly nodded, not quite sure why his Fated wanted the reminder that he'd promised his entire life to another man. He'd probably figure it out later. Right now, he needed one of his novels. With any luck, Yolotzin had packed their decoding book along with all of his other novels. He knew that his best friend had had a hand in sending him his effects, so theoretically the book should be somewhere on his shelves.

He hadn't paid much attention when he'd emptied the trunks, in all honesty. Since Cadeyrn had been talking to him while he had been unpacking his romance novels, he hadn't really looked at what Yolotzin had sent him. In hindsight, he really should have made sure that he'd had his decoder. Of course Yolotzin would send him ciphers at some point. They might not all be so dire. Some might be sent with a playful intent. But not now. Not this one, while King Tonalli was on the warpath.

He flew down the steps to his quarters, startling one of the guards who'd been ascending the staircase. Kajaan managed to keep his feet under him as he reached his door, and he burst inside, making his way to the bookcase a Gaian builder had installed for him a few days after his arrival. Kajaan ran his finger over the spines, not exactly looking at the title names but rather the wear on the spine, and grabbed the book he needed.

Fields of Gold. It was an old pastoral romance and quite battered from use. Kajaan had paid for it to be rebound a couple of times already, but the binding always wore down quickly. He would never replace the book for a different copy. This specific one was far too important.

As Kajaan turned to leave, he detoured to his dresser. He dug into the lowest drawer that held his Averian clothes and fetched the bag that held the napkin ring. Taking a moment, Kajaan opened the bag and dumped the small, tarnished ring into the palm of his hand.

It had seemed so much bigger when he'd been a boy. His father had been furious when Kajaan refused to remove the ring week after week until it had to be cut off by a Healer and Gaian when it started digging into his skin. A small smile graced his face as he tucked the ring back into its bag and got to his feet.

He got back to the office in record time, shut the door behind him, and locked it. Whatever this cipher said, it was probably serious and couldn't leave the room. It would be safest, just in case there were any Averian spies that could report to the king. King Tonalli was probably waiting for Yolotzin to try to send Kajaan information. No need to confirm the man's paranoia.

Hesitating slightly, Kajaan held out the small bag to Cadeyrn. The man carefully took the ring from his trembling hand. He wrapped his hand around Kajaan's fingers and drew him in close enough that he could kiss the back of his hand. The seriousness of his expression told Kajaan that Cadeyrn knew how hard it had been to hand over his prized possession.

Even if it really was a worthless, bent piece of cheap metal.

The acknowledgment warmed his chest, and Kajaan plopped back down on Cadeyrn's lap. Without bothering to ask, he grabbed a fresh piece of paper and the man's ink pen. Kajaan placed the blank page over the cipher so only the first row of markings showed. This handwriting was definitely Yolotzin's. Kajaan could tell by how he wrote his numbers.

"What does a romance novel have to do with anything?" Quillin asked.

Kajaan looked at the first combination and flashed a small smile up at the secretary. "Page number, paragraph, word. It only works with this book. Tzin and I both have this exact copy."

"It's falling apart," Cadeyrn observed.

"Yeah, I should get it rebound again," Kajaan replied absently.

He was already flipping through the book and counting, writing down the word associated with each combination exactly how it appeared in the novel. It was slow going and tedious. He was definitely out of practice. Back when he and Yolotzin passed letters to each other constantly, there were a few combinations he knew by heart. Now he had to search for every word Yolotzin wrote down. They hadn't written a cipher to each other in moonturns. Not since Lady Naias came into their lives. Had she helped create this?

"Or purchase a new one," Quillin said.

Kajaan shook his head. "A newer edition might have revisions. A page might be off, or a paragraph. Even changing a word can mess the cipher up. Something that small might be easily fixed, but if the pages were wrong? It wouldn't be the same message at all. We've had the most success with this book, and believe me, we ran through so many books trying to find the best one."

"You two were very busy boys," Cadeyrn said.

Kajaan snorted. "We were bored. Tzin's smart, so he went through his lessons quickly, and I was often dismissed as being stupid."

"Their loss," Quillin snipped. "I've never seen a more competent secretary from another country."

Blushing, Kajaan bent his head, locating the correct pages and counting. There were a few times he had to pause and not only decipher the word Yolotzin wanted, but the prince's handwriting too. His best friend's hand must have been shaking when he wrote the cipher. The numbers weren't as neat as Kajaan knew Yolotzin's handwriting was.

Either he was scared or had to write his code fast. The pages did tend to stick toward the front of the book, so Kajaan was willing to bet it was probably a combination of both. As the message was decoded, Kajaan's stomach began to hurt. His Fated held him, reaching out to hold down the pages to keep them still and flat while Kajaan worked. Kajaan was grateful for his help and that he seemed to know that to do or offer assistance more would probably end up hindering him.

Finally finished, Kajaan set down the pen he stole from Cadeyrn and sat back, biting his lower lip. His Fated reached out and tilted the page up slightly to read from it.

"Father furious focus King Cows send many eyes desperate gold watch back King Cows children not safe Another Keep Never mount secure send tavern love," Cadeyrn read. He set the paper back on his desk and gave Kajaan a wary look. "Should I be insulted by him calling me King Cows?"

Kajaan snickered. "No. Punctuation is incredibly important when it comes to our cipher which is another reason I can't get a different edition. We never add any articles or punctuation since that would just make the cipher more complicated. Only the first letter matters with words that are capitalized like with Cows, Another, Keep, and Never."

"They're names," Quillin said, sounding awed.

"Exactly," Kajaan replied, nodding. He took the pen and struck out the remaining letters of the capitalized words, leaving just the "C", "A", "K", and "N" remaining. Kajaan slid up the paper and began writing the real message. "Father is furious. He's focusing on King Cadeyrn. Sending spies…."

"Is that the desperate gold part?" Cadeyrn asked.

Kajaan shook his head. "No. If it was just about spies, he wouldn't have included that."

"Desperate gold," Quillin said slowly, frowning.

"Bandits," Cadeyrn said, looking at them. "They're always looking for coin to try and scrape out a living."

"Not bandits. Mercenaries," Quillin said. "They're usually more subtle, and depending on the person, they'll probably do anything for gold. I wouldn't trust a bandit or highwayman for anything delicate like this. Not after they failed to kill Kajaan the first time."

"Mercenaries make sense," Kajaan said. He wrote that down and continued. "Sending spies and mercenaries. Watch your back. King Cadeyrn and his children aren't safe. Asyl, Kende, Naias, and Hariam are secure… or safe. Send tavern…." He trailed off, frowning at the phrase.

Quillin hummed. "Do you two have a bar you go to often?" he asked.

Kajaan shook his head. "That wouldn't be very safe to send letters through anyways."

"The letter was sent with the merchant caravan, not a courier. He didn't want it to be given much notice at all," Cadeyrn said.

"You said Lord Kende addressed the envelope," Quillin said.

Kajaan blinked and crowed in delight. "Of course!"

He grabbed the envelope and flipped it over, showing the seal from Enchanted Waters, and tapped it twice.

"Taverns serve drinks," Kajaan said.

"Wasn't Lord Asyl an alchemist?" Cadeyrn asked.

"Yes. He has a potion shop called Enchanted Waters that is his pride and joy. He and Lady Naias ran it together until she met Tzin and stepped away. If we send any letters there, he'll give them to Lord Kende or Lady Naias, who will get it to Tzin. It's perfect. The castle staff will never be involved. Especially since Lord Kende is planning Tzin's and Lady Naias's wedding. It wouldn't be too suspicious that he'd be summoned to Lord Kende's place fairly frequently or if Lord Kende suddenly showed up to visit Tzin," Kajaan said.

Father is furious. He's focusing on King Cadeyrn. Sending spies and mercenaries. Watch your back. King Cadeyrn and his children aren't safe. Asyl, Kende, Naias, and Hariam are safe. Send any letters to Enchanted Waters. Love, Yolotzin.

Kajaan stared down at the letter and felt his heart ache. This was all his fault. If he'd died, then everything would be all right. Maybe Yolotzin would have been placated by Lady Naias and he wouldn't seek revenge for his death. At least if he did, Kajaan wouldn't be around to see it. But just the thought of putting Prince Thaddaeus, Princess Marika, or the twins in danger made his stomach churn.

"Don't," Cadeyrn said, shifting slightly and pulling Kajaan sideways onto his lap. "It's not your fault."

"If I'd died—"

"Then Tonalli would have figured something else out," Cadeyrn said firmly.

"He's right," Quillin replied. "This ultimately isn't about you. It's whatever King Tonalli has going on in his head, and the perceived slights over the years from Cade rejecting him. Your death would have been an excuse. A means to the end. Being here, alive and able to pass information to the prince will keep us all safe. It's the best insult you can give him."

"What if the letter came too late and the mercs are already close?" Kajaan asked. "You said it yourselves. It came with a merchant caravan, not a courier. Who knows how long it actually took to get here? We don't date these on purpose, so I have no idea when he wrote this. Maybe he wrote it and was delayed in giving it to Lord Asyl or Lady Naias."

"Then we'll do what we can. What matters is that we have been forewarned," Cadeyrn said gently, rubbing his back.

"I can increase security at the Averia–Zothua border to make sure no one without any real purpose to be in our country gets in for a while. We can do the same for Sestella. Only citizens will be allowed in or out without question. Anyone else needs to have a work statement. Then only authorized citizens with a verified letter can come inside Paelfjord," Quillin listed out.

"What about the Healers wing?" Kajaan asked. "Don't citizens use it sometimes without advance warning if it's life-threatening?"

"We can have escorts for the more severe cases," Cadeyrn suggested. "I don't want to put any of my people at risk."

Quillin nodded. "We can bar the door between the Healer's wing and the rest of the castle and post a guard there as well to secure it. We'll move Tamya to a temporary room inside so she'll be able to quickly respond to any injuries. I can also reach out to the desert branch of our military and request a rotating troop of experienced gexena riders to patrol the dunes. That way, if any mercs try to go the long way around, they'll be stopped."

"Good," Cadeyrn said, relaxing back in his chair.

"Do you think any of your staff can be bribed?" Kajaan asked hesitantly.

Cadeyrn scowled, though he didn't seem pissed at his question and gave it the consideration it deserved. He tilted his head back against his chair, staring up at the ceiling, concentrating. It took him a long while before he slowly shook his head.

"I can't think of anyone obvious who could be targeted," Cadeyrn said, looking at Quillin.

"Me neither. However, I can check everyone who works here and their finances or reach out with my Craft to see if I can sense any guilt, stress, or sudden relief," Quillin offered. "I'll get Ameyalli to help. Maybe they'll have a vision or some way to help guide us."

"Good. Kajaan, do you think the prince would want a confirmation letter that you understood everything?" Cadeyrn asked.

"Probably," Kajaan said and slowly smiled. "I'll tell him King Cows is aware of the dangers and has upped security."

Cadeyrn growled at the nickname. "I'm not a cow."

"No," Kajaan all but purred at him. "That you are not."

"I'd much rather be called King Bull," Cadeyrn said, hugging Kajaan to him and nuzzling into his neck.

Kajaan just laughed. "How about King Stallion? That way there's at least the implication that I can ride you."

Quillin burst out laughing as Cadeyrn's face heated against his skin. Oh, he got the king to blush, did he? That he had to tell Yolotzin as soon as he could. Kajaan squirmed out of his Fated's lap, swiping his book off of the desk, and darted to the door. He opened it, turned back to his Fated, and smiled as Cadeyrn grabbed both notes and burned them to ash. A new page slipped into the office since the door was open, approaching the laughing Quillin with a return letter.

"I'll draft up a letter and send it by dinnertime… King Cows," Kajaan said, switching to Averian.

He quickly spun on his heel and ran out of the office, grinning.

"Kaj!" Cadeyrn barked out after him.

Kajaan would have been worried if he hadn't heard the mirth in his Fated's tone, the amusement through their bond, and the roaring laughter of both the king and his secretary echoing down the hall.

Chapter 15

CADEYRN WAS going to lose his mind if he didn't do something soon. Just knowing that Tonalli was plotting something against him was putting him on edge. It didn't matter that Quillin thought he was worrying needlessly after their added security measures or that Ameyalli basically told him the same thing. Both he and Kajaan were taking the letter seriously and making sure that the castle and kids were safe.

That was the nice bit in all of the madness. Kajaan truly did love the children and would verbally take on Wayra to make sure they were secure at all hours of the day. Already once, Kajaan had pinned the captain with his steely gaze and demanded that the man go through all the guards in the castle and check on their vulnerability to bribery after being brushed off.

Kajaan would be a wonderful second father to the kids once they sealed their bond.

Cadeyrn wondered when he should talk to his kids and tell them about Kajaan being his Fated, and that he'd eventually marry him. Sooner than later, too, considering their status in society. Ever since Kajaan had translated the cipher last week, they started to sleep in the same bed, Kajaan curled up in Cadeyrn's arms, which was technically improper during their courting.

His valet, Inti, hadn't said a word in the mornings when he came in to help Cadeyrn get prepared for the day. If anything, he snuck off to Kajaan's rooms first to get him a change of clothes and at least laid those out for the sleepy redhead. Kajaan was too embarrassed to actually have a valet help put himself together, even if he was half asleep when he first got up.

Having the easy support and acceptance of pretty much everyone in the castle had surprised Cadeyrn. Fated pairings were always respected since they were the embodiment of the goddess's will, but that didn't mean they had to be accepted. No one questioned his sudden interest in a man, the fact that Kajaan was a foreigner, or that he'd been held prisoner for nearly a fortnight at first.

Instead, there were rumors flying around Sestella that Cadeyrn had finally found his Fated. Rumors that were happily confirmed by staff or their families who lived in the city. Cadeyrn was getting letters by the day from citizens who were thrilled for their king, congratulating him and wondering when they'd get to meet Kajaan, their future Quenlet. He was even starting to get letters from the farther cities as the news traveled.

Rhionne was the likeliest culprit of who started the rumors. Cadeyrn was pleased that the old woman was who Kajaan chose out of the ones who had responded to his query. She'd trained many young Aquans, specializing in those who struggled with their Craft or needed extra coaching. Her patience was nearly legendary, and she was grateful for the opportunity to be closer to her grandchild.

Granted, from what he heard, Kajaan hadn't exactly been the one to pick her. Rhionne had pretty much picked herself with her insight of Kajaan's problems after he'd rejected the other three. He suspected Rhionne's calm composure and matronly charm went a long way. Cadeyrn wondered, outside of Queen Brekka, if Kajaan had had any older women he'd been able to count on as a boy.

While Cadeyrn hadn't expected a sudden leap of ability, knowing that Kajaan still struggled with his speed and effectiveness was worrisome. He knew that it might be too late, but he'd finally found a way to try and heed Ameyalli's warning that Kajaan's Craft would be vital soon. Hopefully this training didn't break Kajaan's confidence in his Craft and he swore off using it forever.

Kajaan did smile at him every time they retired for the night, even if he was exhausted. Cadeyrn looked forward to that soft, unguarded smile every night. There was always a teaser at the dinner table as Kajaan interacted with the children and other head staff members. His Fated's happiness was a drug, and he thanked the goddess every night Kajaan came to him after the children retired.

Kajaan felt so good in his arms.

It was a bit odd, Cadeyrn would easily admit, though only to himself. Instead of soft curves and silky breasts, Kajaan had firm angles and a flat chest. There was also the matter of what hung between his legs. Of course, Cadeyrn knew damn well how to use his own equipment by himself or with a woman and could probably fumble his way through pleasing his Fated. But he knew there was more, and he wanted to know and be prepared.

Cadeyrn had finally decided to take care of his ignorance and read the book Ameyalli gifted him one evening. To his surprise, it was the same book that decoded Kajaan and Yolotzin's cipher. *Fields of Gold*. The cover was completely different, and the writing was in Zothuan, not Averian. Maybe they'd sensed the book was important to them, but not why.

Hadn't Ameyalli said this featured two men?

His doubts were completely cleared a third of the way through the book. Cadeyrn couldn't help getting sucked into the characters, though he'd disliked one of them initially. He'd been a spoiled gentry brat who'd upended his life and acted better than the villagers who were helping him, and Cadeyrn wanted to smack him a few times for being purposely contrary or rude. That was until he realized where the book was going between the two antagonists. Cadeyrn flushed as the rough and almost violent actions became more and more explicit, painting quite the lurid image in his mind.

That was where he was expected to stick his cock?

Cadeyrn hadn't really cared to compare the size of his manhood to other men, but he seemed a bit thick for what the book was suggesting. A woman's body was at least… made to accommodate such an invasion, preparing itself during foreplay. He highly doubted a man's body had the same response, on account of never feeling anything different in his backside during his romps with Menea.

But to just stick it in with only spit? Wouldn't that hurt? Tear? He had more questions than answers now. With a heavy flush, Cadeyrn had called for Quillin and asked the man to go grab one of the guards, even if he wasn't on duty. With any luck, the man would help answer his questions without too much teasing or embarrassment.

Simthe had a male Fated, and the two of them were fairly active, from what he'd heard from the servants' gossip as they giggled over how vocal the couple got. Clearly they enjoyed their intimate time together, so the book had to have *something* right. Quillin brought Simthe to him, all smiles, and closed Cadeyrn's reception door.

"Can I guarantee your complete discretion?" Cadeyrn asked.

Simthe seemed a little confused, yet he nodded. "Of course, my liege. Is everything all right?"

"I… I would like to know if this author is accurate," Cadeyrn blurted out.

Without thinking about it too much, Cadeyrn shoved the book at Simthe, trying to not blush too badly. He'd bookmarked the pages he wanted the guard to look over so the man didn't have to guess. As he watched the blond open to the right section, Cadeyrn easily caught the small, sharp inhale and slight widening to his eyes. A dark red blush rose on Simthe's cheeks, but he winced at one of the passages.

He cleared his throat and glanced up at the king. "Yes, but no. A scene like this where there's minimal prep and rough handling… could be fine with my Fated and I, as we regularly have sex. But it's probably been quite a while for Kajaan, so I wouldn't recommend it."

"So what—"

"Preparation and slick," Simthe interrupted. He smiled faintly. "Why not ask Kajaan to guide you through it?"

Cadeyrn stared down at the novel and sighed softly. "I wanted to know what I was doing before we went any further."

Simthe's smile turned fonder, and he handed Cadeyrn the book. The king gave him a weak smile in return, running his thumb over the cover as he held the book hard enough that his knuckles were starting to whiten.

"He might enjoy teaching his Fated," Simthe suggested, shrugging. "You should sit with him and talk about it and what he likes and expects. There's no shame in not knowing, and such a conversation might be a nice intimate moment."

"I don't want to hurt him," Cadeyrn admitted.

"You won't. He knows what he's doing," Simthe assured him.

Cadeyrn cleared his throat, unable to lift his eyes from the novel. "Is it really that enjoyable?"

"Oh goddess, yes," Simthe said and grinned, though his cheeks were still a deep red. "I can get you some slick if you don't want to put in a request through Quillin. You'll definitely need that. It'll make it a lot more comfortable for Kajaan."

It took Cadeyrn a moment for him to realize that Simthe assumed he was going to dominate Kajaan. He'd had the same assumptions as well. But what if Kajaan wanted to be on top? The thought made Cadeyrn freeze and stare unseeingly at the front cover of the novel for quite a while. Simthe just stood quietly, waiting for Cadeyrn to figure out that if it made Kajaan happy… he'd try it.

"Um. Another question. Or two, I think," Cadeyrn said.

"Of course," Simthe replied, a ghost of a smile on his lips.

"Kajaan was teased about wanting to be mounted, and he made a comment about wanting to ride me," Cadeyrn said slowly.

Simthe snorted and started laughing. He quickly covered his mouth and shot Cadeyrn an apologetic look when the king glared at him. It wasn't as if Cadeyrn could blame his amusement. This was a little bit of an unreal situation for the guard. It seemed like a conversation like this would be better versed in one of Kajaan's romance books, not real life.

"Sorry, sorry. I don't know what kinks Kajaan likes, but that probably means that he likes to… receive," Simthe explained. "Him riding you would give him control of how quickly he's penetrated, so that could be a good position for your first time together."

Cadeyrn briefly wondered how red his face was, but his cheeks definitely felt like they were on fire. He hadn't been so nervous before bedding Menea for the first time on their wedding night, and he'd been a virgin then. Waiting until marriage, or meeting his Fated, had been a romantic idea he held on to. In reality, he wished he'd played around a bit more just so he knew what to do so that he didn't fail his Fated.

A knock at the door stifled Simthe's snickering, and Quillin stepped inside a moment later. Cadeyrn wasn't sure if he was grateful for his secretary's intrusion or not at the moment. Said secretary looked amused and perhaps slightly contrite.

"Kajaan has informed me to tell you to stop doing whatever it is you're doing since you're interrupting his sessions with Rhionne by making him flustered and unable to concentrate on anything other than carnal pleasures," Quillin relayed, grinning.

Simthe didn't bother holding back his laughter this time. Even Cadeyrn managed to chuckle, though he still felt a little mortified. At least he knew who he could ask for advice when it came to pleasuring his Fated. Even if he was twenty years younger than him.

Some kids got lucky finding their Fated, running into them as teenagers or young adults. Simthe was one of them. He'd married his best friend at eighteen, once they realized they were Fated rather than just instinctively knowing each other's moods really well and refusing to seek out other dates. Their bond had strengthened slightly over the years, from what he knew, but the boys' connection was still weak, and they could rarely track where the other was. Which was much weaker than what Cadeyrn had with Kajaan now, even while unsealed.

Cadeyrn waved the two of them out of his room, hid the book amongst the clutter on his dresser, and took a few minutes of slow, steady breathing to calm himself. Automatically, he tapped into the bond he shared with Kajaan. His poor Fated was getting frustrated with himself over his sessions, and he doubted that accidentally pushing a lot of his unease, embarrassment, and arousal onto Kajaan had helped.

So far, there hadn't been much improvement, and Kajaan was trying to not let it get to him. It was getting harder after each lesson when he felt like he wasn't understanding his Craft. Kajaan could still barely make a wave in the bowl Rhionne was using to teach him. Even his teacher seemed a bit perplexed as to why Kajaan was barely improving and struggling with the basics.

Yesterday, Kajaan had walked directly into Cadeyrn's study after his lesson and crawled into his lap, tucking his face into Cadeyrn's neck. Kajaan hadn't seemed to care that he was in a meeting with Quillin and Ameyalli. His Fated had just needed him and took it with both hands.

At that moment, Cadeyrn hadn't cared about what he'd been doing with his secretary and advisor. He'd clutched his Fated close to him, pressing his face into Kajaan's red hair, and tried to whisper reassurances to his man that he'd have a breakthrough with his Craft soon. Kajaan's mood hadn't improved much since then, and Cadeyrn was starting to get more and more on edge, affected by his Fated's mood bleeding through their bond.

Maybe they both needed a break. Some time together. Alone.

His commission should be coming back later today. Cadeyrn perked up at the thought. Yes, a picnic could be just what they both needed. Cadeyrn waited, a little impatiently, before he sought out Rhionne the moment their lesson was over. Kajaan gave him a quick kiss and muttered something about needing a nap before having to deal with Thaddaeus's tutors adding more classes and adjusting the boy's schedule *again*.

"I'd like to take him out for a day trip tomorrow," Cadeyrn told her.

Rhionne hummed. "Some time away, I think, will help. He's worried about too many things, and perhaps having some one-on-one time with you will help stimulate his Craft. I think what he did before he arrived here has colored a lot of our expectations of what Kajaan can do. He needs to not worry about what we think or expect and just listen to his Craft."

"He's oddly self-conscious," Cadeyrn confirmed, frowning.

"So make sure he understands that he's fine the way he is," Rhionne said.

As if it was that easy.

Still, Cadeyrn nodded and went to the kitchens to let them know of his picnic plans. He spent the rest of the day setting up his outing with the rest of the castle. They needed to know where he was if there was an emergency since they were still under threat, though his request for privacy would be granted. Especially since he was going to be out with his Fated. None of his staff would want to interrupt their bonding time.

It took a few hours to convince Wayra before he reluctantly agreed to keep patrols around the oasis that Cadeyrn was planning on taking his Fated to, far enough away that they'd be out of sight. He wasn't entirely happy about having Cadeyrn almost completely unprotected, just in case. The fact that Cadeyrn was proficient with not only his Craft but a sword did little to ease the man's anxiety.

If the worst would happen, Cadeyrn could always get Kajaan on Maeeri's back and send her back to the castle to try and get help in time. She wouldn't like to leave him alone, preferring to fight beside him instead, but she might understand the importance of keeping Kajaan safe. As long as he could stay on her back during a full gallop.

To his knowledge, Kajaan hadn't been on the back of a gexena yet. Cadeyrn couldn't wait to get him mounted on Maeeri so he could understand the power behind Zothua's pride and joy. There was one hell of a difference between riding a horse and riding a gexena. Though he was fairly impressed with Kajaan riding a horse bareback while seriously injured and panicked.

Every time he saw the scars on Kajaan's arm and his back, Cadeyrn had to fight back a wave of anger and remind himself that the minor blemishes were a small price to pay to have the man in his life. He doubted he'd ever be able to forgive Tonalli for his harebrained plot to kill Kajaan. At least he arrived in time, just barely, but he had. Now he just had to keep his Fated safe and alive until Tonalli stepped down… or died.

CHAPTER 16

IN THE morning, just before dawn, Inti got them both outfitted in practical riding clothes rather than a casual palace outfit. They were heavier and warmer than what they wore every day, and while Kajaan seemed confused at the selection, and that Inti was choosing his clothing, he didn't ask. Once they were properly robed in several layers, along with protective headgear, Inti bowed and retreated into his own room.

Cadeyrn took Kajaan's hand and led him down the quiet hallway. His kids were still asleep, their doors closed and guards posted nearby. As much as he was going to miss Fayette and Rodolfo jumping on their bed to wake them for the day, the silence was nice. It was fun to be sneaking out with his Fated and almost felt illicit. Maybe they could make this a regular getaway, if Kajaan liked the oasis.

They detoured to the kitchen to have the cook give him and Kajaan a breakfast wrap loaded with eggs, bacon, onion, and small cubes of bell peppers. Cadeyrn encouraged Kajaan to eat it as they walked to the stables. The sun was just starting to peek over the Laiyi Desert, catching the shifting sands and making it sparkle and shine as if it were a sea of gold.

Kajaan's breath caught at the sight, and for the first time in a long while, Cadeyrn stopped and appreciated the desert's beauty. The effect was diminished by the stained-glass windows that were built into Paelfjord Castle, so it was likely that Kajaan had never seen the desert reacting to the rising sun. Cadeyrn didn't mind taking a few minutes to enjoy the shimmering sands.

Once the sun rose higher, Cadeyrn gently tugged on Kajaan's hand to lead him on. If they stayed much later, they ran the risk of the kids catching them. The last thing he wanted was a tearful Fayette not understanding why she couldn't come and Rodolfo pouting for the rest of the day. Maybe that was selfish of him, but if they could get away before the kids woke, there'd be less fallout on their return.

Maeeri was already harnessed and saddled by the time Cadeyrn got to the stables. Kajaan had balked at the wide doors, and getting him to actually head inside took some coaxing. The man didn't seem to trust gexenas for some reason, shying away from the occupied stalls. He'd have to figure out Kajaan's aversion if he was going to try and gift his Fated with a colt or filly.

The stablemaster had put Maeeri in her crossties, and Cadeyrn let his Fated's hand go as he approached her. The gexena nosed his chest, snorting when she didn't immediately find any treats. He'd made sure that the cook had packed a few apples into their picnic for her. Rubbing her ears, next to her horns, Cadeyrn gestured for Kajaan to approach.

His Fated kept a wary eye on Maeeri as he came up to stand next to Cadeyrn. Taking the redhead's hand in his, he held it up for the gexena to scent. The beast snuffled a few times and bumped Kajaan's hand with her nose, accepting his presence. She likely would refuse if Kajaan tried riding her without Cadeyrn for a few moonturns, but she would be fine for their little trips.

He led Kajaan around to the mounting block the stableboy had left to one side and instructed Kajaan how to get into the saddle. It took a couple of tries, since Kajaan was unfamiliar with the extra set of legs and additional height. Even with the mounting block, he still needed to brace his foot in the stirrup and swing his leg over, using the saddle and Cadeyrn's strength to make it.

Maeeri simply stood placidly, tilting her head so she could watch, her tail swishing. Finally Kajaan got himself seated, wiggling his hips slightly to get comfortable, and Cadeyrn smiled. While riding gexenas weren't a lot like horses, the basic principle was the same. Kajaan nearly had the perfect posture, and he'd balance just fine without Cadeyrn riding with him.

As if he'd let Kajaan ride Maeeri alone anyway. She certainly wouldn't allow it at any rate, and she'd do her best to throw Kajaan. Cadeyrn swung up into the saddle behind Kajaan and scooted close to his Fated, wrapping his arm around him to hold him close. He pointed out where Kajaan should rest his feet while the stablemaster approached from the side door and released Maeeri from the crossties.

The first few steps she took, Kajaan grabbed at the arm Cadeyrn had around his waist, leaning heavier against him. Maeeri really didn't need reins for him to guide her, but he wasn't sure if directing her without them would unsettle Kajaan. So instead, he held her reins loosely in one hand, though he still directed her with his knees.

He nuzzled into Kajaan's hair and placed a kiss on his temple, trying to let him know he was perfectly safe without speaking. It must have reassured his Fated, as Kajaan slowly relaxed and nestled into him. They carefully plodded out of the stables and away from Paelfjord's gardens and the awakening morning staff.

Cadeyrn clicked his tongue, urging Maeeri to pick up the pace, and she snorted, tossing her head. She was eager to run, but she was too well trained to break into a gallop immediately. Not until they got far enough away from the castle for it to be safe. They'd had one too many close calls with eager gexenas and staff. She sped up into a canter, her body thrumming underneath them.

That was when he heard Kajaan's surprised hum. Maeeri had one of the smoothest gaits out of all the gexenas they'd bred. Riding her was almost like sitting on a chair on solid ground. He wasn't quite sure how her gait was so even despite having chosen her lineage himself. Maeeri certainly didn't inherit it from her sire or dam. Either way, her even gait took the last of Kajaan's wariness away.

They weren't going to go too far, only a couple of hours, and Cadeyrn coaxed Maeeri into a gallop. She set a steady, ground-eating pace, tossing her head in pure joy and prancing when she could from sheer excitement. He really needed to take her out more. He'd been too focused on everything going on inside the castle and trying to win Kajaan's trust to give her the attention she needed.

But now he'd done his homework, Simthe had slipped him a small bottle of a specific lubricant called slick, and they were alone. They could practice consummating their bond while at the oasis. Well, if Kajaan wanted to mess around some. Cadeyrn wasn't going to pressure him, no matter how badly he wanted to explore his Fated's body and how eagerly Kajaan seemed to respond to his touch.

He craved the forged bond that Fated couples talked about. Sure, they could already feel each other's strong emotions and could find each other within the castle, but that was about it. Cadeyrn found that he almost desperately wanted the deeper connection that came with sealing their bond. He didn't know why, but he needed it.

Soon.

They were getting close to summer, and Prince Yolotzin's wedding notice would likely be arriving any day now. It would have to, to make sure all visiting dignitaries had time to travel and arrive. Cadeyrn had the advantage of knowing that the wedding was slated for the end of summer, and he'd received the announcement of Prince Yolotzin finding his Fated a few moonturns ago.

He'd make sure his Fated got to see his best friend's wedding. It was only fair. Though he needed to send out his own notice that he'd found his Fated to the other kingdoms. He was just putting it off to keep Tonalli from potentially retaliating when they visited. They'd have their own wedding soon enough, despite the delay. As long as Kajaan was ready and willing. He absently pressed another kiss to his Fated's temple as they made their way across the sands.

"So," Kajaan said slowly, tilting his head to look at him. "I've got a question about the Laiyi Desert."

"And what would that be?" Cadeyrn asked.

"I never really thought about it, looking at the map of the continent, but it was a bit more apparent looking at the kingdom map that Quillin had out while we were discussing what to do with Lord Neerian. The Laiyi Desert is a perfect circle and topographically doesn't make any sense. This area should be scrubland or open fields based on the surrounding areas. The southern area of Zothua starts to become marshland, which seems completely out of place this close to a natural desert."

Cadeyrn grinned, resting his cheek on the top of Kajaan's head. He didn't know why he hadn't expected this question from his Fated eventually. Kajaan was a smart man; he would have noticed the shape of Laiyi Desert probably within a year. Especially with someone as thoroughly traveled as his Fated. Cadeyrn wasn't one for geography, but apparently Kajaan knew enough to be puzzled.

"I'm not surprised that Averian schools don't teach Zothuan history. To answer your question quickly, no, the Laiyi Desert isn't natural. Hundreds of years ago, before Pemalia started focusing on keeping her people hale and hearty, the king had his eyes on this part of Zothua since it was fertile land. We were a fairly new kingdom, having just separated from Averia—"

"I didn't know they were the same kingdom once," Kajaan interrupted quietly.

"A very long time ago, yes. The king couldn't decide on whether to give Averia to his son or daughter. His daughter was more reasonable, but his son was older. Eventually, they sat down and the king decided to split the country down the middle, using the Reidden Mountains. His son came here, and the daughter stayed in Averia. They were long dead and the familial bonds well muted and forgotten by the time Pemalia tried taking over, so Averia had no compulsion to help.

"So, when the Pemalians tried to take some of our land, the Zothuan king refused. He didn't agree with their proposal and thought that if he gave them some land, they'd come back for more. That spurred a couple of skirmishes just north of here. Neither king wanted to back down, until my ancestor decided he'd had enough."

"So he made the land barren?" Kajaan asked.

"Not him. Even then, the royal family were Ignians. No, it was his general, Laiyi, who changed the land. She was… so incredibly powerful. Stronger than any Gaian I've ever heard of. The fighting had gone on so long, so many were dead and villages razed. That's when she came up with changing the land completely. King Aled Greatblaze agreed with her plan, so she went alone to the center of the land that Pemalia wanted in the middle of the night and ripped open the earth."

"What happened to her?" Kajaan asked, squeezing Cadeyrn's arm.

"She disappeared. It's accepted that she died after altering the landscape so drastically. Doing so would have completely drained her Craft, so she was probably buried in the sands," Cadeyrn said and shrugged slightly. "Ever since, we've had the desert. There've been some species that adapted. Most notably, the han-hans. They were far different back then than what they are now."

"Were they still blue?" Kajaan teased.

Cadeyrn grinned and nodded. "They were. After the desert was made, Pemalia gave up on the area since it was completely barren, and King Aled named it after Laiyi for her sacrifice. Some Gaians have tried to fix it, but whenever they try, more sand gets added and they're nearly fully drained no matter how little of an area they try to change.

"I figure that the desert is here to stay, so I don't bother trying to change it and shut down any petitions for those who want to try and make a name for themselves by returning the desert to its original state. It's not like we need the land for growing crops or raising animals. We've got plenty of farms down south toward Bhyvine and ranches toward Nabene," Cadeyrn said. "Plus the han-han ranches in the desert itself."

"That's…." Kajaan sighed heavily, his head lolling on Cadeyrn's shoulder as he processed the story. He stared ahead of them for a bit before tilting his head and looking up at him again. "I never would have considered that the Laiyi Desert was made by a Gaian."

"It's not really known outside of Zothua. Not all schools teach it here either. The royal family is taught, of course. There's a book or two and ancient maps in the library that have faded ink portraits of Laiyi, along with descriptions and images of the area before she altered it."

"I'd love to read them when we get back," Kajaan said.

"Anything you want," Cadeyrn whispered.

He dipped his head, kissing his Fated's temple, holding him close. Kajaan hummed happily, leaning into him, loose and pliant. They weren't far from their destination now. Cadeyrn could just barely see the palm fronds against the blue sky wavering in the distance. They'd arrive in a couple of minutes. Kajaan seemed comfortable riding on Maeeri, and the heat wasn't bothering him near as much as it had a few weeks ago.

Maeeri slowed as they approached the small oasis that Cadeyrn visited a lot as a young man, her sides heaving from the run. He hadn't been here in several years. Not since Menea had died and left him a widower. His kids had needed him. His people had needed him. The whole kingdom had mourned her loss with him, and he'd focused everything he had into his work.

By the time he'd surfaced, two years had passed, and Cadeyrn hadn't bothered with pleasurable activities, too focused on catching up with his children and running his kingdom. There had been no time to ride Maeeri out to the oasis. At least not until Kajaan came into his life and gave him the perfect reason to step back and take some time off.

Kajaan really was healing him. Damn Ameyalli for always being right. Cadeyrn kissed his Fated's neck, nuzzling in close, and Kajaan tilted his head to look at him curiously. He just smiled and pulled Maeeri to a stop. She bobbed her head a few times and pranced in place near one of the palm trees. Maeeri knew where she liked to graze and was more than fine being left alone while at the oasis.

Cadeyrn got off first, rolling his shoulders after such a long ride, and reached up to help Kajaan slide out of the saddle. Kajaan smiled at him, flopping heavily into his arms, his head tilted upward. Humming, Cadeyrn dropped a kiss on his Fated's lips but refused to get distracted. Once they parted, Cadeyrn showed his Fated how to remove a gexena's saddlebags and handed one to him. Underneath one bag on either side was a sheathed scimitar, and those were handled with care.

Inside the saddlebags was everything they needed for their outing. A blanket, food, drinks, and treats for Maeeri. From the brief glimpse he got inside the bags, they were in for quite the picnic. His cook had really outdone herself this time. There was a good amount of wrapped ice as well that would keep the food from spoiling for a few more hours.

He led him over to the somewhat large pool of crystal-clear blue water and tall, wide-leaf trees. The sparse grass was soft to the touch. Still, Cadeyrn pulled out the large picnic blanket and spread it out, trapping one corner with the now empty bag. Kajaan seemed to understand immediately, using the saddlebag and scimitars he'd carried over to weigh down the other corners of the blanket.

Cadeyrn lay down in the middle with a gusty sigh and reached out for his Fated.

A lazy day was exactly what they needed.

No kids. No secretaries. No lessons. Just them.

The kingdom would survive one half day without them.

Kajaan settled in next to him, curling up on his side to use Cadeyrn's chest as a pillow. For a long time, they just lay quietly together, the trees giving them more than enough cover from the sun and the water offering them a cool breeze when the wind blew. Han-hans chirruped from their nests buried in the sands, calling after their hunting mates to bring them home.

Maeeri snuffled a few times over where they'd left her, nosing and pawing at the lush grass. She wouldn't stray farther than the outer ring of trees. If anything, she'd just graze and nap until it was time to ride back. On rare days, Maeeri would dip into the water and swim around to cool off, though that was as much as she ever did here.

The sand heated up around them slowly in the aging sun's rays. Sweat started to bead on Kajaan's skin under Cadeyrn's hand and where they were lying against each other. His Fated didn't seem inclined to move, much to Cadeyrn's delight. The heat wasn't oppressive for him yet, and they had a pretty comfortable spot right now.

"Is this weird for you?" Kajaan finally said after a long while.

"Is what weird for me?" Cadeyrn asked, lazily running his hand up and down Kajaan's back.

"Me being a man," Kajaan clarified.

He felt his Fated turn slightly to look up at him. Cadeyrn opened his eyes and met Kajaan's worried gaze. Was it weird? Before they'd truly talked to each other, he would have said yes, but likely not for the reasons Kajaan was thinking. Cadeyrn hadn't planned on taking any other lover, at least until his children were grown. Especially not a man when he had littles to take care of.

He'd wrongly assumed that a male lover wouldn't be good for the children. Cadeyrn hadn't wanted to give Kajaan a chance, despite what Ameyalli said and what the goddess had planned for him. That had almost melted away the moment he'd seen Kajaan's fiery red hair, and all but vanished by the time Prince Yolotzin rode away on Hariam with his betrothed. He never wanted to see his Fated so devastated and in tears again.

"Not anymore," Cadeyrn said. "Not since I actually saw you and got to know you."

"My, uh… body doesn't disturb you?" Kajaan asked sheepishly. "It's quite different than Queen Menea's."

"I'm aware." Cadeyrn chuckled. "Though you and her have one thing in common." Kajaan hummed his inquiry, tilting his head slightly. Cadeyrn nuzzled into his Fated's hair and grinned. "You both don't have much body hair."

Kajaan made an indignant noise and sat up, pouting as he folded his arms across his chest.

"You don't have to remind me that I can't grow a beard," he grumped.

Cadeyrn just laughed and sat up, casually stretching. He wrapped an arm around Kajaan's shoulders and pulled him back to the ground, tucking Kajaan underneath his body. He cupped his face, his fingers barely rasping over Kajaan's stubble, and tilted his face up. Cadeyrn kissed him slowly as he leaned over his Fated, pressing him into the blanket. Kajaan arched up into him, sighing happily into the languid kiss.

By the time they broke apart, Kajaan was flushed, and his eyes were slightly glazed over and darkened. Cadeyrn flopped onto his back and held his Fated close to him. Kajaan nestled eagerly right up into him, resting his head on Cadeyrn's shoulder and stretching his arm across his chest. Cadeyrn reached up and gently curled his hand around Kajaan's forearm. He curled his other hand around the nape of Kajaan's neck, slowly running the tips of his fingers in small circles, letting his nails scratch along his skin intermittently.

That made Kajaan shudder and shift closer to him, back arching, his hips pressing tight to Cadeyrn's. Cadeyrn inhaled slowly and deeply as Kajaan let out a small groan, pressing his face into his shoulder, clutching at his thawb. There was a growing hardness making itself known against his hip, and Cadeyrn had to do his best to not laugh. He'd wondered about Kajaan's reaction when Prince Yolotzin had done this to him in the throne room. Now he knew it was one hell of a hot spot.

"Will the kids mind?" Kajaan asked in a near whisper.

Cadeyrn stopped rubbing his Fated's scalp and rested his hand against his shoulder instead. Would they? He doubted that Thaddaeus would, considering he'd been upset when Cadeyrn mentioned to Ameyalli that he might reject Kajaan. Fayette absolutely adored him, and Rodolfo wasn't far behind her. Even Marika seemed pretty taken with his Fated.

Despite all of that, there was no guarantee that the kids would welcome him fully as his Quenlet. There was a major difference between resident and parent. Just because they adored him as their fun secretary didn't mean that would translate favorably to Kajaan becoming their second father. Or they could simply be overjoyed and Cadeyrn was overthinking things as usual.

Cadeyrn took a deep breath and shrugged, ultimately unable to answer the question. He hadn't asked his kids their opinion. Hadn't thought to, if he was honest with himself. All he had to go on was his own observations as an adult and how his kids acted around the two of them.

"I don't think they would. I know they adore you in their own ways, but to see you as another father instead of another member of the castle…," Cadeyrn said.

"They… won't hate me for replacing their mom?" Kajaan asked, not looking up at him.

"You won't ever be able to replace her," Cadeyrn said gently. "She's their mother and will always be a part of their lives. Even if all they know about her is the stories I tell them about her."

"You tell them stories?" Kajaan asked in a somber voice.

"Sometimes, yes. I haven't really since you've arrived, though. They're more taken with you right now and want to know all about you. For the twins and Marika… we'll be the only parents they've ever known," Cadeyrn said.

"I'd love to hear more about Queen Menea," Kajaan said quietly. "I know I would have liked to hear stories about my mother when I was little. Just to get an idea of who she was, rather than hearing how great of a woman she was and how much of a loss her death was when I was older."

"Your mother died in childbirth, right?" Cadeyrn asked slowly.

Kajaan nodded and shivered a little against him despite the heat of the day and his own body heat. He pressed his forehead into Cadeyrn's shoulder, hiding his face as he tightened his hold on Cadeyrn's thawb once more. Cadeyrn held his Fated close, kissing the top of his head. He could feel the deep twang of regret, guilt, and sorrow from Kajaan, but Cadeyrn wasn't quite sure why guilt was a part of the mix.

"Jeryit never spoke of her or told me anything about her. He's hated me my whole life because of what happened. I came too early, and she died of a hemorrhage," Kajaan finally said.

"How did a Healer not save her?" Cadeyrn asked, annoyed. Any Healer worth their weight would easily be able to save a Craft Blessed in a difficult labor. The only exception would be if Kajaan's mother was a Void, but considering Averia's stance on Voids, that was highly unlikely. "Your father was living at the castle, right? There would have been one nearby."

"A Healer wasn't able to get to her in time," Kajaan said hollowly.

That made even less sense. Anxiety spiked through their bond, and Kajaan's breath hitched. He squeezed Cadeyrn tightly to him as if he was going to get up and leave him behind. As if he would mount Maeeri and abandon his Fated two hours inside the Laiyi Desert. His whole body trembled, and Kajaan still refused to lift his face so they could look at each other.

Maybe he felt safer speaking this way. Menea had done the same thing a few times. She claimed that sometimes tough subjects were easier to talk about while not looking at each other. Maybe they were.

"I don't understand," Cadeyrn said, frowning at his Fated.

Kajaan sighed and slowly sat up, immediately hunching over, facing away from him. He hugged himself, running his hands up and down his arms. Cadeyrn just watched him quietly, propping himself onto his elbows, letting his Fated get to the explanation in his own time. There was a lot of guilt and pain that Cadeyrn could feel radiating from his Fated, and he instinctively knew they were misplaced.

"King Tonalli gave Jeryit time off since Mom was getting close to her estimated delivery date. They decided to stay in the country for a moonturn as a last little vacation before I arrived," Kajaan said. "By the time Mom realized she was in labor, it was too late for her to get to a Healer. She had me in the carriage and bled out five minutes away from the nearest clinic."

Cadeyrn sat up and gently pressed his shoulder to Kajaan's. He angled his body slightly away from his Fated, trying to give him some sort of privacy. If Kajaan tilting his head away to block Cadeyrn's line of sight was any indication that he didn't want to be seen at the moment, then he'd try to respect that.

"How early did you arrive?" he asked.

"A moonturn," Kajaan said.

Cadeyrn couldn't help the heavy sigh that escaped him. He closed his eyes and shook his head at the pure stupidity of being so far away from a Healer that close to her due date. Kajaan cringed away, his guilt and shame spiking, probably assuming Cadeyrn was blaming him. Cadeyrn wrapped his arm around his Fated's waist to pull him back into his side and kissed his temple. Kajaan shuddered, tense for just a moment before he melted into Cadeyrn, seeking the comfort that Cadeyrn was pushing through their fledgling bond.

"There should have been no reason whatsoever for Jeryit to take your mother so far away from an available Healer that far in her pregnancy. Children are unpredictable when it comes to their delivery. Thaddaeus was a moonturn late. Marika was exactly on time, and the twins were two weeks early. Your father should have brought a Healer with him during their sabbatical or made sure one was within five minutes," Cadeyrn said with a growl in his voice. "You are not to blame for Jeryit's idiocy and mismanagement of his wife's health. Do you understand?"

Kajaan looked at him, tears welling in his eyes. He bit his lower lip and shook his head in a clear denial of Cadeyrn's comfort.

"I was too big of an infant," Kajaan protested weakly.

"You can't control how big you grow in utero any more than when it was time for you to be delivered. Kajaan, look at me," Cadeyrn said, cupping his Fated's face and forcing him to at least face him. "Your mother's death was not your fault, no matter what anyone says."

"Everyone in Avitou was saying it, though. It wasn't just my father," Kajaan said. "If it wasn't for Tzin, I wouldn't have gotten any education at all."

"I don't understand. You were raised in the castle to be a high-ranking employee. Why wouldn't they have tutors for you to at least learn the basics?" Cadeyrn asked.

"Because I committed matricide," Kajaan murmured. "Why would they want to educate me?"

Cadeyrn closed his eyes and growled, pressing his forehead against Kajaan's, holding his jaw tight. He needed the closeness with his Fated to quell his anger. Needed his lover to know that what he'd just said wasn't true. Cadeyrn didn't understand whatsoever why Jeryit or anyone in the castle had been so vindictive toward a *child*.

Nothing about Kajaan's mother's death had been in any way his fault. So why was he being blamed? Was it truly that easy to scapegoat a child instead of holding the father responsible for his mistake? Yes, it had been a fatal one. And yes, it was a tragic one. But to push all of that guilt onto Kajaan instead of bearing the weight of his decisions?

"What did Prince Yolotzin do?" Cadeyrn asked, trying to distract his Fated. "I need something positive from this, otherwise I'm also going to punch your father during the wedding."

That got a small laugh from Kajaan, as was intended. His Fated slowly rubbed the tips of their noses together before tilting his head, silently requesting a kiss. Kajaan was still a little shy when it came to asking for affection, but Cadeyrn was all too happy to oblige when he did. He pressed a gentle kiss to his Fated's lips, smiling at him.

"Once Tzinny realized I wasn't getting any education whatsoever, unlike him, he got so upset about it. So, eight-year-old Tzin marched right up to his parents while they were in a meeting with some foreign dignitary and loudly demanded to know why I wasn't allowed any tutors or lessons. He figured that he could shame them in front of another monarch and they'd have to agree. King Tonalli tried saying I was going to be a guard, so there was no point in me learning anything but swordplay," Kajaan told him.

"He didn't take that well, I'm guessing," Cadeyrn replied.

Kajaan leaned heavily into him and shook his head, smiling now. He wiped at the few remaining tears on his face and laughed weakly at whatever he was thinking about. Cadeyrn smiled faintly at Kajaan's joy, glad that the memory of Yolotzin bullying his father was cutting through his grief and pain.

"No. Not one bit. He demanded that I stay by his side and that I needed to learn everything he did. He wanted me as his secretary once we were adults rather than the boorish man that was assigned to him," Kajaan said with a laugh. "I think by then we were already mostly in love."

"I wouldn't be surprised. You two shared just about everything," Cadeyrn said.

Kajaan nodded. "Pretty much. We'd never been separated for long. Until… you know."

"I'd say I'm sorry about what King Tonalli had planned for you, but it brought you to me," Cadeyrn said, brushing his fingers down the side of Kajaan's face. "I don't know if I would have ever woken up without you."

Kajaan smiled shyly at him, resting his head on Cadeyrn's shoulder. They stayed like that for a few minutes in the hot air, his Fated sweating a little more in the late-morning heat. Maybe now would be a good time.... Cadeyrn tilted his head and placed a kiss in Kajaan's coarse hair before shifting away. He ignored Kajaan's slightly hurt expression, feeling the faint spike of pain in their bond.

Cadeyrn stood, tilting Kajaan's head up with a finger under his Fated's jaw, rubbing his thumb over his cheek. He offered his lover a soft smile.

"I have something for you," he said.

Kajaan blinked once and cocked his head. "Other than this little retreat?"

"Yes," Cadeyrn replied simply. "Something a bit more tangible. Stay here."

He walked over to their saddlebag and knelt beside it. After fishing inside one of the inner pockets, Cadeyrn pulled out a small velvet bag that he knew Kajaan would recognize immediately. A tangle of nerves settled in his gut as he stood, spinning it in his hands, hoping it would be received well. He returned to Kajaan and knelt in front of him. His Fated was watching him with an anxious look on his face, though he could feel the rumble of excitement through their bond. Did his Fated enjoy gifts? Or surprises? That was something to consider later.

Cadeyrn held out the bag, watching Kajaan quietly. The man regarded him with soft eyes for an extra moment before he looked down. His breath caught, and he frowned ever so slightly in confusion. Kajaan took the bag from him and opened it in a well-practiced movement. He dumped the modified napkin ring out onto his palm and gasped, his eyes going wide as he gaped at the changes.

The Gaian metalworker had done a wonderful job with the commission and Cadeyrn's idea. She'd polished the metal until it was gleaming and hammered out the ring until it was in the shape of a half moon. A dainty metal chain had been added on either side with a clasp in the middle. Small gemstones were inlaid into the bracelet in two distinct colors. Rubies, spinels, and garnets formed a flickering flame that was entwined by a wave of sapphires, aquamarines, and tanzanites. They danced around each other, sparkling in the rising sunlight.

Cadeyrn looked up from the bracelet to catch a tear dropping from Kajaan's eyelashes.

"Kaj?" Cadeyrn whispered.

"It's…. You…." he trailed off, looking up at him.

"Was this all right?" Cadeyrn asked, hoping he hadn't overstepped. He reached out and cupped his Fated's face. "I can have the blacksmith remove the gemstones and reforge the napkin ring if you want it."

"It's perfect," Kajaan choked out. He forced out a breath, and the smile he gave Cadeyrn was nearly blinding with its brightness. "Thank you."

He held out his arm and the bracelet. Taking the hint, Cadeyrn opened the clasp and wrapped the delicate chain around Kajaan's wrist. The bronze ring and chain looked so good against his slowly tanning skin. Once it was secure, Kajaan tore his eyes away from his Fated and ran his fingers over the shining stones.

Cadeyrn watched him with a contented smile on his face, not feeling any of the pain that had been plaguing his Fated earlier in their bond. Instead, all he felt was Kajaan's happiness and joy at the gift. He was glad he didn't overstep, even though he hadn't thought about that as a possibility until he'd returned the bracelet to Kajaan. Cadeyrn felt a sliver of anxiety slip through their bond again.

"I don't have anything I can give you," Kajaan whispered.

"A smile. Your joy. Your love," Cadeyrn replied softly. "You don't need to give me jewelry or trinkets in return."

"What do you give a man who has everything?" Kajaan teased.

"Companionship," Cadeyrn replied easily. "A second father to my children."

Kajaan smiled at him. He cleared his throat and looked down at the bracelet for a minute.

"I think," he said slowly. "I think I can give that to you. I'll do my best to do right by them. And you."

"And any others you might want to have," Cadeyrn said.

His Fated stared up at him with wide eyes, a grin slowly spreading across his face.

"You'd have more kids with me, King Cadeyrn?" Kajaan asked in a sultry tone.

"It would be my pleasure," Cadeyrn murmured. He crawled toward Kajaan, who shifted his weight and spread his legs for Cadeyrn to fit comfortably between them. "Practicing will be fun too."

Kajaan laughed brightly, putting his hands on either side of Cadeyrn's face. He lay back, and Cadeyrn followed him, resting some of his weight onto his Fated's body. Cadeyrn tilted his head and pressed their lips together, smiling as Kajaan sighed happily. He felt his Fated's arms wrap around his head, holding him in place.

They exchanged several soft, slow kisses, reveling in their closeness rather than trying to rile each other up. Cadeyrn eventually lowered himself, relying on Kajaan to support him more.

"Let me talk to the kids before we solidify our bond," Cadeyrn whispered as their lips parted once more. "At least let them know what's going on."

"All right," Kajaan replied, equally as soft. "Your kids have a right to know."

"Our kids," Cadeyrn reminded him. He grinned at Kajaan's wistful expression. Apparently his Fated liked that idea quite a lot. "How many kids do you want?"

"So many," Kajaan said, kissing him quickly, clacking their teeth together with his sudden urgency. "Your four and maybe more?"

"We can put out the call for surrogates after our wedding," Cadeyrn said.

Kajaan squirmed under him, delight pouring through their bond, blinding Cadeyrn to any other emotions his Fated might be having. Their lips found one another again, parted, and tongues darted in to taste each other. Kajaan moaned ever so sweetly, constantly moving underneath Cadeyrn. His hips arching, legs opening, or squeezing Cadeyrn's hips as he practically danced against the ground, Kajaan's fingers constantly running through Cadeyrn's hair.

The next time Kajaan arched into him, Cadeyrn got his arm underneath him, pressing his Fated harder into the ground. His lover whimpered, one hand plucking at Cadeyrn's Bisht even as he bucked. Cadeyrn could feel Kajaan's cock, hard and unyielding, rub against his hip. If he moved his own hips just so, then they could stimulate each other. Their kiss deepened, tongues twisting and tangling as they grasped at each other.

Cadeyrn parted Kajaan's Bisht, pushing the clothing aside to grab at the button of his breeches. Kajaan melted underneath him, moaning eagerly into the kiss, using the hand he had in Cadeyrn's hair to tilt his head any way he wanted. Cadeyrn's body was responding nicely to Kajaan's passion and sun-warmed skin. His blood raced and prick hardened with the ghost of his lover's touch.

Once his pants were open, Cadeyrn slid his hand down the front, groaning at the feel of the sparse pleasure trail and soft muscle. The head of Kajaan's cock bumped against the back of his hand, leaving a small smear of precum behind. Cadeyrn didn't hesitate to wrap his callused hand around the velvety smooth cock, delighted to feel how hot and hard his lover was.

Kajaan gasped, breaking the kiss, arching up into him in encouragement. He was panting heavily, his breath washing over Cadeyrn's lips.

"Cade?" Kajaan whimpered.

"I've got you," Cadeyrn murmured.

Kajaan nodded, his eyes drifting closed as Cadeyrn slowly pumped his length. It felt so nice in his hand. Cadeyrn was suddenly glad he didn't have experience with other men. That he could give his firsts to his Fated, even if Kajaan didn't realize it at the moment. Kajaan's soft moans, breathless sighs, and the small bucking of his hips made Cadeyrn want more.

The bottle of slick that Simthe had given him was still tucked away in the saddlebag. It was out of reach, so they'd have to make do for now. Hopefully he didn't chafe his Fated's cock. Cadeyrn tightened his grip slightly, and Kajaan moaned low in his throat. Kajaan's arms slipped from around Cadeyrn's shoulders to thud to the ground on either side of his head.

Cadeyrn kissed his lover's neck, earning himself a delighted hum from Kajaan. His Fated continued to undulate beneath him in time with Cadeyrn's slow strokes. Kajaan bit his lower lip and smiled shyly at him.

"Trust me?" Kajaan asked, his voice barely above a whisper.

Cadeyrn could only nod, though he was a little curious as to what his lover was planning. Kajaan got his hands underneath Cadeyrn's Bisht and hunted for his riding breeches. Within a couple of seconds, Cadeyrn sighed in relief as his prick slid free. Kajaan gave him a few strokes, sliding his thumb over the head of his length to lubricate his cock with the small beads of precum that were leaking out.

"I have some slick," Cadeyrn said roughly.

Kajaan's face brightened, and he nodded. Cadeyrn stared down at his Fated for a minute before having to tear himself away from him to head back to the saddlebag. He could hear Kajaan moving on the blanket behind him, making him want to turn around. Cadeyrn's hands were shaking by the time he managed to locate and pull out the slick.

When he turned around to see what Kajaan was doing, a groan slipped from his lips. Kajaan had pulled off his breeches and shirt, though he'd put his Bisht back on. The black silk looked decadent next to his golden skin, making Cadeyrn's mouth water. He swallowed hard and walked a few steps back to his Fated, unable to take his eyes off the tantalizing visage.

"Fuck," Cadeyrn breathed out.

Kajaan's face split into a wide grin. He reached up and wiggled his fingers. Cadeyrn handed him the small bottle.

"Take off your pants at least. This might get messy," Kajaan told him.

Unable to tear his eyes away from those glistening fingers, Cadeyrn somehow managed to toe off his riding boots without falling over. His breeches followed suit a moment later as he watched Kajaan rub the slick on the insides of his thighs, close to his hips before briefly stroking his cock with his greased hand. His Fated slowly rolled his balls in one hand, spreading his legs to tease the carefully watching Cadeyrn.

"I would love to have you inside me, but that would seal our bond," Kajaan said. "The kids deserve you to talk to them first."

Cadeyrn smiled, feeling a spark of pride in his chest. Even now, when he could get all the security of bonding with him, Kajaan still put the kids first. Kajaan echoed his smile and held out his arms for Cadeyrn to come closer. Careful of the slick, Cadeyrn leaned over him and slowly kissed him.

"And what is it you want me to do?" Cadeyrn asked.

"Fuck between my thighs," Kajaan said and laughed. "Hence putting the slick there. But it's hard to kiss when my legs are on your shoulders…."

He trailed off and rolled over onto his belly. Kajaan pushed himself up onto his elbows and lifted his hips, the silk Bisht sliding up his back to bunch around his neck. Seeing the tanned expanse made Cadeyrn groan. He reached out and grabbed two generous handfuls of his Fated's backside and squeezed liberally. Kajaan moaned, his head dropping forward to press against the ground. Cadeyrn took his time kneading the soft flesh, running his hands up and down his flanks.

Kajaan's skin was so soft. So smooth. An irresistible urge to bite his flawless skin overcame him, and Cadeyrn gave in to it. He leaned forward and sank his teeth into the meat of his ass. Kajaan gasped and pressed back into his face. Glad that his Fated seemed to enjoy the sharp pain, Cadeyrn took his time, leaving quite a few marks on the man's skin. The brief thought that he shouldn't bruise him so thoroughly for the ride back crossed his mind, and Cadeyrn reluctantly pulled away.

Kissing up Kajaan's spine, Cadeyrn wrapped his arm around the redhead's stomach and slid his weeping prick between his Fated's thighs. Kajaan clamped his legs shut, crossing his ankles to help lock them tight. His lover was right. The pressure felt nice against his aching cock. Moaning softly in Kajaan's ear, he thrust, hips smacking into Kajaan's bruise-warmed ass. He'd taken Menea like this a few times when she wanted sex but at the same time didn't want to put down her book.

He wondered if Kajaan would be the same with his love of reading. Cadeyrn nipped his ear, following it up with a lick behind his earlobe. Kajaan twitched and laughed, jerking his head away. Ticklish, maybe? That would be something to explore later when they had a more comfortable bed.

One of Kajaan's hands slid down to guide the tip of Cadeyrn's prick to rub against his length when he bottomed out. They were already leaking, Cadeyrn's precum mixing with the slick and Kajaan's dripping to the blanket. Cadeyrn moved his hand to tease the tip of Kajaan's prick, dipping his nail to lightly dig at his slit, and was rewarded with a sharp, delighted shout.

Kajaan was quite the vocal lover. Every one of his cries filled Cadeyrn with the urge to hear more. His mind started to cloud with both his own pleasure and what was echoing through his bond from his Fated. Every thrust, every light kiss on his neck or stroke of his Fated's prick seemed to strengthen their connection.

"Oh Goddess," Kajaan whispered, bucking after one well-aimed thrust ground against his prick. "I wish you were inside me."

Cadeyrn couldn't help the low groan that built in his throat with that comment. He dropped his head and bit into the meat of Kajaan's shoulder. Pain that wasn't his own flared bright in the back of his mind, though it quickly turned into a pleasurable burn. That was an easy confirmation that Kajaan enjoyed a bit of rough sex. He'd follow up on that later.

Closing his eyes, Cadeyrn fell into their bond that shone like the sun inside of him. He could feel Kajaan just beneath his skin, could feel his delight at finally having a man holding him down and having his way with him again. Cadeyrn instinctively reached out toward his lover's happiness, wanting to wrap himself in the warmth that it offered. He would do anything to keep his Fated feeling like this. Content. Adored. Loved.

Kajaan was panting, rocking his hips back almost in time with each of Cadeyrn's thrusts, his fingers becoming limp, just providing a hint of pressure. Their movements slowed slightly, finally falling in sync with each other. Being in sync felt more intimate, more significant than their near frantic coupling. Kajaan twisted just enough so they could kiss. Sloppily, but that didn't matter. Cadeyrn shifted and aimed his next thrust to hit Kajaan's perineum.

His Fated shuddered and moaned, his arm giving out and dumping the two of them against the ground. Cadeyrn managed a soft chuckle through the haze. He let go of Kajaan's prick and grasped his hip, helping pull him up to his knees. Neither of them had to ask if their partner was close. Cadeyrn could feel it. He rolled his hips once more, smacking mercilessly into his Fated's body. Kajaan choked out a cry as his body went rigid, and Cadeyrn felt a familiar tingle race up his spine as their bond sparked.

Kajaan spilled onto the blanket, shaking against Cadeyrn as he tried to catch his breath, his eyes heavy and dark. Cadeyrn felt his own release course through him, coating Kajaan's thighs with his cum. They sank to the ground, Kajaan's strength finally giving out and Cadeyrn not caring to hold them up anymore. He was barely aware of how much weight he was putting on Kajaan's body. Not that his Fated seemed to mind one bit.

In fact, he knew that Kajaan loved it. Just as he knew his lover enjoyed being pinned down and letting his partner have his way with him. He could feel Kajaan's body and mind thrumming with happiness and serenity. Their bond was strong, shining bright between them, and Cadeyrn could feel the nuances of what Kajaan was feeling. The slight twinge of guilt underneath his contentment, though it wasn't enough to make Cadeyrn worry about what they'd just done.

The strength and complexity of their bond startled him once he thought more about it. He heard Kajaan grunt in query underneath him, though he didn't seem to have the energy to speak. Cadeyrn searched their bond, confused as to why it was stronger than it had been. He hated the brief flash of panic that coursed through him when he realized that they'd done exactly what they'd been trying to avoid.

Their bond was complete.

Kajaan must have realized something was wrong too. Or rather, not exactly wrong, but unexpected. Guilt flooded Cadeyrn as he pushed up to his knees. He could feel panic and concern emanating from Kajaan, and fear underlying that. Kajaan rolled onto his back and scooted backward, sitting up. He wrapped his Bisht around him tightly, as if it was armor.

"Kajie," Cadeyrn whispered. "I think…."

"But," Kajaan broke in, "it's supposed to be through penetrative sex."

"Apparently not," Cadeyrn replied, hesitating for a long moment.

"Do you… do you regret it?" Kajaan asked in a quavering voice.

His tentative question startled Cadeyrn. Obviously Kajaan could feel his guilt and was trying to interpret the cause of it, or misconstruing it. Cadeyrn cursed himself internally for causing Kajaan unnecessary distress. The last thing he wanted was for his lover to doubt himself and their bond.

"No," Cadeyrn said firmly. He reached out and cupped Kajaan's face, drawing him in for a soft kiss. When they parted, he could see the fear in Kajaan's shining eyes. His Fated looked to be on the verge of crying. Cadeyrn shuffled closer and kissed him again, trying to push as much affection as he could through their bond. "I feel bad because I did want to talk to the kids first. I feel bad because I wanted our bonding to be done in bed where we could take our time and spend hours exploring and learning what each other liked. I will *never* regret tying myself to you."

He nearly held his breath as Kajaan stared up at him. His Fated bit his lip and slowly lowered his gaze. Tears fell to his cheeks, and Cadeyrn brushed them away with his thumbs.

"What if the kids hate it?" Kajaan asked.

"Then they'll have to deal," Cadeyrn said with a heavy sigh. "I doubt it'll be an issue, though. Thaddaeus already knows you're mine."

Kajaan relaxed in Cadeyrn's hands, leaning heavily into him. His Fated gave a weak laugh. The turmoil inside his Fated hadn't eased much, and he didn't seem like he was going to talk anytime soon. It took him another minute observing Kajaan's emotions before he knew that he needed to push.

"Kaj," Cadeyrn murmured. "Talk to me."

His Fated looked up at him with large, watery eyes. He sniffed and rubbed his nose with the back of his hand, ducking his head.

"I feel like such a crybaby these last few moonturns," he admitted.

"Nothing wrong with crying," Cadeyrn said. "I bawled as much as my son did when he was born."

"You didn't faint?" Kajaan teased.

"I might have gotten a bit woozy," Cadeyrn said and grinned. "Especially seeing how much the baby's head stretches—"

"Okay, nope!" Kajaan interrupted and clapped his hands over Cadeyrn's mouth.

He laughed, falling silent at his lover's request.

"We should be present at any surrogate births, if they're all right with us there," Cadeyrn said quietly.

Kajaan blushed and traced Cadeyrn's lips with his fingers almost absently. He took a long minute before he nodded his assent. Grabbing at his lover's Bisht, Cadeyrn pulled him onto his lap. Kajaan wrapped his arms around his neck and settled against his chest. As soon as his lover was secure in his arms, Cadeyrn flopped back onto the blanket.

Kajaan gave a small squeak before laughing quietly against him. His Fated nestled more firmly into him and sighed contentedly. They'd clean up later. Once they both processed the fact that they were now bonded. A small spark of delight burned in Cadeyrn's chest. They were bonded for the rest of their days. He could feel Kajaan's worries, insecurity, underlying fear, and anxiety slowly bleed away.

Then Kajaan gave a small snore. Cadeyrn grinned, glad that his lover had relaxed enough to fall asleep. Maybe a nice nap in the sun was just what they needed. Once his lover woke, they could eat what his chef had made for them and relax a little bit longer before having to head home. Maybe now he'd be able to convince Kajaan to fully move into his rooms.

With that delightful thought at the forefront of his mind, Cadeyrn let himself relax and fell into a light doze.

Chapter 17

Kajaan yawned, arching up onto his toes as he stretched his hands toward the cloudless sky, the oasis water cool against his now clean skin. Somewhere off in the dunes, he could hear a few han-hans chirruping and squawking at each other. He sighed, rocking back onto his feet, and looked over at his Fated before wandering back to their picnic. To his bonded lover. Cadeyrn was a steady, calm presence in the back of his mind, soothing the anxiety that constantly dogged his every step.

They'd just finished their packed lunch that the cook had thoughtfully made for them, having wrapped ice around a covered bowl of sea salt and olive oil hummus so it wouldn't spoil. She'd included several leather bags containing sliced carrots, bell peppers, cucumbers, and celery for dipping. There was a container of something called fatayer, tasty little pastries stuffed with spinach and a creamy cheese. Three types of drinks had been included as well: an apricot drink Cadeyrn called Qamar al-Din and two different lemonades, mint and lavender.

Despite the fairly light fare, Kajaan had managed to stuff himself. Cadeyrn had gladly given him free rein over the fatayer, and Kajaan had found that he adored Qamar al-Din. During their entire meal, Kajaan could feel his lover's pure delight at seeing him enjoying the meal and finding new favorites. If the apricot drink wasn't available at future lunches, Kajaan would be shocked. Cadeyrn did love to spoil him.

Covering his mouth to hide his yawn, Kajaan finally dragged on his clothes. Perhaps that was half of the reason Cadeyrn had been in such a good mood during lunch. Except there hadn't been an overwhelming amount of lust coming through their bond. Before Kajaan could even fully form the thought that perhaps Cadeyrn wasn't interested in him sexually, he felt his lover's powerful body press up against his back.

Gentle kisses in his hair made Kajaan's thoughts scatter, and he leaned back into his Fated, closing his eyes. Cadeyrn was free with his affections, especially now that they were bonded. Several times over their meal, his lover had reached out to wipe up any bits of cheesy spinach or hummus that got trapped at the corners of his mouth. Cadeyrn had casually touched him constantly in between, resting his hand on Kajaan's knee or leg, twining their fingers together, or cupping the back of his neck.

It did a lot to allay Kajaan's nerves over their impromptu bonding. He knew he'd never regret committing himself to Cadeyrn, despite his initial brief panic attack. A sharp nibble on his neck brought Kajaan back to the present, and a small groan escaped him. His knees went weak, and he tilted his head away to offer more room. Instead of teasing him further, Cadeyrn kissed his cheek before patting his flank.

"The sooner we get home, the longer we can spend in bed," he murmured.

Kajaan hummed and smiled up at him. That sounded absolutely lovely, even if he doubted that they'd be left alone once they got home. Between the kids, Ameyalli, Quillin, and Wayra, they likely wouldn't have any time to themselves until the children were put to bed.

"What about the kids?" Kajaan asked. "Will we talk to them today?"

"We should," Cadeyrn said. "Care to join me?"

"If you want me there," Kajaan said.

Cadeyrn rolled his eyes good-naturedly and nodded. He pulled Kajaan in for a brief kiss. They parted far too soon to finish packing up their decimated picnic. Maeeri stood perfectly still as they reattached the saddlebags to her harness. Cadeyrn gave Kajaan the last apple to feed to her while he tightened her belly straps. Swallowing down his nerves, Kajaan offered the gexena the treat, keeping a wary eye on her long eyeteeth.

Her soft lips danced across his palm as she mouthed at the apple, crushing it greedily. She chased the last drops of sticky juice with her long tongue right as Cadeyrn walked up to him. His lover pressed a kiss to his temple before grabbing his wrist and leading him to Maeeri's side. Ignoring the heat in his cheeks, Kajaan accepted Cadeyrn's help in mounting the mare and settled gingerly in the saddle with a wince.

His backside was fairly sore after his lover's exuberant exploration, and while Kajaan wasn't quite looking forward to their ride back, he'd be glad to have padded chairs available. Cadeyrn slid into the saddle behind him, wrapped an arm around his waist, and squeezed Maeeri's sides. The gexena tossed her head and turned back toward home, working herself back up to a canter.

Kajaan leaned back into his Fated, his eyes starting to close. Despite taking a nap under the leafy fronds, he still felt exhausted. Too much emotional turmoil and physical exertion for one morning. Even the tenderness in his ass wasn't enough to stop him from starting to drift. The heat got worse the farther they moved from the oasis, the sun beating down mercilessly upon them, and Kajaan turned his head away to avoid burning his face.

Cadeyrn simply held him, quietly humming some sort of tune. Kajaan wasn't familiar with the song. He wondered if it was a child's lullaby and sighed happily, ready to slide deeper into sleep. His lover went quiet abruptly, and Kajaan opened his eyes, looking up at him. Cadeyrn was staring off toward the center of the desert, squinting slightly. Kajaan followed his gaze, though all he could see was the desert's shimmering haze.

"Everything all right?" Kajaan asked.

"Thought I saw something is all," Cadeyrn said.

Kajaan eyed the dunes warily as he sat up. He wasn't seeing anything concerning, but he wasn't familiar enough with the desert to know what was out of place. Cadeyrn frowned as Kajaan looked back up at him. It took him a long minute before his lover turned away from his vigil, and he urged Maeeri to put on a bit more speed.

"Could it be the extra patrols you set up with Wayra?" Kajaan asked.

"Maybe," Cadeyrn replied and sighed. "Maybe I'm just being paranoid."

"My father always likes to say, better paranoid than dead," Kajaan said and shrugged.

"Not a bad rule to live by as a war—"

Cadeyrn's words were cut off with a pained grunt. Kajaan spun halfway to get a better look at his lover, startled at the wave of pain and fatigue that crashed through their bond. Sticking out of his shoulder was a heavy arrow shaft, the feathers dyed in the Averian royal family colors.

"Fuck," Cadeyrn gritted out.

Maeeri screeched in outrage as she scented her master's blood. She kicked a few times and took off at a dead gallop, though she continued to head back to the castle.

"Cade," Kajaan gasped.

"Get close to Maeeri."

A firm hand between his shoulders pushed Kajaan over the saddle horn and against the gexena's neck. Cadeyrn leaned over him, speaking softly to his mount, urging her to run as fast as she could. A nyala pounded across the sand toward them, her rider garbed in the black linens of a mercenary. He pulled back another deadly-looking arrow and aimed at them.

At Kajaan's startled shout, Cadeyrn twisted so he could shoot out a blast of fire at the approaching mercenary with his uninjured hand. The merc's shot went wide as he jerked back to avoid getting burned. His mount snorted, panicking and bucking as she bounded back and forth a few times, the fur on her face and nose singed.

While the mercenary spent valuable time getting his nyala back under control, Cadeyrn urged Maeeri to ignore the duo and put on a burst of speed. She kept pulling on her bridle to turn and wreak havoc on the man who hurt her master. Kajaan glanced behind them to keep an eye on the archer. Cadeyrn leaned heavier against him, his breath ragged, and the overwhelming presence in his mind was fading.

When the man started galloping after them again, drawing back on his bow, Kajaan's heart skipped a beat. He stretched his hand toward the two, tapping into his Craft. Kajaan wasn't quite sure what he wanted to do, but he had to do something! There was just enough moisture in the air that he could pull on if he timed it just right. He had one shot at protecting his Fated.

The mercenary released his arrow.

Kajaan's fingers stung as if he'd lost circulation, and he desperately pulled on all the water around them that he could. A thin ribbon of water crashed into the arrow's side, causing it to sink harmlessly into the golden sand. Barely holding on to his Craft, Kajaan wielded the water like a whip and cracked it across the merc's face.

The man shouted, and his head jerked back. He lost his seat and fell backward off his mount. The nyala's hoof clipped his face as he fell into a heap with a hard grunt. Kajaan released his Craft, watching the mount spin and bound northward at a fast clip. Poor girl was probably overheated in her thick furs that were far more suited to the cold forests of Valvinte than the desert sun.

Nyalas were the only mount on the continent that had a chance of keeping up with a gexena, though only for a short period of time. The breeders up in Valvinte were doing their best to improve their stamina and speed to try and rival the gexena line. As far as Kajaan knew, they wouldn't hesitate to sell their nyalas to other countries, while Zothua carefully controlled where their mounts went.

"Cade," Kajaan said with a hint of panic in his voice. He could barely feel his Fated in his mind, and his back was sweating profusely from Cadeyrn's feverish skin. Had something been on the arrowhead? "Hold on. I think we're almost back."

His lover didn't respond except for a low groan. Kajaan desperately grabbed Maeeri's reins, though he doubted the gexena needed them to know where she was going. If Kajaan had understood properly, the oasis they'd been to was a place Cadeyrn had frequented often with his wife. In theory, Maeeri should know where she was and would be able to get them home just fine without her rider's input.

Every minute that passed, Cadeyrn's weight got heavier, his skin hotter, and their bond fainter. The relief upon seeing the castle in the distance made Kajaan's head spin. He urged Maeeri faster even though he could feel the fatigue in her muscles. If only he had a way to communicate they needed help even before they got there!

The scimitar. Kajaan managed to lean just far enough that his fingertips brushed against the pommel. It took another minute before he was able to slide it out of the sheath between two fingers. Another fraught few seconds later and he had it firmly in his fist. Kajaan held the blade over Maeeri's head, having basically been pinned completely to her neck, and began tilting it.

He wasn't sure if Zothua used the same distress codes that Averia did. The only reason he'd learned them in his old position was because he'd traveled with Yolotzin extensively. If anything, maybe he'd get a curious guard or two coming out to see what the light was about. If they even cared about light flashes through the desert.

Swearing constantly under his breath, Kajaan continued his frantic signaling until he saw a small dust cloud. Sighing in relief, he rested the sword on the gexena's head as the two groups drew close. Maeeri slid to a halt and pranced on the sand the moment they could see who had come out to meet them.

"Wayra," Kajaan greeted frantically.

"Fuck," the captain spat in return.

"I think it's poisoned," Kajaan said, lip trembling. His voice cracked as he said, "Please."

One of the two guards with Wayra trotted over, her gexena's nostrils flaring at the scent of Cadeyrn's blood. The creature tossed his head, and Kajaan shied away from the duo. Luckily, Maeeri held firm.

"Let's give Maeeri a break," the guard said kindly.

Together, they scooted Cadeyrn from Maeeri's back onto the stallion the guard was riding. The moment he was secure, she and the other guard sprinted back toward the castle. Shrill cries rose from the two, likely some sort of code to ready the castle for their arrival. As much as Maeeri's body thrummed to run after them, she held still, her head dipped low and her sides heaving.

Now that it was just him and Wayra, Kajaan had no reservations about crying. His breathing hitched, and he covered his face with his hands, curling in on himself. Wayra indulged him for a minute, keeping an eye on the desert, giving Kajaan a little bit of privacy.

"He'll be all right, Kajaan," Wayra said softly. The captain reached out and gently gripped Kajaan's upper arm. His voice was kind as he continued. "Whatever poison they used, I'm sure Tamya will be able to neutralize it."

Kajaan sniffed, wiped his cheeks dry, and nodded. He forced himself to breathe slowly until his heart returned to normal and he didn't feel like he'd fall into hysterics from a wrong glance. It took another minute for Kajaan to fully compose himself, while the captain waited patiently. The man was likely plotting his punishment for whichever desert guard was on duty.

Wayra took Maeeri's reins from Kajaan and led the exhausted gexena back to the stables. Kajaan kept quiet as he guided the mare to the mounting block, and he slid off her saddle. The stable hand seemed subdued after he took over for Wayra and walked Maeeri to the crossties to begin removing her tack. Wayra dismounted next to Kajaan and handed his stallion off to another stableboy.

"Do you need another minute?" Wayra asked kindly.

"No," Kajaan said, looking up at him. He let go of the bracelet he'd unconsciously been fiddling with. "Let's go."

The captain gestured for Kajaan to precede him. Without really thinking why, Kajaan walked out of the stables and toward the castle. He barely paid any attention to the other staff members, following the lure to his Fated, despite their bond being muted. It was a bit of a maze to get to him, weaving through different hallways meant to keep Tamya safe in case of an attack.

By the time Kajaan got to the room the Healer was temporarily assigned to, the bond had strengthened once again. Kajaan pushed open the door in relief and saw that Cadeyrn was awake. He looked exhausted, with heavy bags under his eyes, curled up on the exam table and undressed to his waist.

"Cade," Kajaan whispered.

He crossed over to him and without thought, climbed onto the bed. Cadeyrn lifted his arm, and Kajaan nestled into his chest. The puncture wound from the arrow was gone, already expertly healed. Kajaan couldn't help himself, lightly tracing where his lover had been injured, unable to see the scar that sometimes formed during a healing.

"—was on the arrow?" Wayra was asking.

"A strong sedative," Tamya replied and sighed heavily. "King Cadeyrn's body was trying to burn it out, causing his fever. It wasn't poison, or at least, it wasn't meant to be deadly."

"That's a relief," Wayra replied. "Where are the children?"

"Secure with Miski in the king's study," Tamya said. "Along with several guards, of course."

"I'm all right," Cadeyrn murmured, pressing his lips to Kajaan's forehead. "Thank you for getting us back."

"He needs rest. No business for the rest of the day," Tamya ordered. "Just take him back to his quarters and keep an eye on the door."

"What about the kids?" Wayra asked.

"Of course they can stay with their father," Tamya said. "So long as they stay low energy and don't overtire him."

"I'll let Miski know as soon as the king is secure," Wayra said.

Cadeyrn rolled his eyes and smiled crookedly at Kajaan. Likely at the formality that Wayra and Tamya were using instead of speaking casually like how Cadeyrn preferred. After another few minutes of stilted planning that Kajaan wasn't paying attention to, Wayra and Tamya finally approached the bed. The Healer helped Cadeyrn back into his tunic, and Kajaan reluctantly slid off the bed to hold out his hand for his lover to take.

With a helpful boost from Wayra, Cadeyrn got to his feet, holding on to Kajaan. He slid his arm heavily around Kajaan's shoulders, sighing deeply as he did. Wayra took a step back, watching his king carefully as he started to make his way out of the exam room. Caught between the urge to assist Cadeyrn and not wanting him to appear weak, Wayra had a sour look on his face.

It took quite a while for Cadeyrn to lead Kajaan up several flights of stairs and down the long hallway to his chambers. By then, his forehead was covered in sweat and he was leaning almost too heavily on Kajaan. As soon as the door closed behind him, Inti rushed forward and ducked underneath Cadeyrn's other arm. Together, the two of them got the king through the reception room to the bedroom and eased him onto the soft mattress.

"The kids," Cadeyrn murmured, already fading.

"Wayra is getting them," Kajaan soothed him.

Cadeyrn grabbed at his sleeve when Kajaan tried to pull away. "Stay."

"Let me get us comfortable first," Kajaan said.

Changing out of his riding clothes and into lounge wear was a lot faster with Inti's help. Kajaan didn't bother asking the man why some of his own clothes were in Cadeyrn's closet. He knew damn well the man had started moving him in, piece by piece. Sure, it would be his choice to finally give up what was supposed to be a guest suite, but he knew his Fated well enough by now.

"I want to tell the kids," Cadeyrn said when Kajaan crawled underneath the covers next to him. "I wanted to be more coherent when I told them, but…."

"Sooner than later I think would be best in this instance," Kajaan replied. "Are you sure you're up for it? You should rest and get the last bits of that sedative out of your system."

Cadeyrn opened his mouth to reply, only to get cut off by the sound of the door opening. The children were herded in by Wayra, though they were oddly subdued. Well, oddly for Fayette and Rodolfo. Kajaan nestled into his lover's side, awaiting the puppy pile. The children didn't disappoint.

Fayette took her usual spot lying on top of her father, wedged up against Kajaan. Thaddaeus curled up behind Kajaan, with Marika mirroring her brother behind Cadeyrn. Rodolfo lay across everyone's legs, in what had to be the most uncomfortable position. At least there was a blanket between their legs and his jabbing elbows and knees.

"Wayra said you were sick," Marika said in a shaky voice.

"Not exactly, sweet pea. I was attacked with a sedative," Cadeyrn explained. Kajaan kept an eye on his lover's face, a little surprised that he seemed more than ready to tell the kids exactly what happened. "Luckily, Tamya is a fantastic Healer, but I just need to sleep a little more than usual tonight."

"Did you go to the oasis?" Thaddaeus asked.

"Yeah. I went with Kajaan," Cadeyrn said.

Fayette stretched, nearly elbowing Kajaan in the eye as she did. She rolled to fix a serious look at her dad. "Didn't you go there with Mama to be all kissy face?"

"Yes. And I went there with Kajaan to be all kissy face," Cadeyrn replied. His voice sounded so warm yet so casual. As if it wasn't a big deal that he was being romantic with another person. "Is that all right?"

"Of course," Thaddaeus said, albeit a little quickly.

"Kajie is fun," Rodolfo said and shrugged. He pushed himself up onto his hands and peered at the two of them. "He lets me run in the gardens when Miski's not looking."

"Don't tattle on me," Kajaan protested with a laugh.

The twins giggled along with him, completely unbothered by the idea, or at least not understanding the implications of what Cadeyrn was implying. Behind him, he could hear Thaddaeus's unsteady breathing. Kajaan had to remind himself that the boy was well aware of his and Cadeyrn's relationship and seemed to be supportive of them.

"How would you guys feel about having a second daddy?" Cadeyrn asked.

Kajaan wasn't sure if the kids could hear the apprehension in his lover's voice. Maybe it was because Kajaan could feel the anxiety thrumming through their bond, along with an undercurrent of hope that the kids would accept them so easily. Of course, overlaying that was the overwhelming exhaustion from the sedative. Their bond wasn't quite back at the strength it had been, but much better than when Cadeyrn had been unconscious.

"A second daddy?" Fayette asked. "How?"

"By marrying another man," Marika finally said quietly.

Fayette squirmed up to her knees, the boney joints digging into both adults.

"Kajie?" she exclaimed. She had the biggest grin on her face, her eyes wide and bright with excitement. "Really, Papa?"

"Is that okay, sweet pea?" Cadeyrn asked.

Instead of answering him, Fayette flopped down on top of Kajaan, wiggling into him with happy whimpers as exuberantly as only a six-year-old could. Rodolfo crawled up and joined her in Kajaan's personal puppy pile, making him groan with their combined weight and heat. With Thaddaeus behind him, he had a feeling he'd overheat far too quickly.

"Marika?" Cadeyrn asked hesitantly.

"Yeah," she whispered. "I'd be okay with Kajaan as a daddy."

Kajaan felt a flood of relief pour through their bond. He smiled, managing to turn his head just enough to look at the twins grinning down at him. After pulling his arms out from under them, he wrapped them around the two and rolled over further, crashing them into Thaddaeus. The eldest yelped, though he dissolved into laughter along with his twin siblings.

Gentle fingers plucked at the hem of his shirt, contentment thrumming through their bond loud and clear. Kajaan scooted back slightly, keeping as much contact as he could with his lover. Cadeyrn's hand slipped under his shirt, resting on his stomach.

"Kajaan is my Fated," Cadeyrn said, his voice dropping down toward a whisper. "We sealed our bond today. Meant to talk to you kids first, but… I'll make sure the bonding conditions are clearer when you four are old enough."

"I'm glad you finally claimed him," Thaddaeus said.

"When will you two get married?" Marika asked.

"Winter or spring, probably," Cadeyrn said. "I don't want to compete with Prince Yolotzin's wedding. Especially since I promised Kaj that we'd go."

Kajaan smiled at the three kids looking up at him expectantly. He gathered as much of his joy as he could and pushed it through their bond. Cadeyrn deserved to know how delighted his consideration and forethought made him. Kajaan released his hold on the children and managed to squirm back enough to press a kiss on his lips. Cadeyrn sighed happily and buried his nose into Kajaan's hair. The remnants of the sedatives were taking a heavy toll on him, and he was fading fast.

"Can I help plan the wedding?" Fayette whispered, loud enough to not even be considered a whisper.

"You'd have to ask Quillin," Kajaan said. "I don't know the ins and outs of a Zothuan wedding and what is socially acceptable. I'm sure your papa won't mind your ideas."

Fayette grinned. "On a gexena! Maeeri would want to be a part of the wedding."

"I don't have a gexena," Kajaan said nervously.

"We've got plenty in the stables," Thaddaeus said, heedless of Kajaan's spike of nerves. "We've got a couple of unbonded ones too, so even if you're not their rider, they'll behave."

"Maybe I should get my horse while we're in Averia. That way I can be on horseback while Cade is on Maeeri," Kajaan suggested.

"Maeeri is too tall! How will you kiss?" Fayette gasped, her eyes wide.

"We'd only ride them down the aisle," Kajaan said. "Unless it's different here?"

"No. Two stable hands would take them once you reach the altar. No one wants to have the wedding interrupted if the gexena starts to urinate or defecate," Marika piped up from the other side of the bed. "That would be unsanitary."

Kajaan looked over his shoulder to see Marika sitting up to see them. He glanced down at his lover and smiled, seeing Cadeyrn's face lax and peaceful as he slept.

"Well, we can talk more about it later. I'm sure Quillin has a lot of things he needs to do in preparation, and it'll take a while. We have time," Kajaan said. "Thank you for accepting me into your family."

"You make Papa happy," Fayette said, as if it was the easiest thing in the world.

Thaddaeus smiled. "He's been happier since you've gotten here. Except when you were in the dungeons, of course."

Of course. Kajaan smiled at his soon-to-be stepchildren, and his heart warmed. He didn't know how soon it would be before he and Cadeyrn would start having children of their own, but even if they didn't, these four would be enough. Maybe it was a remnant of being an only child, but he'd always wanted a large family.

Kajaan lay back down, sighing happily from being surrounded by his new and not quite official family. The napkin ring bracelet hung heavily on his wrist, pulling his thoughts toward his oldest friend. While Yolotzin would always be a part of his life, it really was time to move on. He had his own Fated. His own husband-to-be. His own lover, who wouldn't think to stray from their bed.

Happy seemed like too small of a word to describe how he felt. Elated? Blissful? Marika would probably know the best descriptor.

One by one, the kids started dropping off. Ensconced in the pile of sleeping Greatblaze children, Kajaan found himself more than content for the first time in a long time.

Chapter 18

Yolotzin's bootheels echoed down the marble hallway as he strode toward his father's office. There was something horribly wrong. He could feel it. The energy in Avitou had shifted dramatically ever since he came back from Zothua without Kajaan or news of his death. His father had been nearly beside himself with rage when he learned that the redhead was alive and well despite Yolotzin's joy.

The fact that Kajaan and King Cadeyrn were apparently Fated was something Yolotzin kept quiet, not even risking telling Kende or Naias. Especially since Kajaan was a little freaked out by the idea of being King Cadeyrn's Fated. Or perhaps not as much anymore considering their latest cipher.

Thanks for the warning. Security will be tightened over here. Cadeyrn and I are kissing. He's very warm. I'm training and trying to get stronger. Miss you. Love, Kajaan.

Of course, it didn't explicitly say that. He'd hidden his copy of *Fields of Gold* in his room. Though if Naias found it, he'd tell her why he had it while they walked together in the park. Away from the castle. She seemed fairly easy with his and Kajaan's relationship, not harboring any jealousy, which was a huge relief. Maybe watching Asyl and Kende fall in love had helped with her acceptance.

Naias was such a wonderful lady.

Which was why Yolotzin was refusing to move her into the castle. Her parents didn't understand why he was holding out, insisting that they spend as much time together as possible to strengthen their bond. Naias did deserve that, so they'd compromised and Yolotzin slept at her home these days, despite both of their parents' ongoing confusion. He hated being in the castle right now. It felt so oppressive.

Most of the negative energy came from his father and his study. Yolotzin stood on the other side of the wooden door, taking in slow, deep breaths. He knew his father knew he was outside his door. Heat signatures were something no one could hide, and his father was quite skilled at locating them, even through obstacles. Yolotzin placed a hand on the handle, steeled himself, and opened the door.

Inside the dark room, barely lit by Ignis lamps, were his parents. His mother sat by the back wall, her eyes a little glassy and vacant as usual. She'd been so full of life when he was little, encouraging him and Kajaan to play together and forge a nearly unbreakable friendship. Sometime around his Awakening, she'd changed. Yolotzin still had no idea what had happened, but after that, he knew she no longer shared a bed with his father.

King Tonalli sat at the heavy dark wood desk that took up a good chunk of the room. Imposing and meant to intimidate whoever entered his study, including his children, who rarely visited. His father always wore his regalia, no matter whether anyone was around. King Tonalli's everyday crown sat firmly on his head, and his cape was draped over his shoulders, though he was careful not to splatter any ink on it. He was working on something even as Yolotzin approached.

"You called, Father?" Yolotzin said slowly.

"Yes, good. Sit," his father ordered him.

Yolotzin quietly sat in one of the uncomfortable wooden chairs and waited, listening to the quill pen scratching across the paper. He slowly unleashed his tightly controlled Craft, sending out feelers into the room. Past the first strong wave of fury from his father, Yolotzin could detect glee, apathy, boredom, and passion. He did his best to not wrinkle his nose in disgust. Had his father brought a mistress in here? When he took over, he was going to have the room gutted, cleaned, and get all new furniture. Maybe knock a hole in the wall to put in a window.

He loved the stained-glass windows in Paelfjord Castle. Maybe he could get ideas from King Cadeyrn along with those little fire bubbles that hovered at the ceiling of every room. Kajaan still hadn't written about them. Maybe the fascination of the things had slipped his mind. After all, he'd be used to them by now. Yolotzin's heart ached. He missed his best friend.

For better or for worse, right?

It really felt like worse right now. They'd made the promise a lifetime ago, in boyish fantasy and ignorance of the world around them. The two of them had been so convinced that they'd be together forever, riding the high of his eldest sister's wedding and vows. Now they were separated by hundreds of miles, a country border, and a very real threat on Kajaan's life.

If he ever came back over the border without protection, he'd be charged and killed for the improper use of his Craft. Yolotzin had found King Cadeyrn's immunity request for his visit and accepted it behind his father's back. He wanted to see his best friend. Wanted his best friend to be here for his wedding. Kajaan couldn't stand with him anymore, which hurt to no end, but he could at least be present.

Then they could celebrate together. He could celebrate with Kajaan about him finding his own Fated. And inheriting four kids who probably already adored him. That was good. Both he and Kajaan had wanted large families and planned to have as many children as they could. Filling the whole nursery full of little bundles of joy they could cherish for the rest of their lives. Luckily, Naias seemed to be of the same mindset.

Kajaan had been right during their last night together, and that sense of loss sent a pang of regret through Yolotzin. Years from now when he finally took over for his father, when he could pardon and recall Kajaan, Yolotzin would probably have children. Seeing that would hurt Kajaan more than anything, even if he wasn't Fated to King Cadeyrn. At least over there next to the desert, Kajaan had the opportunity to raise four children.

Maybe even have some of his own, if King Cadeyrn was open to surrogacy. Yolotzin truly did want little copies of Kajaan to spoil. Maybe once their kids got old enough, they could do an exchange or some sort of boarding for each other. That way, his children could know their uncles and know that if there were ever any problems here, they'd always be welcome at Paelfjord Castle. And of course, any of Kajaan and King Cadeyrn's children would be welcome here in Avitou.

"Done," King Tonalli grunted.

He poured his gold shimmering red wax on the bottom of the paper, and Yolotzin realized he had just drafted a proclamation. The overwhelming joy he felt from his father was terrifying, and Yolotzin swallowed hard. He did his best to not flinch when his father's beady eyes fixed on him. Long ago, when his mother still laughed, his father's blue eyes had been soft and kind. Now they were as sharp as chipped ice. How had he not seen that detachment before?

"You summoned me, Father," Yolotzin said instead, hoping his voice didn't shake too much.

His father grinned at him. Clearly he hadn't been quite successful enough. Shit.

"Yes. What's with this nonsense of not moving Lady Naias into your quarters? She needs to be by your side and share your bed. Neither of you are getting younger, and if you want children, the sooner the better," his father said.

Yolotzin blinked slowly and flexed his hands into fists. Digging his nails into his palms helped center him, focusing on the pain. He glanced at his mother, who was still staring at nothing. Seeing her in such a state made his heart ache so much. She'd been an immensely strong woman and was now reduced to nothing more than a ghost. Yolotzin forced his eyes back to his grinning father.

"I will speak with her about it. I know her parents would be overjoyed," Yolotzin said slowly. "However, she is a few years younger than I. Her body and spirit are strong, so I have no doubt we'll have problems there."

"Good. One of the few things women are good for. A king must have a healthy broodmare for his offspring," King Tonalli said.

Yolotzin outwardly winced at that. He looked at his mother again, who hadn't even blinked at his father's words. Trying not to alert his father, Yolotzin reached out to her with his Craft. She was empty. No emotions. No thoughts. Nothing. She was simply breathing. Existing. Oh Goddess, what had happened to his mother?

"If you say so," Yolotzin finally said. "Naias is everything to me."

Something flashed in his father's eyes, and that smile twisted a little more. Fear curled in his belly, realizing just exactly what he'd given his father. He'd freely given him leverage to make Yolotzin do whatever he wanted. When had he become scared of his father? Did his sisters feel the same way? Why hadn't he realized Kajaan's reluctance to be near King Tonalli might be more than just him being an Ignis?

He should have listened to his best friend better. The continual snipes to his Craft had closed him off from using it, but perhaps that had just put him in more danger in the end. Not even his dear Kajaan had been subject to his Craft lately, though he hadn't noticed. Not even Naias had noticed that he barely used his Craft from what was essentially shame.

"I do say so. Even if I have to hand the throne to a worthless non-elemental Craft heir. Maybe at least she'll pop out one or two proper heirs and restore our status," Tonalli said. "She is an Aquan, so at least one of you is strong."

The barb was meant to hurt, and it did. The implication there was clear, and Yolotzin did his best to hold back the choking pain. Had his father always thought he was weak? What was changing him so much? He didn't understand.

He wanted Reina to marry Thaddaeus despite their massive age difference, potentially crippling Zothua's prince.

Ten years ago. Could that have changed everything? Surely not. His mother had been fading for longer than that. Yolotzin didn't know what to think anymore. Yannat slipped into the office, quiet and sneaky as ever. He took the document that Tonalli had just finished with a satisfied smile on his face.

"Make sure that new law goes into effect before I retire tonight," the king said.

"Yes, Majesty," Yannat said.

Yolotzin missed the casual way King Cadeyrn had his people address him. There wasn't much standing on formality unless it was important business. Hell, some of his staff had even called him Cade. Tonalli would never let anyone in the castle call him by a nickname, Yolotzin included.

"New law?" Yolotzin asked as Yannat left the room.

A wicked smile spread across his father's face. One that made Yolotzin shudder and wonder again how depraved the man had become. Pure malice poured from him, so strong that it overrode the hold he kept on his Craft.

"Lady Ilfa and Mr. Gaten will be released and pardoned." Yolotzin shot to his feet, but his father wasn't finished. "They had the right of it. Voids are a plague among us. All Voids are to be rounded up and put into prison until they can be processed. They'll either be neutralized or have the pleasure of volunteering their bodies for Ignian inventors and Healer scientists. Flesh is always in demand to advance our knowledge and prowess."

"That's horrific!" Yolotzin snapped. "Voids can harness Craft energy and use it to enhance their own bodies or transfer that energy into another person. Asyl did that to save Kende's life."

"Then he should have died," Tonalli replied flatly. "I already have a few men ready to arrest Asyl. He'll go to the inventors. I've got a friend lined up ready to experiment with him."

The words made Yolotzin's stomach churn, and he clapped a hand over his mouth, swallowing down the bile that rose in his gut. He shook his head, staring at the man who fathered him. The man who'd loved him for years stared back with dead eyes and a cruel, twisted grin.

"This is genocide," Yolotzin said.

"Careful," Tonalli growled. "I can easily remedy the law to add sympathizers on there too."

No one would be safe without carefully defined parameters that Yolotzin was sure would be left off "accidentally." It would put Naias, Kende and his household, and countless others at risk. Olire's family would be hit for trying to protect their son. The women who work at Enchanted Waters, along with Asyl's sometimes bodyguard Tsela, would be arrested immediately. Lord Lairne and his brood wouldn't be safe either, despite his caste.

Yolotzin turned and fled from the office, hearing his father's cackle echoing in his head.

CHAPTER 19

THE LAST two days had been wonderful. Blissful, even. Once Cadeyrn recovered from the strong sedative and was reassured by the children that, yes, they really were thrilled to have Kajaan as a second father, there was an added stability to their relationship. Neither of them had to feel as if they were sneaking around the children's backs, though the twins perpetually ewww'ed when he and Cadeyrn kissed, no matter how chaste it was.

Kajaan had fully moved into Cadeyrn's suite, with the kids' help. He got his own closet that was hewn into the sandstone. Or rather, the doorway was reopened, since it had been closed up after Menea passed away. It was too large for what Kajaan currently owned, but he had a feeling it would fill up quickly.

Cadeyrn was a generous lover, and he was getting spoiled. Last night, a new set of clothes had been left for him on the bedspread. They were incredibly lightweight and felt as if he wasn't wearing anything. If it wasn't for the quiet swishing that the silk made, Kajaan could easily believe he'd forgotten to dress that morning.

Summer clothes, Cadeyrn had told him with an indulgent smile. When Kajaan put them on, the flowing garment let in enough air that he knew he'd be cool, but it would also wick away any sweat from his body. Kajaan requested some sleep pants to be made in the same material, making Inti crack a grin and nod knowingly.

Kajaan had wondered why Cadeyrn didn't sleep in the nude. It would have been more comfortable in the long run, and Kajaan chafed at having what he viewed as an unneeded layer. He realized why the next morning when Fayette and Rodolfo tumbled into the bed, giggling madly and jumping on them. Kajaan laughed, snatched up the twins, and squeezed their little bodies tight to his, kissing their temples.

Rodolfo tried squirming away, claiming cooties, putting his hands over Kajaan's mouth. Oh, poor baby didn't know better. Kajaan licked his palm, and Rodolfo screamed. Cadeyrn took his son, laughing, and headed back to the twins' room with Fayette following him.

Rodolfo constantly wiped his soiled hand on Cadeyrn's bare shoulders, faking a few gags to try and get some sympathy from his father.

Kajaan flopped back onto the bed and sighed happily, closing his eyes for a minute. The two liked to get up right at the crack of dawn. He didn't mind, really, but sleeping in was nice, and he realized how much he missed it. Kajaan heard Inti enter the room, and the valet chuckled. Probably from seeing him stretching out on the bed.

"Morning," Kajaan said, yawning.

"Laughter is always a good thing to wake up to," Inti said, already heading to Cadeyrn's closet.

"It is," Kajaan confirmed.

Kajaan rolled onto his stomach, nestling back into the sheets with a low groan. He'd get up in a little bit. Cadeyrn came back and said something to Inti, low enough that Kajaan couldn't hear it. Their bedroom door opened and closed one more time. It was completely silent. Once that would have worried Kajaan, not knowing who was in the room or if he was going to be attacked. Now he knew that the staff harbored no hatred toward him.

It didn't hurt that he had a man who so clearly adored him.

The bed dipped and weight settled on his legs, pressing up to the curve of his ass. Kajaan tilted his head and cracked open an eye to smile up at his Fated. He could feel his lover's contentment and a slow buzz of arousal through their bond. His lips quirked in a small smile.

"Hey," Kajaan murmured.

"Good morning," Cadeyrn replied thickly.

Oh. Oh yes, it was a good morning now. He felt a familiar rod digging against his crease. Kajaan groaned and pushed back with his hips, wiggling as best as he could. Cadeyrn grunted above him and thrust down, shoving Kajaan into the mattress. Kajaan moaned, arching at the pressure, delighted with Cadeyrn's rough handling.

"Please," Kajaan gasped out. "You're ready?"

"More than," Cadeyrn purred in his ear.

His Fated began kissing his neck in a trail down to his shoulder, where he gently nipped him. The man's weight left his legs briefly, and then Cadeyrn tugged his pants down and off. Kajaan kicked the silk away, not caring at all where it went. The next time Cadeyrn lowered himself, he could feel his lover's bare skin. Kajaan moaned into the pillow, pushing up into him, wanting that friction.

He felt empty as the need for Cadeyrn to take him sparked deep inside of him. Two strong, capable hands ran up his back on either side of his spine, heavy and firm. His Fated was finally confident about what he was going to do. It made Kajaan's heart swell, and he stretched underneath his lover's touch.

"How do you want me?" Cadeyrn asked softly.

"Like this is fine," Kajaan replied. "It'll be easier for your first time."

Cadeyrn pinched his ass, making him jump and laugh.

"I'm no virgin," Cadeyrn growled.

"For this, you are," Kajaan teased. "Fuck me into the mattress, love. You don't need to be gentle."

They hadn't exchanged "I love yous" yet despite the deep current of affection that flowed freely through their bond. Cadeyrn leaned over him, and their lips clashed together. By the time he pulled away, Kajaan was panting hard.

"I love you too," the king murmured.

Kajaan gave him a stupid grin and dropped his head back to the pillow, folding his arms underneath it. He pushed up with his hips again, groaning as Cadeyrn's heavy cock slid into his crease. Cadeyrn was already leaking and was leaving behind a trail as he rocked his hips. Sighing contentedly, Kajaan arched, unable to help himself. He wanted more, and soon.

Two wet fingers slid between his cheeks, and one plunged into his hole. Kajaan bucked and buried his face into the pillow, sighing as the burn quickly turned into pleasure. The first finger was joined by a second, diving deep into him. Kajaan rocked with Cadeyrn's thrusts, impaling himself on his hand as much as he could, seeking for that specific spot that would bring him ecstasy.

"Eager," Cadeyrn murmured softly.

A sharp slap to his left asscheek made Kajaan pop his head up, gasping. He let out a choked moan, wiggling his hips, trying to entice him further. Cadeyrn's fingers left him, and Kajaan cried out, far too empty for the promised pleasure his lover would bring him. His Fated couldn't leave him riled up like this. He started to reach down to grab his prick, needing the extra stimulation.

Kajaan stilled when he felt Cadeyrn's weight shift above him and a thick, warm, blunt object pushed against his hole. So much better than fingers and nowhere near as sharp. Cadeyrn pushed, and Kajaan willed himself to relax and take the invasion as painlessly as he could. The stretching pulled a groan from deep within his chest as Cadeyrn's cock popped inside of him.

Cadeyrn didn't stop, didn't give him a moment to breathe. He pushed in deep, bottoming out in one long, steady thrust. Kajaan pushed up on his elbows, panting hard, trying to clear his mind from the blast of need through their bond to participate. Blessedly, Cadeyrn waited for a moment, letting the burn change to pure pleasure. Kajaan finally shivered and nodded, letting his Fated know he was all right.

His lover pushed him down to the mattress and almost pulled out. He thrust back in, and Kajaan shouted, his eyes rolling back. It didn't hurt, not for a second. It felt right… perfect. Like this was exactly what he was made for. Cadeyrn wasn't gentle, having taken Kajaan's request seriously. His Fated built up to a rough pace, the wood bed frame protesting slightly.

Kajaan put one shaking hand out onto the headboard to steady himself and try to push back into each slam. He hadn't quite expected Cadeyrn to go so hard immediately. Maybe being rough was what his lover needed too. Kajaan let out a string of low moans, gasping every time Cadeyrn dove home. He squirmed a little, reaching back and patting his Fated's knee.

"Let me up a little," Kajaan managed to say.

Cadeyrn slid out and backed up, giving him room. Kajaan got his knees up underneath him and wiggled his hips, silently telling Cadeyrn that he was ready. Strong hands gripped his waist, and Kajaan reached back, guiding Cadeyrn's cock back to his hole. The next second, he was full again, his lover's cock stretching him thoroughly. Kajaan moved with Cadeyrn, their skin slapping together, filling the room alongside their cries.

He bowed his back, and Cadeyrn's next thrust hit his prostate. Kajaan yelped and his lover chuckled, only to repeat the motion. Pleasure clouded his mind, and he began moving on pure instinct, chasing his orgasm. He was so close. Kajaan pushed back and sat up, falling back onto Cadeyrn's lap. They groaned together, the change pushing Cadeyrn in just a little deeper. Precum dripped down Kajaan's prick in a slow rivulet as he shuddered from the overwhelming pleasure.

Kajaan hooked one arm back to grab Cadeyrn's beautiful silky hair. His lover wrapped his arm around his waist, helping hold him steady. Kajaan rested his other arm on top, twining their fingers together. They rocked slower now, shallowly pulsing up into him rather than long thrusts. Cadeyrn nuzzled into his neck and Kajaan turned his head. Their lips met in a sloppy kiss, though neither of them really cared.

"Cade," Kajaan groaned low in his throat. "Please."

A spark of arousal surged through their bond. His lover grabbed Kajaan's cock, pumping him hard in time with his languid thrusts. Kajaan tightened his hand in his hair, panting as Cadeyrn moved faster, pulling out further each time until only the tip remained inside him. One more hit to his prostate and Kajaan's breath caught in his throat as he spent in thick ropes. Pleasure cascaded through his mind, spinning the world around him.

Kajaan slumped boneless against Cadeyrn, moaning brokenly as his lover thrust a couple more times up into him. Cadeyrn shouted his release, and Kajaan felt his lover spill deep inside of him. The man's hips stuttered against his, and Kajaan whimpered, feeling Cadeyrn's orgasm crashing through their bond. His cock gave one more pulse, valiantly trying to come again. He wasn't sure how long he floated from the echoing waves, basking in the afterglow.

Cadeyrn groaned behind him, and he felt himself falling. Kajaan gasped, slamming back into himself the moment they hit the mattress on their side. His lover had even angled him so he didn't end up in the wet spot. They lay together, panting and trying to recover from their lovemaking. Kajaan squeezed the hand he still had in his and hummed happily.

"Goddess," Cadeyrn murmured.

Kajaan chuckled and snuggled deeper into his lover's chest. He hummed his agreement, his throat a little too sore to speak at the moment.

"If I knew it would feel that good, I would have jumped you moonturns ago," Cadeyrn said, snickering.

Kajaan couldn't stop the laugh that bubbled up inside him. They lay together in perfect silence for a few more minutes, Cadeyrn slipping out of him at some point. Kajaan was too blissed out to really think too much at the moment, and in his stupor, he must have fallen back asleep. The next time he opened his eyes, the room was brighter, and the cum on the sheets had dried. He was warm, sated, and so incredibly happy.

His lover was slowly running his fingers through his hair. Kajaan stretched, groaning as he felt the soreness in his lower back. His ass still felt a little numb, and he figured he'd be feeling Cadeyrn's club of a cock for the rest of the day. That would be one hell of an ache he'd cherish.

"Will you be all right?" Cadeyrn asked.

"Yeah," Kajaan said through a yawn. "Might walk funny for a bit, but I'll be fine."

Cadeyrn hummed and rolled Kajaan around, tucking him in under his chin. Kajaan chuckled and nestled into his Fated, draping his arm over his waist. Outside, he could hear the children laughing and screaming. Likely the twins escaping from their nanny once again. Kajaan couldn't help his grin, listening. Yes, that was absolutely Fayette squealing.

"When did you realize you wanted kids?" Cadeyrn asked.

"I've wanted a whole gaggle ever since I was a teenager. Tzin and I had plans on two surrogates, either once we felt the Fated bond or when we got married. We wanted our kids to be a mix of the both of us," Kajaan replied.

There was a long moment of silence between them again, letting in more of Fayette's squeals. Rodolfo shouted at something, but it wasn't quite clear what.

"Would you want to do the same here?" Cadeyrn asked. "I'm sure we could find an approved surrogate that we could have legally recognized so the kids from you would be part of the royal lineage."

Kajaan's breath caught in his throat, and he looked up at Cadeyrn in surprise. He blinked a few times before a smile spread across his face. They'd briefly touched on the topic a couple of days ago, but the oasis trip almost felt like a dream now. Maybe they could solidify their plans a little more.

"Do you really mean that? You want more babies?" Kajaan asked.

"I would love more kids," Cadeyrn said with a smile. "Menea and I were trying for another when she got sick. I miss the baby smell sometimes."

"Then I would love to start looking," Kajaan replied, wrapping his arms around Cadeyrn's neck and kissing him quickly. "Shouldn't we get married first, though?"

"We should," Cadeyrn said and huffed. "So much political nonsense. I don't care about parties, and the lords are going to have to deal with the fact that you're my Fated no matter what they think."

"You just don't want me near Lord Neerian," Kajaan teased him.

"Oh Goddess, don't remind me," Cadeyrn groaned, flopping onto his back. Kajaan followed his love and curled up into his side. "His response came back yesterday, saying I was *unfair* and that I would *bankrupt* him with all my unfounded fines."

Kajaan snorted. "I bet Quillin's having a field day with that."

"Completely," Cadeyrn replied with a laugh.

The commotion outside changed. Instead of peals of laughter, more urgent shouting echoed through the halls. The two looked at each other and leaped out of bed. Kajaan took a few wobbly steps, his body suddenly rebelling about having to support his weight. Cadeyrn quickly helped him dress before he took off outside.

Kajaan was on his heels, keeping one hand on the wall as he followed him. They ran to the great hall, and Kajaan stopped in his tracks, stunned at the sight before him. Lord Asyl and Olire stood in the hallway, the older Void's face reddened as he shouted at Quillin.

"I don't *want* to be here!" Lord Asyl was saying. "That's what I'm trying to tell you! I need to talk to King Cadeyrn!"

"I'm here," Cadeyrn said, trying to keep his voice calm.

Lord Asyl turned and seemed to sag in relief. Olire slumped down next to a small bag he'd dropped and curled into a ball as he burst into tears. Something very bad had happened. Kajaan approached quietly, watching Lord Asyl slap the tears off his cheeks.

"Tonalli is a bastard," Lord Asyl said flatly once he and Cadeyrn got closer. "He's passed a new law to incarcerate Voids and give them to psychopathic scientists for whatever experiments they dream up for *science*. If we don't cooperate, then we'll be murdered like chattel."

Kajaan blinked once and stared at the man before him, completely stunned. He knew King Tonalli was a heartless ruler these days, but Kajaan never thought he'd stoop so low. Trying to wipe out a whole portion of his population? For what purpose?

"You can't be serious," Cadeyrn snarled. He spun to Quillin. "Please tell me we opened the borders to Voids."

"We did," Wayra said, nodding. "One of the first Voids brought a flier with the new law, so we decided to open the border and settle them in Kierton for now. I just got a report a few hours ago."

"Why wasn't I told this?" Cadeyrn said, actually sounding mad.

Kajaan walked over to his lover and slid his hand into Cadeyrn's, wincing at the rage he felt building through their bond. He had to breathe in slowly to push back the panic that started to tug at his mind. The contact alone calmed Cadeyrn, and he closed his eyes, pinching the bridge of his nose. Their bond quieted, allowing Kajaan to feel his Fated's despair.

"You were occupied this morning," Quillin said dryly.

That made Cadeyrn's cheeks flame, and he slowly nodded, sighing. He rubbed the back of his head and nodded again.

"All right. Get Lord Asyl and his young friend set up with rooms here. These two will stay here and be treasured guests," Cadeyrn said.

"What about Tzin?" Kajaan asked. "Can't he get it reversed?"

Lord Asyl shook his head. "Tonalli threatened him that if he got involved or tried to oppose him, he'd include sympathizers. He'd be able to imprison Yolotzin, Naias, Kende… my family. Olire's family. Who knows what the hell those insane assholes have planned for the other Voids."

"Is anyone pushing back?" Cadeyrn asked.

Lord Asyl nodded. "Kende is. He and Macik are banding together and gathering a lot of support within the gentry with both of our fathers' help. Yolotzin is… technically not involved."

"But he is," Kajaan said with a small smile.

His idiot best friend. He was going to get himself killed. Lord Asyl nodded and turned to Olire, pulling the teenager to his feet. The boy wasn't far past his Awakening, from what Kajaan understood. Damn it. There should be no reason why this poor child had to flee his kingdom because his king was going insane. Kajaan turned to his Fated, taking in the murderous look on his face.

"Is there anything we can do?" Kajaan asked softly.

"We can support the Voids coming across the border. I'll confer with the other monarchs I know well to see what we can do," Cadeyrn said and sighed heavily. "Maybe we can appeal to the council and get Tonalli dethroned. I'm sure Prince Yolotzin would be a far better ruler."

"How are Voids treated in other countries?" Lord Asyl asked.

"Just like any other citizen," Cadeyrn replied. "Only Averia is backwards with suppressing their Voids. You have an important role in society. It's not your fault that Tonalli can't see that."

Olire slumped against Lord Asyl, sniffling and burying his face into the man's shoulder. Kajaan's heart ached for the boy, and he took a step toward him to comfort the fellow redhead. Thaddaeus beat him to it, trotting over with a big smile.

"Want to see gexena?" Thaddaeus asked in clipped Averian.

"Gexena?" Olire asked.

"It's what we rode in on. Yolotzin gave us Hariam to ride here," Lord Asyl explained.

They must have ridden Hariam to the edges of his stamina to get here so quickly. Kajaan didn't know how good of a rider Lord Asyl was, but he felt a bit of pride for the young man, and he smiled sadly. Hopefully Yolotzin wouldn't need the gexena for himself and Lady Naias if the two of them needed to flee Averia as well.

Olire looked at the prince and slowly nodded. Thaddaeus grinned and held out his hand, bouncing slightly on his toes. As soon as Olire took the offered gesture, he was tugged toward the side door that led to the gardens. Like a hunting pack, Marika, Rodolfo, and Fayette trailed after them. The three looked worried. Though they hadn't been able to follow the conversation, they'd been able to pick up on the tension in the room just fine.

Maybe Thaddaeus would explain to the three once Olire was resting. The boy looked beyond exhausted. So did Lord Asyl, underneath his anger and frustration. Kajaan looked back at the man, who was currently fighting a yawn.

"How hard did you ride?" Kajaan asked.

"We didn't stop," Lord Asyl said. "Whenever Hariam needed a break, we'd just walk for a few miles. He was a huge sweetheart and made sure we were safe from the Averian guards that tried to come after us."

"He didn't mind carrying you two without Prince Yolotzin?" Cadeyrn asked.

Lord Asyl shook his head. "Not at all. I think Yolotzin talked to him with his Craft to explain the situation. We had to leave quickly. According to Yolotzin, Tonalli had officers ready to arrest me as soon as the law went into effect."

"Why?" Cadeyrn asked.

Lord Asyl shrugged. "Fuck if I know. Probably some sort of personal vendetta. Or Duke Ruvyn is still pissy about Kende being my

Fated and marrying me, but that wouldn't make sense since he seemed just as stunned about the law as we were."

"How is Lord Kende doing?" Kajaan asked.

His question seemed to cut right to Lord Asyl's heart. The man curled in on himself, an agonized look on his face. He shook his head and pressed his fists to his eyes.

"He's really upset," Lord Asyl said. "He doesn't want to be apart, but he knows I have to be here to be safe. Same with Olire's family. I had to practically drag him out of his home to get on Hariam. The police know who he is because of me, so he wouldn't be safe trying to hide. We had to leave, and his parents put him under my care."

"We will keep him safe, Lord Asyl," Cadeyrn said kindly.

"Please, stop with the Lord bullshit. I haven't felt like one in my entire life," Lord Asyl said weakly. "And I know you will. Kajaan is healthy and happy. But what about when you leave to attend Naias's wedding?"

"Do they finally have a date?" Kajaan asked.

Lord Asyl nodded and riffled through the bag at his feet. He pulled out an envelope sealed in red wax that shimmered gold in the noonday sun. Cadeyrn took it and popped open the invitation. It was beautifully made, the handwriting flowing with several loops and swirls, though it wasn't hard to read.

"Two moonturns away," Kajaan said, reading over his Fated's shoulder.

He waited for the announcement to hurt. It didn't. Instead, all he felt was joy for his childhood friend. He understood what it meant to find the one who was made just for him, and there was nothing Kajaan would do to interfere with that. A gentle hand slid to his lower back, and Kajaan looked up at Cadeyrn, who was watching him.

"I'm okay," Kajaan said gently. He got on his toes to kiss Cadeyrn on the cheek. "Really, I'm happy for him."

Cadeyrn nodded and smiled, dipping down and placing a soft kiss on his lips.

"This will give us time to have your introduction," Cadeyrn said. "There will be a lot of interested parties, and it'll be fairly involved."

"I thought you wanted to keep me away from Lord Neerian," Kajaan teased.

"I do," Cadeyrn replied, raising an eyebrow. "But you arriving at the prince's wedding as my recognized Fated will be better than as my unofficial lover."

"Kajaan!" Rhionne's voice cracked through the great hall like a whip. "Stop slacking and get over here for your lessons!"

Both he and Lord Asyl jumped at her voice. Kajaan leaned up and gave his love another kiss before scurrying off after his Aquan teacher. He trusted Cadeyrn and Quillin to get Lord Asyl and Olire settled. Hopefully they'd find some peace here while Averia tore itself apart.

CHAPTER 20

LORD ASYL and Olire weren't integrating into the castle well. Not like how Kajaan had seemingly fit in without any sort of monumental effort. Almost like he'd been destined to be a part of Paelfjord. Olire was prone to fits of high emotion, often ending up with him crying or running away to scream in his room. Cadeyrn didn't know how to help, often deferring to Lord Asyl once Olire's cheeks started to flush. Sometimes the older Void was able to calm his friend, sometimes it took Thaddaeus to calm Olire, and sometimes the boy was replaced by a banshee.

For the longest time, Cadeyrn wasn't sure why Lord Asyl kept Olire with him and talked fondly about the boy if he was so temperamental. That was, until he learned the boy's story. Olire had been one of the few who'd been disowned by his family for Awakening as a Void. Lords Kende and Asyl had taken him in for a few moonturns until his family called him back home after Lord Asyl's engagement.

In short, Olire hadn't had much time to reconcile with his family before this new law went into effect, throwing his whole life into disarray once more. He missed his parents fiercely and didn't harbor Lord Asyl and Kajaan's faith that the law would be reversed within the year. Olire simply believed that he was separated from his parents even more permanently than before.

Cadeyrn ended up sending the boy to work in the stables with the gexena underneath his stablemasters' watchful eye. It seemed the beasts, labor, and stability were doing him some good. By the end of the moonturn, Olire had calmed down and started playing with the other children in Paelfjord. He and Thaddaeus were forming a tight friendship that, in a way, Cadeyrn hoped would resemble Prince Yolotzin and Kajaan's.

Lord Asyl wasn't faring much better with his separation. If he wasn't hiding in his assigned room, he was either reading in a quiet corner of the library or hiding in the gardens. The Void's retreat into himself had struck Cadeyrn as odd, since Lord Asyl had seemed fairly lively and outgoing during his last visit. Except, his last visit he'd been with his husband. Maybe it was Lord Kende's presence that brought Lord Asyl's personality forward.

As much as Cadeyrn wanted Kajaan to spend time with Lord Asyl, he couldn't. Between running Thaddaeus's schedule, his own training, and starting to interview tutors for Marika, Kajaan's days were beyond full. More times than not, Cadeyrn felt Kajaan's frustrations at either himself or others. During those times, Cadeyrn pushed as much confidence and affection as he could through their bond, hoping that it would settle his lover. It worked about half of the time.

Ameyalli had come to Cadeyrn a few days ago, cackling with something his tricky Fated had done. Cadeyrn left the hiring of tutors completely to Kajaan, trusting him to know best, especially since Marika was fond of her second Papa.

His faith was well rewarded.

Kajaan had rejected a good number of tutors based on presence alone. If they seemed threatening or snobby, Kajaan thanked them for their time and sent them packing. The ones he thought would be a good fit got an intensive interview. Kajaan would pretend to not know much Zothuan, struggle with basic questions, ask the tutor to repeat themselves several times, and generally did his best to piss them off.

Many of the tutors who applied passed his tests, and he was even called out on his act by a Sympathetic history tutor. At that, Kajaan had just grinned and let him know that only the best would be chosen for Marika, since she was a delicate soul who needed a gentle tutor. There'd been one who'd lost their patience in quite the memorable way, cussing out and yelling at Kajaan, demanding to know why he was Marika's secretary if he didn't have any brains.

Kajaan dropped his pretense between one breath and the next and asked the guards to escort the tutor out. No further questions. No niceties. The tutor had been grabbed and forced to leave even after she tried to babble out an apology. The fact that she was an Ignis hadn't been lost on Cadeyrn, though he hoped his Fated remembered that not all Ignians were short-tempered and prone to shouting.

If their nights were anything to go by, Kajaan had most definitely found a way to no longer be wary of Cadeyrn's Craft. Kajaan often initiated their lovemaking, either by posing near the bed suggestively and wiggling his hips or simply dropping to his knees in front of Cadeyrn.

Either was quite the obvious hint of what his Fated wanted. Cadeyrn thoroughly enjoyed his lover's amorous nature, being fairly tactile himself. He could touch and kiss Kajaan for hours.

That urge was what drove Cadeyrn out of his study and into the gardens. He knew his lover was amongst the flowers, able to smell their sunbaked scent through their bond while the invisible cord tying them together drew him to Kajaan's location. Lord Neerian had sent his reply to Kajaan's introduction party—they'd both agreed to not do a gala, but rather a formal dinner—and his letter was quite scathing. Sure, the man didn't have any real reason to like him right now, but Quillin assured Cadeyrn that their rebuilding and updating project was benefiting everyone so far.

The most important thing was that his citizens were taken care of. None of them were starving or put out in the elements for too long, with the secretary they hired finding places for the displaced to stay. The laborers were swift, well paid, and sympathetic to the victims of the disaster. Some of the victims even pitched in to help rebuild homes, silos, and businesses. If Lord Neerian didn't want to see the goodwill the townsfolk were displaying and how it was helping their community, it was his problem.

Right?

Goddess, he just didn't like Neerian at all. Cadeyrn needed to clear his head. So of course that meant finding his Fated and nestling into him. Maybe see if they could slip to their bedchambers and cloud his mind with more pleasurable thoughts instead. Kajaan would forgive him for upsetting his afternoon plans, even if it was one of his rare moments that he got to himself.

Cadeyrn didn't have to go far into the gardens before he saw Lord Asyl. The Void was sitting underneath one of the large frond trees, his eyes fixed on the glittering gold sand of the Laiyi Desert. Cadeyrn watched his guest for a while, reaching out with his Craft to take stock of the man. A moment later, he snorted to himself for his idiocy. Lord Asyl was a Void. There wasn't a way for him to check on the man's temperature and make sure he wasn't overheating or sick.

Instead, Cadeyrn walked toward him, glad he'd swapped his long-sleeved shirts for short now that they were in early summer. He sat down next to Lord Asyl, watching his guest carefully. The man's blue eyes barely flickered toward him. Only the slight frown that tugged at his lips and tensing in his shoulders told Cadeyrn that Lord Asyl knew he was there.

"Are you well?" Cadeyrn asked, switching to Averian.

"Well enough," Lord Asyl replied flatly. "Thank you for taking care of us."

"It's my pleasure. Any friends of Kajaan's are friends of mine," Cadeyrn said. "I'm sorry I can't do more about King Tonalli."

The Void snorted and rolled his eyes, finally looking at him. His eyes were puffy, and there were bags under them that Cadeyrn hadn't quite noticed. With a flash of intuition, Cadeyrn realized that Lord Asyl wasn't sleeping well. How much agony must he be in from being separated from his Fated for an indeterminate amount of time? Cadeyrn remembered how awful it had been when he'd first lost Menea and winced.

Was Lord Asyl's suffering worse than his own had been? Their circumstances weren't quite the same, considering Lord Kende was still alive, but Cadeyrn wasn't sure what a prolonged separation did to a Fated bond. He should check with his Healers and make sure that Lord Asyl was going to be all right. In no way did he want to risk the Void's health.

"Who can?" Lord Asyl asked. "He's a king. Goddess forbid someone tell him he can't do something."

"That's what the world council is for," Cadeyrn replied gently.

"And what are they going to do? Say that it's his country, so it's his rules? They won't care about Voids," Lord Asyl said acidly. "No one cares about us."

"What happens to Voids in Averia isn't the truth everywhere else," Cadeyrn scolded him. "I have plenty of Voids staffed here in the castle. A few of them work with my Healers. Just because you don't have a Craft Mark doesn't mean that you don't have abilities."

Lord Asyl's lips twitched in the barest hint of a smile, his eyes growing distant for just a second. Some sort of memory, perhaps. Had Lord Asyl mimicked a Craft Mark at some point to hide his Void status? He wouldn't have been the first one to do so.

"Tell that to Tonalli," Lord Asyl muttered.

"I will when I see him at Prince Yolotzin's wedding," Cadeyrn said, shrugging.

Just the mention of the wedding sapped whatever strength Lord Asyl got from arguing with him. The man's shoulders slumped, and he turned to stare out at the desert again. It was a long while before Lord Asyl spoke again.

"If I didn't know how busy Kende was, I would have been upset that he hasn't come after me," Lord Asyl finally said. "I would have taken it as a sign that he really didn't love me and it was all an act."

"Why so cynical? You two are Fated, aren't you?" Cadeyrn asked.

"Yes. It took me a long time to believe it. We have some sort of bond, I think. He's not very happy these days, so I can't hear him. Of course, I don't know if it even works over such a distance," Lord Asyl replied gloomily.

"It should," Cadeyrn said kindly. "Your bond isn't constant?"

Lord Asyl shook his head. "I know the vague direction he's in, but if I'm upset, I can't pinpoint his location. We can feel each other's emotions, and Kende can read me like an open book. He likes to send me a lot of love through the bond, but I'm not very good at doing that.

"I can only hear him when I'm happy, but he can track me through the city and tell where I am based on sound and scent. It's a little annoying and makes it hard to truly surprise him. He knows if I've swung into the bakery or florist on the way home, and it ruins the excitement of an impulsive gift."

Cadeyrn smiled softly, watching the Void next to him. Only being able to feel the bond during moments of happiness was horrifying to him. He couldn't imagine not feeling Kajaan's moods through the whole day and trying to temper his downward swings. Or missing out on his amusement with the tutor interviews. Even Kajaan's frustration during his training was something Cadeyrn would hate to miss. Then there was Kajaan's pure joy of riding Maeeri, who had accepted Kajaan as a rider and was teaching him that gexenas really weren't terrifying.

He really needed to get Kajaan his own gexena. If breeding and rearing one didn't take so long, he'd offer to breed Maeeri for him. Cadeyrn didn't want to wait three years to give Kajaan his own mount. They'd have to go to auctions and breeders to check out young stallions and fillies to see if a gexena accepted Kajaan as their rider immediately. That way Kajaan could have as strong a bond with his mount as he had with Cadeyrn.

"Us going to the wedding isn't helping, is it," Cadeyrn asked.

Lord Asyl shook his head. "No. I know Kende will be there, so it makes it worse, knowing that you'll be able to see my husband, but I can't."

"What if you could?" Cadeyrn asked, remembering the diplomatic immunity paper he'd gotten a fortnight past.

Quillin had carefully examined it and told him that the immunity extended to the whole wedding party, which was a surprise. That included his entire retinue, though Cadeyrn wasn't too worried about his people breaking laws. When Cadeyrn had showed Kajaan the form, his lover examined the signature and laughed until his eyes filled with tears.

"King Tonalli didn't approve this," Kajaan had said, needing to take several deep breaths to talk. "See how the hyphen in his name connects with both the 'e' and 'h'? King Tonalli's doesn't. Otherwise, I wouldn't have known it was Tzin's forgery. He's getting scary good at it."

Cadeyrn smiled softly at the memory. The two of them had laughed while Quillin paled at the idea of Prince Yolotzin forging the king's signature. If the forgery was ever called into question, there might be problems, but Cadeyrn would figure it out if it happened. He wasn't going to borrow trouble.

"Tonalli can't arrest you if you're with us, and Kajaan could use his own valet. Inti has enough on his plate with me for weddings. I'm sure he could train you how to properly dress the king's fiancé," Cadeyrn suggested.

For a brief second, Lord Asyl looked elated. He sat up straight, and a hopeful gleam sparkled in his eyes. Then it was replaced with wariness, and he frowned at the king.

"And what do you want in return?" he asked.

"To help Inti get Kajaan and I ready for the ceremony. Once that's done, you can run off and find your Fated for the evening. You may have to return before long, but a couple hours in his arms might do some good for the both of you," Cadeyrn suggested.

The hopeful look came back, and Lord Asyl smiled.

"I would like that," he said. "Thanks."

"Don't say that just yet until you see what Kajaan is going to be wearing," Cadeyrn teased him.

"What am I wearing?" Kajaan asked, strolling over to them.

"Clothes," Lord Asyl supplied helpfully.

Kajaan gave a short laugh and sat on Lord Asyl's other side. His skin was sun-kissed, the scars on his arms shimmering, and there was a bit of pinkness to his cheeks Cadeyrn didn't quite like. He reached out with his Craft, avoiding the vacuous space that was Lord Asyl, to check on his love's temperature. It was quite elevated, and the slight fevered look spoke of a potentially serious ailment. Cadeyrn immediately used his Craft to lower the temperature surrounding them.

"Hello, love," Cadeyrn said warmly. "Lord Asyl and I were just discussing him being your valet during the wedding so he can come with us since the immunity is for the whole party."

"Just Asyl, *please*," the Void begged.

"That's a fantastic idea," Kajaan said with a smile. "What about Olire?"

"He could be an extra pair of hands to help with the twins," Cadeyrn said, shrugging. "I'm sure Miski would relish the help."

"Fay and Rod do like him," Kajaan agreed with a smile. He gave a gusty, overexaggerated sigh and simpered at Asyl. "Our men know how to make us happy, Lord Asyl."

Cadeyrn felt his cheeks heat even as he preened slightly at Kajaan's words. Asyl just looked annoyed as he glowered at Kajaan.

"No titles, for Goddess's sake. It's just Asyl, *Prince* Kajaan," Asyl shot at him.

Kajaan went completely still for a minute. He blinked and looked up at Cadeyrn. The complete surprise and bafflement on his face made Cadeyrn burst into laughter.

"Yes, love. You will have a title. It's Quenlet, though, not prince, since you'll be ruling by my side," Cadeyrn said.

This time it was Asyl's turn to cackle as Kajaan's face paled. Clearly everything that came with being Cadeyrn's Fated hadn't registered to Kajaan yet. Marrying into royalty wasn't easy. It came with a lot of rules, many of which the two of them had broken during their courtship. Though that would be overlooked solely based on them being Fated and that Cadeyrn was already an established king with heirs. Usually they wouldn't be sharing a bed until after their marriage or allowed to be alone without a chaperone.

"Quenlet Kajaan," Asyl said slowly and smiled at him. "I'd say lucky man, but I don't envy how busy you'll be. My shop will be enough for me whenever I get back. Especially since I'll have to build my reputation up again."

"I'm sure Lord Kende will help you there," Kajaan said absently, turning to stare at the sand.

Asyl looked between the two of them and sighed, shrugging. Apparently he was picking up on Kajaan's overwhelmed thoughts. Cadeyrn wasn't about to pick through their bond just yet. Not with Asyl still here, though he seemed a bit more hopeful than he'd been a mere hour earlier.

"I'll meet with Inti and talk to him about me being Kajaan's valet. Then I'll hunt down Olire and tell him our plan to have him help out with the twins," he said, standing. "Thank you, King Cadeyrn. You have no idea how much this will mean to us."

Cadeyrn simply nodded at the man with a faint smile. Asyl turned and left the two alone without another word. Silence stretched between Cadeyrn and Kajaan, and Cadeyrn found himself at a loss on what to do. Eventually he reached out and took Kajaan's hand into his, twining their fingers together. The quiet allowed Cadeyrn to check on the cooling field he had around them and how much longer he could sustain it. Another hour at the most, and then he'd have to rest.

He lifted Kajaan's hand to his lips and kissed it gently, eyeing his Fated carefully.

"I didn't realize," Kajaan finally said in Zothuan. "I mean, it's stupid to be surprised, right? But I never really thought I'd be your equal."

"Of course you will be," Cadeyrn said gently. "You'll be my husband, and we'll help our citizens together. I'll listen to what you have to say, and if I'm indisposed, then our people will look to you for guidance and help."

Kajaan inhaled slowly and nodded, blinking finally. It took another minute for Kajaan to look at him.

"That's scary," he said. "I'm nobody, Cade. I wasn't raised to be special or important."

"But you are," Cadeyrn replied. "You're everything to me. If I lost you or any of the kids, I'd… I don't know what I would do anymore. Your kindness and empathy will serve you well and will help me bring Zothua to the best she's ever been."

"Don't you understand how terrifying that is?" Kajaan said weakly. "To put so much hope and faith into me? I'm a motherless child whose own father couldn't care less about him, and I latched on to Yolotzin because he was kind to me. Just as I've latched on to you."

"You're my Fated, Kaj," Cadeyrn murmured. He wrapped his arm around his lover and pulled him in close, kissing his temple. "Of course you'd latch on to me. I can't imagine my life without you. I want you by my side even when we're old and gray, criticizing Thaddaeus and his Queen or Quenlet. I want to have more kids with you. I want little redheads running around Paelfjord, causing trouble and living up to the Greatblaze name."

Kajaan looked up at him with flushed cheeks. He sighed and wrapped his arms around Cadeyrn's neck, wiggling into his lap.

"Oh, Cade. What if I mess up and get people killed?" Kajaan asked weakly.

Cadeyrn took a moment to kiss his Fated, sliding his tongue in to taste his love. Kajaan must have had something spicy recently, the flavors bold and nearly overwhelming. Cadeyrn slid his arm down to hold Kajaan around his waist and pulled him tight to his chest. His lover returned the kiss, easily opening and submitting to him. It took Cadeyrn a few minutes to break away, breathing heavily.

"Everyone makes mistakes," Cadeyrn said, dropping his head to press their foreheads together, rubbing Kajaan's nose with his own, drawing a smile from him. "I won't lie. It's awful, and a horrible feeling, knowing you made the wrong decision. But it's better than being paralyzed with fear and unable to do anything. I have to weigh the options before me and try to make the choice that results in the least amount of life lost. Sometimes the right answer is to do nothing. Sometimes doing nothing will get more people killed than if I'd intervened. It's a fine line to walk, and it's hard.

"But that's what Ameyalli is there for. They're there to help with the really hard decisions. The ones that could end in a total disaster. Our advisor will help us see the problem objectively. Your input will be even more helpful since you were raised outside of Zothua, so you see things differently than we would."

"Just don't be indisposed for a long time when you bring me into the decision-making," Kajaan said with a weak smile. "I'll need to watch and listen to get a feel for everything."

"That's the plan," Cadeyrn murmured, kissing his lips lightly.

Kajaan sighed, his eyes fluttering closed. The anxiety that had been building to near overwhelming levels slowly eased, and Cadeyrn could feel his lover's muscles begin to relax. His poor Fated. Kajaan still struggled with his self-worth and place in society, despite all the reassurances Cadeyrn tried to give him. Cadeyrn had accepted his lot in life a long time ago. But then again, he had always known he'd be the next king of Zothua. Kajaan's prospects had been slim while he was in Averia and only expanded recently.

Cadeyrn wrapped his arms around Kajaan's ass and stood. His lover yelped and flung his arms around Cadeyrn's neck, giving him a slightly terrified look. Cadeyrn just smiled and walked back toward the castle.

"Cade?" Kajaan asked softly.

Cadeyrn kissed the tip of his nose. "I think I want some alone time with you."

Kajaan flushed and smiled before leaning into him. None of the staff said a word as Cadeyrn carried his Fated up the staircase to their bedchamber.

CHAPTER 21

CADEYRN WAS slowly getting more tense the closer it got to Yolotzin's wedding, when hopefully the threat against them would be addressed and nullified. Kajaan couldn't lie that he was tired of constantly being wary of anyone he didn't know approaching him while in the castle. He wasn't permitted to leave Paelfjord to wander Sestella unless he was with Cadeyrn or Wayra, either. The restrictions chafed slightly, but Kajaan knew it was for his safety. At least Wayra seemed to know what was happening at the border almost constantly.

Kajaan did his best to keep himself occupied these days, which really wasn't too hard between his secretarial duties to the older children and his own training. His introduction dinner was looming on the horizon, and just after that was Yolotzin's wedding. At least his training with Rhionne had a breakthrough. After weeks of fighting his Craft, trying and mostly failing to move the water in the bowl, his tutor started one morning with the simplest question.

"How have you successfully used your Craft before?" she asked.

So he described how he'd changed the composition of the wine at Tillet's party to alter the alcohol content, and then eventually include a sedative. His middling success with the Craft vehicles that were popular within the gentry in Alenzon had been embarrassing to admit. Heating or cooling a small amount of water, such as his tea that had gone cold or a beer that had warmed too much, was a handy trick he'd learned yet rarely used. Then he described getting away from his would-be assassins, which was something completely out of the norm for his abilities. Pulling water from the air for the mercenary felt a bit truer to what he could do.

His descriptions seemed to spark something within Rhionne. She got to her feet and left him in the room, only to return with several covered tankards a few minutes later. The lids were marked with numbers, and Kajaan figured that his mentor knew what was inside, but she refused to let him pop open the lids to smell the contents. Rhionne set the tankards down and pushed the bowl of water aside with no more regard to it.

"Reach in with your Craft and see what the composition of the liquid is," she told him firmly.

Kajaan stared at her for a long minute before nodding. Why not fail at something else? Maybe after this she'd give up on him too. He took the first tankard into his hands and focused on his Craft. The tingling in his fingers came with barely a thought, his Craft eager to be put to work. It was almost as easy as breathing now. Kajaan closed his eyes to block out all other distractions and felt the ripples of the hidden contents. He delved further, smaller, to the molecular level.

He could taste tannins on the back of his tongue, his Craft intuitively working with his knowledge to tell him what he was experiencing. It recalled a fruity scent that filled his nose, and even the warmth that spread through him once he started to get buzzed. For a second, it felt as if his head was swimming. The feelings faded, only lasting a split second, though long enough for Kajaan to understand what his Craft was telling him.

"It's wine," Kajaan said, blinking at his tutor.

She nodded and handed him the second one. He repeated the process, identifying the other unknown liquids with ease. Water. Beer. Another wine. Water again, but different… salt water that he'd expect to get from the ocean. Oil. Slick. Rhionne had him compare the two wines again and asked him for the difference between them. Since he wasn't much of a sommelier, Kajaan was lost until she told him one was a red wine and the other a white. Then she took the white from him and took a generous swig.

That was when the situation hit Kajaan. He would never be an Aquan who could draw water from wells or redirect rivers. His Craft specialized in minute details, the smaller the better. Kajaan took the fresh water tankard and concentrated, thinking about how the beer felt across his senses and what it was made of. For a long while, he sat there with the tankard in his hands, thankful that Rhionne was giving him free rein.

Slowly, he could feel the composition of the water changing to mimic the beer. Cautiously optimistic, Kajaan flipped back the lid and inhaled. It smelled like the beer that Rhionne had brought him. It tasted just about the same too. Kajaan tamped down on his excitement and looked up at his mentor.

Rhionne just grinned at him, true joy and pride sparkling in her eyes. She took his hand, hauled him to his feet, and pulled him from the room. To Kajaan's mortification, Rhionne began hitting the marble floor with her cane to drum up her own version of a fanfare. Kajaan flushed a deep crimson all the way to his ears, unused to the excitement being centered on him. He supposed he'd have to get used to it. Especially once he married Cadeyrn.

Speaking of… his lover descended the stairs, looking as if someone had summoned him from his office. He looked a little bemused when he caught sight of the two of them, and his posture remained open. Rhionne beamed at him and squeezed Kajaan's hand in a reassuring manner.

"What?" the king asked, a smile tugging at his lips.

"Tell him what's in the tankard," Rhionne told Kajaan.

With a shy smile, Kajaan handed him the covered tankard and took a breath to steady his nerves. "It's beer."

Cadeyrn gave him a confused look and opened the lid, sniffing. He nodded his agreement, though Kajaan could still feel his lover's bewilderment through their bond.

"That it is," he said simply.

Kajaan shook his head and reached out, flipping the lid shut again. He wrapped his hands over Cadeyrn's and looked him in the eye.

"Cade. It's *beer*," he stressed.

It took his lover a full minute before his eyes widened.

"You identified it?" he asked.

Kajaan nodded and gave Cadeyrn a shaky smile. It was so stupid, something that a teenaged Aquan could do, but he hoped that his lover would be excited and supportive. He shouldn't have worried. Pride flowed through their bond, bolstering his confidence.

"Yes, but also, it was water before. I never looked inside it until after I changed it. Rhionne got me all these different tankards and had me identify what was inside without looking," Kajaan said, growing more excited with his explanation.

Cadeyrn grinned and dipped down, hooked his arm around Kajaan's hips, managed to pick him up, and spun him in one complete circle. Kajaan couldn't help but laugh, wrapping his arms around Cadeyrn's neck. He leaned in, and the two exchanged a gentle kiss even as he was deposited back on the ground. If he'd thought Cadeyrn was proud of him before, that was nothing compared to what was coming through their bond now.

"I always knew you'd figure out your Craft," Cadeyrn murmured against his lips.

"He's most certainly not a typical Aquan," Rhionne said, breaking into their revelry. "But I think his Craft will serve you well."

Cadeyrn nodded almost absently and cupped Kajaan's face, planting another kiss on his forehead. Kajaan hesitantly pulled at their bond, trying to see past the pride to see if there was anything underneath. Despite his minor worries, all he could feel was Cadeyrn's love for him. Nothing said that he was scheming about something. Kajaan chided himself. Hadn't his lover proven himself enough? That Kajaan would be safe with him? Not like how he'd been back in Alenzon.

"It feels weird knowing that I wouldn't have flourished under Torbid's training. I was never meant for the scenarios he wanted me to perform under," Kajaan said softly.

"That's why it's so important to be trained with someone who shares your Craft," Cadeyrn said firmly. "No other Craft tutor could realize that your abilities were so specialized."

Kajaan just smiled up at him. He closed his eyes and sank into his Fated's arms and warm body. Of course he'd always known that Cadeyrn believed in him and knew that he'd figure out how to harness his Craft. Knowing that and having it be proven to him were two completely different things. Rhionne tapped his calves with her cane as she walked past them and took the tankard from Cadeyrn's hand.

"Tomorrow we'll delve a little deeper into molecules and the like. How to separate them, identify different structures and foreign materials," she said with a grin. "This is going to be loads of fun. I've trained one other Aquan like you, and she was incredibly powerful."

"What does she do?" Kajaan asked.

"She brews alcohol. Beer and mead mostly," Rhionne said with a chuckle. "She loves it."

At that, the woman sauntered off, a spring in her step that hadn't been there after all their other failed sessions.

"I want to go see Tamya," Kajaan said, gently pulling away from his lover.

"Why?" Cadeyrn asked, looking confused.

"I want to see if this revelation has affected my reservoir," Kajaan told him, grinning. "I feel full of energy, and I'm not tired at all like I thought I would have been."

Cadeyrn simply nodded, and the two walked toward the room that Tamya was temporarily placed in. Rumors must have already been making their rounds, as the Healer met them outside her door, a huge grin on her face. Or perhaps Rhionne had swung by her granddaughter's office before leaving the castle. Either way, Tamya eagerly waved them into her room, nearly bouncing her way to the exam table.

Kajaan reluctantly sat on the minimally padded surface and tucked his shaking hands between his legs. His lover hovered near the door, arms folded across his chest, yet he couldn't stop the excitement and anticipation that thrummed through their bond. Kajaan was sure he was sending the same, with a hint more anxiety, of course. Tamya touched his temples with her fingers, and Kajaan did his best to not pull away or fight her when she dove into him.

Her touch felt so much different than Kende's. Kende was warm and slow-moving, as if he made sure that his power wasn't overwhelming. Tamya was equally gentle, but her Craft felt like he swallowed a beehive. The buzzing sensation centered in the center of his chest around his Craft, then withdrew after a minute or so. Tamya blinked to come back to herself and smiled at him while Kajaan fought the need to escape her.

"Your reservoir is growing. Slowly, but it's beginning to fill the space that it should. I think after your training with Rhionne, you'll be where you should be as an adult," she said.

Joy exploded inside of Kajaan, both from him and his lover's bond. Tamya backed away hastily as Kajaan slid off the exam table and bounced over to Cadeyrn. He flung his arms around his Fated, grinning and ignoring his love's deep chuckle. Not much could make him happier than he was now.

"Bed," Kajaan said firmly.

The Healer behind him burst into laughter even as Cadeyrn flushed slightly. Their sex life was fairly active, especially since their bond made everything so much more extreme and pleasurable, yet his lover was still shy about openly talking about their bedroom activities. Cadeyrn growled low in his throat and swept Kajaan up into his arms. He grinned, hooking one arm around the man's neck and using the other to rub Cadeyrn's jawline, down his neck, and over his collarbone.

By the time Cadeyrn managed to get their bedroom door shut behind them, Kajaan had riled himself up to a boiling point. He was aching to an almost painful level, needing his Fated in a way he couldn't quite understand. Cadeyrn dumped him onto the bed, and Kajaan immediately parted his legs as his lover fell upon him. Their kiss was fierce, not taking any time for a slow seduction as they tore each other's clothes off.

Kajaan managed to get Cadeyrn on his back and straddled his hips, panting with his sudden abundance of energy and desire. If he didn't know any better, he'd almost think that Cadeyrn was heating his core temperature. He hadn't felt so flushed in bed with another man in so long. Not even when he and Yolotzin read their favorite erotic passages from their romance books while touching and building the tension for hours before finding release.

This was going to be quick and dirty, Kajaan knew instinctively. He didn't want to wait for any finesse. Cadeyrn handed him the bottle of slick, and with a grin, Kajaan poured some onto his hand. He teased his lover's thick cock, using just the tips of his fingers first, making the man beneath him groan and squirm. Watching his chest rise rapidly was an aphrodisiac all its own. Once his lover was coated, Kajaan held him steady and shifted his hips back.

Kajaan loved riding. It really didn't matter what kind of riding either. Horses, gexenas, or his lover's prick… all were about the same. Well, that wasn't true. One was quite a bit more fun and pleasurable than the others. Kajaan sat fully on Cadeyrn's length, luxuriating in the burning stretch, sighing happily and feeling complete. He finally understood his Craft, he had his Fated, his place in life, a purpose, and children to adore.

He was home.

So completely and utterly home. Kajaan got his knees under him and braced his hands on Cadeyrn's chest, even as his Fated cupped his legs right under the curve of his ass. Together, they set their rhythm for the afternoon, quick and punishing. Kajaan couldn't help the whimpers and moans coming out of him any more than he could the slapping of their connecting hips. His Fated knew exactly where to touch him that would make him go out of his mind with pleasure.

Cadeyrn wasn't faring much better, grunting as he pounded up into him, sweat beading along his forehead. Precum formed on the tip of Kajaan's prick in a perfect, pearlescent bead, dropping to Cadeyrn's stomach on their next impact. More leaked from him as he rushed toward orgasm, dragging his lover along with him.

One good hit to his prostate had Kajaan jerking upright and arching back, clapping one hand over his mouth to mute the scream that threatened to leave him. Another shot lighting up his spine, past the sweat dripping toward the bed, his flesh erupting into goose bumps. The third made his balls draw up tight and the muscles in his lower abdomen clench in anticipation of the next hit.

Kajaan gripped Cadeyrn's wrist tight, digging his nails in with his lover's final thrust. His body exploded, and he barely recognized the shout that escaped between his fingers even as he emptied onto Cadeyrn's stomach. Heat rushed up inside of him, coating his insides as Kajaan ground down into his lover's hips, wanting more.

He started to tilt backward when Cadeyrn quickly braced him, drawing him toward his chest instead. Kajaan was still flying, the giddiness of their coupling no less potent now than it had been for their first time. He groaned softly, nestling into the sweaty warmth of his lover, not caring that some of the dampness was his own seed. Slowly he came back to himself, his breathing returning to a more normal level.

"Better?" Cadeyrn asked.

Kajaan laughed and nodded. The sense of completeness didn't leave when Cadeyrn slipped from his channel, his lover's hands roaming up and down his back. Maybe today's breakthrough was the last piece of his puzzle he needed to finally settle in. As they lay together, Fayette and Rodolfo's shouting drifted up from the garden, Olire and Thaddaeus's voices joining them a moment later. Kajaan couldn't help the grin that split his face wide.

It was good to be home.

CHAPTER 22

THE DAY for Kajaan's introduction dinner finally arrived, dawning bright, muggy, and warm. His poor Fated was uncomfortable in the growing heat, tossing and turning in their bed except for the deepest parts of the night. Cadeyrn had eventually put on his warmer clothes and forwent a blanket while Kajaan wore nothing.

That seemed to help, but Kajaan was still miserable when Inti roused them. Summer was in full swing, and it was clear to Cadeyrn that his lover would struggle with the season for years to come. He couldn't always alter the temperature around his love due to proximity and his own limitations. Kajaan would have to adjust eventually, but today would be an exception. Today wasn't going to be an exercise in adjusting to the heat. All of Kajaan's energy needed to be directed to the dukes and lords that were arriving.

Once Cadeyrn wrapped Kajaan in a cooling aura, his exhausted lover just smiled at him instead of demanding why he hadn't done so earlier. It made Cadeyrn glad to know that Kajaan didn't expect him to manipulate the temperature around him just because he could. As soon as they were dressed, Cadeyrn in his full regalia and Kajaan in a colorful, lightweight caftan that accentuated his hair, Inti placed a diadem on Kajaan's head, made of a warm gold that all but glowed against his tanning skin and framed his Craft Mark beautifully.

Cadeyrn stared for a long time, his memories pulling him back to the last time he saw his promised wearing the diadem. Menea had been standing in the hallway, a shy smile on her face as she ducked her head. The diadem was a bright streak in her dark hair, accenting her deep green eyes perfectly. Cadeyrn had been struck speechless then, just as he was now. The reality of everything came crashing down around him.

Kajaan was going to be his husband, his Quenlet. The partner who would be by his side for the rest of their lives. For a second, fear raced through his thoughts. Would Cadeyrn be good enough for Kajaan? Could he keep his Fated safe through all the political subterfuge that plagued them? Would the dukes and lords truly accept Kajaan simply because they were Fated?

His lover must have felt his distress through their bond as Kajaan approached him cautiously. Kajaan lifted onto his toes, rested his hands on Cadeyrn's chest, slid them underneath the shimmering Ignis cape he wore, and placed a light kiss on his lips. Cadeyrn let out his breath in a rush and offered his Fated a gentle smile. Comfort flooded into him along with a healthy dose of love, chasing away the doubts that churned in his mind.

"Sorry, my love," Cadeyrn murmured. "I was thinking of the first time I saw Menea with that diadem on and lost myself."

Kajaan gave him a sad smile. He trusted his Fated to not begrudge his dead wife. They both had a history with an important lover whom they'd lost. Though Kajaan's loss was far more recent, Cadeyrn had never truly accepted and moved on from Menea's death until Kajaan fell into his life.

"I do wish I could have met her, even if it meant that I'd be your side piece rather than your husband," Kajaan said gently. "The kids deserve their mother."

"The kids deserve loving parents," Cadeyrn corrected gently. "I have every faith in you stepping into that role."

"Papa," Marika inquired softly, tapping on the door as she opened it.

Reluctantly pulling away from Kajaan, Cadeyrn walked to his daughter and smiled. She was wearing a pretty frock that was dyed in a green gradient to show off her eyes. Marika was currently barefoot, holding two different pairs of shoes in her hands. He knelt down in front of her so he could speak on more equal terms with his little girl.

"I don't know what to wear," she said, holding them up.

One was her comfortable pair of sandals she wore every day, and the other were jewel-colored slippers that matched the dress. Obviously she didn't find the slippers very comfortable if she was asking him about what to wear. He knew how to read what his daughter wasn't saying, and right now she was telling him how uncomfortable she was with her footwear.

"Sweetling, you should wear the slippers," Cadeyrn said softly.

Marika's eyes filled with tears, confirming his suspicions.

"But they hurt my feet," she complained.

"How so?" Kajaan asked, crouching down next to Cadeyrn.

"The sides of my toes and the back of my heels," she said, blinking a few times, tears dropping to her youthful chubby cheeks.

"Sounds like they need some stretching," Kajaan said with a smile. He held out his hand, and Marika gave him the shoes. Kajaan inspected the material before smiling and winking at her. "I think your papa can help."

"Can I?" Cadeyrn asked.

"It's silk. If you warm it up, we can manipulate it and stretch out the toes and heel a little bit," Kajaan said with a smile. "Tzin and I did this a few times when we were younger and he didn't want to get rid of a favorite pair of shoes. Though we'd always use coals instead of Craft and were more likely to burn holes in the shoes instead of actually altering them."

Marika giggled and put her hands over her mouth, the sandals forgotten at her feet. Cadeyrn smiled and took one slipper from Kajaan. With his Fated's help and a dowel Inti produced from somewhere, they stretched the silk to better fit his daughter's feet.

"When were these made for you?" Kajaan asked as he handed the first slipper back to Marika.

The girl shrugged. "Maybe three seasons ago?"

"Has it really been that long?" Cadeyrn asked. "Sweetling, you're growing bigger. You'll need new shoes as you get older."

"Will I get as big as you, Papa?" Marika asked, rolling onto the balls of her feet to test out the altered slippers.

"Maybe," Cadeyrn said with a smile. "Your mother was fairly short, though, so it'll be interesting to see where you stand in ten years."

"Ten years," Marika whined. "That's so far away!"

"I know, sweetling," Cadeyrn said gently. "But you've got to take it slow."

"Why can't I just be big tomorrow?" Marika asked with a pout. "At least that way I can get the books I want to read easier."

"If you're big, how would you be able to cuddle into your papa when he reads you a story?" Kajaan crooned gently. "Being little has its advantages. Just ask Ameyalli. I'm sure they'll tell you."

Marika rocked back on her heels and nodded, rubbing at her eyes that so resembled her mother's. Cadeyrn reached out and planted a kiss on her forehead, cupping her sweet face.

"Dry your tears, sweetling," Cadeyrn said softly. "Don't think about the future. Tonight you'll get to see some of your distant friends and have a wonderful meal."

His daughter gave him a wobbly smile and nodded, her wavy brown hair bouncing around her face. Marika bent over to grab her sandals and skittered off down the hallway to her room. The two men stayed where they were for a minute before Cadeyrn sighed heavily and smiled at Kajaan.

"Loving parents," Cadeyrn murmured.

"She is a dear," Kajaan replied. "Though I might disown the twins if they become more of a terror than they are now."

Cadeyrn laughed and got to his feet, helping his lover up. They exchanged another kiss and walked toward the reception room hand in hand. There, several of the dukes, duchesses, lords, and their heirs had arrived. Thaddaeus was already amongst the gentry, smiling and acting like the perfect crown prince. Cadeyrn couldn't be prouder of his son as he watched Thaddaeus hug one of the Lansonds's boys who wasn't much older. The two had been pen pals for years, only able to meet during high-profile parties.

Their arrival into the chamber garnered some polite interest, though they weren't immediately swarmed. By the adults at least. The younger children didn't really know better, their youth overcoming their manners. All they saw was a man with a queen's diadem on his head and were absolutely fascinated. Kajaan just grinned and crouched down to address the kids and answer their questions to the best of his abilities.

What was his name? Did he have any siblings? Were his parents here? He was so tall! How tall was he? Why was his hair red? Why did it feel funny? His Fated was inundated with nearly a thousand questions, and while Cadeyrn could see and feel that the probing questions about his family hurt, Kajaan never dropped his smile. In the end, one of the little girls who was about five ended up on his knee, and the other children dropped in a half circle in front of him.

Kajaan was telling them a story of one of Yolotzin's pranks. Apparently the young prince had been about as much of a nightmare as the twins were now. At least Kajaan had some experience in dealing with crafty children. Kajaan pantomimed Yolotzin mixing up a "potion" using random berries, herbs, and pure water they'd stolen from the kitchens. Cadeyrn hadn't heard many of these stories yet, so even he was enthralled. With the looks on some of the other adult's faces, he knew he wasn't the only one.

His Fated paused dramatically once he described the finished "potion" with a sly smile on his face. He continued his story when some of the kids began to get antsy. Yolotzin dumped his mixture into his father's wine while he was distracted by his wife. King Tonalli hadn't understood his children's giggling when he took a drink, though it was very obvious that it had been tampered with. The kids near Kajaan were dead silent, enraptured by the story. Kajaan grinned at them.

"—and then, King Tonalli gagged, grabbed his throat, and started choking," Kajaan said, making choking noises and pretending as if he'd been poisoned. He stopped and winked at the five-year-old on his knee, who'd started sucking on her thumb, her eyes wide. "But all that changed was his mouth turning bright han-han blue, and it stayed that way for moonturns until the Healers could finally replicate the potion that Prince Yolotzin made and was able to reverse it."

The kids broke out into giggles and started peppering him with more questions. This time about his story and if it really did happen. Cadeyrn smiled at their enthusiasm, though he sadly wondered what had changed with the Averian king. The way Kajaan told it, Tonalli hadn't been a bastard for years and had loved his children dearly. So what changed that turned him into a heartless monster who had tried to kill his son's best friend and the boy his wife had all but raised?

Duchess Eilone wandered up and gently swept her daughter from Kajaan's knee, the other fascinated children breaking apart. His Fated stood, smiling a little nervously at her, not sure if he'd overstepped, a flutter of anxiety blooming in their bond. As soon as the girl was settled on her mother's hip the woman addressed Kajaan.

"You tell a wonderful story," she said with a smile. "Were you a writer back in Averia?"

"No, Duchess," Kajaan said respectfully. "I was Prince Yolotzin's secretary. I had a lot of time on my hands while he was occupied at socials, so I tended to read."

"Well, if you ever do write a wondertale, please let me know. I would be delighted to read what your mind comes up with," she replied.

The woman curtsied as best as she could with her child and swept off back to her husband. Cadeyrn just smiled as Kajaan's story had seemingly broken the ice, and several others wandered up to talk to his Fated, doing their best to not crowd him. His gentry were a kind lot for the most part, and Cadeyrn always did his best to rule fairly and compassionately. Something that Tonalli had lost these last ten years.

As such, those under Cadeyrn flourished, passing on his benevolence to their own people. His citizens' happiness was something that Cadeyrn took seriously. Of course, there would always be strife and those who would never be happy, but as a collective, he did his best by them. Kajaan's open personality and need to be needed and loved was both a boon and a curse. He'd do his best in everything yet worry whether he did the right thing.

Which was why Cadeyrn was there. He would help guide his Fated to being the best Quenlet that Zothua would ever have, and together they would bring the kingdom to untold prosperity. At least that was his hope. Cadeyrn finally moved close to his Fated once he saw the slight panic in his eyes and rested his hand at the small of his back. Almost immediately, Kajaan's shoulders that had tightened relaxed, and his smile came easier.

Of course that's when Lord Neerian arrived with his non-Fated wife and daughter. He was nearly fashionably late, as the meal would be called soon, leaving barely any time to mingle and get to know Kajaan, which had been the whole damn point. Cadeyrn did his best to keep his mouth shut, though he freely glowered at the man when Neerian started in on thinly veiled insults and jabs at his Fated.

Oddly, Kajaan didn't seem to either notice or mind. Instead, his Fated just smiled sweetly at the tardy lord and bowed over his wife and daughter's hands, showing them a deference that wasn't quite proper, yet flattering either way. A tic developed under Lord Neerian's left eye that he had to rub away, betraying his irritation with Kajaan not getting defensive or sniping back. The man was the last relic of Cadeyrn's father's era. Lord Neerian hadn't aged well, his hair completely gray, the skin around his jowls sagging, and his eyes were getting cloudy.

Out of everything Healers could do, muscle degradation was one of the few things they couldn't help with. There wasn't anything to heal when what they were trying to fix had eroded away. Lord Neerian would have to step down soon, solely because of his failing vision. Sure, he could have plenty of secretaries and scribes to help him with reading and writing letters and whatever else the man did, but it wasn't a viable option. Sooner or later, his daughter would have to take over.

If she hadn't already. Lady Laillya was a shrewd woman, watching and listening before saying a word. When she did speak, it was soft but direct, almost to the point of rudeness. She never rambled and seemed to choose her words carefully. Lady Laillya would be a formidable enemy if she walked in her father's shoes, though she was already giving Kajaan a faint smile even as he ignored Lord Neerian's jabs about his breeding. Lady Neerian, however, regarded Kajaan with open disdain.

Finally dinner was called, and the children who hadn't gone through their Awakening were ushered and tended to the adjoining room. To Cadeyrn's dismay, Lord Neerian was seated across from Kajaan, who was at Cadeyrn's right. They'd long abandoned the king's seat at the short end of the table, instead preferring a round one where it was easier to speak and hear everyone else. Of course, that meant that everyone could hear Lord Neerian try to tear down Kajaan on everything he did and said.

Cadeyrn wasn't a saint. By this point, he was seriously debating how he could force Lord Neerian to step down tonight and throw the doddering old fool under Maeeri's sharp hooves. Kajaan continued holding his soft smile, projecting calm through their bond. With a jolt, Cadeyrn realized he recognized his Fated's smile. It wasn't one of polite interest. No, it was the same smile he'd given all the tutors he'd interviewed for Marika.

Kajaan was *playing* with Lord Neerian. He was feigning innocence against the insults to piss the lord off. Cadeyrn fought his grin, instead dropping his hand onto his lover's thigh and squeezing gently. His Fated looked at him, and his smile morphed into a true one, leaning into his side briefly. Lord Neerian grunted at that as he speared a chunk of han-han meat.

"No need to ask if you've perverted our king and the sanctity of royal courtship," the man said in a drawl.

"Surely you understand the bond Fated couples have and how important it is to have contact during the first few moonturns," Kajaan said, feigning surprise. "Isn't your lovely daughter the product of such a union?"

At that, Duchess Eilone tittered. "Lord Neerian chased away his Fated when they first met. Lady Laillya is born from his current wife."

"Chased her away?" Kajaan gaped, the act dropped for a second. "How did that happen?"

"She wasn't suitable to become a lady. Much like how you're not suited to be our Quenlet," Lord Neerian snapped.

"Why do you say that? Cadeyrn and I are Fated, so it's only natural I'd take on the title when we wed," Kajaan said, his mask dropping back into place.

"Because you're a meddling foreigner. I wouldn't be surprised if you haven't been tampering with potions or charms to make our king think you two are Fated," Lord Neerian said.

"It's true I wasn't born a Zothuan citizen, but that hardly matters when it comes to the will of the goddess," Kajaan said, blinking innocently. "She sends us where we're needed and to who completes us."

"I will not see my king married to a harlot such as yourself," Lord Neerian snapped.

"Watch your tongue," Cadeyrn snarled.

His grip on Kajaan's thigh tightened, and his lover covered Cadeyrn's hand with his own. The gentle gesture made him relax, and Cadeyrn took a slow breath, reaching for his wine chalice.

"I may be younger than Cadeyrn, but I'm hardly a harlot," Kajaan said with a smile. "Being Tzin's *personal* secretary really didn't leave me much time for other activities."

Lady Laillya's eyes snapped up to Kajaan's the moment she registered how informally the man spoke about another kingdom's prince. Her shoulders tensed, and she looked at her father, clearly trying to warn him off without speaking. Either he ignored her or didn't notice as he leaned forward.

"So you were a prince's plaything. Looking to climb the ranks by slipping into bed with a widowed king, taking advantage of his grief?" Lord Neerian said.

Hurt flashed in Kajaan's eyes, and Cadeyrn gave his leg a quick squeeze, pushing reassurance through their bond. It didn't matter what Neerian thought of their relationship. The two of them knew the truth, and that was enough.

"Considering how low the beds are here, I would hardly call it climbing," Kajaan jested with a false smile. A couple of the other guests chuckled, helping release some of the tension built in the room. He shrugged elegantly. "Tzin and I parted ways amicably. I'm quite looking forward to his wedding next moonturn and seeing him once again."

"How can I trust your innocence when you just so happened to part ways with the Averian prince and fell into King Cadeyrn's bed? You're looking forward to the wedding so you can tell him everything about Zothua," Lord Neerian snapped.

"I am," Kajaan replied, grinning genuinely now. "I get to tell my best friend all of the twins' antics and how they're driving their nurse mad. I get to brag about Thaddaeus and how he's flourishing with his schedule and how he's going to be an amazing king when it's his time. Of course, then there's Marika, who is a brilliant young thing and quite liable to put her tutors out of a job within a year. We'll get to swap stories about how good being with your Fated feels in *every* aspect of the relationship. I'll probably bring him a book or two as well since the novels here are quite different from those in Alenzon and I'm sure he'd relish them."

Lord Neerian's face faded into a nearly comical look of horror as he realized just what Kajaan was saying.

"Prince Yolotzin… is your best friend?" he asked slowly.

"Not just," Kajaan said, stretching slightly and sighing as he settled back in the chair. His expression had gone cold and his tone sharp. "Queen Brekka nursed me herself after my mother died and raised me alongside Tzin. We were inseparable as boys."

And lovers as teenagers and adults. Kajaan didn't say it, but Cadeyrn knew that was on his mind. Leaving it there was enough for Lord Neerian to understand the weight of his words.

"You don't look like an Averian," Lord Neerian said flatly.

Kajaan tilted his head to the side. "That's true. I only know of one other redhead, and that would be Lord Asyl's young friend. Presumably one of his parents has red hair as well, but I don't know them personally."

"So not only are you a foreigner here, but you don't belong in Averia either," Lord Neerian said, his lip curling. "You don't belong anywhere, you motherless whelp. I bet your birth killed her."

It took all of Cadeyrn's strength to not stand up and smack that smile off of the man's face. Duchess Eilone dropped her silverware with a clatter and openly sneered at the man. Many of the women had the same naked fury on their faces, and he was glad to see several of the men looked annoyed as well. Being parents, Cadeyrn would bet they were enraged by Lord Neerian's implications that Kajaan was to blame for his mother's death. The room fell completely silent, and Kajaan sighed heavily.

"You know, once that would have hurt and torn me up inside, reminding me that my mother died bringing me into this world. But in the end, the fault lies with my father for not ensuring her safety during the last two moonturns of her pregnancy. Cadeyrn helped me see through the grief and torture I experienced all my life in Avitou Castle from the beatings and burns from careless Ignian men," Kajaan said slowly. "I can't help what I am, and I won't apologize for being Cadeyrn's Fated. I won't step down and be his dirty non-secret, and I most certainly won't be intimidated by you."

"You need to respect your betters," Lord Neerian sneered.

"Respect is earned, not owed," Kajaan snapped at him, finally dropping his act. "I don't owe you a thing after you've been insulting me all night when I've done nothing toward you except breathe." Lord Neerian got to his feet, his face contorting in anger. He froze at Kajaan's lazy grin. "King Tonalli plays this game much better—and deadlier—than you ever will. Tzin had better insults when he was ten. You're living proof that older isn't always wiser. The citizens you nearly killed with your greed and reckless disregard for safety proves that."

Lord Neerian snapped and flung his arm out, fire erupting from his palm. Without thinking, Cadeyrn surged to his feet and intercepted the white-hot blast, absorbing the energy before it could get to his Fated. He redirected the flames and sent a bolt with twice as much ferocity at Lord Neerian. The old man tried to deflect but ended up screaming and collapsing as the heat blistered his forearms and the parts of his face that had been left unprotected.

His daughter, who was a Healer, stared at him dispassionately even as Lord Neerian screeched for her to help him. Wayra stood over the man's prone body, his face firm and disapproving. None of the other nobles even tried to get near their fallen acquaintance. Not after he'd tried to attack Kajaan.

Cadeyrn turned away from the man, his concern limited to his lover. He couldn't feel Kajaan in his bond at all, and that worried him. Looking at his love, Kajaan had his head tilted upward in a proud, defiant pose despite his hands shaking. Cadeyrn could easily see the tightness in his shoulders, his lips pressed together in a thin white line, and eyes slightly widened.

Cadeyrn recognized the look, and his heart dropped. Kajaan was well on his way to a massive panic attack, if not a complete shutdown. Cadeyrn tried pushing as much compassion and calm into their stunted bond as he could. He pulled out Kajaan's chair, angling it toward him, and crouched down next to his Fated. Kajaan barely reacted, his eyes darting around frantically and his breathing starting to get heavy.

"Shit," Cadeyrn cursed under his breath.

He reached up and cupped Kajaan's face, trying to break through that deadness in their bond. If he could just push hard enough, maybe he could feel his lover again and understand better how to help him. This was far worse than the previous few times he'd seen his Fated panic when he got too overwhelmed by memories. Why hadn't he talked with Tamya about how to help the last time this had happened?

Cadeyrn looked up at Duchess Eilone, who was cautiously approaching him. He'd always liked her, and she was the more sensible one between her and her husband.

"Can I help in any way?" she asked softly.

"He's either blocking me or shutting down," Cadeyrn said, hating how small his voice sounded.

The woman rucked up her skirts and knelt next to him. She didn't touch Kajaan and began to murmur gentle endearments to him. Only when Kajaan's eyes started to lose that wild edge and his breath began to even out did Cadeyrn start to relax. He stood and leaned in, pressing a kiss to his lover's sweaty forehead. Kajaan flinched when Neerian let out an agonized yelp.

"He needs to be somewhere quiet," Cadeyrn said to Duchess Eilone.

The duchess nodded and smiled. "Would the kids help?"

"Possibly," Cadeyrn said, rubbing the back of his head. "I'm not sure what to do with a panic attack. Last time I just held him, but…."

She nodded. "Leave it to me."

Duchess Eilone returned her attention to Kajaan, still speaking in her soft voice. When Cadeyrn backed up, a couple of the other ladies wandered over and sat near him, joining the duchess with soft encouragement and praise. He watched for a bit longer, noting Kajaan's shoulders starting to loosen and relax.

Cadeyrn left the ladies to their task, rounding the table to where Lord Neerian lay gasping on the floor. The remaining lords hovered in a semicircle around him, some holding their older sons and heirs next to them while others had their daughters nearby. Cadeyrn wished that he could promise the children that this would be the only time they'd see violence, but he was no fool.

Lady Laillya hadn't moved from her chair, sitting properly and facing across the table where Kajaan was slowly crumbling in on himself. Her posture was rigid, though not quite tense as though she was offended. If anything, she seemed to be waiting patiently. Beside her, Lady Neerian had slumped back, her manners completely broken as she appeared exhausted yet relieved.

Cadeyrn turned his attention to the charred man at his feet.

"Lord Neerian," Cadeyrn said flatly. The man's good eye rolled up to see him, and he groaned low in his throat, though it ended in a gurgle. "You are to be denied a Healer much like Kajaan was when he was purposely burned as a boy. A salve will be provided to you for your burns, but don't expect any further help. For your crime in attacking my Fated and fiancé in rage, you are to be imprisoned and stripped of your title."

He looked up to Lady Laillya, who had finally turned and was watching her father dispassionately. She sighed, raised her eyes to Cadeyrn, and shrugged, a faint smile tugging at her lips.

"If he can't handle being insulted, perhaps the former lord shouldn't have picked a fight," she said serenely.

That was all he needed to hear. Cadeyrn smiled weakly and nodded. She would be nothing like her father, for which he would be eternally grateful. Even though she was a Healer and should be sent to the colleges to take up some sort of medicinal profession, she was also Neerian's only heir. How Neerian had sired Lady Laillya was beyond him.

"Will you need help with your affairs? I can send a secretary with you to smooth over the transition," he offered.

Lady Laillya gave him a genuine smile this time and said, "I wouldn't say no. I intend on removing all of the secretaries the former lord had employed and bringing in new people. I would like for the one coming with me to be familiar with the secretary who's been working on the rebuilding efforts. That way there's already a good relationship between them. I would also like to keep the laborers on after the current rebuilding has been finished if they wish, and make sure all the other businesses and farms are up to date with safety measures."

"That may be costly," Cadeyrn said slowly.

"It's worth it to keep my people safe," Lady Laillya said. "There are many outdated buildings that need to be restored, and far too many living in squalor due to needlessly high taxes. I intend to put that money back into our communities."

"Please keep me updated, and don't hesitate to reach out for help or advice. I will gladly help however you need to my ability," Cadeyrn said.

"I appreciate your assistance, King Cadeyrn. I wholeheartedly welcome your future Quenlet. Kajaan seems to be a wonderful and sharp man. I'm only a little jealous he's yours," she teased.

"I am doubly blessed by Ilyphari to have such a wonderful Fated," Cadeyrn said.

"I can take things from here so you can attend to our future Quenlet," Duke Lansonds said.

Neerian had gone quiet, though the rattling breaths he drew between his chapped lips signaled he still lived. Cadeyrn nodded his thanks to the duke and looked to Lady Neerian. She simply inclined her head toward him, looking decades older than she had when they'd arrived. A quick survey of the room revealed that Kajaan had been moved. Simthe nodded toward the door he was stationed next to, obviously knowing who Cadeyrn was looking for.

Relieved, Cadeyrn swept past the remaining gentry and his guards to the room where the children had been eating. He was beyond grateful that they'd been in a different room altogether and hadn't had to witness Neerian's stupidity, though he had no doubt they heard some of it. The rooms weren't completely soundproof, and there was a small gap underneath the door.

Inside, Kajaan was curled up on the floor against the wall. Fayette was in his lap, leaning up against him. Thaddaeus on one side, Marika on the other. Rodolfo was in his older brother's lap, holding Kajaan's hand, a worried look on his face. The other children had sat close, all of them in different stages of mess from dinner. Kajaan was surrounded by affection, and the room was oddly silent. Almost as if the children knew that too much stimulation wouldn't end well for their storyteller.

Duchess Eilone approached him, leaving the other three women behind, who were watching the kids with careful eyes. Duchess Lansonds was among them, her young son standing next to her, biting his lower lip. Kajaan hadn't seemed to register the children's proximity, just sitting quietly with his head down.

"How is he?" Cadeyrn asked.

"I think he needs you," the woman said softly.

Cadeyrn nodded. He approached the gaggle of children and smiled faintly, remembering Kajaan's wish to have his own offspring and how excited he was to look into surrogates. After tapping Marika on her shoulder, Cadeyrn slipped into her place. Without a word, Marika crawled into his lap and clung to his regalia, her eyes fixed on Kajaan. Cadeyrn gently took his Fated's hand in his, lifting it and kissing his knuckles.

"Look around you, my love," Cadeyrn said softly. "This can be our future in a decade or two. More kids than you can count, especially if we try for a baby every year. Two different surrogates. One that has my coloring and one that has yours. That way our babies will be a mix of us."

The complete change in subject got Kajaan to blink and raise his head. He looked over at Cadeyrn and took a shaky breath. Their bond opened slightly, giving Cadeyrn a glimpse of the guilt, shame, and fear that had shut down his lover so thoroughly.

"I'm sorry," he said, his voice trembling.

"There's nothing to apologize for," Cadeyrn murmured, wrapping an arm around Kajaan's shoulders and pulling him in close. "Lady Laillya had it right. Neerian shouldn't have started something he couldn't handle."

"He looks like Torbid," Kajaan said quietly.

"Papa?" Thaddaeus asked.

"Later, son. We'll all sit down and discuss what happened. No secrets," Cadeyrn replied.

His boy simply nodded and adjusted his glasses before leaning back into Kajaan's side. Kajaan started trembling as he came down from his shocked state, and Cadeyrn rocked him, planting a kiss in his beautiful red hair. Some of the gentry kids gave an automatic "ewwwww" at the gesture. That startled a laugh out of Kajaan, and he quickly dissolved into tears. He hid his face behind his hands even as Cadeyrn held him close.

"It's okay," he whispered. "Let it out."

The bond opened fully, and the rush of Kajaan's emotions nearly barreled Cadeyrn over. He was grateful he was sitting, though he'd never admit that he might have been taken out by the overwhelming dread that

Kajaan was feeling. Holding his Fated tight to him, he focused on sending back all his affection to his love, not bothering to subdue anything that Kajaan was working through. If all he could do was support his man, then that's what he would do.

Several of the smaller children lost interest, wandering off to play with their toys or being collected by the remaining women as they started to fuss. Cadeyrn's four were still firmly rallied around Kajaan, though Thaddaeus looked more and more worried by the minute. Fayette eventually fell asleep, exhausted by everything while nestled firmly in Kajaan's lap. It took his Fated a quarter hour before he pulled himself together and sat up, his eyes red and puffy.

"I'm okay," Kajaan croaked.

Cadeyrn nodded and picked Marika up as he stood. His eldest girl clung to his sleeve as he perched her on his hip, and he held out his hand to his Fated, feeling the exhaustion that was pulling at him. Kajaan cradled Fayette to his chest and accepted his love's help to stand. As soon as he had the young girl settled in his arms, Kajaan ruffled Thaddaeus's hair. Holding his younger brother's hand, the six of them returned to the dining hall, where Neerian had been removed.

The ladies who had stuck close to Kajaan walked back to their seats and perched on the edge as if nothing had happened. The remains of their dinner had been cleared away, and as soon as Kajaan and Cadeyrn sat, dessert was served. Kajaan found himself with Thaddaeus in his lap alongside the sleeping Fayette, where Cadeyrn had Rodolfo and Marika. The children were treated to a few bites of the rich mousse, Marika bouncing excitedly on his lap.

None of the gentry mentioned what had happened with Neerian, and Lady Neerian was absent. Lady Laillya sat quietly in the place she'd been assigned. All the chatter was light and friendly, far from what it had been before, and Cadeyrn watched his lover's shoulders relax further. Fayette woke near the end of dessert and was about ready to pout at being left out. Kajaan scooped up the last bit of what was in his cup and offered it to the little girl.

Mollified, Fayette munched on the chocolate and raspberry mousse. Thaddaeus slipped off Kajaan's lap, and the parents who brought their younger children rounded them up from the adjoining room. The farewells were brisk, though friendly. No one seemed to be annoyed at Kajaan for what happened, to which Cadeyrn was grateful. Duchess Eilone winked at the two of them and kissed Kajaan on the cheek.

"I look forward to seeing you at the socials," she said happily. "I've been needing someone to practice my wit with."

Her husband gave a bark of laughter. "My dear, you'd end up cutting yourself if you sharpened your wit any further."

The duchess rolled her eyes with a smile and followed her husband and daughter out of the castle. Alone at last, Cadeyrn took Kajaan's hand and led him upstairs. The children followed close on their heels all the way into their bedroom. The family settled in bed together, in one giant, twisted pile that made no logical sense. Finally, after Kajaan's permission and a long moment of gathering his thoughts, Cadeyrn told the children about what happened to his love when he was a boy.

They talked at length about trauma and how it affected someone for the rest of their life. Naturally, Kajaan's mother came up, and he spoke about how he'd been blamed unfairly for his mother's death. That led to Cadeyrn telling the children extensively about Menea's death, despite the ache in his chest. He still missed his wife, but the pain was nowhere near as awful as it used to be.

Finally, their curiosity sated, the children dropped off one by one. Cadeyrn kissed his lover lightly, and Kajaan nestled into his side as much as he could with the four children sleeping on top and around them. Needing to reassure himself, Cadeyrn kissed Kajaan's temple before allowing himself to start to fall asleep, not caring one whit that he was still in his regalia.

CHAPTER 23

KAJAAN WAS returning to Averia in style. The coach they were taking was extra large, likely to compensate for the gexenas that pulled them. While the door was still in the front, padded benches stretched along the sides and around the back, where a table had been bolted into the floor. It comfortably fit Cadeyrn, his children, Asyl, Olire, and Kajaan. Granted, it helped that most of the children were still small.

The castle had been a hive of activity during their departure and drew the attention of the nearby citizens of Sestella. By the time they were ready to go, the royal procession had quite the crowd to wave to. Out of the hundreds of faces, one stuck out to Kajaan. The man stood near the edge of the crowd, holding on to the reins of his gexena. That wasn't remarkable in itself. What was, however, was the snow-white mask covering his whole face.

A shiver ran down Kajaan's spine as he stared at the masked man, feeling as if he was being watched and judged. Fayette squealed inside the carriage, pointing excitedly toward someone who had their arms full of a fat, lazy cat, distracting Kajaan. By the time he looked back, the masked man was gone. Cadeyrn didn't seem worried when Kajaan mentioned the masked man and told him that they'd deal with it if there was a problem later.

Even though the two of them were still worried about King Tonalli's reception, Cadeyrn was adopting the "don't borrow trouble" mantra. Kajaan understood, but at the same time, he couldn't help but worry as he settled on the bench seat and pulled out one of his books to pass the time.

Thaddaeus had brought along a deck of cards and was teaching Olire how to play a game that involved a lot of quick flipping of the cards, slapping the table, and laughter. Kajaan had tried to make sense of the game but quickly gave up as the boy's hands grew red from accidentally smacking each other. The twins eventually got involved with the game, and the racket redoubled.

Marika sat quietly with Asyl, the two reading a book together. Their tones were quiet, often drowned out by the hooligans in the back of the carriage. From what Kajaan could hear, Marika was teaching Asyl how to read Zothuan. The young princess had been quite upset; she was only allowed to bring three books with her instead of the ten she wanted and was near a meltdown before Kajaan bribed her with the promise of purchasing her a book in Alenzon. Of course, he was debating about slipping into Yolotzin's quarters and seeing if there was an appropriate book there he could steal instead.

Yolotzin wouldn't mind, he knew. The two of them had been stealing and borrowing things from each other for decades. Many times Kajaan would be looking for his favorite fountain pen only for him to find it in Yolotzin's hands as he drafted a letter. Or he'd steal one of Yolotzin's scarves that he adored and wear it when he had to accompany his best friend to a party before hiding with the coachmen.

Neither of them really thought about it. It was just something they did.

The one thing Kajaan never truly filched was jewelry. He hadn't ever had his ears pierced, didn't quite care for necklaces, and rings made holding his pen awkward. Yolotzin had tried giving him jewelry as a gift for a few years before he realized that, while Kajaan loved looking at the sparkling gemstones, he simply didn't wear any of it.

But now he was expected to. The only exception was the napkin ring bracelet that Cadeyrn gave him, which never came off except when he bathed. He was getting used to putting on the diadem in the mornings, though he didn't really have to deal with it consistently throughout the day like he did the engagement ring. Kajaan spun said ring on his right hand, still unused to the weight even after three weeks. Cadeyrn's official proposal hadn't been overly romantic, which was fine with Kajaan. He really didn't need the pomp and circumstance that many couples wanted when it came to exchanging rings.

His true proposal had been quiet. They were in bed together, not quite yet retiring for the night, and Cadeyrn had lowered the temperature around them so they could cuddle as they sat against the headboard. Kajaan was between his Fated's legs, his bare back against his lover's chest. They were reading together, switching off narration between chapters, and each grabbing different characters to voice with amusing effects. Cadeyrn had a perfect nasally voice that he liked to use with characters he didn't care for.

They'd just finished reading a romantic scene between the two main men, and Kajaan had been playing with Cadeyrn's fingers behind the book. Now he knew it was a distraction and an excuse for his lover to be touching his hand. When Kajaan had gripped the book to flip to the next page, he'd felt the weight on his finger and instead closed the book to reveal the ring. His heart had pounded as he turned to look at Cadeyrn in surprise, even though rationally he knew that they were going to get married.

Cadeyrn just kissed him, told him how much he loved him, before taking the book out of his fingers and rolling them to the bed. Afterward, when they were catching their breath, minds hazy from bliss and bodies sated, Cadeyrn told him that the wedding ring would be more elaborate. Kajaan couldn't bring himself to care.

"Everything all right?" Cadeyrn asked, leaning into Kajaan and breaking through his memories.

Kajaan stopped spinning the gold ring, smiling down at the line of tiny sapphires bisecting the band. He looked up at his lover and shook his head, knowing he probably looked silly with his sappy smile. Instead of replying, Kajaan leaned in and placed a light kiss on Cadeyrn's lips, curling up into his side. Since they were around the children and Asyl, neither of them really took their affection further than a few chaste kisses.

Four days of this would be torture in the end, Kajaan knew. They were traveling between two other carriages. One held Wayra and a few of his guards, along with Quillin and Ameyalli. The other had Inti, the twins' nurse, and a few other supporting staff. All of their luggage had been evenly split between the three carriages, never wanting to overburden one of the gexenas that pulled their carriages.

Cadeyrn had been talking about having Kajaan meet up with some gexenas that hadn't been bound to a rider yet. While Maeeri was all right with Kajaan riding her, she much preferred it when Cadeyrn was around. He still wasn't quite sure, still a little nervous around the massive beasts, but Kajaan figured his lover knew what was best. Besides, it would be nice to have his own gexena around to ride during his growing free time.

He wasn't as busy now that Rhionne was no longer tutoring him. She'd been around for a few more weeks after his breakthrough, teaching him everything she knew and could think of to train him on for his specialized Craft. It had been an intense schedule, but one they were both quite happy with. Kajaan didn't have to think at all to invoke his Craft anymore. It was as natural as breathing, just like how every other Craft Blessed described it.

The tension in the carriage rose the closer they got to Alenzon and Avitou castle. They'd passed over the border just fine, the guards barely inspecting the carriages before waving them through. Clearly, they were foreign dignitaries here for the wedding of their beloved prince. Kajaan hoped that their own guards would be a little more cautious who they let in when it came time for his wedding.

On their last day of travel, when they'd clambered back into the carriage after spending the night in an inn, Cadeyrn cleared his throat and demanded everyone's attention.

"Ameyalli came to me last night," Cadeyrn said slowly. Kajaan nodded, having remembered the Seer knocking on their door and asking to speak with Cadeyrn privately. "They said that we must be very careful during our stay. I don't want any of you running off on your own without me, Wayra, or one of his people beside you. If someone you don't know approaches you and tries to get you alone, you scream like hell and get back to Kajaan or me."

"My parents," Olire said in a broken voice.

"I'm sorry. You need to stay close by to make sure you're safe. Of course we'll try to host your parents for as much time as we're able, but at the end of this visit, you will be coming back to Zothua," Cadeyrn said gently.

"Unless, of course, the Void law is repealed," Kajaan interjected. "I know many of the monarchs who're attending aren't pleased with what King Tonalli has done, and there will be pressure for him to dismiss the law. Several other Voids will be in attendance from the other kingdoms."

"Last winter, Siora had told Kende that she saw a mass grave of Voids, with Olire and I as two of the victims," Asyl said. "I thought it was over when Ilfa and Tillet had been arrested, but I suppose not. We'll do our best to be safe. As Kende's husband, I *will* be by his side during the ceremonies. But I'll do my duties as planned, and… come back with you two when it's time to leave, if needed."

"I'm sorry, Asyl," Kajaan said, reaching out and taking the young man's hands in his.

Asyl smiled weakly at him. "Just a few hours with Kende is a blessing. It'll be hard to leave, but at least I'll have been able to say 'farewell for now' on my own terms."

Kajaan nodded and smiled at him, squeezing his hands before letting go.

"Anything else?" Thaddaeus asked, blinking owlishly behind his glasses.

"Be on your best behavior," Cadeyrn said sternly. "Kajaan, is there anything we should know?"

"Yannat, King Tonalli's secretary, is also his confidant. If he tells you something, it's probably a direct order from King Tonalli himself, so respect it, but don't act rashly. Jeryit is his captain of the guard, and he's massive. Don't make him angry. He's likely to trap you in an earthen cage until he has the time to come back and let you out. And trust me, he doesn't have a lot of time on his hands."

"Did he ever do that to you?" Cadeyrn asked, his voice tinged with anger.

Kajaan hesitated before answering. "Once. Tzin threw a massive fit and screamed his head off until Jeryit was found and I was released. Tzin refused to leave my side until it was over."

"Your father sounds like a piece of work," Asyl muttered.

Thaddaeus blinked and straightened. "That's your dad? Why wasn't he one of the ones who came with you to Zothua if your message was so important back in the spring?"

Kajaan looked at Cadeyrn, not quite sure how to proceed here. His Fated cocked an eyebrow at Kajaan and nodded hesitantly. This had been something neither of them had talked to the children about yet. Not so much as they were keeping the truth from the children, but rather they hadn't wanted to worry them.

"Cadeyrn and I have reason to believe that I was sent here under false pretenses to die," Kajaan said. "King Tonalli wanted an excuse to attack Zothua and was using me to do so. Of course, Tzin didn't know or have time to object to the plan since I was thrown out of the castle in the dead of the night after he retired. I still don't know what all my father knew of his plan, but I have to believe he was aware of at least some of it, considering some of the king's guards came after me to try and finish what the coachman started."

Thaddaeus paled slightly, and Fayette whined, climbing into Kajaan's lap. He hugged the little girl, pressing his face into her hair and breathing in. She was little enough that she still had the baby smell around her that Kajaan adored.

"As far as I know, neither Kende nor Yolotzin have been able to find out either," Asyl said with a grimace. "I'd like to believe he didn't know any of the details, but…."

"I know. It honestly won't be a disaster if he was complicit. He may have taken part in making me, but when it came to raising me, he gladly left it to Tzin's mother and nurse while ignoring me," Kajaan said.

"That's awful," Marika said, her eyes wide. "I can't imagine Papa doing anything like that."

"Because I would never," Cadeyrn said firmly.

With that assurance, the carriage fell into an uneasy silence. Thaddaeus shuffled his card deck and started playing solitaire, frowning down at the cards. Olire shifted to sit next to Asyl and struck up a quiet conversation with him in Averian. Mostly about what to do when he saw his parents again and what was proper at court. Kajaan kept quiet, slumping into his Fated.

Already Kajaan was looking forward to getting back to Zothua. Just being inside Averia's borders was exhausting. He no longer felt any grief over the fact that he would never get to stay. Even if the Void law was struck down, Kajaan would still leave his home kingdom behind. He wanted to be by Cadeyrn's side, travel with him everywhere he wanted to go, see whatever he could see, and raise many more kids with him.

He was holding Cadeyrn to the words he spoke last moonturn while Kajaan struggled through another panic attack. A specific and approved surrogate for each of them with the potential for a baby every year. Even though they'd brought it up a few times during their stolen moments together, Kajaan had been hesitant to begin planning their family. But clearly the big man loved children as much as he did.

Kajaan shifted his head to look up at Cadeyrn, who smiled and dropped a kiss on his lips. He couldn't wait to get started on having children. They just had their pesky marriage to arrange first so none of their littles would be bastards. That hadn't stopped either of them in looking for and vetting the women who would carry their children.

As soon as the wedding license was signed, they'd begin trying for a baby.

The thought rattled around Kajaan's mind, warming him, until the carriage rolled to a stop. Asyl took a deep, fortifying breath and plastered on a gentle smile.

"Ready?" Cadeyrn asked his kids. "Be on your best behavior."

The door opened, and Cadeyrn stepped out first, his cape billowing behind him. He'd worn his less ornate crown, but he still cut quite the imposing figure. Cadeyrn turned and held out his hand. Kajaan took it, stepping carefully from the carriage before he slipped his arm into his Fated's as was proper in Averia. Asyl and Olire were next, helping the children get out and quickly stretch. The two Averians would walk behind the royal children in their intended roles of personal assistants.

Wayra stood to Kajaan's side with Quillin stationed next to Cadeyrn. Ameyalli walked near the kids, and the rest of their entourage went with the carriages to get everything unloaded into their assigned rooms. The footman opened the door to Avitou Castle, looking startled at seeing Kajaan again. Kajaan caught the sneer before the man adjusted his expression to professional apathy, and a pang of hurt tugged at his heart.

Even now, he was still going to be hated. He wondered if any of the staff here would truly believe that he was Fated to Cadeyrn, or if they had the same beliefs that the former Lord Neerian did. That he purposely went from a prince's bed to a king's. Cadeyrn squeezed his hand, sensing his distress, though he clearly hadn't seen the footman snubbing Kajaan.

Jeryit was waiting for them in the grand hall, and his posture went rigid as soon as he caught sight of the approaching party. Cadeyrn went tense next to Kajaan, examining Jeryit, and his face settled into hard disapproval. Despite Kajaan looking nothing like his father, Cadeyrn obviously knew enough of Jeryit's countenance. Granted, he'd been to Avitou before, so perhaps he was more familiar with the guard captain than Kajaan knew.

Their small party came to a halt in front of the massive Gaian. Behind Kajaan, Fayette whimpered, and a quick yet quiet shuffle ensued. The little girl was obviously intimidated by the man who was nearly twice her height.

"King Cadeyrn," Jeryit managed to say in Averian with a tense smile. "Pleasure to see you in the castle again. May I get the name of your fiancé so I can make sure he'll be announced properly at the gala tonight?"

"Kajaan Pernoac," Cadeyrn said in a clipped tone. "Though I believe you already knew that."

Jeryit's eyes flashed with anger, and his smile dropped. His eyes fastened on Kajaan, who quickly dropped his gaze, beginning to tremble. Kajaan had thought he was strong enough to encounter his father. What a fool he'd been. Small arms wrapped around his waist, and Kajaan looked to see who it was. Thaddaeus was hugging him tight, glaring daggers at Jeryit. His brave, sweet boy.

"Good to see you home and in good health, Kaj," Jeryit said.

"Avitou isn't my home," Kajaan snapped, looking at him. "Paelfjord is my home, and this is my family."

A surge of pride came through his bond, bolstering Kajaan's resolve. It was beyond time to put Averia behind him. Jeryit opened his mouth and took a step forward. Wayra moved to stand in front of Kajaan and Cadeyrn, his hand resting casually on the hilt of his sword. Their Gaian captain was quite a bit shorter than Jeryit, yet his stance clearly said to not mess around with him.

"Is there a problem with my king's fiancé?" Wayra asked in a deceptively calm voice.

"No. I'm sure I'll speak with my son later," Jeryit said.

"Only when King Cadeyrn or I are in attendance," Wayra said firmly.

Jeryit gave another stilted nod and rattled off where their assigned rooms were. His father gave him a baleful look and a crooked smile.

"I'm sure you know where it is," he said.

Kajaan simply turned without comment and tugged on Cadeyrn's arm lightly to get his love to follow him. If that's how this visit was going to be played, then he would learn their rules.

Normally they would have gotten a servant to escort them to their rooms, but Jeryit was seemingly fine ignoring that part of his hosting duties. If the footman's reaction to him was any indication, he couldn't rely on any of the staff being polite toward him, whether his Fated was with him or not. Despite his position in Zothua, he was still nothing here, and clearly his father thought he could treat Kajaan like he had before.

Somehow carding his hand through Thaddaeus's hair kept Kajaan's anger in check as they walked through the castle that Kajaan had once called home. As soon as the door to their extensive suite was shut behind them, Cadeyrn let loose a snarl and turned toward Kajaan. Fayette was in Asyl's arms, refusing to get down, her face streaked with tears.

"Is he always that much of a bastard?" Cadeyrn asked, switching back to Zothuan.

"Towards me, yes," Kajaan replied and huffed. "Now you know why Tzin and I were so close and I had no other friends. I only wanted to come back for him."

"You're much happier in Paelfjord," Quillin remarked.

Kajaan nodded and sighed heavily, looking around the spacious room. They'd been put up in one of the finer wings, and their party essentially got the whole corridor along one side. He wondered who they'd be sharing the floor with, though he quickly found he didn't care. Kajaan wasn't going to leave the rooms without Cadeyrn or Wayra at his side, or perhaps not at all.

Despite the pretty tapestry, large windows, and comfortable furniture, it was still a prison.

Wayra and Ameyalli left them to inspect the rest of their quarters, and Kajaan wandered over to a soft-looking settee. He sank onto the cushion, unsurprised to find Thaddaeus in his lap a moment later. Kajaan gathered the boy up in his arms and squeezed him gently, pressing his face into Thaddaeus's shiny black hair.

"I'm sorry," Thaddaeus said softly. "I can't imagine growing up with him as a dad."

"Well, he wasn't much of a dad, I'll tell you that much," Kajaan replied with a small chuckle. "Don't worry about it. Just keep quiet as much as you can, and don't trust anything the Averian gentry says unless it's Yolotzin, Kende, or Naias."

While he knew there were others he could trust, Kajaan wasn't going to overload the boy's mind by giving him more names to try and remember. He looked over at Cadeyrn, who was talking quietly with Quillin, tension pouring off the king. Olire plopped down on the ground with a still shaken Fayette and Rodolfo, who was doing his best to put on a brave face as he held his sister's hand. Marika had taken residence on another settee with her third and final book while Asyl was tugging at the hem of his tunic, pacing the room as he looked around.

He wasn't pacing for long. There was a knock at the door, and Wayra immediately came back into the main room, waving off Asyl, who'd gone to answer it. The guard barely cracked the door to speak to the person outside, using his body to block any line of sight their visitor might have inside their suite.

"I was told Asyl was here?" Kende's voice came in stilted Zothuan, sounding nervous. Behind Kajaan, Asyl gasped. "I'm his husband."

"Let him in," Kajaan called over to Wayra.

Wayra looked over his shoulder at him and nodded. He stepped back, opening the door, and Kende rushed in. Asyl all but flew into his arms, and the two embraced like they were both starving men stumbling upon a feast. In a way, they probably were. Fated couples weren't meant to be apart for long. It was likely only due to Asyl being a Void that they hadn't been driven to insanity from starving their bond.

Kende briefly lifted Asyl off the ground so only his toes were touching the floor, eliciting a giggle from the Void. The two stood there in the middle of the room, just holding each other tight, relishing in the contact and rejuvenating their bond. Kajaan tore his eyes away from them and looked to Cadeyrn, who was watching him with a soft smile. He grinned at his Fated and squeezed Thaddaeus.

"That's what you get to have when you're older," he murmured to the young prince. "After your Awakening, you'll start traveling as a part of your training and hopefully find the one who's your Fated."

"What if I never find her?" Thaddaeus asked.

"Then your papa and I will look for a bride suitable for you, or maybe there will be a lady who catches your eye that we can consider. Your mother wasn't Cadeyrn's Fated, and from all that I've heard, they had a beautiful relationship. You can still be happy even if your spouse isn't your Fated," Kajaan replied. "But we have many more years before then. In three, you'll Awaken, and five more after that is when we'll start seriously looking towards marriage."

"But isn't Prince Yolotzin much older than eighteen?" Thaddaeus asked, his brows knitting together in confusion.

"Yeah. Part of that is my fault. We kept hoping we'd become a Fated couple, and he wanted to hold off to find the other half of his soul. Since Tzin has sisters who have children, I think Tonalli didn't really care for him to marry early," Kajaan said and shrugged.

"The throne not going to the eldest child is still a bizarre concept to me," Cadeyrn said, sinking onto the settee next to Kajaan.

"Yeah, well, Uncle Tonalli has always been weird," Kende said, emerging from his bliss of being reunited with Asyl.

"*Uncle*?" Quillin demanded.

Kende looked a little sheepish. "Um. Yeah. He's my father's brother. Yolotzin is my cousin."

"This isn't news to you," Cadeyrn said, looking at Asyl.

The Void shrugged. "I knew that Yolotzin was his cousin, but that was about it. No wonder your dad was a dick."

Kajaan snorted, trying to not burst into laughter. Quillin didn't have the same luck, and Cadeyrn simply grinned. Kende shook his head and pulled his Fated back into his arms.

"Would you two like some privacy?" Cadeyrn offered.

Asyl's eyes shone. "Could we?"

"Go to the room you'll be sharing with Inti, and he'll give you time to be with your Fated," Cadeyrn said.

Asyl took a step away from Kende, grinning from ear to ear. He held up his hands in a pose that Kajaan recognized as the follower's waltz and Asyl wiggled his fingers at Kende in a silent request. The lord stepped forward into the leader's position, their fingers entwining. Just like that, the two were in their own world, foreheads touching and lost in each other's gaze as they swayed for a few steps. Kende dipped and swept Asyl up into his arms, making Asyl shriek with laughter.

The two headed down the hallway where Asyl was theoretically staying for the next few nights. Thaddaeus's nose scrunched slightly, and he frowned.

"They're not just going to do some boring dances are they?" the boy asked.

"Absolutely not," Kajaan said. He ignored the warning glance he got from Cadeyrn and rolled his eyes at his Fated. "Asyl is a fantastic dancer and was a treat to watch at his Introduction Gala. There's a style here among the Voids that's very high-energy that he taught Kende."

"Maybe we should ask for lessons for Fayette and Rodolfo so they don't keep running through the gardens," Thaddaeus said and nodded.

With the perfect ten-year-old logic that determined once something was decided it needed to happen immediately, Thaddaeus started to slip from the settee. Kajaan snickered and grabbed the boy, hauled him into his lap, and hugged him tight.

"Maybe let them dance together in private for a bit first," he suggested. "They've missed each other, and they should be able to have some alone time before subjecting them to your siblings."

"Ohhhhh. Yeah, good point," Thaddaeus conceded and leaned against Kajaan.

Biting his lip, Kajaan looked at his Fated and managed to suppress his wild laughter into an undignified snort. Cadeyrn simply shook his head, his slightly panicked expression melting into a gentle fondness as they exchanged smiles.

Dancing indeed.

CHAPTER 24

THE REST of the evening went by smoothly, the luggage delivered and unpacked, and everyone settled in. There was enough room for the kids to have their own beds, though the twins refused to sleep separately. The closer it got to the formal dinner, the more nervous Kajaan became. He held on to Cadeyrn's calm demeanor as much as he could, and he knew his Fated was concerned about his growing anxiety, based on the amount of reassurance his lover sent through their bond.

Just being back in Avitou was enough to make him jump when someone touched his arm. It didn't matter if Kajaan had clocked the person coming up to him. If he wasn't being approached directly, then he ended up getting startled. The kids didn't seem to understand that he was on edge, constantly grabbing at him.

After the eighth time, Cadeyrn grabbed his hand and seemed content to not let go, casually giving Kajaan strength. Asyl and Kende finally surfaced after several hours, both looking flushed and a little rumpled, though quite relaxed. No one said anything about their appearance, and the two joined Kajaan and Cadeyrn in the sitting area, casually talking about their households and projects. Eventually, Asyl started talking about Enchanted Waters and the potions he was researching.

"Oh, I'll get the notes and books you've been using packed up and sent here so it can go back with you," Kende said, though his tone was distraught.

"Thanks. I haven't been able to even think about picking up where I've left off. It's been too painful to think about," Asyl said quietly.

"Your patrons will be very happy when you come back," Kende said. "I get letters daily asking if you've been able to return and fulfill their orders. They've had to go with inferior quality potions and they know it. A lot of the gentry are pissed at Uncle Tonalli."

"I was training Tsela," Asyl said with a frown. "Is he not making anything?"

"He's not able to keep up. Tsela doesn't have the speed or experience that you do," Kende explained. "The most he's been able to do is keep the store sparsely stocked."

"What are you researching?" Marika asked, her head popping up from her book.

Asyl smiled at his fellow bookworm. "Regeneration of the eyes."

"But that's impossible," Cadeyrn said, frowning. "What's been lost can't be restored."

"By a Healer," Asyl said with a sly grin. "I want to make a rejuvenation potion to work on restoring the ligaments, muscles, and nerves of the eyeballs, and hopefully the connection it has with the brain. Otherwise, the eyes could be perfect, but if the brain can't interpret anything, there's no point."

"That seems dangerous," Cadeyrn said. "It could be an easy slide into trying to create immortality."

Asyl shook his head. "It wouldn't be able to heal any major damage. If an eye is lost, it won't regrow. But reconnecting or strengthening what's eroded is more of the idea."

"But then couldn't you make a potion that could do the same for the heart or lungs?" Cadeyrn asked.

"Theoretically, maybe. The eye is an incredibly complex organ, so others would likely be easier to help repair. But that's not to say that what I want to do will even work. I could be researching something that will never come to fruition," Asyl replied, shrugging. "Even if this does work, we could always have an ethical argument about how recovering eyesight isn't creating long life, but rather ensuring quality of life."

"I suppose that's a good potion to have. Something that wouldn't extend a person's lifespan, but make it comfortable," Cadeyrn said.

"But don't Healers disregard someone's lifespan every day, then?" Kajaan asked, frowning. "Healing mortal wounds?"

"The difference lies with a natural death," Kende said. "Saving someone's life from being cut short is different than an old man trying to cheat death after a long life."

"If this works, I'd love to try and look into repairing ears," Asyl said, nearly bouncing now. "Though there's a lot of tiny bones in the ear, so maybe some of my bone growth tincture."

The Void trailed off and folded his arms across his chest as he slumped back into the settee, his eyes unfocusing as he thought about his new project. Kende chuckled, gripping his Fated's thigh as he watched him with a soft smile. The casual movement and fond look told Kajaan this was a regular occurrence and something Asyl was prone to.

"Can I train under Asyl?" Marika asked, her sharp eyes focusing on her father.

Kajaan didn't bother hiding his snicker.

As the sun dipped in the sky, it was time for them to get ready for the feast. Tomorrow was the wedding and reception, and they would leave late the day after. While Kajaan would love to stay longer, he really didn't want to tempt King Tonalli into arresting him despite their immune status. There was no need to have anyone really examine the signature on their documents and have the forgery discovered. As much as it hurt, leaving quickly was their best course of action. He'd much rather hide from King Tonalli as much as he could so the man would forget about him.

Instead, Kajaan quickly worked with Asyl to get dressed in a simple pale gold caftan, a flowing Bisht that complemented Cadeyrn's fiery ensemble with a water motif, his slippers, jewelry, and correct the diadem so it was sitting properly on his head. The Void had his own outfit that Kende brought with him to change into, and he needed to focus on his own grooming.

Kajaan joined his lover in the main room. His cloak had been removed, and he wore a gorgeous burgundy tunic and loose-fitting pants underneath his glittering Bisht. Even after looking at him for so long, Cadeyrn still took his breath away. Kajaan smiled, trotted up to his love, and nestled into him. He sighed and luxuriated in the tight hug that Cadeyrn always gave him without reservation.

"I will never regret leaving Avitou, even though the circumstances under which I did weren't ideal," Kajaan said. "But I don't miss being scared all the time, and I love you and the kids so much."

"You've made my life so much better these last few moonturns. I've felt like I'm actually living again after Menea passed on," Cadeyrn murmured. "I'm so glad you feel safe at Paelfjord. I love you so much."

Once the kids, Miski, and Olire joined them, the party left their suite. Wayra followed behind them with Asyl and Kende a few paces back. In addition, Wayra had assigned Kajaan and Cadeyrn their own personal guards tonight, so the two weren't tethered to the entire Zothuan envoy. Splitting up wouldn't be ideal, and Cadeyrn had requested that Kajaan stay by his side. Cadeyrn didn't trust King Tonalli or Jeryit not to pull something while everyone else was distracted.

The ballroom had exploded in colors since the last time Kajaan saw it moonturns ago. Lords, ladies, kings, kinlets, queens, quenlets, dukes, and duchesses from all over the continent were in attendance. If his eyes weren't playing tricks on him, Kajaan thought he spied a few from the council as well. Yolotzin was plotting something in inviting them, he was sure. Speaking of.... Kajaan looked around, trying to locate his best friend. He wasn't too worried about finding the prince right away. There was plenty of time before the dinner.

Theoretically per caste seating, he and Cadeyrn would be close to the royal table where Yolotzin and Naias would be sitting, along with King Tonalli and Queen Brekka. Naias's parents would be up there as honored guests. Kajaan wondered if he hadn't been part of an assassination plot if he'd be up there too, as Yolotzin's guest of honor, or if he'd be shunned as Yolotzin's dirty secret. He couldn't wait to see his best friend again.

Couldn't wait to show him the bracelet and ring that Cadeyrn had given him.

He'd have to make sure that Yolotzin would be an honored guest for his own wedding. Though if he knew his Fated, Cadeyrn was already planning on such an honor for the prince. Hell, Kajaan wouldn't be surprised if Yolotzin, Naias, Asyl, and Kende would be invited for an extended stay. That would be so much fun, and Kajaan could pick Naias's brain on how she used her Craft to see if he could expand his own control.

Maybe by then he'd even have his own gexena so he and Yolotzin could go riding together. Hariam was a sweet gelding with a near perfect temperament now that he was bonded, even though he'd been separated from his master. Kajaan figured he should finally tell his lover he was ready to have his own mount.

Kajaan was too far in his head thinking about when Cadeyrn would trot him in front of unbonded gexenas that he missed someone calling his name. His Fated gently nudged him, and Kajaan blinked a few times to bring himself back into the present, realizing he'd really lost himself. Approaching the two of them was a man who was just shy of six feet, bright red curly hair on the top of his head with the sides shaved, and bright blue eyes. His Craft Mark identified him as a Harvester.

"That is you, right? Kajaan?" the man asked.

He was dressed in the layered robes of Valvinte, each one designed to keep the chill out despite the fact that it was late summer in Averia. Valvinte was a cold country, far to the north at the edge of the continent. Kajaan was grateful he didn't have to endure such a distance for this wedding. He couldn't imagine spending more than four days in a rocking carriage, no matter how nicely furnished it was.

Yet there was something about this man that made Kajaan hesitate to reply. It wasn't so much as he felt like a threat. Rather, the complete opposite. This newcomer almost felt familiar, like they could be best friends, if only Kajaan had the confidence to reach out. Taking a breath and trusting his instincts, Kajaan smiled at the redhead.

"I am, yes. I'm afraid you have me at a disadvantage," Kajaan replied kindly.

A quick glance toward Cadeyrn got him a small shake of his head. So his lover didn't know who this man was either. Kajaan wanted to be on guard and wary of the new male, but he couldn't. Everything he felt and read from the man's body language was acceptance and excitement. Especially after Kajaan's confirmation.

"Oh, we thought you were dead!" the man said, sounding jubilant. "Ever since you disappeared from the castle in spring." A dark look crossed his face then, and he shook his head before that smile reappeared. "But now you're back, and with the Zothuan king no less! Oh, Auntie is going to be so excited! Stay here!"

Before either of them could protest, the redhead scurried off, slipping through the crowd almost effortlessly. Kajaan stared after him in bewilderment and turned to look at Cadeyrn. His lover looked amused, and Cadeyrn folded his arms loosely across his chest.

"Do you know who that is?" Kajaan asked.

"No. But I'm guessing his 'Auntie' is a diplomat, if not the queen of Valvinte," Cadeyrn said. "Brace yourself, love. I think these people know you, even though you don't know them."

"Over here, Auntie!" the young man was saying.

The redhead was holding on to a woman's hand and pulling her through the throngs of people, some of whom had paused to watch the spectacle. The woman herself was alabaster pale, her skin creamy and clear of any imperfections. She had deep red curls with streaks of white that cascaded down her back to her hips, and her green eyes sparkled with good cheer. Even if Kajaan hadn't seen that, the sweet smile on her face confirmed that she wasn't upset about being led around haphazardly by her nephew.

Her dress was regal indeed, a beautiful silver silk that hugged her ample curves, flowing all the way to the ground with a slit up the side to midthigh. Earrings dangled from her ears, and the bangles on her wrists clacked together in a musical harmony, imitating birdsong. The diadem on her forehead glittered around her Gale Mark, signaling her as royalty as much as her demeanor did.

Then she looked up and saw Kajaan. Any color on her beautiful face drained away as her eyes widened and began to fill with tears. Almost as if she'd seen a ghost of someone she'd loved.

"Auntie, Kajaan," the boy said in a half-made introduction.

"Oh Goddess, it is you," she said with a tremor in her voice.

Just as Kajaan was about to lose his manners and demand an explanation, another woman wearing a similar frock stepped up to her. This second lady's dress was a deep sage, complimenting her graying rusty brown hair and dark eyes. Her features were even more delicate than the first lady, though her skin was a bit darker. She, too, wore a diadem, and had an Illusionist Mark.

Kajaan did his best to not shy away from the women who were staring at him with equal expressions of joy and sorrow.

"Beg pardon, Queen and Kinlet of Valvinte," Cadeyrn said smoothly. "We are both a little baffled as to what you are to my Fated, though it is clear that Kajaan means a great deal to you."

"You're Sinelle's boy, aren't you?" the Gale asked.

"Who?" Kajaan asked, wincing.

The Illusionist looked a little pained. "My little sister. She found her Fated here in the castle when we were visiting once. She was claimed by the captain of the guard, though his name is escaping me right now."

"Jeryit?" Kajaan asked, his tongue going numb.

They couldn't be.

Could they?

"Your mother," the Illusionist said, her voice choking. "My sweet Sinelle. You look so much like her. Oh, the goddess has blessed me with seeing you alive and well."

The woman stepped toward him, and Kajaan took an unconscious step back. As much as he believed her—she had all the markings of telling the truth—she was still a stranger. Right now, he didn't trust anything in Avitou. Not with Ameyalli's words of warning ringing in his ears. Could this be some elaborate trap King Tonalli set up?

"My Fated and I are a little confused," Cadeyrn said, coming to his rescue again. "I don't believe he was ever told he had a family, and none turned up when I looked for more information on his mother."

The Illusionist slapped a hand over her mouth, her watery eyes going wide.

"Wasn't he? Oh, my sweet nephew," she said. "I'm your Auntie Ellenis. This is my Fated and Queen of Valvinte, Terenna. Her nephew, Basren, is accompanying us this year."

Kajaan nodded slowly, staring down at Ellenis. His aunt. He had an aunt? Why hadn't his father ever told him about her? Had he not wanted Kajaan to be able to move somewhere else and be out of his control? Kajaan slowly looked toward the front doors where Jeryit would be standing.

"I don't understand," Kajaan said slowly. "I thought my mother was an only child."

"Is that what he told you?" Queen Terenna spat. "I knew their match wasn't a good one, love. Jeryit never gave us details on how Sinelle died. Just that she had after giving him a son. Through inquiries, Kajaan, we were able to learn your name and that you resembled a Valvintette, but not much else. We were going to confront King Tonalli about your whereabouts tonight, and if you weren't needed at the castle any longer to bring you back home, where you should have come after Sinelle's death."

Kajaan felt the breath leave his lungs as old fears came rushing back. Would these two blame him for his mother's death? They clearly deeply cared for Sinelle, to the point where they'd even argued against a Fated bond. They'd wanted to take him to Valvinte after his mother's death, but Jeryit had either hidden him or blocked their pleas. Yet his father seemed to despise his very existence.

"I'm so confused," Kajaan finally said, putting a hand to his head. Cadeyrn gently rested his hand in the small of his back and rubbed in small, slow circles. "I-I don't.... Jeryit always seemed to hate me. Why wouldn't he just give me up after Mother died?"

"I can't answer that. Though I most definitely want to put your father in his place after hearing this new information," Cadeyrn said.

"Kajaan," Aunt Ellenis said softly, "please, do you know how my sister passed?"

Bile rose in the back of his throat, even as he gave a jerky nod. Only the reassurance and calm from Cadeyrn stopped him from fleeing the room. Well, that and the fact that Wayra would probably catch him and pick him up off the ground to keep him in sight and safe. Wouldn't that be a wonderful introduction as a Quenlet?

"She… hemorrhaged while… giving birth to me," Kajaan managed to choke out.

Aunt Ellenis gave a small sob, and both hands covered her mouth and nose, tears gathering in her eyes. Clearly the pain was still there and would likely always be. Queen Terenna closed her eyes briefly, rage crossing her timeless features for a moment. She glanced toward the front doors, and Kajaan very briefly wondered if his father was in danger from two or three angry monarchs. He didn't know why he cared.

"Sinelle gave the world a wonderful gift," Queen Terenna finally said, releasing a slow breath. "And I'm not just saying that because you're King Cadeyrn's Fated."

A gentle smile curved her lips again, and she approached Kajaan, who'd begun wringing his hands. With a gentle touch, she parted them and took both hands in hers. Her skin was cool to the touch, helping push back the nausea and panic that had been building inside of him despite Cadeyrn's best efforts.

"Truly," Aunt Ellenis said, sniffing and flapping her hand in front of her face. "King Cadeyrn, would it be all right if we accompanied you to Paelfjord for a week or so after the ceremony? I would very much like to get acquainted with my nephew."

"It would be my honor to host the Queen and Kinlet of Valvinte, along with their entourage," Cadeyrn replied kindly.

"Please, your marriage would make us related. You can just use our names," Queen Terenna said slyly.

"Then you must drop the honorifics for me as well," Cadeyrn said, grinning in turn.

"Do…. Do I have any other relatives?" Kajaan managed to ask.

"Oh, sweet," Aunt Ellenis said and nodded. She took one of Kajaan's hands from her Fated and stared down at the back of his hand, almost as if she couldn't believe he was real. "Your grandmothers and one grandfather are still alive. You've got me, two other aunts, and five uncles. Countless cousins, married-in aunts and uncles, and I believe some of your direct cousins have been having children as well."

A dizzy spell spun Kajaan's vision, and he blinked, realizing his knees had locked. Cadeyrn's arm slid around his waist, holding him up so he didn't faint like a noblewoman overdressed in summer.

"So many," Kajaan said weakly.

Aunt Ellenis gave him a gentle smile. "It will be a huge reunion when you're able to visit."

"Which we will. I've always loved Valvinte in the winter," Cadeyrn said. "I'm sure the kids will enjoy seeing the snow instead of sand for once as well."

Queen Terenna blinked slowly before tilting her head. "That's right. You had four kids with Queen Menea, didn't you? Where are they now? Prince Thaddaeus is what… eleven?"

"Almost. His birthday is in late summer," Cadeyrn said and smiled as only a proud dad could.

Kajaan had never had that expression turned to him by his own father, and his heart ached with desperate longing. He'd missed so much of his life. Over thirty years, and he'd never once known that he had aunts and uncles, cousins, grandparents…. Hell, his aunt was a Kinlet! Marrying royalty seemed to be a habit of their family.

He stifled the laugh that started to bubble up his throat, knowing it would probably sound a little unhinged. He was already stupefied; he didn't need his aunt… aunts to look at him like he was insane. Maybe they'd forgive him this once if he broke a little.

The boy, Basren, slipped forward and grabbed Queen Terenna's hand, smiling at her. They were nearly the same height, Kajaan noted dimly.

"Auntie, I think Kajaan is a little overwhelmed," he said.

Kajaan blinked once, looking at the boy. He most definitely was, and the Harvester had somehow picked up on it. Hell, Kajaan had almost forgotten he'd been there with how quiet the young man had been throughout their conversation. Though the wide smile still on Basren's face betrayed his excitement.

"Oh. Oh, my sweet, I'm so sorry," Queen Terenna said gently. "This has to have come as a shock to you. I shall leave the travel arrangements between our secretaries."

Cadeyrn nodded. "Quillin is my secretary. I'll make sure he contacts yours before the night is out."

Queen Terenna smiled before her face went completely cold. Ellenis seemed to notice the change in her Fated, and she cast her a worried look. His aunt gently tugged him down and planted a gentle kiss on his cheek.

"I'm looking forward to getting to know you, nephew," she said.

With that, the two women clasped hands and walked toward the front hallway. Kajaan winced, figuring he knew who Queen Terenna had seen, and Basren winked at him before trotting off after his aunts.

"Oh Goddess, please tell me she was including Queen Terenna's family when she told me how many relatives I have," Kajaan said in a rush, turning to his lover. "How did I not run into any of them despite the amount of times I was in Valvinte? I know I avoid the castle and the parties Tzin attends, but if I have that much family? There's no way I have that many relatives!"

Cadeyrn laughed and shrugged, pulling him into a gentle hug. "Valvintettes have massive families. I'm sure making love is a great way to keep warm during the deep winter."

Kajaan groaned and dropped his face to his lover's shoulder. The man snickered and hugged him close, rocking slightly. Kajaan sighed heavily, sliding his arms around his Fated's waist. So many new relatives. How would he be able to keep them all straight? Would he be expected to keep in touch with them? How was this going to affect their relationship with Zothua?

Kajaan knew all the monarchs didn't get along. King Tonalli was living proof of that. At least Queen Terenna seemed amicable and even kind when speaking to Cadeyrn. Unless she was one of those underhanded and manipulative queens. Kajaan really hoped she wasn't. But the thought wouldn't go away.

"How do I know they're telling the truth?" Kajaan asked.

"I'll bully the information out of Jeryit," Cadeyrn replied, shrugging. "After dealing with a pissed-off Terenna, I'm sure he'll be glad to deal with me."

"Is she scary?" Kajaan asked.

"She can be as frozen as the Valvintette ground in deep winter if she wants to be," Cadeyrn said and chuckled. "That woman is a force of nature. I've always done my best to be polite towards her."

"Oh, sure that's the only reason," Kajaan teased.

"Completely. What if she snowed out the Laiyi Desert? All the han-hans would die, and you wouldn't have your favorite breaded dish anymore."

The impracticality of someone freezing the desert did what Cadeyrn had intended. Kajaan laughed and pulled away from his grasp. His lover's eyes were sparkling with amusement as he dipped down and pressed a gentle kiss to his lips. A moment later, they were bombarded by their twins, Olire right behind them, and their assigned guard behind him.

Kajaan picked up Fayette, whose mouth was a deep blue from eating some sort of fruit. A moment too late, he realized her hands had met the same fate, and he got a tiny handprint on his shoulder for his troubles.

Absolutely worth it.

Chapter 25

Later in the evening, the bell was rung for dinner. Kajaan still hadn't been able to locate Yolotzin, though he knew his best friend was somewhere in the throng of people. He put Fayette and her sticky hands back on the ground, much to her displeasure. Olire had tried to clean her hands from the fruit juice, but she managed to evade the teenager, fascinated at how her palms stuck together when she clapped.

Olire took over the twins again and, like during Kajaan's introduction dinner, led them to the children's area. There, they sat with their caretakers while the adults sat in long rows, perpendicular to the royal table with the couple and their families. Kajaan's heart thumped when he finally got a look at his friend. Yolotzin looked tired with bags under his eyes, but he was smiling. Beside him was Naias, who seemed to be suffering from the same affliction.

Of course, Kajaan knew full well it was because they were fighting King Tonalli's Void law. Still, the sight of his first love struggling and clearly backed into a corner rankled him. He wished he could be here fighting too but knew he couldn't. If he stayed past the wedding party, he'd be at risk of being arrested and probably executed within the hour with the charge of Craft misuse. That was if Cadeyrn let King Tonalli's guards anywhere near him.

Kajaan, Cadeyrn, and Thaddaeus were sitting at one of the closer tables, where he could easily see Yolotzin standing next to Naias. Cadeyrn was seated between him and Thaddaeus, with Kajaan being to his right. Across from them were Asyl and Kende, for which Kajaan was grateful. Farther down the table were Queen Terenna, Aunt Ellenis, and Basren. His aunt's eyes were red, and Queen Terenna looked downright murderous. No one near them said a word.

Amongst those gathered, Kajaan recognized several of the Averian gentry, including Duke and Duchess Ruvyn. Why Kende wasn't seated with them, Kajaan wasn't quite sure, but it made him nervous. Lord Seni was sitting near the duke with his fourteen-year-old twin boys, Arik and Alyn. The twins were clearly unhappy about being separated from their older brother, making upset faces at their father and grabby hand motions toward Asyl, who smiled sadly at them.

King Tonalli shuffled to his feet and raised his hands for silence. He thanked those in attendance and spoke at length about how proud he was of his son, how excited he was for the marriage, and the joy of Yolotzin finding his Fated. For a moment, it almost felt like King Tonalli from half a lifetime ago. Kajaan wanted to believe the man truly meant his words, but the flinty look in his eyes spoke differently. He was just putting on an act… as usual.

Beside him, Queen Brekka sat listlessly, her shoulders slumped, staring quietly off into the distance. What had happened to her? He hadn't seen her in a long time, but the last time he had, she'd still been vibrant and full of life, if not slightly depressed. True, she hadn't had kids after Yolotzin and lost far too many pregnancies, but when she and King Tonalli had made the decision to stop trying, she'd still been a wonderful mother.

Finally, the guests shuffled to sit once Tonalli's long-winded speech was finished. Servants made their way down the aisles, filling the goblets with wine. The kids over at their tables got nonalcoholic sparkling cider just so they felt included in the ceremonies. Kajaan finally caught Yolotzin's eye, and he knew his friend registered his presence by his strained smile morphing into something more genuine.

Kajaan discreetly pointed at him and made a thumbs-up motion. *You okay?*

Yolotzin glanced at his father and licked his lips before shrugging. His own gestures were so minimal, Kajaan doubted anyone else casually watching him noticed them. *Not really.*

Worried, Kajaan swiped his hand over his eyes, nodded toward Yolotzin, and tapped the table a few times. *See you later tonight?*

His friend stared at him for a minute, and Kajaan briefly worried he hadn't understood. Then Yolotzin raised his hand and tapped the ring on his finger and his wrist before nodding toward him. Oh! He hadn't really had time to write to his friend and let him know that he was engaged. Kajaan couldn't help the grin that spread across his face. He pretended to yawn, covering his mouth and purposely wiggling his fingers to get the stones on his jewelry to shine.

Yolotzin's smile grew, and Naias leaned into him, obviously asking what was going on. He tilted his head and whispered to her. Her head snapped toward him, and Kajaan waved at her. The blond's smile nearly split her face, and she hugged Yolotzin's arm. If it had been proper for her to leave her seat, Kajaan had no doubt he'd be swept up into a hug. It was then that he realized there was no animosity between him and Naias, and he would eagerly take the gift of her friendship.

Beside her, Yolotzin traced his lower lip and nodded at him.

I'm happy for you.

Tears gathered in Kajaan's eyes, and he buried his face into Cadeyrn's shoulder.

"How are you two communicating?" his lover asked.

Oh, of course he'd picked up on it. Kajaan laughed weakly and sat straight, smiling at him.

"I have to keep some of our secrets," Kajaan teased him.

Apparently Cadeyrn was completely fine with that answer as he chuckled. "I was a little worried that you were tiring until I saw Lady Naias move at the table and realized you two were gesturing at each other."

"Tzin is going to come by later tonight, probably with Lady Naias. He's going to be ecstatic about our engagement," Kajaan said. "And I can't wait to show off my bracelet."

For a moment, Cadeyrn looked confused, but he shrugged and smiled. Clearly he hadn't realized how in-depth Kajaan's conversation with Yolotzin had been, as simple as it was. A servant finally came by to fill their goblets. King Tonalli got back to his feet and raised his cup in a toast. Kajaan twined his fingers with Cadeyrn's and cupped the goblet with his other hand.

"To my son and daughter-in-law's health, prosperity, and marriage filled with love," King Tonalli said and drank.

Kajaan brought his goblet to his lips, unconsciously diving into the wine to see its composition. It was a habit he'd formed once he realized where his Craft specialty lay. He'd thoroughly enjoyed how different drinks had been put together, and sometimes he could even tell where a new bottle of wine came from after knowing the company. This wine, though…. It was wrong.

Not just wrong.

Poisoned.

At the time, Kajaan hadn't understood why Rhionne had him identify different toxins in their pure form, and then again after they'd been imbued in a drink. Some of the poisons had changed chemically, and Kajaan was tasked to find which goblets had been poisoned or if they'd been mixed with something benign like juice or sugar. Learning the poisons and their effects had been a part of his training, and Kajaan was never more grateful.

Then his brain caught up and he realized that if his goblet had been poisoned, then….

Kajaan dropped his cup, not caring about it spilling, and slapped the one out of Cadeyrn's hand, who had hesitated after picking up on his distress through their bond.

"The wine's been poisoned," Kajaan shouted.

Cadeyrn's eyes went wide, and he hastily grabbed the cup from his son, turning Thaddaeus's head toward him, ignoring where he'd effectively thrown it onto the table. Asyl lowered his goblet, a bead of wine resting on his lower lip. Kajaan's heart plummeted. At the table, King Tonalli stood, his heavy chair scraping back, a snarl growing on his face.

"You dare disrespect me in my own hall?" Tonalli snarled.

"Father," Yolotzin said, rising as well. "Give Kajaan a moment to explain."

The prince set his goblet on the table just as a cry from the other side of the room went up. Yolotzin turned toward the distressed noise and wavered. His brows knitted together, and he grabbed the back of Naias's chair. She looked up at him, worried, and opened her mouth to say something. Only a handful of heartbeats after his plea to his father, Yolotzin collapsed.

Oh Goddess, no!

No!

Naias's scream was drowned out by the others whose loved ones were collapsing.

"Tzin!"

Kajaan was on his feet before he knew it, rushing up to the table, not caring about the exploding chaos. There were sobs already echoing through the room and the children were wailing, refusing to be consoled by their caretakers. Chyrdatyl, a fast-acting necrosis poison that was absorbed into the bloodstream, was rare and incredibly deadly. It was made from some sort of plant that Kajaan couldn't remember at the moment, and it was one of the few poisons that changed composition after being dissolved in a liquid.

He'd be using his Craft on Yolotzin, and he could only hope he would be able to isolate the poison and draw it from his body. If it wasn't too late. *Please, don't let it be too late.* Kajaan dropped to his knees next to Naias, who was valiantly trying to not break down into tears. She had only just now found her Fated, and he was potentially dying. Any young bride would be beside herself.

She was going to be so perfect for Yolotzin. Just as long as he survived this. Kajaan would do anything to make sure he would. He reached out and put a hand on his best friend's chest, trying to dive into his body much like a Healer would. His senses kept getting pulled back every time he pushed, and Kajaan looked up to try and figure out what was blocking him. Naias was touching her Fated's face, gently stroking his pale cheek.

"Naias," Kajaan said. When she looked at him, he smiled faintly. "Please don't touch him."

For just a second, an indignant look crossed her face until she spotted Kajaan's hands on Yolotzin's chest. She finally nodded and withdrew from her Fated. Kajaan looked back down at Yolotzin and dove into him with ease, searching for the strands of poison. It was water-based, so he knew he'd be able to find it. The poison changed composition again after being imbibed, but Rhionne had thought of that and trained him for a worst-case scenario. Kajaan hated the need of using small animals to know how Chyrdatyl evolved, though in this moment, all he could do was praise his tutor.

"What have you done?" Queen Brekka's voice rang out over all the screaming and crying. "Tona, *what have you done*?"

"I don't know what you mean," Tonalli's response came, sharp and decisive. "We have a traitor in our midst!"

"There's no traitor!" Brekka screeched. "This was Yannat's task, wasn't it? I was there when you asked him if the correct goblets had been taken care of. You… you poisoned our *son*!"

A rush of skirts and a new spark of energy pulled Kajaan from Yolotzin's body. He'd been so close! He'd just started to see the spread and to isolate it, and now he was being ejected. On her knees beside Yolotzin was the queen, roused from her eternal stupor, tears streaming down her face as she grabbed at her son's hand and face.

"Baby boy, please, please wake up!" she cried.

"Queen Brekka!" Kajaan shouted, trying to get her to hear him. The longer this took, the higher chance Yolotzin had of dying. It took a lot of power to recover from Chyrdatyl, and he wasn't sure how many Healers there were in attendance or how long it would take to rally all the ones within Alenzon. She shook her head, subconsciously reacting to Kajaan. He took a breath, and tears pricked his eyes when he called out, "Mom!"

The woman started and looked at him, her eyes wide. He'd never once called her that, always deferring to be polite and proper, keeping his distance. Once, when he and Yolotzin were five, he'd asked his best friend if he thought the queen would be all right with him calling her Mom. Yolotzin hadn't seen the problem with it, was even excited by the concept, but Kajaan had been too scared to do so in the end.

"Mom, please. I'm trying to save him. I'm familiar with this poison. My tutor had me study it. I just can't have anyone touching him right now, it pulls me out," Kajaan said. "Please, trust me."

"I do," Queen Brekka said, nodding as she slowly composed herself.

Rage overtook her fear and shock. She spun to her feet and started shouting and screaming orders, even as the panicking gentry and dignitaries started to rally. Kajaan tried to block it out and dove into Yolotzin's body for a third time. He was able to find the branches of the poison much faster this time. It had activated the moment it hit his saliva and had been absorbed into his tongue and esophagus. Already the poison had leaked through the muscle to his lungs, leaving a wake of dead tissue behind.

It was heading for his heart and reservoir.

If the poison even so much as touched it, Yolotzin would die. Even a Healer couldn't repair that much damage. A loud screech jarred Kajaan, and he twitched, ducking his head to one side, trying to reduce the amount of external noise. He and Rhionne had always practiced in an isolated room that had been dampened for sound. Just now he realized what a mistake that was.

Once they got back to Paelfjord, he'd write to his tutor and suggest she train her future students in a noisy environment near the end of their training. If they got back. Kajaan knew there were members of the council in attendance. Not all of them, but enough. It would be obvious to them that Kajaan wasn't a Healer, so he shouldn't be using his Craft to draw the poison from Yolotzin. He was breaking every law an Aquan could, but Kajaan found he didn't care.

As if he would wait for however long it would take for a Healer to help his best friend. He would call him his brother, but… well, that was a little awkward after sharing his bed. His concentration waned, and he struggled to maintain the connection through the cacophony.

Small, warm hands cupped his ears, blocking out most of the noise. Kajaan relaxed, and he focused on his task. The poison burned a baleful green in his senses, the withered tissue a deathly gray and the healthy tissue a soft pink. He didn't have long, and he needed to work quickly.

Kajaan strengthened the cell walls that were in the pathway of the Chyrdatyl, stopping it in its tracks. He slowly worked outward, preventing the poison from trying to seep around, isolating it. By this point, the damage was getting extensive. Almost half of one of his lungs had been damaged. Would he ever be back to full health after this? Unshed tears burned his eyes, and Kajaan did his best to ignore his morbid spiral.

Finally, after what felt like hours, Kajaan had the poison completely isolated. It still saturated the necrotic tissue, but at least it couldn't spread further. Yolotzin's heart was slowing from its rapid pace, but it wasn't returning to a normal beat. It was stopping. He needed to remove the poison quickly. Making the cells stronger was putting too much strain on the prince's body.

Kajaan worked through the dead tissue, pulling the poison from each cell. As soon as he got the aptitude for it, he was able to work faster. He held out his free hand, and someone placed a bowl into it. Kajaan brought the poison through the initial path to reduce any further damage, out of his lungs, up his throat, through where it had hit his tongue, relaxing his hold on the cell walls as he retreated.

The amount of poison he finally extracted was misleadingly small, and Kajaan dropped it into the bowl, exhaustion claiming him. Whomever gave him the bowl took it out of his hands. He looked up to see Cadeyrn's gentle smile and turned to see who was covering his ears. Thaddaeus buried himself in his side, his face stained with tear marks. Kajaan wrapped his arm around the boy and flopped back on the ground, not wanting to move.

Chapter 26

Cadeyrn couldn't be prouder of his Fated. Without hesitating, not caring about making a scene, he'd prevented a larger disaster than the one that was currently being resolved. Luckily, there were a good amount of Healers amongst those gathered, and even the servants had jumped in to help. Someone had the idea to sound the alarm for any nearby Healers, so they'd gotten help by the time those present were tapering off with exhaustion.

But it had been his beloved who'd had the ability to save the prince. Once Prince Yolotzin had collapsed, Cadeyrn knew nothing would pry Kajaan from his best friend's side. Not until the Sympathetic died or stabilized. Kajaan was a sweaty mess, his face completely white as he lay on the ground with Thaddaeus on top of him. Once the prince was tended to, Cadeyrn was going to have a Healer check on Kajaan's Craft and make sure he hadn't overdone it and put himself at risk.

"Lungs," Kajaan rasped out. "I may have overtaxed his lungs."

Lord Kende was at Prince Yolotzin's side in an instant, a determined look on his face. The man already seemed exhausted, sweat beading his forehead. He'd likely been using his Craft to heal others who had imbibed varying amounts of poison. Cadeyrn wasn't sure what it was, but the rapid delivery made him nervous. This dinner could have ended far differently, and with his Fated as a victim.

Right now, Queen Brekka had taken charge and had her husband subdued. Not exactly arrested, since there didn't seem to be much point in it if he could get free with the help of a loyal guard or two, but restrained. The council members present were some of the ones poisoned and weren't in any position to pass judgment or bring a prisoner back to their quarters. Queen Brekka got the young kids sent back to their rooms with their nurses or elder siblings, and those who were healthy out of the hall.

Fewer people meant less chaos. Theoretically. Cadeyrn hadn't met Queen Brekka much, and the knowledge he had about her during this last decade was of a woman dispossessed. That broken, listless woman he'd seen before the toast was gone, burned away in the wake of her rage. Menea would have done the same if Thaddaeus was on death's door.

Cadeyrn leaned down and placed a gentle kiss on Kajaan's sweaty forehead, smiling down at him. His Fated was starting to regain some color in his cheeks and lips, mollifying his fears that Kajaan had overextended himself. If he'd drained his well so thoroughly, he wouldn't be able to recover naturally.

"You're amazing, my love," he whispered.

Lord Kende grunted, and Cadeyrn looked up at the Healer. The man's face was pale, and his hands shook.

"I don't have enough energy," Kende said. "Is there another Healer available?"

Standing above him, Lady Naias pressed her hands over her mouth and nose, a sob finally breaking free from her carefully maintained composure. Asyl crouched next to his lover with an anguished look on his face, tugging on the hem of his tunic. There was a look in Asyl's eyes that Cadeyrn recognized as determination and fear. Asyl had been learning under Tamya and her Void twin Maya to control his unique gifts better. More importantly, how to not absorb energy from Craft-powered objects.

But the most important thing was that they still had a chance to save Prince Yolotzin.

Asyl caught Cadeyrn's eye and nodded slightly. Squeezing Kajaan's hand, Cadeyrn got to his feet, eyeing the worried families standing around their recovering loved ones, and those grieving. There was a small contingent of people hovering near the royal table, all family of the prince. Wayra, Simthe, and Jeryit were nearby as well.

"We need those who can donate their energy to do so to save the prince!" Cadeyrn bellowed.

Lady Naias was the first one to leap forward, blinking out of her panic. She grabbed Asyl's outstretched hand, and Cadeyrn could almost feel her pushing her Craft into him. Kende's pinched expression eased, and his eyes slid closed. Likely diving deeper into Yolotzin to heal the damage. Cadeyrn hoped it wasn't too late.

The woman's eyes slowly drooped, and she stepped back, a little unsteady on her feet. Princess Reina took over, a worried look on her face as her eyes fixated on her baby brother. A slow procession of the royal family came forth to donate as much energy as they could, even the older teenagers. Cadeyrn lost track of everyone who assisted in saving Prince Yolotzin's life, checking in on his own love, who was watching his best friend, crying silently.

Finally Queen Brekka approached and offered her own Craft, though she didn't seem to have much to spare. When she moved back, Cadeyrn reached out and took Asyl's hand. The Void smiled faintly at him, and Cadeyrn pushed his energy into the young man in a sudden rush. Asyl's eyes widened at the influx of power, and his irises started to take on an ethereal glow. Cadeyrn grinned despite the severity of the situation. He knew how big his reservoir was, and he'd just filled the Void's completely.

Yolotzin's chest was rising steadily now, though he was still deathly pale and unmoving. Lord Seni and his twins stood nearby next to Duke and Duchess Ruvyn, who'd also lent their strength. Queen Terenna and Kinlet Ellenis had donated as well, refusing to leave the son of the one Kajaan called mother in danger.

He'd have to explore that relationship a little more once things weren't so dire. Sure, Cadeyrn knew that Kajaan had practically been raised by Queen Brekka, but he hadn't realized how deep Kajaan's feelings ran for the queen. Cadeyrn would encourage that relationship as much as he could. His lover deserved to have a mother in his life.

Captain Jeryit stepped forward, looking down at his exhausted son with something akin to fondness or pride in his eyes. He turned his intense gaze to the Void, who looked positively tiny next to the captain, and reached out. Asyl flinched back, snapping his hand to his chest and pressing into Lord Kende's side.

"Please save the man who brought comfort to my son for so many years," Jeryit said.

Cadeyrn stared at the mountain of a man, stunned. He hadn't thought Jeryit would have bothered to offer or cared about how much Yolotzin meant to Kajaan. From everything he'd heard and witnessed about the man, Jeryit had been a fairly distant and somewhat abusive or neglectful father. This was a surprising development that Cadeyrn wasn't quite sure how to process. He wouldn't suddenly encourage Kajaan to have a relationship with his father after this. But Kajaan did deserve to know that his father helped save Prince Yolotzin's life.

Asyl nodded slowly and took Jeryit's hand. His eyes had lost their luster; the energy Cadeyrn donated was already processed and given to

Lord Kende. Asyl was surprisingly adept with Craft transference with how little he'd trained. The glow came back with a vengeance, and Asyl flinched, his body going taut.

"Too much," the Void gritted out.

Jeryit simply nodded, and the muscles in his arms relaxed. He must have adjusted how much he gave at a time, as Asyl didn't pull away. Color rose in Prince Yolotzin's cheeks, and Lord Kende heaved a massive sigh, his eyes finally opening nearly an hour after he'd taken over.

"That's as good as I can get it," he said. Asyl immediately dropped Jeryit's hand and turned to Kende, hugging him tight. "Yolotzin needs rest and careful monitoring. I suggest Healer Gojko attend to him."

"We'll get it done," Queen Brekka said, her eyes brimming with tears as she knelt next to her son. "Thank you, Kenny. Thank you so much."

Lord Kende smiled brightly at her and nodded, sweeping Asyl into his arms and kissing his temple.

"Couldn't have done it without you," the man murmured.

He stood, bringing Asyl with him. His Fated immediately latched on to him, wrapping arms and legs around him and holding on tight. Cadeyrn looked down at his own Fated and smiled, seeing the peaceful look as Kajaan continued to sleep through the proceedings. Thaddaeus was watching Kajaan intently, as if making sure he wasn't going to suddenly die in his sleep.

Cadeyrn slipped his arms underneath Kajaan's shoulders and knees. Thaddaeus slid off him as Cadeyrn lifted Kajaan, cradling his lover close to his chest. An older man crossed the room, flanked by two castle guards, his Healer's Mark prominently displayed. He got to one knee and placed a hand on Yolotzin's chest. A moment later, he nodded.

"Get the prince to his chambers. I will treat him there. He'll heal better when he's in his own bed," the Healer—presumably Gojko—ordered. "Kende, with me."

Jeryit and Wayra stepped forward. They shared a brief hard look, sizing each other up, before they knelt and picked up the unconscious prince together. Kende followed them, still carrying Asyl, looking as if he would never let his beloved go. If Cadeyrn was in their position, he knew he wouldn't. He smiled at his lover in his arms, feeling the pride of Kajaan's actions swell in his chest.

Following the rest of the attendees, Cadeyrn nudged Thaddaeus and walked out of the ballroom. They split from the majority of the group, heading back to their assigned rooms. Marika and the twins were there waiting for them with Quillin and Ameyalli. The kids were beside themselves with anxiety, and Fayette was on the verge of a breakdown. She wailed, seeing Kajaan unconscious, unable to be consoled even when Miski told her that Kajaan was just asleep. Her little brain couldn't process everything that had happened and was far past the point of being overwhelmed.

Cadeyrn made sure Kajaan was tucked neatly into their bed before returning to his children. He gathered them onto the couch with him, and his whole body began to shake while he held all of his kids tight as the realization of how close to death he'd come finally sank in. If he'd drunk some of the poison, he would surely be dead. Not that he believed Kajaan wouldn't have tried to save him, but the poison had done severe damage to the prince in a short amount of time.

Cadeyrn didn't even know how many people had died or who they were. He'd been so focused on his own family by the time the chaos started, and he hadn't seen who'd been affected. After everything, Cadeyrn was beyond grateful that his family and those closest to Kajaan had survived. Cadeyrn was glad he could even say that after seeing how close Prince Yolotzin had been to dying on the cold marble floor.

At least it seemed the poison didn't affect Voids or those who hadn't Awakened yet. He'd noticed that Asyl had drunk some of the wine and was just fine. Or maybe his goblet hadn't been poisoned, since according to Queen Brekka, not everyone was to be targeted. Cadeyrn didn't know, and he didn't want to dwell on it.

Everyone here was safe, and in the morning, Kajaan would be right as rain.

CHAPTER 27

KAJAAN WAS beyond exhausted. His shoulders were tense, his eyelids drooping, and a headache throbbed with every heartbeat. The new papercuts he acquired on his fingers weren't helping either. Somehow Kajaan had even managed to slice his upper arm, which was a feat, since he was wearing longer sleeves. After living in Zothua for almost two seasons, Averia felt a little too cold. Which was vaguely hilarious that his body was protesting the cooler air while also rioting over Zothua's summers.

He'd adjust. Eventually. At least Cadeyrn was confident that after the next couple of years, Kajaan wouldn't struggle with the high-summer heat. Kajaan wasn't a fan of doubting his fiancé, so he did his best to not complain about the heat—and of course, now the cold. Not that he felt it too much while he was running around with Queen Brekka's orders and digging through endless piles of papers and ledgers. Trying to piece everything together was its own form of hell.

Though it wasn't like Kajaan could complain.

Ten people were dead.

One was a councilman that Yolotzin had befriended during their travels. The man had come with his wife and children all the way from Nabene. They'd been thinking about moving to Bhyvine or Zothua to escape the kingdom's rampant homophobia, since their daughter had started to express interest in other girls. Now it was up to his wife to keep their family safe.

Another victim was the princess and heir of Bhyvine. She hadn't even reached her twentieth birthday and was of no apparent threat to King Tonalli, other than being a bit more headstrong than her peers. Princess Aurea returned to Bhyvine wrapped in a white shroud and surrounded by her grief-stricken parents and siblings. Kajaan had found the seating chart Tonalli drafted up and kept the knowledge of Princess Aurea swapping places with her mother to himself.

The other eight deaths were Averian gentry who had protested a little too loudly about the new Void laws and had worked openly to protect any Voids who hadn't had the means to run. Apparently King Tonalli had thought to take care of his dissenters during his son's wedding while so many dignitaries were present. Kajaan still wasn't sure if it was supposed to be a show of power or if he was trying to somehow keep suspicion off himself, since Yolotzin was one of the victims.

Olire's father had been among those targeted. Lord Ebornzaine had been blessed with an unusually strong Craft, so he'd succumbed quickly to the Chyrdatyl poison. He hadn't suffered, but his wife and son were trapped in a waking nightmare. Olire left Avitou Castle with his mother, took his place as head of the house, and began organizing his father's funeral. Kajaan, Asyl, and Kende's letters were all going unanswered. Asyl had plans to go see his protege tomorrow, though Kajaan wouldn't be surprised if Kende told him that Asyl took off in the middle of the night to bang on Olire's door until he got an audience.

If there was any consolation in any of this madness, it was Queen Brekka ripping up the Void law and opening up the royal coffers to any Void who'd been captured. Those that had been displaced were also compensated, though there weren't that many that were coming forward, despite Asyl and Rojir reaching out to their community. Since they weren't making much headway in that direction, Queen Brekka had pledged a generous amount of gold to Rojir's community center in addition to her offers to try and help.

Yannat had been arrested and was being studiously ignored despite kicking up a fuss of epic proportions in the dungeons. Since he hadn't bothered to even try and stop King Tonalli and was actively helping in locating the Chyrdatyl poison, Queen Brekka wasn't showing an ounce of mercy toward him. She'd threatened anyone who even went to see him outside of delivering him meals with exile, and was actively hunting down any other conspirators.

King Tonalli was sequestered to a bedroom and bathroom within his quarters. He had no access to his study, library, or anything that could be seen as extra comforts. There was a posted guard that, under pain of death, wasn't even allowed to acknowledge the king. How Queen Brekka was ensuring their compliance, Kajaan wasn't sure, and he wasn't sure he even wanted to know. He'd always respected her as a child, and now he was slightly terrified of her. Which probably hadn't been her intentions, but she was trying to keep her children safe, even if it was nearly two decades late.

Princesses Reina and Saian had surprised Kajaan, showing up at the quarters the Zothuan delegation had been moved to with armloads of toys, games, and books for the children. They'd both smiled at Kajaan for the first time in their adult lives and had even hugged him in front of some of the castle staff that were still glowering at him. One maid had dropped the tray she'd been carrying in shock and scuttled away with one well-practiced sneer from Saian. Kajaan had laughed, unable to help himself.

Then there was his wonderful Fated. Cadeyrn was so incredibly supportive, and even offered to help in whatever capacity he was able to. Quillin worked half days with Linel and Siora, responding to panicked letters delivered to the castle and reaching out to help organize, or at least pay for, the funerals of the ten that had died. Wayra had taken over castle security with Queen Brekka's blessing while her investigation of Jeryit was ongoing.

When Kajaan had confided in Cadeyrn about his fears of his father having been complicit in everything, and that he'd lose his father permanently, Cadeyrn hadn't scoffed or rolled his eyes at him. Instead, Cadeyrn had held him close and kissed the back of his head.

"Why are you so scared?" Cadeyrn asked kindly.

They were curled up in their large guest bed, completely nude for the first time all week.

"It's stupid," Kajaan muttered, pressing his face into the pillow.

Cadeyrn's arms tightened around his chest and nuzzled into Kajaan's hair.

"Things that frighten you aren't stupid," Cadeyrn chastised.

Kajaan scowled. He huffed and looked over his shoulder to glower at his fiancé. "If Jeryit dies, then that means I've lost both of my parents and I'm alone. But that doesn't make any sense because I have Aunt Ellenis, and you, and the kids, and Tzin. It's not like Jeryit was even really ever a proper father."

"He's still your father," Cadeyrn said, his voice going soft. "Even though he mistreated you while you were a boy, he was your anchor alongside Prince Yolotzin. There's no shame in being worried about his involvement and what his future will look like."

Kajaan hated that his lips quivered as he held back his tears. He sniffed, perhaps a little too loudly, and wiggled back into his fiancé.

"I don't want to think anymore," he pleaded.

"Are you sure?" Cadeyrn asked. Kajaan lunged forward and grabbed the slick from their nightstand and thrust it into Cadeyrn's hands. Cadeyrn snorted and pressed a kiss underneath Kajaan's earlobe. "As you wish, my love."

Kajaan's body melted into the mattress as Cadeyrn hiked Kajaan's leg over his hip. His love's grip was firm without bruising, and it was only seconds later when the rest of Kajaan's thoughts fled from his mind. After several hours, Kajaan dropped off, still sweaty and sticky from their lovemaking, his mind blessedly silent.

The relief Cadeyrn gave him at night helped Kajaan focus during the next day, even if it was a little uncomfortable to sit in the morning. Today he'd read through several of King Tonalli's journals, taking notes of days and events that seemed even slightly suspicious. Kajaan had learned that his own murder had been planned for years in advance, and the poisoning started the moment Yolotzin introduced Naias to his father as his Fated.

Kajaan wished he could talk to his best friend. Cadeyrn was a great person to talk to, but the man wanted to try and help and fix the issues Kajaan discussed with him. While his expertise would be nice, Queen Brekka was slow to trust him, despite him being Kajaan's Fated. Kajaan couldn't quite blame her, since he'd unearthed far too many secrets that he probably shouldn't have ever learned. Especially since he wouldn't be a citizen of Averia for much longer.

As much as Kajaan wanted to stay and fix his birthplace, he knew they needed to leave soon. Aunt Ellenis and the rest of the Valvinte delegation had left after the first few days. That had been two weeks ago now, and Cadeyrn, Quillin, and Ameyalli were starting to get antsy. Kajaan couldn't put off the children's lessons for much longer either, and Miski was in desperate need of a break.

So they were leaving tomorrow. Kajaan had compiled his notes for Queen Brekka so she'd be able to easily pick up where he'd left off. She'd already said goodbye after dinner, hugging him for a long time and tenderly kissing his forehead as she blinked back tears. Kajaan wouldn't be surprised if they found some presents in their luggage when they got back to Zothua. Queen Brekka had insisted that she needed to make up for all the birthdays she'd missed and, naturally, his engagement.

Yolotzin was still asleep. Gojko wasn't worried just yet, but Kajaan could see the Healer's jaw tighten the longer Yolotzin slept. The prince was losing weight even with the nutrient-dense water they trickled down his throat at mealtimes. If Yolotzin didn't wake soon, he'd be in danger of wasting away. Despite Kende's assurances that he'd write no matter what happened, Kajaan had begged Cadeyrn to leave him behind.

His Fated simply kissed him and told him no.

Kajaan understood. He was needed back in Zothua, with his own wedding to plan and surrogate to find. The kids needed him. Cadeyrn needed him. But Yolotzin needed him too. So did Naias, Kende, and Queen Brekka. But Kajaan knew the truth. He'd be on the carriage in the morning, leaving Avitou and her slumbering prince behind.

As he did every night, Kajaan nodded to the guards standing outside of Yolotzin's rooms and headed inside. He rolled his shoulders in a desperate bid to try and get them to loosen up as he crossed the room. The air was stuffy with the fire already going despite it not having gotten that chilly during the day. Gojko was taking no chances for Yolotzin to catch another illness while he recovered.

Naias was slumped on the settee, a book on the floor next to her feet. Her mouth was open, and she was drooling in quite the unladylike fashion. Kajaan would have laughed, if it wasn't for the dark bags under her eyes. She was as exhausted as the rest of them, doing her best to handle all of Yolotzin's affairs in case the worst happened.

Kajaan quietly approached her and took her pulse, just in case. When he determined that she was simply sleeping, he gathered the book, straightened out the pages, and set it on the low table in front of her. Kajaan placed a featherlight kiss to her brow and left her to rest. If he tried to move her, she'd likely wake, and Kajaan didn't want to deal with a grumpy, overtired Naias on his last evening in the castle.

Instead of sitting in the chair next to the bed, Kajaan crawled on top of the covers and flopped down next to his best friend. There was a healthy color to Yolotzin's cheeks, though his face was starting to get a bit gaunt. Kajaan reached out and placed his hand on Yolotzin's chest, sighing heavily as he did so.

"We're leaving in the morning," Kajaan said, keeping his voice low so as to not wake Naias. "I wanted to stay longer, but of course, I was overruled. You haven't met Fayette yet, but she's persuasive when she wants something. Which, right now, is to go home. Marika is in love with the library, though. I wouldn't be surprised to see half of it come with us when we finally load up the carriages. Rodolfo has streaked through the gardens about ten times already and has probably scandalized every staff member you have. I know he's not exactly happy here—it's too cold for the kids—but he's trying to be a good sport about it. Thaddaeus is doing really well, at least. He's been staying in the library, but he's reading books about Averia to learn more and how to help improve our kingdom's relationships.

"Though, that won't really be much of a problem once you wake your lazy ass up and take the crown. You and Cadeyrn already like each other all right, so we'll be great allies. But you need to be in charge. I know Mom would be great too, but could you imagine Saian's eldest stepping up to be king? He has no sense of humor at all, but I blame Saian's Pemalian husband for that. Reina's son would be a much better bet. She's slowly bringing her kids around to visit Mom for the first time. Can you imagine meeting your grandmother and then having your Awakening in a few moonturns? I think that'd be pretty damn scary."

"I can think of a few things that'd be scarier," Yolotzin commented.

Kajaan snorted before he froze. While he'd been talking, Kajaan had closed his eyes and curled up next to his best friend. He bolted upright and stared at Yolotzin, who was awake.

"Naias!" Kajaan shouted.

His breath caught in his throat, and Kajaan collapsed on top of Yolotzin, hugging him tight. Yolotzin chuckled when Naias fell off of the settee with a loud thump. Chapped lips pressed against Kajaan's temple as he sobbed in relief. He couldn't respond to Naias's panicked inquiries, then her own desperate cry when she saw her fiancé awake.

As soon as her weight piled on top of Yolotzin beside him, Kajaan flung his arm around her shoulders, bringing her close. She burrowed in, wrapping an arm around his waist. Yolotzin wiggled underneath them both, and a moment later, he joined in on the embrace.

"I'm here," he whispered.

"You very nearly weren't," Naias choked out. "Thank the goddess that Kajaan was there."

Yolotzin gave a quiet noise of inquiry, but Kajaan shook his head. They could talk about it later. They could talk about it later! Yolotzin was awake, and though his recovery would take a long time, there wasn't much danger of a relapse.

The door clicked open, and Kajaan looked up to see Queen Brekka and Gojko come through. Of course the guards would have heard the shouting and sent for the Healer. Kajaan reluctantly stepped aside to give Gojko access to his patient, and retreated next to the queen. She wrapped her arms around Kajaan and laid her head on his shoulder, not bothering to hide her tears. Kajaan hugged her close, scrubbing his face with his sleeve.

"Well," Gojko finally announced, "he's as good as expected at this point. Lots of hearty, bland food to wake his stomach back up. Bedrest for now, I think, until we get some strength back into you. Then we can see about walking you to your lovely living space and back to bed for the next week. After that, we'll revisit how much stamina you have and see about longer excursions."

"Bedrest?" Yolotzin protested.

"You're welcome to try and get up before I authorize it, but then you're going to have to haul your scrawny ass back into bed," Gojko threatened, raising an eyebrow.

Yolotzin snickered and grinned up at the Healer. His smile faded, and he sighed softly. "Thank you."

"Your young man and Kende did most of the work. I just swept in at the end to take the credit," Gojko replied. "Rest. The more you rest now, the faster you'll recover. Now, if you'll excuse me, Your Highness, I believe your family needs some alone time. I'll go speak with the cook about your meal plan."

Kajaan escorted Queen Brekka to the chair, and she sat with a heavy sigh, folding her hands in her lap. Naias was refusing to leave Yolotzin's side, holding on to him as if he'd disappear if she let go. Once it was the four of them, Kajaan leaned against the wall next to the bed and dropped his head back.

"What's happened?" Yolotzin asked.

The pause after his inquiry was a bit uncomfortable, and Queen Brekka cleared her throat. She caught Yolotzin up on the deaths and what was being done to Yannat and King Tonalli. While Queen Brekka was telling him about the safeguards she had in place so they weren't liberated, Yolotzin held up a shaking hand.

"The Void law?" he asked.

"Shredded," Queen Brekka snarled. "We're working on reparations."

"And Jeryit?" Yolotzin asked.

Queen Brekka hesitated, glancing at Kajaan. When he made a move to leave, she shook her head.

"As if Yolotzin isn't going to just tell you. We believe Captain Jeryit is largely innocent. I think he got caught up in everything and was in survival mode," Queen Brekka said. "I've ordered him to stay in his rooms until tomorrow afternoon."

So after the Zothuan delegation left. Kajaan smiled faintly at her, hoping he was conveying his gratitude and relief at not having to interact with his father.

"Tillet?" Yolotzin asked.

Kajaan growled and banged his head against the wall. It didn't help with his headache, nor did it make him feel any better. At least it wasn't the sandstone of Paelfjord that would have cracked open his skull.

"As soon as I saw the pardon papers, I had Macik rally his old team and try to hunt him down. He and Ilfa are gone. Possibly even out of the kingdom," he groused.

"They'll get their comeuppance," Naias muttered.

A firm knock on the door silenced any further conversation. Any tension Kajaan might have released came right back when Jeryit hovered in the doorway.

"May I interrupt?" Jeryit asked.

He and Queen Brekka shared a meaningful look, and she sighed but nodded. She got to her feet and smoothed out her skirts, offering Kajaan a wobbling smile.

"Listen to him," she implored.

"Can you send Cade?" Kajaan whispered.

Queen Brekka nodded. She tugged him down to her height and placed a kiss on his forehead, then did the same to Yolotzin and Naias. Queen Brekka ran her hand through Yolotzin's hair and left the room. Jeryit approached the bed and stopped several feet away. He bowed properly to Yolotzin, though his eyes stayed on Kajaan.

"I expect you have questions," he said.

"They can wait until Cadeyrn gets here," Yolotzin muttered.

The room fell into silence. While they waited, the prince dozed off, having reached the end of his meager energy supply. Kajaan's skin felt too tight. He didn't want to listen to his father despite yearning to know why Jeryit hated him so much. If it really was as simple as Sinelle dying bringing him into the world.

Cadeyrn entered and shot Jeryit a fierce glare. He walked over to Kajaan and cupped his face to tilt his head up and kiss his lips. Cadeyrn led him to the chair that Queen Brekka had so recently vacated and sat, pulling Kajaan into his lap.

"Hello, King Cadeyrn," Yolotzin said quietly.

"Good to see you awake, Prince Yolotzin," Cadeyrn replied kindly.

"Talk," Yolotzin demanded.

"It's about your father, the king," Jeryit said. "Though I suppose everything that's happened these last two seasons all tie together."

"That's generally what happens when a monarch goes mad," Cadeyrn said coldly. "Though I'm quite proud of the queen for taking charge like she did."

"The last seventeen years has been a near absolute hell," Jeryit intoned. He sighed heavily and scrubbed his face with his hands. Suddenly he looked far older than his sixty years, staring at a spot on the floor. "As you know, Brekka has had trouble conceiving and carrying her pregnancies to term. When she lost the child shortly after Sai's wedding, they decided to stop. Considering she was in her early forties, it was for the best.

"Then… six years later, she told Tona and I that she was expecting again."

Cadeyrn tensed, and Kajaan stared at Jeryit in disbelief.

"Mom was never pregnant again," Yolotzin said, his voice starting to sound a bit stronger. "I would have known. Especially after my Awakening."

Kajaan gasped as a long-buried memory came to the forefront. Jeryit caught his eye, and the small smile on his face confirmed his suspicions.

"There never was a Teenaged Sympathetics Jamboree, was there?" he asked.

"You mean the one I went to when I was fourteen and managed to drag you along?" Yolotzin asked.

"The very same," Jeryit confirmed. "Tona got a lot of the gentry boys who were at the cusp of their Awakening that you weren't familiar with and organized a retreat. The counselors would paint their foreheads every morning, and made games designed for you to train and control your Craft."

"A win-win," Cadeyrn said, albeit grudgingly. "Pretty clever."

"But it was also to hide Mom's pregnancy," Kajaan said. "Tzin would have sensed it, so he needed to leave. Sai was off in domestic bliss, and Reina was too focused on her studies to realize what was going on."

This time Jeryit smiled a little more at Kajaan. His expression was soft, making Kajaan's heart ache. He wished he'd gotten that look from his father as he'd grown up. Not now. Not when it felt like too little and far too late.

"Only three people knew. Brekka, Tona, and myself. I only knew so I could keep an extra eye on Brekka because she was of the age where being pregnant could be dangerous."

"Then she miscarried," Cadeyrn said.

Jeryit nodded slowly. "Two moonturns later. It… it broke Brekka. They had such high hopes that the baby would be their little miracle. A blessing from the goddess herself to give them one last child. Brekka just stopped caring about anything. No mind Healer could help. She actively locked herself away, though it doesn't surprise me that she'd been listening all these years.

"Then Tona turned to Tratane. He couldn't function between trying to help his wife, run the kingdom, and handle his own grief. The drugs helped boost his mood, and I suppose he thought that the low doses he took would be safe enough."

"What about you? Where do you fit in all of this?" Cadeyrn asked.

"I begged Tona to leave the drugs alone. He started pushing me away, telling me to take care of his wife since he needed to focus on the kingdom. When I recognized Brekka's total despondency, I realized one very important thing. I'd done the same damn thing when Sinelle died. Except I took my feelings out on my son. I promised to do better, to try and make up for the shit I'd put him through, even if he never forgave me," Jeryit said.

"He's right here," Yolotzin grumped.

"But you didn't," Kajaan growled. "You just went from actively telling me how much you hated me to ignoring me completely!"

"Tona hired Yannat shortly after he got addicted to Tratane," Jeryit said. Cadeyrn hissed and hugged Kajaan tight for a moment. Kajaan could feel his Fated's rush of frustration at Jeryit ignoring Kajaan again. "I never liked him, and I tried getting him fired several times. Never worked. He started whispering in Tona's ear, getting him to change policies, feeding his paranoia while he was high. Sometimes he'd bring in sex workers while Tona was compromised, and Yannat often made sure Queen Brekka was in the room. Once he was sober, Tona would be devastated, so he chased the Tratane high more frequently, putting him more firmly in Yannat's hands.

"The few friends and confidants I had in the castle vanished. Less and less of the royal guards listened or reported to me, and I was being cut out of security meetings while I was resisting the changes. Yannat finally told me that if I stepped out of line, you'd be his next target, Kajaan. So I did everything I could to push you away. To try and keep you safe."

"Did you know about the assassination?" Yolotzin asked.

"Not fully," Jeryit admitted.

"Not fully," Cadeyrn repeated with a scoff.

"What would you have had me do? Learned everything and told Kajaan, risking them finding out and changing their plans while you operated on outdated information? I overheard them mentioning that the route they were having the driver take was dangerous and isolated, but they were very careful to not say anything around me. The only time I was able to warn you was when I followed you to the carriage, and that was because they thought I knew nothing at all past the missive being blank," Jeryit protested. "You have no idea how relieved I was when Prince Yolotzin came back with the news that you were safe and… that you'd found your Fated."

"I never—"

"You were overheard telling Lady Naias," Jeryit interrupted kindly.

Yolotzin huffed and pressed a hand over his face. Naias sat up and fixed a death glare on the captain.

"There had to have been time between Yannat being appointed secretary and his total control over you. Why didn't you get Kajaan out then?" she demanded.

"In the beginning, I didn't realize what was happening. The changes happened slowly at first. Then by the time I realized how bad it had gotten, it was too late to try and smuggle him out."

"You could have sent him to Queen Terenna. She would have kept him safe and even probably would have tried to extract you too," Cadeyrn said.

"And started a war? Yannat would have gone after Kajaan under the guise that Queen Terenna was holding him hostage due to his proximity to the royal family. We both know how she'd take that," Jeryit replied.

"They started making plans fifteen years ago," Kajaan said, hating how his voice started to shake. "You said the miscarriage was seventeen. There were two years where I could have had you as a father, but you were too caught up in your job to even look at me. You didn't even give a shit to say goodbye the first time Tzin and I started to travel."

"I managed to get Tona to agree to that and override Yannat's protests about keeping you close. You were able to leave because of me. Because I surrendered more power to him in exchange for your freedom. You were the safest with Prince Yolotzin, always moving and learning more about the world," Jeryit snapped, his patience finally wearing thin.

Kajaan flinched back, and Cadeyrn's arms immediately wrapped around him and squeezed, cocooning Kajaan in warmth and safety.

"You will keep your tone even when talking to my fiancé," Cadeyrn said coldly.

Jeryit closed his eyes and visibly got himself back under control. He finally inhaled deeply and nodded. When he raised his head, Kajaan avoided Jeryit's gaze, focusing on his best friend. Yolotzin had pulled Naias to his side again, rubbing her back as he stared at the ceiling, contemplating something. She was watching him, her eyes sharp and body tense, as if she was waiting for Yolotzin to need something.

"One year," Yolotzin finally said. He looked at Jeryit, his voice cold. "You have one year to train your replacement, and then you will retire. I don't care what you do after that, but you will be forbidden to return to the castle. I understand that you were put in a hard place and you did your best to survive, but you were my father's personal guard. You failed him the moment he got hooked on Tratane. You said yourself there was a two-year gap in between Father starting to take Tratane and you handing over your power to one who deserved none of it. There was time, and you mismanaged it, putting the whole kingdom at risk.

"Because you didn't actively participate and tried to minimize as much damage as you could, I won't pursue charges against you. If I find out that you knew more about the assassination on Kajaan's life than what you've told us to try and save face, I will exile you with nothing but the clothes on your back. If I find out that you have lied about anything when it came to you trying to protect Kajaan, I will drag you out of bed and exile you. Do I make myself clear?"

"Yes, Your Majesty," Jeryit said quietly.

"You're dismissed."

"For what it's worth. I'm very proud of you and the man you've become," Jeryit said, locking eyes with Kajaan for just a second.

Jeryit bowed to Yolotzin, then turned and left. The click of the door sounded too loud as none of them responded to the captain's final words. After a minute, Kajaan gasped in a hard breath and let out a sob. He hadn't even realized he'd started crying. Cadeyrn gently shushed him, moving Kajaan around so he sat sideways in Cadeyrn's lap, facing Yolotzin, and was gathered in a near bone-crushing hug.

"Do you believe him?" he managed to say, looking up at his Fated. "Was he really trying to protect me?"

Kajaan wasn't sure what he wanted the answer to be. He clutched at Cadeyrn's shirt, feeling far too vulnerable after everything his father had told them.

"It's possible," Cadeyrn said gently. "He did appear to be telling the truth."

"I've never heard of someone using Tratane for nearly two decades," Naias said with a small growl. "Especially regularly like he claims King Tonalli was doing."

"Actually, it makes sense," Cadeyrn replied. He sighed heavily and began rubbing a small circle into Kajaan's low back. "It's slow, but long-term use eats away at the brain. It begins with a heightened sense of paranoia, and that's when they're highly susceptible to manipulation, like what Yannat was doing. The mood swings start to become more severe, and their original personality starts to disappear. They become erratic, usually on the crueler side, and most times end up developing psychosis."

"That's where he's at now?" Yolotzin asked.

"Yes. It happens probably closer to ten to fifteen years after regular use," Cadeyrn said. "The long-term effects aren't well known, as those who usually get hooked are those who are destitute or have suffered a great loss but don't have a reliable or safe supply, so they pass away after two or three years. I assume Yannat knew someone who could get him high-quality Tratane without any dangerous fillers, and regulated the doses to keep Tonalli under his thumb for as long as he could. You would have needed a regent for four years before you stepped in, and he couldn't risk that. He wouldn't be able to take the role, and you'd fight the policies he'd want to enact."

"So what happens now?" Yolotzin asked in a small voice.

"There's no fixing him. If you don't continue to give him Tratane, he'll die from the withdrawal. But if you continue to give him the drug, he'll deteriorate further to the point where he'll essentially go comatose and waste away. I don't think he's got much time left before he reaches that state," Cadeyrn explained.

"Is that why Yannat drugged Yolotzin?" Naias asked. "He knew he wouldn't be able to control Yolotzin, and he didn't have much time left with King Tonalli. So he tried taking out the crown prince to get one of the princess' boys, who haven't been trained to take over a kingdom, in order to control them."

"Probably."

Silence descended on them once again for a long time. Kajaan fought off a yawn, pressing his face into the side of Cadeyrn's neck.

"I think it's time to go to bed," Cadeyrn murmured.

Kajaan shook his head. "I'm not ready."

The moment they went to bed, he would have to leave his best friend behind. They wouldn't have time in the morning to come visit and say goodbye. It had to be now.

"Kaj," Yolotzin murmured, "I'll see you again soon. You're free to stand in my wedding now. I'm sad I didn't get to meet your kids, but I'll have to monopolize your time on your next visit. Now come give me a kiss and let your man take you to bed."

Kajaan glanced up at Cadeyrn, who smiled fondly at him. He slid off of his Fated's lap and walked over to Yolotzin's bedside. Kajaan leaned in and placed a soft kiss on the prince's lips, fighting back another wave of tears. Naias leaned in and kissed his temple, smiling at him when Kajaan looked up at her in surprise.

"Travel safely. Love you," Yolotzin said, his voice slurring.

"Love you too. Heal quickly," Kajaan whispered. He looked at Naias. "Thank you."

"Thank you," she replied. "We'll see you again soon."

Kajaan straightened up and turned around to regard his Fated. After a moment's deliberation, he held up his arms. The feeling of vulnerability was hitting him hard, and Kajaan just wanted Cadeyrn to take care of him. A second later, Cadeyrn had swept him off his feet and strode out of the prince's bedroom. Kajaan relaxed into his lover, closing his eyes, and sank into their bond, seeking comfort.

He twitched in surprise when his back hit a mattress. Cadeyrn wasted no time stripping him and then pulling off his own clothing. He left them where they fell on the ground and crawled into bed. Cadeyrn manipulated them so they lay on their sides, facing each other, with Kajaan's legs draped over Cadeyrn's hips. Cadeyrn wrapped his arms around Kajaan's chest and held him close, tucking Kajaan's head under his chin.

For a long time, neither of them spoke. Kajaan closed his eyes and thought back on the entire conversation they had with his father. Everything had gone wrong so quickly by trusting one person who should have never been in a position of power. Had Jeryit really ever cared? It felt weird even considering that perhaps his father really had been trying to protect him.

"It's all right if you never forgive him for how he treated you as a child," Cadeyrn said. "Despite his grief, and then desire to protect you, he still failed the first rule of being a parent."

"And what would that be?" Kajaan asked.

"Protect your kid," Cadeyrn replied. "You have permanent scars on your arms because he checked out and left you in the hands of those who didn't care about you. He didn't spirit you away the moment he sensed some sort of danger, putting you at an even higher risk. Just because he's now saying how proud he is of you doesn't erase his neglect."

Kajaan nestled into his lover, sighing heavily. "How do I know I won't hurt the kids?"

"You're not your father," Cadeyrn replied. "Your experiences are vastly different. If I were to pass away, you'd have Quillin and Ameyalli at your side to help with the kids. Jeryit had a newborn and no other family to lean on. It's not comparable."

After a long moment, Kajaan said, "I don't think I want to talk to him again. At least… not for a while."

"Then don't talk to him," Cadeyrn said. "He made his bed. It's time for him to lie in it."

Kajaan pulled away just enough so he could look up at his lover. He smiled faintly and leaned in to kiss him. Cadeyrn squeezed him tight for just a moment before rolling onto his back, bringing Kajaan with him. He began running his fingers through Kajaan's hair, luring him to sleep.

"Once we get back, we should start screening surrogates while we plan our wedding. Maybe we should start trying sooner than later," Cadeyrn murmured.

Kajaan wiggled as close to his Fated as he could, unable to stop himself from grinning. The dread he'd felt earlier about their departure was gone, leaving only excitement behind. What Jeryit had done and what his motivations were didn't seem to matter so much to Kajaan anymore. He had a family to plan for. To treasure and hold until his final breaths. It was time to let go of what-ifs.

He wasn't going to waste his chance at his forever.

Epilogue

SNOW DRIFTED to the ground as the royal marriage procession made its way down the street to the church. Normally, the parade would wind around the main city streets, offering every citizen the opportunity to see their crown prince in decent health, hand in hand with his bride. It was a time-honored tradition that went back far more generations than what was written down. Since Yolotzin was still recovering, even eight moonturns later, the procession had been limited to only a few blocks near the church.

Naias wore the most beautiful, pure white gown with gemstones embedded in the bodice, long flowing sleeves, and pearl-hemmed veil. She had a heavy white fur cloak on to keep her warm, her train sweeping out behind her by several feet. The only concession the tailor made to the weather was a pair of sturdy fur-lined boots that would be swapped out for white slippers once they got to the church. Her fine golden hair had dozens of tiny braids, making it look elegant without being busy.

Yolotzin was a vision in his white tux that had gold highlights, his hair neatly combed to one side. He'd chosen to have a tailcoat that mimicked Naias's train, though it wasn't nearly as long, only dragging a few inches along the snow. His cloak was the exact copy of Naias's, and he had been outfitted with a pair of slim white boots, though his weren't fur lined.

Because of the extensive damage done to his lungs, Yolotzin had fought long and hard with Gojko to even be able to take part in this tradition. The Healer had finally thrown up his hands in frustration and demanded that Yolotzin at least take a cane with him. The white marble tapped against the stone road, the sound dampened by the thick snow.

Just like Yolotzin promised, Kajaan walked a few paces behind the prince in his position as his best man. He had worked with Cadeyrn's tailor to get clothing that would be warm enough for the wedding, but still have Zothuan aspects. The resulting outfit ended in a close-fitting long-sleeved gold shirt with a thick white vest and pants. It was a bit restrictive but definitely cozy, with the addition of his cloak. He wore his quenlet diadem, despite not having had his own wedding yet.

Beside him, as Naias's best maid, was Asyl. The Void walked proudly behind the woman with perfect posture, his circlet showing off his bare forehead. He had a loose white tunic with gold highlights, matching Yolotzin's tux. His pants were form-fitting, and Asyl had a new brace that blended in perfectly with the white fabric. Luckily, any whispers of having a Void in the procession were drowned out with the cheers of the people seeing their crown prince.

By the time they reached the church, Yolotzin was flagging, and Asyl had developed a bit of a limp from walking on a slick, uneven surface. The bride's party was ushered to a side room while Yolotzin and Kajaan were brought to another. Yolotzin sat heavily on the bench and huffed out a breath, looking up at Kajaan.

"How're you feeling? Ready to let Gojko tell you 'I told you so'?" Kajaan teased.

Yolotzin snorted and said, "Absolutely not. Just need a minute."

Servants bustled in with large fluffy towels. They got to work patting down both of their legs and shoes so they wouldn't track water in the worship hall. As soon as Kajaan was dried off, he leaned forward and placed a kiss on Yolotzin's forehead.

"See you at the altar," Kajaan said.

Yolotzin smiled up at him, and Kajaan left the side room. Asyl waited for him in the foyer, looking a little pale, sweat beading at his temple. Without commenting on the pinched expression, Kajaan simply held out his arm. Asyl took it with a small smile and leaned heavily on Kajaan. They waited for several minutes until their music cue played through the church. Asyl stood up straight, though he didn't let go of Kajaan's arm.

They walked slowly down the aisle, passing pew after pew of gentry and dignitaries. The church was nearly insufferably hot after the long walk in the snow. Maybe having the wedding in the dead of winter hadn't been the best idea, but Kajaan knew there was a reason Yolotzin and Naias weren't putting it off much longer. It was the same reason Kajaan and Cadeyrn's wedding was in only a few more moonturns.

Usually royal weddings weren't so close together, as they were expensive and time-consuming. If Yolotzin had gotten his way, both he and Kajaan would be married to their Fated on the same day, at the same time, at the same altar. Cadeyrn had shut that down faster than Maeeri taking off across the Laiyi Desert. Zothua had its own traditions for the royal wedding, and he refused to set them aside just to have a joint wedding.

Kajaan couldn't wait to be officially tied to his Fated. He gave Asyl's hand a small squeeze as they parted once they stepped up onto the dais at the base of a statue of Ilyphari. She stood tall, head tilted back and hands clasped over her breast, ignoring the wedding that was taking place.

A few minutes later, the music swelled again, and Yolotzin walked down the aisle next, with Regent Queen Brekka escorting him. She wore a proud smile, tears streaming down her face. They exchanged a brief kiss once they got to the end, and Queen Brekka went to sit in her assigned space.

Almost right when she sat, the doors opened once more. Lady Naias was accompanied by her father, who was in no better condition than Queen Brekka. He held a handkerchief to his eye as he sniffled, his lips and chin quivering as he tried to stifle his happy tears. Naias carried a bouquet of lewisias, daisies, and carnations. Father and daughter embraced gently before he handed her off to Yolotzin, who looked as if he would also burst into tears at any given moment as he smiled at her.

With the whole wedding party present, the priest began the ceremony. He talked for what seemed like hours about sacred bonds and how it was a blessing for Fated soulmates to find each other. Kajaan tuned him out, instead scanning the gathered crowd to find one particular Ignis.

The first row was dedicated to the bride and groom's immediate family. Behind that were their extended relatives, which included Duke Ruvyn and his brood. Then the foreign dignitaries. King Cadeyrn was dressed in his full regalia like all the other kings and queens were, with their spouses and children. Remarkably, King Cossus had returned as well, despite the loss of his daughter, to celebrate Yolotzin's wedding.

Kajaan locked eyes with his Fated and couldn't help his smile. From what he understood, their wedding would have a lot less pomp and circumstance. It was far more informal, and the major party members would be mounted on a gexena. Once their rings were exchanged, they'd race across the Laiyi Desert—literally riding into the sunset together. It was far more romantic than the stately wedding that Kajaan had once pined for.

He clued back in just in time to stand forward and give Yolotzin the ring. His best friend smiled at him, and Kajaan knew that if they didn't have thousands of eyes on them, the crown prince would have hugged or kissed him. Cadeyrn had been surprisingly fine with Yolotzin declaring "cuddle time" and spiriting Kajaan away for a couple of hours while they curled up together and caught up with the things that couldn't be sent in letters. It usually amounted to a lot of raunchy jokes and Kajaan rambling about how much he loved his kids.

Said kids who were doing so well sitting quietly in the pews. Even the twins, newly seven, were behaving for once in their short lives. Kajaan pulled his focus back to the ceremony as it came to a close and Yolotzin was able to kiss his bride. He handed his cane back to Kajaan and lifted Naias's veil. She grinned up at him, a mischievous sparkle in her eye as she flung her arms around his neck, nearly hitting Kajaan with her bouquet, and they came together hard enough that Yolotzin had to take a step back.

Laughter echoed through the hall while Kajaan put his hand on Yolotzin's back to help his best friend not fall on his ass during his own wedding. The laughter evolved into wild cheering, and Kajaan tilted his head to get a better look to discern why so many Averian gentry were losing their minds.

Naias had taken Yolotzin's hand and placed it on her low belly.

It was the perfect announcement for the new couple. In the next few days, Yolotzin would have his coronation, and the babe that Naias carried would be the kingdom's heir regardless of sex. Yolotzin squeezed Naias to him and picked her off her feet, his joy infectious as he held his wife. They only had eyes for each other, Yolotzin's full of wonder as he regarded his Fated.

Kajaan managed to get Yolotzin to take his cane before they walked down the aisle to leave the church. Asyl followed, his eyes suspiciously wet, though he still giggled and nodded at the forgotten bouquet at Kajaan's feet. Kende slipped from the pew and walked alongside Asyl hand in hand as they followed the couple. Kajaan waited for a beat and did the same.

He grinned at Cadeyrn when his Fated left the children in Ameyalli and Quillin's expert care, though Kajaan did give them a quick wave and blew them a kiss for behaving so well. Cadeyrn grabbed Kajaan's hand and twined their fingers together. Sighing happily, Kajaan leaned into his lover, his focus turning back to the man beside him rather than the one walking in front of him.

“Think everyone will cheer like this when we announce our pregnancy?” Kajaan asked.

Cadeyrn grinned down at him. “I have no doubt. Our surrogate wishes to remain anonymous to the people, but she’s given us her blessing to announce that she’s carrying Zothua’s heir. Have you told Yolotzin yet?”

Kajaan snorted. “Absolutely not. I figure he can learn the same way he meant to tell us. The only way I found out sooner was because I caught Naias getting up close and personal with the castle’s new plumbing.”

The two chuckled as they exited the church and were greeted with a rare sight. The skies were clear and the sun shone down on the wedding party, making the snow sparkle as bright as the Laiyi Desert. Yolotzin helped Naias into a waiting carriage, and the coachman pointed the horses toward the castle.

As guests made their way out of the church, Cadeyrn pulled Kajaan off to the side to wait for their kids. Kajaan hummed happily and wrapped his arms around Cadeyrn’s neck, leaning into his Fated. Cadeyrn hugged him close and pressed a kiss to the top of Kajaan’s head. They had only a few minutes before Fayette barreled into them, giggling endlessly.

Shouts rose up from the side of the church where children of varying ages were letting off some steam with a snowball fight after sitting still for so long. Their boys were in the midst of the battle while Marika stood on the sidelines, critiquing her brothers. For kids who rarely saw snow, they were holding their own fairly well against the Averian and Valvintette children.

It was hard for Kajaan to believe that only a year ago he’d been heartbroken and had no idea what his future looked like. Now he laughed with his Fated as Rodolfo got a snowball to the face and fell backward onto his butt. Kajaan would never be alone again. He had friends and family to lean on if he lost Cadeyrn. He’d never be in the position to neglect his children.

Now the only thing he had to worry about was… how many kids could they have before Cadeyrn told him no?

Who's Who

Kajaan Pernoac—Aquan, 31—Raised in the castle alongside Yolotzin after his mother's death, he and the prince grew up together. As such, he fell into the role of being Yolotzin's lover and personal secretary. He's friendly, though reserved, and can't abide seeing someone hurt. Former lover of Yolotzin Navarre-Hamonn. Fated to Cadeyrn Greatblaze.

Cadeyrn Greatblaze—Ignis, 40—Growing up an only child, Cadeyrn knew he was destined to take over his father's throne. For the most part, Cadeyrn is easygoing, though prone to anger when innocent people are harmed, especially when his family and friends are threatened. Formerly married to the late Queen Menea. Fated to Kajaan Pernoac.

Thaddaeus Greatblaze—Unawakened, 10—A restless young boy, Thaddaeus would rather ride his gexena than be cooped up in a room trying to learn mathematics. He's shy, though he loves to make friends with kids his own age. Especially if they like to ride horses like him. While he's Cadeyrn's firstborn, he needs to Awaken as an Ignis first, if he wishes to become king.

Marika Greatblaze—Unawakened, 8—Studious and shy, Marika is happiest when she's in the great library, surrounded by leather-bound books. If her father would permit it, she'd even read during family meals and fall asleep with one on the bed next to her. Marika has no interest in becoming queen, so she's hoping one of her other siblings will take the role.

Fayette Greatblaze—Unawakened, 6—Wild child extraordinaire, Fayette adores being outside underneath the sun, surrounded by the castle's gardens. She seems to have boundless energy, always keeping her nurse Miski on her toes. Although she's little, Fayette is already a romantic, adoring weddings and the idea of falling in love. Twin of Rodolfo.

Rodolfo Greatblaze—Unawakened, 6—Always ready for chaos, Rodolfo prefers to spend his days under the sun in his birthday suit. When he's not being a terror to his nurse, Rodolfo is fairly quiet and would rather play with building blocks… and then destroy what he's built. Twin of Fayette.

YOLOTZIN NAVARRE-HAMONN—SYMPATHETIC, 30—The crowned prince of Averia, Yolotzin is a kind soul who waits for as much information as possible to present itself before he reacts. He's frequently ruled by his heart when it comes to those he loves, even if that means he doesn't see their flaws. Former lover of Kajaan Pernoac. Fated and married to Naias Elrel.

QUILLIN FAERING—SYMPATHETIC, 25—A kind and quiet man, Quillin worked hard to become the best secretary available. He was young when he went into Cadeyrn's employ, and has proved himself several times over. It takes a lot to make him angry, and he's a terror once he's on a roll. Fated and married to Ameyalli Faering.

AMEYALLI FAERING—SEER, 24—Somehow always in a good and serene mood, Ameyalli takes life one day at a time. They absolutely adore children, and love Cadeyrn's kids as if they were theirs and would spoil them rotten if Quillin didn't step in. Ameyalli does their best to not be too disheartened with their infertility, choosing to believe they'll become pregnant when the time is right. Fated and married to Quillin Faering.

TAMYA LALTINE—HEALER, 30—Tamya all but fled Averia to protect her Void twin, Maya, knowing her Healer status would be enough to take care of them no matter where they settled. Her dedication to her patients and devotion to her sister caught Cadeyrn's eye, and she was quickly snapped up as the royal family's Healer.

WAYRA SURRAL—GAIAN, 35—A direct descendant of the great general Laiyi, Wayra possesses an exceptionally strong Craft, though he doesn't use it often. He's wary and isn't shy to use spies to keep an eye on the kingdom to keep his charges safe. It takes a bit to earn his trust, but when it's been earned, Wayra is a steadfast ally. Has his eye on courting Tamya Laltine.

ASYL RUVYN—VOID, 27—Formerly Lord Asyl Seni. Alchemist and researcher, Asyl strives to keep his medicines as cheap as possible to help those in need despite his shop now being located in a wealthier district. He's hired on new staff to keep up with the influx of orders, yet still struggles because of his Void status. Fated and married to Kende Ruvyn.

KENDE RUVYN—HEALER, 33—The youngest son of Duke Kiyiya Ruvyn. Known to his family and the higher gentry as the one to go to for planning parties, though he runs charities and benefits consistently to try and get the gentry to help the city. He wants what's best for the destitute of Alenzon, and works hard to keep the city in good health. Fated and married to Asyl Ruvyn.

NAIAS ELREL—AQUAN, 27—Asyl's best friend and unofficial caretaker when Kende isn't around. Even though she no longer works at Enchanted Waters, she still keeps meddling with the business, in addition to her new royal duties. She dreams of traveling and having a large family. Fated and married to Yolotzin Navarre-Hamonn.

OLIRE EBORNZAINE—VOID, 13—A timid young man who was disowned once his Awakening failed. He's academically smart and picks up alchemy quickly. Olire tries to stay hopeful about the future, though he gets overwhelmed fairly easily. He views Asyl like a big brother and looks up to Kende for what he did to help him.

RHIONNE LALTINE—AQUAN, 86—Mother of Gojko and grandmother of Tamya and Maya. She's observant and knows how to read between the lines of what people say to try and get right to the heart of the issue. Teaching kids how to use their Aquan Craft brings her immense joy, even if she is a bit of a taskmaster about it.

INTI BROACHE—ILLUSIONIST, 35—Content to just be King Cadeyrn's valet, Inti classifies himself as a selective mute. He mostly only ever talks to Cadeyrn and, more recently, Kajaan. Inti enjoys listening to all of the castle gossip and likes to investigate to see if the more spicy rumors are true before he brings them to his king or Wayra.

MISKI ABRIES—GALE, 42—Almost always being run ragged on her feet, Miski struggles to keep up with the terrible twins. She's strict with her charges, though she loves them dearly. Miski applied to become the castle's nanny after her own left the nest and is terrified with the prospect of Cadeyrn and Kajaan planning on having an undetermined number of children.

SIMTHE CRELIEU—HARVESTER, 23—Young and in love, Simthe is a happy-go-lucky guard who believes that everyone should find their Fated. He found his own happiness as a teenager, and the couple is well known for their amorous nights. While Simthe isn't a strong fighter, Wayra keeps him around for his exceptional riding skills.

TONALLI NAVARRE-HAMONN—IGNIS, 66—King of Averia and Kiyiya's elder brother. It's said at one point, he loved his children dearly and ruled the kingdom kindly. Somewhere within the last twenty years that changed, and Averia's laws have gotten harsher. The reason for his change of heart is unknown, as is the reason why his wife has been absent for the same amount of time.

Jeryit Pernoac—Gaian, 60—After losing his wife, Jeryit threw himself into his work to try and dull his pain, despite having a newborn to take care of. He was grateful when Queen Brekka intervened, and let her take care of his son without complaint. By the time Kajaan was grown, Jeryit regretted his apathy, but kept up the ruse so Tonalli wouldn't have any leverage over him. He's proud of the man Kajaan has become despite everything. Fated and widower of Sinelle Pernoac.

Yannat Tadi—Ignis, 58—A highly unpleasant man who enjoyed watching people squirm. Yannat constantly spied on his coworkers, and anything that could be exploited was reported back to Tonalli. He encouraged Tonalli to ignore his queen after her last miscarriage and did his best to tear them apart. Just because he could.

Brekka Navarre-Hamonn—Harvester, 65—For the first many years of her marriage to Tonalli, Brekka was happy. She bore him children that she took an active role in raising, even when she got sick after Yolotzin's birth. After that, she was unable to bring another child into the world, though not from a lack of trying. Her spirit broke from miscarriage after miscarriage, with Tonalli pulling away further each time. It was easier to stay in their rooms than face the man she'd disappointed so many times, and to not think about anything than face his infidelity and her pain.

Saian Navarre-Hamonn—Gale, 45—Even though Saian is the firstborn of Tonalli and Brekka, Saian was never destined for the throne, despite her fury over the injustice when she was a child. She made it her mission to marry to become queen or kinlet instead, but found her Fated in a lesser Pemalian noble. The two have four kids together, and Saian runs an export company with an iron fist.

Reina Navarre-Hamonn—Ignis, 40—As a child, Reina was closer to her father than her mother. She watched as Yannat pulled her parents apart, yet couldn't figure out how to stop it or who she could tell. Once she found her Fated, Reina distanced herself from the family completely, rarely interacting with her little brother, especially once she had her own kids to protect.

Ellenis Saskia-Kaja—Illusionist, 59—When she was barely out of her teens, Ellenis persuaded her little sister to apply to work in the Droskyn castle with her. Barely a year later, Terenna came into the larder where the sisters were working, and Ellenis got pulled into a whirlwind romance. She takes her role as Kinlet seriously, and she's known as the warm heart of Valvinte. Fated and married to Terenna Saskia.

TERENNA SASKIA—GALE, 65—Terenna was crowned queen of Valvinte when she was barely ten, after her parents died in a bandit ambush gone wrong. Despite having a steward, Terenna pushed hard to have the bandits found and executed, gaining her ice-cold reputation. Only her Fated and children know how loving and gentle she can be with her loved ones. Fated and married to Ellenis Kaja.

SINELLE PERNOAC—SYMPATHETIC, 28, Deceased—Ever the romantic, Sinelle ignored her sister's warnings when she found Jeryit during one of his visits to Droskyn Castle. She wanted what Ellenis had and happily went with Jeryit, spending several years in bliss as his wife. All she wanted was to be a mother and wife, and even with her last breath, never blamed Jeryit for accidentally isolating them. Fated and married to Jeryit Pernoac.

MENEA GREATBLAZE—SEER, 30, Deceased—Daughter to one of the chiefs of Pemalia, Menea's marriage to Cadeyrn had been an arranged one, though they eventually fell in love. She was incredibly smart and was delighted to take on the challenge of bettering Zothua beside her husband while bearing him children they both loved. She fell severely ill with an unending fever, and though it broke her heart to leave her husband behind, it was a relief to let go. Married to Cadeyrn Greatblaze.

What's What

(and other worldbuilding info)

Concerning Crafts;

Awakening—Upon a child's thirteenth birthday, at the exact second they first drew breath, their Craft becomes accessible to them. There's no real explanation as to why the child doesn't have access to their Craft beforehand. Many kingdoms treat the occasion as a ceremony, often resulting in a several-hour party. Traditionally, the child will tilt their face to the heavens to receive their Craft, though it isn't necessary.

Fated—Believed to be two halves of a whole; Fated soulmates. The tug that many describe only occurs when the two are ready to meet, even if they already know each other. This tug can expand over several miles. Once established, the two share a connection, able to locate their Fated many miles away and can feel their current emotions. The strength of the bond depends on the cumulative strength of the individual. In very rare circumstances, the bond can be rejected. If done so by both parties, the break is clean. Otherwise, the one rejecting their Fated is subjected to heartache.

Craft Mark—Upon Awakening, the Mark appears in the center of the forehead. It is a simple symbol, easily recognizable at a glance. For the most part, the mark is slightly darker than the skin, like a mole or blemish. For those with darker skin, the Mark is a few shades lighter. Some cultures paint their Craft Mark to match what they're wearing for the day.

Craft Blessed—References anyone who has gone through their Awakening. Some religious sects claim that Voids aren't a part of the blessed and preach against them. Most believe that the Craft given to an individual is predetermined, while very few insist that it's based on their actions as a child and potential or intent.

Aquan—Someone who can manipulate not only water, but all liquids. They're able to locate water sources deep underground and even pull moisture from the air. A more uncommon talent is being able to breathe underwater. One of the rarest abilities is to be able to manipulate liquids on a molecular level.

Gale—Manipulators of air and other gases. They're often guardians of the sky and will be the "canary" when it comes to mining expeditions. Rarer talents run toward being able to manipulate the air around to make people and objects fly. Even rarer is being able to use their Craft to manipulate the weather, though those individuals are heavily regulated.

Gaian—Movers of earth and metals. Gaians can form the earth beneath their feet at a whim, and the stronger individuals are able to manipulate the hardest metals. Some Gaians are able to identify the composition of an area immediately to know where to plant to yield the best crops without the aid of a Harvester.

Harvester—Attuned to all plant life, Harvesters are able to coax plants to grow without blight and on minimal resources. Many tend to stay within the agricultural professions and take pride in sustaining their communities. Strong Harvesters can grow a plant from a seed with just a whisper, though it's rare to be able to do so.

Healer—The one Craft that is bound together by a guild. Healers are only able to go into some form of healthcare, whether that's general or private practice, alchemy, or research, with very few exceptions. They're enrolled in school from the moment they Awaken to learn anatomy and psychology. Their Craft allows them to "dive" into a Craft Blessed patient to get an itemized list of ailments to then invoke healing. Children and Voids are unable to be healed this way and must rely on mundane medicines. While children are completely unaffected by healing, Voids absorb whatever the Healer pours into them, though to no effect.

Ignis/Ignian—Tamers of fire and energy. Ignians can call flame from nothing via their Craft, though trying to burn something that's not flammable is a greater energy drain. Some Ignians have figured out how to use their Craft to heat or cool the air around them. A very few Ignians are fireproof and have been rumored to be able to alter lava flow.

Illusionist—Often viewed as the most useless Craft, Illusionists are able to create images of varying detail that hang in the air. Some use their Craft as a substitute for fireworks during burn bans. A few Illusionists can create lifelike illusions that can move in a realistic way. The talent to be able to conjure sound with their illusion is almost unheard of.

Seer—Depending on the person, Seers can be the most annoying Craft Blessed solely based on the unpredictability of their Craft. Their abilities range far, from seeing multiple futures but being unable to act upon any of them, to seeing one single critical point, but not knowing the circumstances around it. Most of the time, Seers are awake and are taken to a fugue state where they have their Vision and are released. Some have their Visions as dreams instead.

Sympathetic—Always able to feel the emotions around them, Sympathetics are nearly impossible to lie to. They're eerily good at reading people and drawing out their true intentions. To some, emotions are a specific color aura or shape, whereas others describe it as a type of scent or tone. Very few Sympathetics can read thoughts at the base level, though that tends to be draining.

Void—The unofficial tenth Craft. Voids are unique, as they have no well to replenish their reservoir. Instead, they must rely on outside Craft Blessed to give them energy to manipulate. Voids can either take the energy as is from the individual or strip it down to its pure form. They can use this energy to either enhance their own bodies to give them better strength, speed, or senses, or they can transfer it into another Craft Blessed. In an energy transfer, the receiver either must be the same Craft as the donor, or the Void needs to strip it to pure energy.

Reservoir—An innate pool of ready-to-use power by the Craft Blessed. Larger reservoirs usually denote stronger individuals who can either use that energy in a single strong burst or sustain a smaller effect for longer. Smaller reservoirs hold less and therefore tend to leave their hosts in a weaker capacity. Continual training after Awakening until about twenty is essential to maximize the size of a reservoir, though some claim the size is predetermined.

Well—The size of the well determines how fast the reservoir is refilled. Larger wells naturally hold more and can produce energy faster than a smaller one. Voids are the only adults who don't have a well and have no natural energy regeneration. If a Craft Blessed drains their Craft well all the way down to their core, they run the risk of stripping their souls and ending their life.

Gexena—A specially bred Zothuan mount that's remarkably fast, with high stamina and cloven hooves. They are distinguished by their six legs, long neck, and striped brown, black, and gold pelt, along with their long, sharp eyeteeth and antlers. They are omnivores, but a vegetarian diet is best for their health. Gexenas stand roughly 20 to 22 hands. They mature at two years of age, have a lifespan of 30 years, and their gestation is 11 moonturns.

TRATANE—INTRAVENOUS DRUG, upper. Offers the user a euphoric release while potentially causing hallucinations. Highly addictive and popular amongst those who live in squalor. It's also an appetite suppressant, often causing the user to rapidly lose weight. The effects of a dose can last anywhere from three to eight hours depending on quality, quantity, and the person's metabolism. No restrictions on those it can affect.

CHYRDATYL—NECROTIC POISON, usually orally ingested, odorless and tasteless. Chyrdatyl only affects those with a Craft, as it targets the well. The stronger the victim is, the deadlier the poison. The poison naturally occurs in the stamen and berries of the Itonnelle plant. This incredibly rare plant grows deep within the swamps of Bhyvine. There are no known antidotes.

ILYPHARI—GODDESS OF all Craft Blessed. Her priests usually preach about kindness, love, and acceptance, except in Averia, where Voids are shunned. She's always depicted as a mother and never has had a Craft Mark placed on her forehead.

KINGDOMS;

AVERIA—THE SOUTHWESTERN most kingdom. Stretches further north and south than it does east to west. The eastern border pushes up to the Reidden mountain range. The western and southern edges of the kingdom lead to the Duparthon Sea. To the north is the kingdom of Pemalia. Unfriendly toward Voids. Claims more Seers than any other kingdom. The king lives in Castle Avitou, located at the center of Alenzon. Her king is Yolotzin Navarre-Hamonn, temporarily ruled by regent Queen Brekka.

ZOTHUA—A MASSIVE desert kingdom that stretches across most of the continent. A large chunk of the kingdom is claimed by the Laiyi desert. To the east is Nabene, southeast Bhyvine, north Pemalia, and west Averia. Claims more Aquans than other kingdoms. The kingdom's capital is Sestella, home to Paelfjord Castle. King Cadeyrn Greatblaze is her current ruler.

PEMALIA—A HARSH, landlocked barren kingdom. From the western to eastern border is Valvinte, south Zothua, southwest Averia, and southeast Nabene. Filled with arid hills and fallow plains, Pemalia doesn't have much to boast about, except for the pride of her people. Claims more Ignians than other kingdoms. The Royal city of Cleroux encompasses Parandor Castle. Ruled by Queen Linriyo Dallae.

VALVINTE—A KINGDOM to the far north, frigid and covered in snow and expansive forests. North, east, and western borders lead to the icy, perilous Cresok ocean. To the south is Pemalia. Produces the most Harvesters. Droskyn Castle is nestled inside the city of Evigoza, which is built into the Okapi Forest. Currently ruled by Queen Terenna.

BHYVINE—NORTHWEST BORDER leads to Zothua and east to Nabene. The rest of the western and southern border leads to the Duparthon Sea. Most of Bhyvine alternates between plains and marshland. Produces a large amount of Gaians. The capital is Khathen, home to Ichepi Castle. Ruled by King Cossus Verulus.

NABENE—A FAR eastern kingdom. Northwestern border leads to Zothua and southwest to Bhyvine. North border leads to Pemalia. East leads to the expansive Haeftanne Sea. Fairly flat, Nabene raises a variety of animals and is known as a pastoral kingdom. Unfriendly toward queer couples. Produces the most Gales. The capital is Oviedura, home to Draris Castle. Ruled by King Henrik Gyula.

See how the story started in
A Broken Spirit
by AR Bryant!

Prologue

ASYL HAD always wanted to be special.

He was the apple of his mother's eye, his father's pride, and beloved lordling to the servants. For the last thirteen years of his life, Asyl had been groomed to take over his father's business. Well, not all thirteen, truthfully. Ten, perhaps. He was the heir to their family, the only child who made it out of infancy, so a lot rested on his shoulders.

Today was his thirteenth birthday, and the hour grew ever closer to his Awakening. At the exact second that he drew breath in this world, he would be blessed by the Goddess Ilyphari with a Craft. There were nine Crafts he could be blessed with, guiding the rest of his life with a related career he would naturally excel in.

Most, if not all, parents wanted their children to be blessed with an elemental Craft. Harvesters controlled plants, able to encourage them to maturity from a simple seed and will. Gaians could move the earth under their feet with just a thought, shaping the land and finding precious metals and stones. Aquans ruled the oceans and rivers with the ability to breathe underwater, able to locate and call upon underground reservoirs. Ignians were fireproof, able to call upon flames at will—or smother them. Gales could summon the winds ranging from a small breeze to massive storms.

The most coveted of the non-elemental Crafts were the Healers, who were able to pour their Craft into their patients to speed up recovery time. Secondly were Seers, able to see into the future, even if their Visions weren't exactly clear in their meaning. Sympathetics were strong empaths, able to read the emotions of those around them, discerning truth from lies as easily as breathing. The least wanted Craft was to be an Illusionist, able to make fantastical images out of thin air, often working as storytellers or actors.

Though being blessed with any Craft was nothing compared to the excitement of finding one's Fated—the one person made specifically for him that he would find when the time was right. The Fated bond was established at the same time as the Craft blessing, though there were academics who claimed the bond was forged at birth, simply maturing when the child reached thirteen.

Asyl had grown up with stories of how his mother bumped into his father on the street and upon looking at each other, they'd felt the tug of their Fated hearts. Perhaps they'd made their way to the street by the urging of their bond, whispering for them to alter their usual routines. Some people talked as if the tug on their souls was physical, while others just likened it to an awareness.

His parents had been married within a year, as most Fated couples were, and he was born ten months later. It wasn't uncommon for couples to have children quickly and often, and many couples who could afford it ended up with large families. Being an only child was the one thing that Asyl wished he was able to change. He would love to have younger siblings to spoil and look after, taking away the sadness in his mother's eyes.

As it was, he would stand with only his parents on his thirteenth birthday, sans siblings. Awakenings were massive affairs, friends and family invited to join in the anticipation and celebration. The child would be showered with gifts and a feast containing their favorite foods spread out along countless tables. Depending on the season and time of the Awakening, sparklers would be passed around to the children for them to run around with.

Then when it came time for the Awakening itself, Asyl would stand between his parents and tilt his head to the heavens as the revelers counted down the seconds. His Craft Mark would be revealed in the center of his forehead, a few shades darker or lighter than his skin tone, and he would learn his path in life. Of course, his father's political friends were exchanging coins, betting on what Asyl would be blessed with.

At least Asyl had his one childhood friend in attendance. Lady Naias Elrel, who had Awakened as an Aquan eight moonturns ago, was just as eager to see what he would be blessed with. They stood quietly by the buffet tables, despite the other kids running around and adults chatting excitedly to each other. Asyl held Naias's hand tight, his body vibrating with fear and excitement.

The suns were setting, lighting the clouds with pinks, oranges, and purples. His backyard had a warm glow to it, giving all the decorations an orange hue. Tables were adorned with white cloth, held down with platters of his favorite meals. Colorful candies in small glass bowls fit in wherever there was space. His Gale father had set up special torches to keep mosquitoes and wasps from getting close to the backyard. It smelled wonderfully of the forests to the west that they'd visited a couple of years ago. His Harvester mother had outdone herself, cultivating the most beautiful plants and delicious fruits for the party.

After the last two hours, the tables were no longer groaning with food, almost picked entirely clean by Asyl's family and his father's contacts. The second of his first breath was rapidly approaching.

He couldn't wait.

He was terrified.

Asyl eagerly ran over to his parents when his father gestured for him to join them, a smile on his father's handsome face. His mother dipped down and covered his face in greasy kisses, leaving lipstick smudges behind as he giggled and squirmed away from her. His parents took a hand each, and he bounced on the balls of his feet, closing his eyes and tilting his head to the sky, feeling the radiating warmth of the setting sun on his skin.

All around him, the revelers counted down the seconds, and Asyl took a deep breath and held it in anticipation. Would it hurt when his Craft unlocked? If it did, would the pain be only for a second? How would it feel to be a non-elemental? Asyl squeezed his parents' hands tight, the countdown falling into single digits.

Naias had whispered excitedly to him that she'd briefly felt dizzy, suddenly aware of the moisture in the air and how much water the clouds above were carrying. She'd explained that she felt like she was underwater when the days were humid, though she was learning to block out the overwhelming sensations with the help of her tutor.

Father told him he'd felt the currents in the air, all the way up to the highest cloud level. He could feel the vibrations in the air of the larger fowl flying within a couple of miles, and his skin had buzzed with the proximity of insects. He too had training to block out the constant overstimulation his Craft bestowed upon him.

Mother had felt a rush of life. Surrounded then as he was now by shrubbery, flowers, and trees, she had immediately learned which ones were healthy, which ones needed a little bit of help, and which trees were reaching the end of their lifespan. Somehow, she'd instinctively known that she could coax the slightly blighted plants back to perfect health with a song or praise. She hadn't bothered to learn how to block out what her Craft told her, not minding feeling the status of every plant within fifty yards.

Three.

Asyl bit his lip, practically dancing in place. He heard his mother laugh at his excitement, her voice high and bright. His father chuckled, running his thumb over the back of Asyl's fingers.

Two.

Naias shouted out encouragement to him, whooping and hollering. She stirred up the other kids who'd accompanied their families, and Asyl grinned at the cracking adolescent cheers.

One.

Asyl breathed out, his whole body relaxing as he anticipated the rush of his Craft coming to the forefront. He was ready. Elemental Craft or not, he would be the best person he could possibly be. He'd be the son his father wanted. Make his mother proud. Once he was old enough, he'd seek out his Fated and bring him home. Live his life in bliss.

Asyl had always wanted to be special. He opened his eyes, confused after a few seconds had passed. He didn't feel any different. Didn't feel any sort of power welling up inside of him. Hadn't become aware of the wind, water, earth, heat, or flora surrounding him. No one had told him that wishes tended to find loopholes.

His mother dropped his hand as if it had burned her. Asyl turned to her, startled, his eyes wide. Panic started to rise inside of him, and he looked around wildly. Something had to have gone wrong, right? Maybe the hour was incorrect. Minute. Perhaps the Healer transposed a number or two. Even as he frantically cast his mind about for a logical answer, he knew the truth.

His Awakening had failed.

How could his Awakening fail? He'd never heard of something like this before.

"Mother?" Asyl managed to squeak out.

His mother backed away from him, shaking her head as she pressed her hands over her mouth. Tears welled in her eyes, and she shook her head. Her sob echoed through the backyard, breaking the stunned silence that had fallen over everyone.

"What's going on?" Naias demanded. "Where's Asyl's Mark?"

Behind him, his father stepped away, leaving him to stand in the center of the backyard alone. The adults regarded him with something akin to fear on their faces. Parents grabbed their children, stopping them from moving close. Clearly frustrated, Naias started to rush toward him.

"No!" Lady Elrel cried out, grabbing her daughter.

"He'll steal your Craft," Lord Elrel spat.

Asyl took a few steps back, looking between all those who'd been smiling and laughing just moments ago. One of his father's associates clapped his father on the shoulder, an agonized look on his face.

"Do we kill it?" the man asked.

It. What was it? His breath caught when the man looked at him, his eyes sharp and filled with hatred. He… was the it?

"Father?" Asyl implored him, taking a step toward him.

"Stay back," the associate said, his voice colder than Valvinte in winter. "What do you want to do, old friend?"

"Everyone leave," Father said briskly.

The backyard emptied with a dizzying speed. Parents scooped up their confused children or hauled their elder ones away. His grandmother moved forward in the crowd, and for a second, Asyl thought she was heading for him. Instead, she spat on his face and hurried over to her daughter and sat next to her. Stunned, Asyl brought his hand up, lightly touching the spittle running down his cheek.

"No!" Naias shrieked as her mother tried hauling her away. "Tell me what's going on! He's my best friend!"

"The goddess has looked into his soul and found him tainted. She refused to bless him. A Void," Lord Elrel sneered, his impressive mustache curling. He turned to Mother, who was openly yet silently weeping. "My condolences. I hope you're able to carry a *proper* child to term."

His best friend screamed at her father that there had to have been a mistake. Naias tried to rush toward him and was lifted off her feet by her father. Her defiant shouts echoed through the silent backyard, demanding that her father put her down. There clearly had to have been a mistake!

"My friend," the associate began.

"Please leave," Father murmured.

The man simply nodded, casting another frigid glare at Asyl, and followed the rest of the revelers out of the garden. They were alone now. Or rather, as alone as one could get in a manor. Servants stared at him from the deck and many windows. The faces of the maids that had been with him his entire life were ashen, and Asyl could see that one or two of them were crying.

His father's butler, on the other hand, was a different story. He openly glowered at Asyl, as if he hadn't cheerily given him a gift only a half hour ago: a beautiful pocket watch that showed the heavenly bodies, telling him the time with the greatest accuracy Gale inventors could determine.

"What do you wish, sir?" the butler asked.

Father stared down at Asyl, and he stared right back, terrified. He still didn't understand what was happening. What was a Void? He'd never heard of such a thing until now. But that… that wasn't possible. His father told him everything, even if Asyl was too young to fully understand the nuances of his business deals.

"Father, please," Asyl said, his voice trembling.

"Get out," his father snapped. Asyl jerked as if he'd been stabbed. His fingers and toes were growing cold, even as his stomach rebelled and warned him that he was going to vomit, making him break out into a sweat. "Get the *fuck* out of our lives. You are no longer my son."

Tears sprang to his eyes, and Asyl's throat closed. He tried stammering a plea, wanting to change his father's mind. Hadn't he been a good son? He'd done everything his father asked of him, even eating foods he hated, simply because he wanted to please the man. He was good at his studies, though he found it hard to socialize with the others in his classes. He treated the servants well, respected his parents and the adults in his life.

What could there possibly be within him that marked him as tarnished? Unworthy? He'd read novels and watched plays where the villains were Craft Blessed. Surely the Goddess would have seen the corruption within their souls and denied them a Craft. But what had he done?

"Father," Asyl tried again, his vision blurring, "what have I done wrong?"

"You survived," Mother snarled from behind him. "Why did you live when your siblings didn't? Saddling me with a useless, damned child, giving me false hope that I could have a wonderful family. You disgust me."

"You're not wanted," his grandmother sniffed, glowering at him. "Get out before we have Kusinut fetch the police."

Trembling, his legs barely supporting his weight, Asyl stumbled to the garden gate. He put one hand on the white-painted wood and looked back. Father was staring at him, his eyes completely blank. It was the same look he'd had when Asyl's paternal grandfather had died. A shudder ripped down his spine, and Asyl slipped out of the gate.

It swung shut behind him with a finalizing clang, physically and emotionally cutting him off from his family. Fear gripped him as he stared down the darkening street, paralyzing him for just long enough to hear his father try to comfort his grieving mother.

"It's okay, my dear," Asyl heard him say gently. "I know seeing so many friends with kids is hard. But we're still young, and we can keep trying."

AR BRYANT has frequently been accused of having their head in the clouds, and quite frankly, it's a lot more fun up there! For as long as they can remember, they have loved telling stories. They wrote their first story in the third grade, and it involved the Backstreet Boys going to the moon. AR is a PNW cryptid who loves the rain, windstorms, sandy beaches, and redwood forests.

They currently guard their book hoard alongside their dog while their two cats get annoyed when AR tries to write, reducing their lap time. If they're not reading or writing, AR is likely playing on their Switch, cross-stitching, or playing their ranger-druid in D&D with their friends. Their favorite genre, in basically everything, is fantasy. More dragons please!

While AR finds social media exhausting, they'd be glad to hear from you at arbryant91@gmail.com!

Follow me on BookBub

SHADOW'S WOUND

ELEMENTAL THRONES
BOOK 1

SARIA BRYANT

With the realm teetering on the brink of magical annihilation, Callith Ratearynn, the reluctant heir to the Sun Throne, is thrust into power centuries too soon. With his father dead and corruption tearing the kingdom apart at the seams, Cal must battle rising racial tensions and unravel a dark conspiracy. Justice, a manipulative human official, has stirred hatred between humans and the magical community, using enslavement collars and control over the Black Sun—an elite group of soldiers loyal to the Shadow Throne.

Just as civil war seems inevitable, Cal's Fate string—a magical bond tying him to his soulmate—leads him to a grim prison where he finds Haru, his bonded, broken and tortured. But Fate has more in store. Cal discovers he is bound not to one, but two: Rashi, a fox shifter, and Haru, a fierce dragon warrior. Together, this reluctant triad must face cult attacks, dark rituals, and the creeping Wound, a void threatening to consume their realm.

Cal's new reality is one of impossible choices—between duty and heart, loyalty and passion. As war looms, the only hope lies in Cal's ability to trust in his newfound soulmates and uncover the depths of the corruption before it's too late.

stasis
flux
equipoise
kim fielding

Prosperity comes at a price. In Praesidium, that price is freedom. Strict laws and a harsh penal code ensure ordinary criminals become bond-slaves. But the most serious traitors are turned over to the wizard to be suspended in a dreamless frozen state known as Stasis.

Miner is one such criminal, suspended forever—until Ennek, the youngest son of Praesidium's Chief, stirred by the horror of Miner's fate, sets him free.

Ennek has always skirted the edge of the law. Now he finds himself a fugitive, friend of a traitor. He and Miner must rely on each other if they are to overcome the challenges facing them. Though their deepening relationship offers them both support, Miner grapples with the consequences of his enslavement, while Ennek struggles to control his newfound wizard powers. Seeking balance for themselves and their world, they learn the greatest challenges sometimes come from very close to the heart.

Contains the novels Stasis, Flux, and Equipoise.

Former chef Jasper Wight has been magically ensnared in his apartment for over three months. Cabin fever doesn't begin to cover it. All he can do to pass the time is indulge in his hobby—painting portraits of his neighbors. But once a handsome new man moves into a swanky nearby penthouse, Jasper is no longer content merely to watch. Following his gut, he reaches out through astral projection….

Finn Anderson is the CEO of a food app funded by his parents, but he struggles to believe in the dream. When a mysterious someone starts leaving messages on his mirror, he learns the world holds more possibilities than he ever imagined.

When a chance encounter brings Finn to Jasper's door, the pair are soon as enamored with each other as Finn is of the magic he's just discovering. But navigating a relationship that spans two worlds is only the tip of the iceberg. They still have to figure out how to free Jasper from his apartment, how to make Finn's business into a success, and whether an outsider can be trusted with the secrets of the magical world.

AMY LANE

Sometimes the
best magic is just
a little luck…

THE RISING TIDE

THE LUCK MECHANICS  BOOK ONE

The tidal archipelago of Spinner's Drift is a refuge for misfits. Can the island's magic help a pie-in-the-sky dreamer and a wounded soul find a home in each other?

In a flash of light and a clap of thunder, Scout Quintero is banished from his home. Once he's sneaked his sister out too, he's happy, but their power-hungry father is after them, and they need a place to lie low. The thriving resort business on Spinner's Drift provides the perfect way to blend in.

They aren't the only ones who think so.

Six months ago Lucky left his life behind and went on the run from mobsters. Spinner's Drift brings solace to his battered soul, but one look at Scout and he's suddenly terrified of having one more thing to lose.

Lucky tries to keep his distance, but Scout is charming, and the island isn't that big. When they finally connect, all kinds of things come to light, including supernatural mysteries that have been buried for years. But while Scout and Lucky grow closer working on the secret, pissed-off mobsters, supernatural entities, and Scout's father are getting closer to them. Can they hold tight to each other and weather the rising tide together?

The Wanderer
Rowan McAllister

Chronicles of the Riftlands: Book One

After centuries of traveling the continent of Kita and fighting the extradimensional monsters known as Riftspawn, mage Lyuc is tired and ready to back away from the concerns of humanity.

But the world isn't done with him yet.

While traveling with a merchant caravan, Lyuc encounters Yan, an Unnamed, the lowest caste in society. Though Yan has nothing but his determination and spirit, he reminds Lyuc what passion and desire feel like. While wild magic, a snarky, shapeshifting, genderfluid companion, and the plots of men and monsters seem determined to keep Lyuc from laying down his burden, only Yan's inimitable spirit tempts him to hang on for another lifetime or so.

All Yan wants is to earn the sponsorship of a guild so he can rise above his station, claim a place in society, and build the family he never had.

After hundreds of years of self-imposed penance, all Lyuc wants is Yan.

If they can survive prejudice, bandits, mercenaries, monsters, and nature itself, they might both get their wish… and maybe even their happily ever after.

www.ingramcontent.com/pod-product-compliance
Lightning Source LLC
Chambersburg PA
CBHW060227100726
47907CB00003B/538